William John Johnston

Lightning flashes and electric dashes

A volume of choice telegraphic literature, humor, fun, wit & wisdom

William John Johnston

Lightning flashes and electric dashes
A volume of choice telegraphic literature, humor, fun, wit & wisdom

ISBN/EAN: 9783741182594

Manufactured in Europe, USA, Canada, Australia, Japa

Cover: Foto ©Andreas Hilbeck / pixelio.de

Manufactured and distributed by brebook publishing software
(www.brebook.com)

William John Johnston

Lightning flashes and electric dashes

The Telegrapher's Dream.—Drawn by J. J. Calahan.

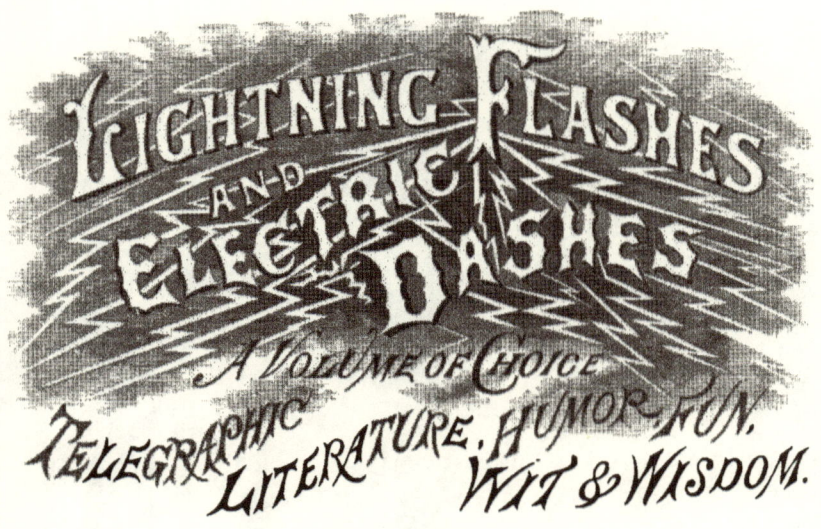

LIGHTNING FLASHES AND ELECTRIC DASHES

A Volume of Choice Telegraphic Literature, Humor, Fun, Wit & Wisdom.

COMPILED BY

W. J. JOHNSTON,

EDITOR OF "THE OPERATOR,"

WITH CONTRIBUTIONS FROM THE PENS OF ALL THE PROMINENT WRITERS
IN THE RANKS OF TELEGRAPHIC LITERATURE,

As Well as Several Well-Known Outsiders.

PROFUSELY ILLUSTRATED,

PRINCIPALLY BY MEMBERS OF THE TELEGRAPHIC PROFESSION.

NEW YORK:
Copyright, 1882, by
W. J. JOHNSTON, Publisher,
NO. 9 MURRAY STREET.

PREFACE TO THE THIRD EDITION.

To the many thousands scattered over the country who are engaged or interested in the art of telegraphy, this book will probably need neither preface nor apology. Its object is to present articles from the pens of each of the principal telegraphic writers, as well as a few on telegraphic subjects from prominent *litterateurs*—all well worthy of preservation, and written in such a manner as to combine entertainment with instruction.

LIGHTNING FLASHES as originally published appealed more particularly to the members of the telegraphic fraternity, from whom it has received a very hearty welcome. The demand for copies from persons outside of the profession, and the unanimity of the press in commendation of the work, have encouraged the compiler and publisher to prepare an edition that can be understood and appreciated by the non-professional reader as well as by telegraphists.

This edition is intended both for those connected with telegraphy and also for the general reading public—for people who have no knowledge whatever of the art or business of telegraphy—and will be found free from technical terms and professional idioms not familiar to those unconnected with the business.

The book has been entirely rearranged for the present edition, and a large amount of additional matter, as well as several new pictures, added. It is therefore hoped that LIGHTNING FLASHES in its present form will prove of very considerable interest to the general reader, and afford a comprehensive and instructive insight into the mysteries of the electric telegraph, and of the inner life of that great and growing fraternity, the telegraphists, in reference to whose highly interesting history so little is known to the outside world.

CONTENTS.

LIGHTNING FLASHES AND ELECTRIC DASHES.

Some Curious Anecdotes of the Wire.

THERE is probably no better place in all this world for studying human nature than in a telegraph office. You are brought in contact with so many different people, made a confident of in so many important transactions, meet so many peculiar people, and see so many strange messages passing over the wire, that you feel as if from some loophole of retreat you were viewing the world shorn of its shams and its pretences. Perhaps no class of men enjoy a good joke better than telegraphers, and they certainly often find in the ordinary routine duties of their position many dispatches calculated to provoke a smile. For instance, a Massachusetts man recently telegraphed to his son: "I am dying; come immediately," which elicited the very sympathetic reply: "Cannot come. Let me know when you die." A message was sent not long since to a doctor in this city from the husband of one of his patients, which read: "Please come down right away; wife very ill," and fifteen minutes afterward another, merely saying: "You need not come. Funeral Tuesday!" The following message, addressed to an insurance agent, recently passed through the Western Union general office in this city:

"Have you received proofs of my death? They were forwarded sixty days ago.
(Signed)   JOHN BAIRD, deceased,
                        per Mary Baird."

As the operator always "follows copy," and senders are often a little excited, very queer messages are sometimes sent; for ex-ample this one: "Cousin: Go for Auntie. Father is dying as soon as possible." An Irishman—of course—in Palmer, Mass., sent the following message to his brother in New York: "Your wife died yesterday. We will wake her to-night. Come home. P. S. Don't open this for two hours, so as to prepare yourself for the melancholy news."

But the most laughable messages are generally those from love-sick swains to their sweethearts. A gentleman in the South not long since telegraphed to his affianced in Maine: "Your life is a rich bouquet of happiness, yourself the sweetest flower. If Northern winds whisper Southern wishes, how happy you must be! Good night. Happy dreams, sweet love!—Frank." The following message recently passed through the Chicago office: "I lent you one year ago to-night four dollars eighty-seven cents. If you have not had it long enough, please keep it one year longer." To this delicate hint this answer was returned: "Had forgotten it, and hoped you had. Let her run another year."

Mr. Beecher, years ago, when he was but little known outside of New York or Brooklyn, received a telegram from a Y. M. C. A. in the West asking him to come on and lecture for fame. His reply created a hearty laugh in the telegraph office; it was, "Yes, I will lecture for F. A. M. E.—fifty and my expenses."

Operators occasionally encounter some very strange people in the way of customers. It is quite astonishing what crude ideas many even intelligent people have of the telegraph. A German once brought a message to one of the branch offices in this city for transmission. It was so indistinctly written that the operator couldn't read it, and asked to be enlightened. Hans studied it carefully for some time, but couldn't make it out either. After awhile, however, his face brightened up and he said: "Oh, well, just send it that way; he'll understand it!" A porter belonging to one of the city hotels one night handed the operator a message and a two dollar bill. The operator returned him the change, and was not a little surprised to see him walk off with both change and message.

"Arn't you going to have the message sent?" he inquired.

"Oh!" replied the porter, "I thought you had sent it. I supposed that all you had to do was simply to look at it!"

A lady of color once asked what the tariff was to Portsmouth.

"What Portsmouth?" asked the operator.

"Why, just Portsmouth."

"What State is it in?"

"The—U-nited States."

"Yes, but there are over thirty States. Which particular one?"

"I never heard of any Portsmouth but the one." And she looked like it

After a little questioning she spoke of Richmond, and he concluded it was Virginia.

"Seventy-five cents for ten words."

"Well, what's a word? I want to say 'Arrived safe, but my trunk hasn't come on. Please forward it at once by express, care of Mrs. Julia Johnson, without delay. I'll write as soon as ever I have time.' Is that more than one word?"

He thought it was.

Not long since a man stopped at the little window of a branch office in the "Hub," the inhabitant evidently of a little sphere of his own, outside of which he was lost in the mazes of life.

"Is this the telegraph office?" he asked, hesitatingly.

The young lady operator satisfied him or this fact.

"I want to telegraph," he proceeded, growing confidential, "I want to telegraph to my wife and tell her I missed the train."

"You will have to write it on one of those blanks," said the operator, coolly, entirely unimpressed by the (to the sender) exciting event.

"Oh! well. I guess you'd better write it. I can write," (evidently thinking it necessary to establish this fact before proceeding farther), "but" (flatteringly) "you can fix it up better than I can."

"Whom is the message going to?" asked the operator, as she armed herself with pen and blank.

"To—my wife—in Providence," he replied, with the most sublime innocence.

The operator looked at him doubtfully.

"What is the address? To whom is the message going?"

The man eyed her with great astonishment. "I told you," he said, raising his voice as if he thought her afflicted with deafness, "to my wife in Providence."

"I am afraid," the operator replied, trying to speak ironically, "that the message might not be received if addressed in that way. Providence is a small place, I know, but it might possibly go to some other man's wife."

The story of the Irishman who hung his boots on the telegraph wire is laughed at, but is not really believed, any more than many other tales of people who imagine everything is transmitted bodily over the wires. Yet parallel cases are constantly occurring. A young woman brought a letter, sealed, directed to the same telegraph office to be "telegraphed," she said. "Shall I open it?" inquired the operator, thinking perhaps the message was inside. The young woman looked insulted. "Of course not!" It was to be "telegraphed" just as it was, of course! "Don't you send letters by telegraph?" she asked, with her nose in the air. The operator advised employing the United States mail in the transmission, and the young woman departed with the evident impression that telegraph institutions were all nothing more or less than "frauds."

Another young woman came into the Boston office above mentioned. The inevitable "I want to send a telegram," brought the operator to the window, when, after explaining all the whys and wherefores, and relating the family history for the past three generations, she dictated the message while the operator wrote. When finished, the young woman took the document, scrawled in the operator's "third best" handwriting—the one that "no one but herself could read"—examined it critically, pointed disdainfully to a spider-like word, as she asked: "What's *that?*" crossed a few t's, dotted a few i's, rounded some o's, and finally flung down the message angrily, exclaiming to the wondering operator: "John never will be able to read that; I shall have to write it myself," and she did.

How often the operator in leisure moments ponders upon the sequel of some story of sorrow, of joy, of strange mystery, perhaps of crime, a part of which, and a part only, comes to his knowledge! But for him the unfinished tale is never completed, the mystery never solved. With all his sympathies aroused, he wonders what became of the poor woman who telegraphed a friend to meet her late at night in a strange city, and departed on the train. What did she do when she found no one there, as the operator knew, too late, would be the case, from receiving word that the message was undelivered, "no such person to be found?" And the man who was "in a terrible fix, come quick;" what had he done, and how did he come out?

What with the responsibilities always resting on his shoulders, the constant wear and tear of nerves and patience, the fear of making some mistake that may prove of the most serious consequence, the irksome confinement, the small compensation, troubles on the wire, etc., there is more of prose than poetry in the life of the translator of dots and dashes.

A few months ago a darkey came into the office at Bainbridge, Ga., and said he wanted to send an "expatch" to his girl. "Very well," said the operator, reaching for a blank, "what do you want to say to her?" "Now that's cool," remarked the ebony customer, "I ain't gwine to tell you what I want to say to her, I ain't no fool, I ain't," and he put his quarter back in his vest pocket and marched off.

Speaking of customers, a story is told of a man who came to send a message—evidently his maiden effort in that direction. He had on an overcoat reaching nearly to his heels, and there were other signs about him reading, "I live in Illanoy." He entered the telegraph office, sat down to the table, and covered four blanks with writing. When he had read them over he signed his name, and, walking to the window, shoved the sheets in and said:

"There— I guess that'll ease the ole woman's mind."

"Fourteen dollars and twenty cents," said the clerk, as he counted the words.

"Charge it!" replied the stranger.

"This company doesn't trust," said the clerk.

"Ain't I good for fourteen dollars?" demanded the stranger, in a loud voice.

"You may be, but the rules of this—"

"Rules be hanged!" interrupted the Illinoisan. "Don't I own a six hundred acre farm? Don't I own twenty-eight horses and forty mules? Haven't I been Supervisor, Overseer of Highways, and Town Assessor? And am I going to run away on account of fourteen dollars?"

"I don't mean to say— "

"Yes, you do!" put in the stranger, getting red in the face. "You mean that I'm a sneak and a shirk! You mean to say I'd run away for fourteen blasted old dollars?"

"You see," began the clerk in a soothing voice, "you see that—— "

"I see them sheets!" exclaimed the stranger, reaching in after them, "and now, young man, I want to tell you something. I'm as liberal as the next, and I wouldn't kick at six shillings for that telegraph. You thought I was green, and you piled it on, but you went a leetle too far. I'm going right home and set up a telegraph myself, and if I don't run you and your old company under ground in less than a year, I'll donate the best jackass in Illanoy to any orphan asylum you may pick out!"

Another one, also very good, is told of a man, a stranger in town, who entered the office of the Western Union Company one morning, and wanted to know if he could send a dispatch to Fayette, Ohio. He was told that he could, and he asked:

"If I send a telegraph to my wife will she answer it?"

"I can't say as to that," replied the clerk. "If you ask for an answer I should think she would reply."

"If I ask for twenty dollars will she send it?"

"I can't say as to that. You ought to know best about it."

"Isn't she obliged by law to send it?"

"No, there is no law about it."

"You won't guarantee that she'll send it?" continued the stranger.

"How can I?" answered the clerk, smiling at the idea.

"Then I won't telegraph—no, not a cent's worth! I know the old woman, know her like a book, and I know that if you don't send a man up to the house to choke it out of her, I might telegraph from Dan to Besheby, and she wouldn't forward a shilling!"

He went out, but returned in a few minutes and whispered:

"Mum is the word. Don't say that I said anything about her. She's awful when she's roused, and though I've got my opinion of her and all her relations, I don't care to have my home turned into a raging paradise!"

Operators sometimes take great delight in playing practical jokes upon persons whom they consider green. About as good a joke of this kind as has come to light lately, oc-

curred a few months ago at Norwalk, Conn. One day, a gaunt, slab-sided chap, with particles of hay-seed on his coat and in his tow-colored hair, stepped up to the telegraph office at the railroad depot, and asked if the boss was in. The operator assured him that he was, and his rural friend went on to relate that he lived up in Danbury, had come down from there that morning and had intended bringing his brother's dog, which a man in Norwalk wanted to buy, but had forgotten it, and wanted to know if the dog could be sent down from there by telegraph. The man of lightning seeing a good chance for a little fun, at once answered, "Certainly, sir, that is a matter of daily occurrence; all that is necessary for you to do is to give me a description of the dog so that no mistake can be made; call again in about half an hour, and the dog will be here. "It is a yellow dog with small ears, and is about so high," said the Granger, placing his hand about eighteen inches from the floor. He then took his departure with the remark that he would call again pretty soon. The operator then sent his message boy to look for a dog as near the description as possible, which he soon succeeded in finding. It was at once brought to the office and secured to the operator's desk by means of a piece of telegraph wire. After a little coaxing the dog was made to lie quietly down and everything was in readiness for our rural friend. Punctual to the time appointed he made his appearance, and asked if the dog had come. "I will see," said the operator, and stepping up to the instrument he tapped a few times on the key, at the same time inserting his leg under the desk, and managing to step on the dog's toes, which caused the canine to yelp. "Ah! he's coming," said the operator, and then tapping more furiously on the key, he, at the same time, kicked the dog clean from under the table, who, not relishing this kind of treatment, barked furiously and ran around the office with the wire attached to his neck. "Fifty cents, sir," said the operator, turning around to the countryman. "Uncommon nice dog, must be worth fifty dollars; but he is the hardest dog I ever received over the wires; he is so muscular, you see, that he broke the wire, in fact a piece of it is now attached to his neck, which he broke off." During the whole of this operation the countryman gazed on the operator with eyes wide open and full of surprise; but when the dog came from under the table and was seen by the countryman, that was the culminating point, and he was struck with unbounded amazement. After looking at the dog a moment or so, he said, "Say mister, he ain't so big as he was, and he is darker, how is that?" "Oh! that is easily explained," said the operator; "you see the chemicals employed in making electricity of course darkens his original color, and the velocity with which he passes over the wire causes him to contract in size; but after you expose him to the air for a short time he will soon assume his original size and color." "Du tell!" said the countryman, and, after placing fifty cents on the counter, he picked up the dog and walked out of the office, remarking that "the man who invented them telegraphs must be a very knowledgeable man."

The first public telegraph line in this country was erected in 1844, and ran from Baltimore to Washington. In the following year —thirty-two years ago—a single wire was erected to an obscure office beneath the *Express* office at 16 Wall Street, New York, and two wires from Washington terminated in a small room over the ferry house in Jersey City, where three operators easily, and not very continuously, performed the whole telegraphic business of the city of New York. The entire telegraphic system of the United Kingdom consisted at the same time of a single line to Nine Elms, and a small office at 334 Strand, London.

Things have changed very materially since then. One company alone in this country now operates about 250,000 miles of wire, nearly 8,000 offices, and handles about 25,000,000 messages a year. The Western Union main office in New York has 500 employés, including about 125 ladies. In the central office in London, as many as 1,500 persons, including 850 ladies, find employment. The number of words which pass through this one office alone in a week, is equivalent to several hundred thousand messages. These immense establishments are but the growth of a little over a quarter of a century; for, as we have seen, it is only about thirty years since a small room in West Strand and another in Wall Street represented the headquarters of the telegraph system of the Old World and the New.

But no great invention steps at once, like Venus from the foam of the sea, or Pallas from the brains of Jove, into being completed at its birth. That such was the case with Prof. Morse's great achievement is practically explained by the following account of blundering by electricity during the early days of the business.

It was about twenty-five years ago. Telegraphy had scarcely outgrown its swaddling clothes, and the wires had only reached as far west as St. Louis. The operators were still comparatively inexperienced, and the public more so, many people regarding with incredulity the stories about the wonderful rapidity of transmitting messages. Gustave Bender, a rising young merchant of St. Louis, was one of the latter. He had come to America and gone to the Far West with his parents years before even the word telegraph had been whispered, or the name of Prof. Morse was known outside the small circle of his immediate friends. Bender's partner, John Stuts, on the contrary, was a firm believer in the new invention. He had been in New York and Baltimore when the wires were first used, and was slightly acquainted with the working of the instruments. Bender and Stuts had many disputes in an amicable way about it, the one declaring it all a humbug, the other stoutly protesting the truth of the amazing things published in the journals concerning it. Just as the telegraph was completed to St. Louis, Bender received by mail a letter from his wife, who had gone on a visit to the fatherland, informing him that she would sail from Liverpool on a certain day in the steamship Baltic, for New York. The letter had been delayed on the road, and the steamer was nearly due at the port of her destination when Bender received it. "The very thing, Gustave," said John Stuts to his partner, "is to try the telegraph and convince you of its efficacy." "Well," replied Bender, "I know it's all a humbug, and if you want to throw away any money on it, do so, I'll not give a cent." "See here, Gustave," began John, somewhat angered at his partner's obstinacy, "I'll bet you fifty dollars that I will send a message to our friend Heil, in New York, and get an answer from him before you are ready to start on your proposed trip to that city to-morrow morning. What say you?" "All right," replied Gustave, and the bet was duly agreed to. John went to the desk and wrote out in plain words the following message:

CARL G. T. HEIL, No. 45 Beaver Street, New York: Gustave Bender's wife and sister on board the Baltic, from Europe. See them, and forward safely. JOHN STUTS, St. Louis.

"And you think that letter will go through the wire to New York, John?" asked Gustave "Surely it will, word for word, and it will be in Heil's hands before two o'clock this afternoon," said John. "Then I'll bet you another fifty to make you pay for trying to fool me," exclaimed Bender; and that second bet was also taken, and both walked to a telegraph office, where John delivered his message, paid the charges, and was told that it would be sent on at once.

That same afternoon Mr. Heil was in his Beaver Street store in New York, when a messenger brought him a dispatch. He signed a receipt for it, opened and read it—read it twice, three times; burst into a violent fit of laughter; read it again, but could make neither head nor tail of it. The following was the way in which the message of Stuts had been transcribed in New York and delivered to Heil:

CARL G. T. HEIL, No. 45 Beaver Street, New York; Just on a bender. Live on blisters. Round to Baltimore on new rope. Season forward. Rate high. JOHN STUTS, St. Louis.

Now, Heil knew John Stuts well as a sober, sedate, industrious man, and concluded at once that there must be some mistake. Presuming that either some important business matters were hid under this meaningless jungle of words, or that the operators must have made havoc with the dispatch as intended to be sent by his friend, he resolved to make inquiries at once by telegraph, and forwarded from New York the following:

JOHN STUTS, St. Louis: Repeat what the devil you mean.

CARL G. T. HEIL, 45 Beaver St., New York.

Bender and Stuts were closing up their store on the evening of the same day, and the former was continually poking fun at his partner on account of the telegraph, Stuts simply replying: "Wait till to-morrow morning, Gustave, and you'll talk otherwise," when a messenger approached them, inquiring for Mr. John Stuts, and saying that he was from the telegraph office with a message from New York. "Oh!" cried John, "now I have got you, Gustave; the reply comes earlier than even I thought it would." He snatched the envelope from the messenger, put his name hurriedly to the receipt, hastily unfolded the paper, but the evening was too dark to read the faint writing, the gas lamps in the streets not having yet been lit. The two walked briskly into an adjoining saloon, and there proceeded to ascertain the remarkably quick answer of their friend Heil, in New York. Stuts read as follows:

JOHN STUTS, St. Louis: Reptile; watch devil, you mean cur. Go to h—l. Forty-five pounds bear's grease, New York.

Stuts was amazed; he trembled with rage; but Bender quietly remarked, "Didn't I tell you it was all a humbug?" Yet John did not see it in that light. He felt convinced that one of the telegraph clerks whom he knew was only playing a trick on him, and he would at once get even with the villain.

"Let's go to the telegraph office, Gustave," he said ; and both went. Here John met the young man whom he sought, and holding the offensive dispatch before his eyes, asked who sent it. "Dunno," said the clerk ; "it came from New York." "It did?" howled John ; "then take that from New York, too," and knocked the poor clerk down. Cries of "Help!" "Murder!" "Police!" were raised, and both John and Gustave were arrested and locked up for the night. Next morning the two got out on bail, and an investigation during the day, by repeating the two messages between St. Louis and New York, set matters right. John won his bet from Gustave, and the latter never again doubted that the electric telegraph was, indeed, a wonderful reality.

This recalls many amusing mistakes, or "bulls," as they are technically called, that have been made from time to time in the transmission of messages over the wire. Telegraphy, as at present practiced, is simply the art of instantaneously conveying to distant places the first elements of written language. In transmitting the letters of the alphabet, either visual or acoustic means can be employed. Most of the telegraphs in Great Britain appeal to the eye ; in America nearly all appeal to the ear. The sending of messages from place to place is dependent upon mere transitory signals, which in many cases are similar to each other ; and it is not therefore surprising that errors occasionally occur.

Anna Dickinson was once telegraphed to by a lecture committee, inquiring the subject of her lecture. She replied that it would be "Breakers Ahead." The committee telegraphed back, "All right; come and lecture on 'Break his Head,'" which was what the message read after being "improved" by ye intelligent operator.

A "bull" was also perpetrated last winter in connection with the title of a lecture by Hon. Sunset Cox, of New York. Mr. Cox telegraphed Mr. Bain, of Atlanta, that his subject would be "Irish Humor," but when the message reached Mr. Bain, it read "Just Human." When the lecturer took his stand, he said : "the message was only bulled, ladies and gentlemen, but I am sorry to say that it was certainly an Irish bull."

On one occasion the message "Arrived all right," dispatched by some ladies, was delivered "Arrived all tight." In another case a husband who had gone to the seaside to engage apartments telegraphed "All right; come to-morrow." He was astounded that his wife did not come to him, but the mystery was explained when it was discovered that "All right; home to-morrow," had been the message actually delivered. A member of the Masonic fraternity once telegraphed to a friend to "make room for ten Royal Arch masons, coming to-day;" and on his arrival found a neat pen erected in the yard, the message as delivered asking for accommodations for ten "rams." A gentleman in California was much astonished to receive a message informing him that "David goes up this evening on a spree." The dispatch originally read, "This evening on Osprey." An Associated Press dispatch published some years ago contained the clause: "Col Gilbert, a fierce editor of the Valparaiso *Vidette and Republican.*" As filed it read, "Col. Gilbert A. Pierce, editor, etc." A New York merchant was once considerably puzzled over a message he received from a correspondent South, saying: "It don't rain mush here" A gentleman in Poughkeepsie, not long since, received a message reading, "Father is singing. Come." A repetition, however, dispelled the poetry, as the message then read: "Father is sinking. Come."

A rather inexperienced operator, whose knowledge of legal phraseology was more or less limited, was one evening heard to struggle for a considerable time over a long message from the Western Union Company's lawyer. After the sending operator had slowly and carefully repeated the word "Supersedeas" at least two dozen times, the operators at the other offices along the line, who had been listening to the two, were much amused to hear the youthful disciple of Prof. Morse request the sender to "go ahead, after 'supper for six!'"

A grocer who had pursued a runaway clerk named Galusha, and found him with the money, and repentant, telegraphed to his (the grocer's) anxious wife: "Found Galusha. Hope for better things." When she got the missive it read; "Found girl; shall elope and get her things." She started for the scene of action by the first train.

A very ludicrous telegraphic mistake occurred a short time after the escape of Ex-Boss Tweed, which led the detectives and Chief of Police of Philadelphia a wild-goose chase which they probably did not quite relish. The Chief sat in his leather-cushioned chair, and deliberated. The cause of his deliberation lay on the table before him. It was headed, "Western Union Telegraph Company," and below the printed words was a message, very short but very significant. Half an hour before, the message had been handed to the Chief by one of Philadelphia's most distinguished citizens, who protested on his word as a poet and a statesman, that its contents were so much Choctaw to him, and that why such a dispatch should be sent to him he could not imagine. The message, which was a firebrand both to the recipient and the Chief, was as follows:

New York, December 7.— *To General H. H. Bingham, Philadelphia:* Meet me at the 12 o'clock train.　　　　　　　　　　　　　Tweed.

The dispatch, unfortunately, had not reached Philadelphia until 11:30, and the State House clock struck twelve while a messenger was hastening to deliver it. An hour or more was then lost in astonishment, and it was fully one o'clock before the police knew that the Ex-Boss, with his confidence thus betrayed, was probably in the city. It was too late to capture him in the depot, and the escaped convict, on finding that his friend was not on hand in reply to his dispatch, had undoubtedly taken secure quarters, unknown alike to the police and the public.

A tap on a very rusty bell summoned a boy to the inner sanctum of policedom, and the Chief ordered that a messenger should instantly be dispatched for Captain Heins. Meanwhile General Bingham dropped in to inquire what had been done.

"I can't make my plans public," the Chief replied, in answer to the General's questions; "but every point is thoroughly covered, and if Tweed is in the city we'll have him before dark. I am very anxious to lay hands on him myself, for I haven't a man about me I can really trust in a big case like this. How is it about the reward, General? Is that a sure thing?"

The General assured him that it was.

"Then," said the Chief standing up and striking an attitude, "Tweed is nabbed, and these strong hands shall drag him to a felon's cell before yon sun goes down beyond the muddy Delaware."

The door had hardly closed behind General Bingham before Captain Heins entered, cap in hand, and saluted his chief. The Chief speedily explained matters to the Captain. When the latter was made to understand, the three blonde hairs on the top of his head bent and swayed in their fruitless endeavor to raise his policeman's cap. But before he could reply, the Chief went on: "There's no time to be lost. Some fool of a patrolman, or, more likely, an obscure citizen, may stumble on him, and then where's our divvy? At twelve o'clock this afternoon the Boss was in the West Philadelphia depot, intending to go to General Bingham's. The General gave him the cold shoulder, and now there's no knowing where he is. But he may find his way to Bingham's yet. You must go to the depot, get on his track and follow him. I will go to Bingham's, shadow the house, and take him in if he shows up. But I depend most on you, and— remember!" and the wink was as good as the nod which followed.

Captain Heins' inquiries in the depot disclosed the fact that a very large, tall man, in every way answering to Boss Tweed's description, had arrived in the twelve o'clock train, and, the janitor thought, had taken a Market Street car for the city. Inquiry among the conductors showed that "the large, tall man" had gone to the end of the route, and then disappeared down Front Street, and the "conductor" of the Smith's Island boat had no hesitancy in saying that the supposed convict had gone over with him on his last trip, and had not come back. Captain Hein at once rose twenty-seven degrees in his own estimation. By his detective skill he had found the distinguished fugitive, traced him, and now had him safely caged on a desolate island in the middle of the Delaware. The boat made a quick trip to the island, and the first person that the captain met was the "large, tall man." In his left hand was a gingham umbrella, and in his right a canvas satchel. The detective approached him, and was just screwing up his courage to the point of making him a prisoner, when the "large, tall man" walking slowly into the neighboring saloon, stepped behind the counter and deliberately helped himself to "ein," "zwei," "drei," in rapid succession. The satchel was tossed under the counter, the umbrella laid on the shelf, and the tired and dusty Tueton explained to his son, who stood behind the bar, that his mission to Newark to buy lager had been eminently successful. The idea of the beer-swelled Teuton being mistaken for the Boss was so very funny that even the disgusted detective could not help but smile, even while he was warming his hand in his empty pocket. The captain's journey back to headquarters was a slow one, but when he arrived he found the Chief there before him in a paroxysm of rage. Always grand in repose, the Chief was magnificent in his anger, and the detective hesitated to approach. At length he mustered courage to whisper, "I had a fine clew, but it fizzled out."

The Chief paused in his rapid march up and down the room, threw himself once more into his chair, and beckoned the detective to his side. "Heins," he began, "if anybody

ever hears of this afternoon's work, you and I will be the laughing stock of the town. Listen, but what I tell you is never to be whispered to mortal man. Bingham has promised to hush it up on account of some work I got my men to do for him recently, and if you don't mention it we're safe. I went to Bingham's house an hour ago, and there sat Thurlow Weed, and he and Bingham were splitting their sides with laughing. It was Weed that sent the message—T. Weed.—don't you see? And the d——d operator here ran the letters together, and made it Tweed. They're laughing about it yet, but I'll show them they must not keep the Philadelphia police running around all day after a mare's nest." Captain Heins was at last accounts still trying to get the joke through his head.

Some grotesque errors are sometimes made in messages going to newspapers, most of which, however, are noticed by the news editor, and corrected before reaching the public. For instance, in the early part of the present year, the manifold paper upon which such messages are written, revealed to the eyes of the smiling news rectifiers the information that "President Grant had transmitted to Congress a special *sausage* on the resumption of specie payments." Of course it was printed *message*. Some ten years ago there came over the wires an account of the proceedings of a National Temperance Convention, concluding with the announcement that the "meeting was very *parsimonious*." Laughingly, the news editors substituted *harmonious* for the last word, and thus spared the feelings of the teetotalers.

In the English system of telegraphy, the letters y and x, are so nearly alike as to sometimes be curiously confounded one with the other. Over and over again jaded railroad officials have been caused fruitless searches after a missing "black boy" through this want of power, on the part of the telegraph to discriminate between y and x. The stories current on this point are numerous, but the best is probably the following : Some time ago a station-master received a telegram from a lady, stating that she had left at his station "two black boys" in the waiting-room, she believed, and tied together with red tape; would he please forward them at once. The astonished official caused search to be made; but instead of boys he found two boxes in the waiting-room, as described, which were duly forwarded. From a similar cause on the part of the electric fluid, a lady received from her son-in-law a telegram which astonished her not a little. It stated that his wife had presented him with a "fine box."

A good story is told of Lawrence Barrett and his friend Stuart, the theatrical manager. It was during the war, and Barrett and a number of other pleasant fellows had been invited to spend the Sunday and dine with Stuart, at New London. As no okra was to be had in New London, Stuart wrote Barrett to try and obtain some at Washington Market, and telegraph, announcing his success or failure before leaving New York, so that if necessary, the carte for Sunday's banquet might be amended. Barrett procured the necessary vegetable, and went to the telegraph office, where he found the wires so crowded with war news and government business that it would be impossible to get off his dispatch for some hours, if at all. He bribed an operator to send the telegram as if it was a private matter of his (the operator's) own, in which case the freemasonry between telegraphers would certainly insure its getting through. The message consisted of three words; " Stuart— Got okra." Meanwhile Stuart after being in suspense till late in the afternoon, determined to go down to the telegraph office. There he saw a crowd gathering around the bulletin board of the newspaper office, on which was displayed in huge letters : "Important War News—Another Reverse for the Union Arms—General J. E. B. Stuart Captures Okra," and so on. Stuart understood it at once. The operator had kept faith, and sent on Barrett's dispatch, but the man at New London received it, "Stuart got Okra," and took it for a war bulletin

announcing the capture of the important village or town of Okra, not down on the map, by the great rebel raider.

It was reported to one of the chief physicians in Blockley Almhouse, Philadelphia, a few months ago, that there was a man lying in one of the wards in a comatose condition. The nurse declared that he had been insensible for twenty-four hours, and she had tried in vain to rouse him. The doctor said that it was probable that the patient was under the influence of some powerful narcotic ; perhaps he had taken a large dose of laudanum. He said it was imperatively necessary that the unfortunate man must be resuscitated at once by some powerful stimulant. Accordingly he directed two of his assistants to take a strong galvanic battery and apply it to the patient until he recovered. The assistants went into the hospital with the battery, while the nurse stopped for a few moments in the laundry. When they reached the man's bedside they placed the battery on the floor, and baring the patient's ankle they wrapped the wire around it. When everything was ready they turned on the current full head. A second later the prostrate form of the patient bounded about four feet into the air, and as it came down upon the bed a second shock sent it up again, the patient meantime exclaiming :

" Yow-wow-wow ! Oh, murder ! murder-r-r ! Oh ! Oh ! Oh ! Thunder and lightning ! Murder-r r ! Yow-wow-wow ! Grashus ! Let up on that ! Ow-wow-wow ! Another one of them'll kill me. Oh ! Merciful Moses ! stop that."

When he came down the fourth time the doctors turned off the current, with the remark that they guessed that would be about enough. Then one of them asked the patient how he felt, and attempted to feel his pulse, but the patient, furious with rage, said :

" You diabolical scoundrel, what d'you mean by hitching that thing to me in that manner ?"

" Now, be calm," said the doctor ; " it's all right ; you'll be better directly."

" But it isn't all right. I've a mind to knock your head off for blowing me up with that infernal machine. What d'you do it for ? "

" My friend, don't excite yourself," said the

doctor. "You've been in a very bad way, and we ran the current through you to bring you back to life."

"Bring me back to life? Why, you must be crazy! Back to life? I was no more dead than you were!"

"Now, keep cool. You have been unconscious for twenty-four hours. Narcotic poisoning, no doubt. We saved you from an early grave. It was the closest shave I ever saw ; it was, upon my honor."

"Well, well, if this don't beat all the —. You took me for the man in ward 49. Why, I'm one of the keepers of the asylum, and I laid down on this bed for a nap. The fellow you're after is over yonder. An early grave! Well, now, I've heard of foolishness in my life, but this takes the rag right off. And I give you warnin' that if you come around yer with that apparatus again tryin' experiments on me I'll wrench your brain pan for you."

Professor Morse and the Telegraph.

SAMUEL F. B. MORSE.

In the year 1811, Benjamin West, the President of the Royal Academy of Fine Arts, and then past seventy years of age, was enjoying the noontide splendor of his fame as the great historical painter of England. During his presidency the Academy had a high reputation, for he was an eminent instructor, and young men from many lands went to it to learn wisdom in Art.

On a bright autumnal morning in the year just mentioned, West's beloved American friend, Washington Allston, entered the reception-room of the venerable painter, and presented to him a slender, handsome young man, whose honest expression of countenance, rich brown hair, dark magnetic eyes and courtesy of manner, made a most favorable impression upon the president. This young man was SAMUEL FINLEY BREESE MORSE. He was then little more than nineteen years of age, and a recent graduate of Yale College. He was the eldest son of Rev. Jedediah Morse, an eminent New England divine and geographer. Rev. Samuel Finley.

D.D., the second president of the College of New Jersey at Princeton, was his maternal great-grandfather, from whom he inherited the first portion of his name. Breese was the maiden name of his mother.

At a very early age young Morse showed tokens of taste and genius for art. At fifteen he made his first composition. It was a good picture, in water colors, of a room in his father's house, with the family—his parents, himself and two brothers—around a table. That pleasing picture hangs in his late home in New York, by the side of his last painting. From that period he desired to become a professional artist, and that desire haunted him all through his collegiate life. In February, 1811, when he was nearly nineteen years of age, he painted a picture (now in the office of the Mayor of Charlestown, Mass.) called "The Landing of the Pilgrims at Plymouth," which, with a landscape painted at about the same time, decided his father, by the advice of Stuart and Allston, to permit him to visit Europe with the latter artist. He bore to England letters to West, also to Copley, then old and feeble. From both he received the kindest attention and encouragement.

Morse made a carefully-finished drawing from a small cast of the Farnese Hercules, as a test of his fitness for a place as a student in the Royal Academy. With this he went to West, who examined the drawing carefully, and handed it back saying, "Very well, sir, very well; go on and finish it." "It is finished," said the expectant student. "O, no," said the president. "Look here, and here, and here," pointing out many unfinished places which had escaped the undisciplined eye of the young artist. Morse quickly observed the defects, spent a week in further perfecting his drawing, and then took it to West, with confidence that it was above criticism. The president bestowed more praise than before, and with a pleasant smile handed it back to Morse, saying, "Very well indeed, sir; go on and finish it."—"Is it not finished?" inquired the almost discouraged student. "See," said West, "you have not marked that muscle, nor the articulation of the finger-joints." Three days more were spent upon the drawing, when it was taken back to the implacable critic. "Very clever indeed," said West, "very clever; now go on and finish it."—"I cannot finish it," Morse replied, when the old man, patting him on the shoulder, said, "Well, well, I've tried you long enough. Now, sir, you've learned more by this drawing than you would have accomplished in double the time by a

dozen half-finished beginnings. It is not numerous drawings, but the character of one, which makes the thorough draughtsman. Finish one picture, sir, and you are a painter."

Morse heeded the sound advice. He studied with Allston and observed his processes; and from the lips of West he heard the most salutary maxims. Encouraged by both, as well as by the veteran Copley, he began to paint a large picture for exhibition in the Royal Academy, choosing for his subject "The Dying Hercules." Following the practice of Allston (who was then painting his celebrated picture of "The Dead Man restored to Life by touching the Bones of Elijah"), he modeled his figure in clay, as the best of the old painters did. It was his first attempt in the sculptor's art and was successful. A cast was made in plaster of Paris and taken to West, who was delighted. He made many exclamations of surprise and satisfaction; and calling to him his son Raphael, he pointed to the figure and said: "Look there, sir, I have always told you that any painter can make a sculptor."

This model contended for the prize of a gold medal offered by the Society of Arts for the best original cast of a single figure, and won it. In the large room of the Adelphi, in the presence of British nobility, foreign ambassadors and distinguished strangers, the duke of Norfolk publicly presented the medal to Morse, on the 13th of May, 1813. At the same time his colossal painting, made from this model, then on exhibition in the Royal Academy, was receiving unbounded praise from the critics, who placed "The Dying Hercules" among the first twelve pictures in a collection of almost two thousand. So began, upon a firm foundation, the real art-life of this New England student.

Encouraged by this success, Morse determined to contend for the highest premium offered by the Royal Academy for the best historical composition, the decision to be made late in 1815. For that purpose he produced his "Judgment of Jupiter," in July of that year. West assured him that it would take the prize, but Morse was unable to comply with the rules of the Academy, which required the victor to receive the medal and money in person. His father had summoned him home, and filial love was stronger than the persuasions of ambition. West and Fuseli both urged the Academy to make an exception in his case, but it could not be done, and the young painter had to be contented with the assurance of the President afterwards, that he would certainly have won the prize (a gold medal and $250 in gold) had he remained.

West was always specially kind to those who came from the land of his birth. Morse was such a favorite with him, that while others were excluded from his painting-room at certain times, he was always admitted. West was then painting his great picture of "Christ Rejected." One day, after carefully examining Morse's hands, and observing their beauty and perfection, he said, "Let me tie you with this cord and take that place while I paint in the hands of the Saviour." It was done, and when he released the young artist, West said to him, "You may now say, if you please, that you had a hand in this picture."

Fuseli, Northcote, Turner, Sir Thomas Lawrence, Flaxman, and other eminent artists ; and Coleridge, Wordsworth, Rogers, Crabbe, and other distinguished literary men, became fond of young Morse, for with an uncommonly quick intellect he united all the graces of pleasant manners and great warmth and kindliness of heart, which charmed the colder Englishmen. And when in August, 1815, he packed his fine picture, "The Judgment of Jupiter," and others, and sailed for his native land, he bore with him the cordial good wishes of some of the best men in England.

When Morse reached Boston, he found that his fame had gone before him, and the best society of that city welcomed him. Cards of invitation to dinner and evening parties were almost daily sent to him. He was only in the twenty-fourth year of his age, and was already famous and bore the seal of highest commendation from the President of the Royal Academy. With such prestige he set up his easel with high hopes and the fairest promises for the future which were doomed to speedy decay and disappointment. The taste of his countrymen had not risen to the appreciation of historical pictures. His fine original compositions, and his excellent copies of those of others (among them one from Tintoretto's marvelous picture of " The Miracle of the Slain"), which hung upon the walls of his studio in Boston, excited the admiration of cultivated people ; but not an order was given for a picture, nor even an inquiry concerning the prices of those on view.

Disappointed, but not disheartened, Mr. Morse left Boston, almost penniless, and in Concord, N. H., commenced the business of a portrait painter, in which he found constant employment at $15 a subject, cabinet size. There he became acquainted with a Southern gentleman, who assured him that he might find continual employment in the South at four-fold higher prices for his labor. He appealed to his uncle, Dr. Finley of Charleston, for advice, who cordially invited him to come as his visitor and make a trial. He went, leaving behind in Concord a young maiden to whom he was affianced, promising to return and marry her when better fortune should reward his labors. That better fortune soon appeared. Orders for portraits came in so thickly (one hundred and fifty, at $60 each) that he painted four a week during the winter and spring. In the early summer time of 1818, he returned to New England with $3,000 in his pocket, and on the 6th of October following his friends read this notice in the *New Hampshire Patriot*, published at Concord :—

"MARRIED, in this town, by Rev. Dr. McFarland, Mr. Samuel F. B. Morse (the celebrated painter) to Miss Lucretia Walker, daughter of Charles Walker, Esq."

Four successive winters Mr. Morse painted in Charleston, and then settled his little family with his parents, in a quiet home in New Haven, and again proceeded to try his fortune as an historical painter, by the production of an exhibition picture of the House of Representatives at the National Capital. It was an excellent work of art, but as a business speculation it was disastrous, sinking several hundred dollars of the artist's money and wasting nearly eighteen months of precious time. No American had taste enough to buy it, and it was finally sold to a gentleman from England.

Morse now sought employment in the rapidly-growing commercial city of New York. Through the influence of Mr. Isaac Lawrence he obtained the commission, from the corporate authorities of that city, to paint a full-length portrait of Lafayette, then in this country. He had just completed his study from life, in Washington city, in February, 1825, when a black shadow was suddenly cast across his hitherto sunny life-path. A letter told him of the death of his wife. There is a popular saying that "misfortunes seldom come single." The popular belief in the saying was justified in Mr. Morse's case, for in the space of a little more than a year death deprived him of his wife and his father and mother. Thenceforward his children and art absorbed his earthly affections, and he sought in a closer intimacy with artists the best consolations of social life. By that intimacy he was soon called upon to be the valiant and efficient champion of his professional brethren in a bitter controversy between two associations, in this wise :—

The American Academy of Fine Arts, then under the presidency of Colonel John Trumbull, was in a languishing state, badly managed and of little use to artists. Indeed, the artists complained of ill usage by the directors, a majority of whom were not of the profession ; and Thomas S. Cummings, a spirited young student with Henry Inman, drew up a remonstrance and a petition for relief. Morse took a great interest in the matter, and called a few of the artists together at his rooms to discuss it. At that meeting he proposed as a remedy for the fatal disease of which the old Academy was dying, the formation of a society of artists for improvement in drawing. This was done in November, 1825, at a meeting held in the rooms of the New York Historical Society, at which the now venerable Asher B. Durand presided. The new organization was named "The New York Drawing Association." Mr. Morse was chosen to be its president. Its members were immediately claimed to be students of the Academy, and Colonel Trumbull endeavored to compel their allegiance. The artists were aroused, and the subsequent action of the Academy determined them to cut loose from all connection with it.

At a meeting of the Drawing Association in the following January, Mr. Morse, after a short address, proposed by resolutions the founding of an association of artists, far wider in its scope than the one over which he presided. He foreshadowed in a few words its character. The resolutions were adopted, and on the 18th of January, 1826, the new association was organized under the name of THE NATIONAL ACADEMY OF DESIGN. Mr. Morse was chosen to be its president, and for sixteen successive years he was annually elected to that office. Mr. Durand and General Thomas S. Cummings (the latter for forty years the treasurer of the new association) are the only survivors of the founders of that now flourishing institution.

The friends of the old Academy were very wrathful, and assailed the new association with unstinted bitterness, in which personalities were indulged. A war of words in the public press was carried on for a long time, which Mr. Morse, as the champion of the new society, waged with the vigorous and efficient weapons of candor, courtesy, and dignified, keen and lucid statements and arguments, which finally achieved a complete victory. *

Mr. Morse inaugurated a new era in the history of the fine arts in this country, by calling public attention to their usefulness and necessity, in a series of lectures on the subject before the New York Athenæum, to crowded audiences. These were repeated before the students and academicians of the National Academy of Design. ·

In 1829 Mr. Morse made a second professional visit to Europe. He was warmly welcomed and duly honored by the Royal Academy in London. West had been dead nine years, and Fuseli was no more ; but he found an admirer in Sir Thomas Lawrence, West's successor, and many friends among the younger academicians. During more than three years he made his abode in various continental cities. In Paris he studied in the Louvre, and there he made an exhibition picture of the famous gallery, with beautiful miniature copies of about fifty of the finest works in that collection. It failed as a speculation, and finally went to Hyde Hall, the seat of Mr. George Clarke, on Otsego Lake.

In November, 1832, Mr. Morse landed in New York, enriched by his transatlantic experience and full of the promise of attaining to the highest excellence in his profession. Allston, writing to Dunlap in 1834, said : "I rejoice to hear your report of Morse's advance in his art. I know *what is in him*, perhaps, better than any one else. If he will only bring out all that is *there*, he will show powers that many now do not dream of."

A higher revelation than art had even given it was now vouchsafed to the mind of Morse through Science, its sister and coadjutor. For several years his thoughts had been busy with that subtle principle, by whatever name it may be called, which seems to pervade the universe, and "spreads undivided, operates unspent." The lectures on electro-magnetism by his intimate friend, J. Freeman Dana, at the Athenæum, while he (Morse) was giving his course there on the Fine Arts, had greatly interested him in the subject, and he learned much in familiar conversations with Mr. Dana. Even at that early day, Dana's spiral volute coil suggested to Morse the electro-magnet used in his recording instruments.

While on his second visit to Europe, Mr. Morse made himself acquainted with the labors of scientific men in endeavors to com-

* A record of this controversy, with the newspaper articles of the combatants, may be found in that rare and valuable work, *Historic Annals of the National Academy of Design*, by Professor Thomas S. Cummings, N. A.

municate intelligence between far distant places out of the line of vision by means of electro-magnetism, and he saw an electromagnetic *semaphore* in operation. He was aware that so early as 1649, Strada, a Jesuit priest, had in fable prophesied of an electric telegraph; and that for half a century or more, philosophers had been, from time to time, partially succeeding in the discovery of the anxiously-looked for result. But no *telegraph* proper—no instrument *for writing at a distance* —had yet been invented.*

In the ship *Sully*, in which. Mr. Morse voyaged from Havre to New York in the autumn of 1832, the recent discovery in France of the means for obtaining the electric spark from a magnet was a fruitful topic of conversation among the cultivated passengers ; and it was during that voyage that a revelation was made to the mind of Morse, which enabled him to conceive the idea of an electro-magnetic and chemical *recording* telegraph, substantially and essentially as it now exists. Before the *Sully* had reached New York, he had elaborated his conceptions in the form of drawings and specifications, which he exhibited to his fellow-passengers. This fact, proven by the testimony of those passengers given in a court of justice, fixes the date of the invention of Morse's electro-magnetic recording telegraph at the autumn of 1832.

Circumstances delayed the construction of a complete recording telegraph by Mr. Morse, and the subject slumbered in his mind. During his absence abroad he had been elected to the professorship of the Literature of the Arts of Design in the University of the City of New York, and this field of duty oc-

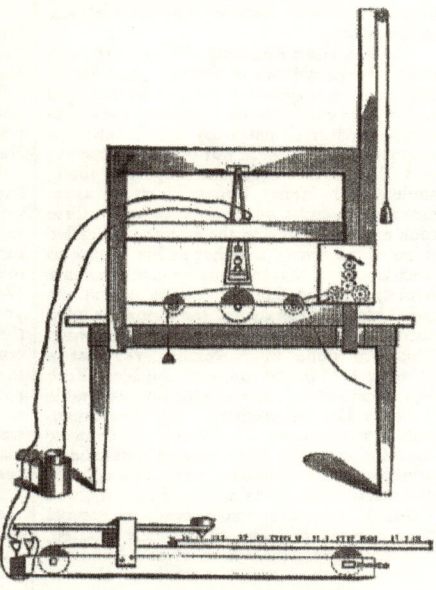

MORSE'S FIRST RECORDING TELEGRAPH.

cupied his attention for some time. Finally, in November, 1835, he completed a rude telegraphic instrument—the first recording apparatus—which is now in the library of his country-seat near Poughkeepsie. It embodied the mechanical principles of those now in use in every quarter of the globe. But his whole plan was not completed until July, 1837, when, by means of two instruments, he was able to communicate from as well as to a distant point. In September, hundreds of people saw it in operation at the University, the larger portion of whom looked upon it as a scientific toy constructed by an unfortunate dreamer.

In the following year Mr. Morse's invention was sufficiently perfected to induce him to call the attention of the National Congress to it, and ask their aid in the construction of an experimental line between the cities of Washington and Baltimore. Late in the long session of 1838, he appeared before that body with his instrument. Before leaving New York with it he invited a few friends to see it work. The written invitation ran thus, —I copy one now before me :

" Professor Morse requests the honor of Thomas S. Cummings, Esq., and family's company in the Geolo-

---

* In 1774, Le Sage constructed an electric semaphore with twenty-four wires corresponding to the 24 letters of the alphabet. In 1793, Claude Chappé established an aërial line of electric semaphores. From 1780 to 1800, German, Italian, and Spanish philosophers made interesting experiments in this direction. In 1810 Schweiger discovered the multiplying power of the magnet by an electric coil, and in 1819 Oersted perfected the discovery of electro-magnetism. Ronalds constructed an electric semaphore, which made signals at a distance of eight miles, in 1816. In 1825 Sturgeon invented the electro-magnet. In 1830 Professor Henry applied Schweiger's coil to Sturgeon's magnet, and wonderfully increased the magnetic force which Morse subsequently used. Arago, Faraday, Ampère, Gauss and Weber, and Steinheil had made many valuable advances towards the great discovery, and Wheatstone very nearly reached it.

gical Cabinet of the University, Washington Square, to witness the operation of the electro-magnetic telegraph, at a private exhibition of it to a few friends, previous to its leaving the city for Washington.

"The apparatus will be prepared at precisely 12 o'clock, on Wednesday, 24th instant. The time being limited, punctuality is specially requested.

"NEW YORK UNIVERSITY, *June* 22, 1838."

One of the first messages on that wire was given to Mr. Cummings (yet in his possession) in these words : "Attention the Universe—By Kingdoms, right wheel—Facetiously." It may be explained by the fact that Mr. Cummings had just received military promotion to the command of a division. It is probably the first message by the recording telegraph now extant, and how prophetic !

Professor Morse found very little encouragement at Washington, and he went to Europe with the hope of drawing the attention of foreign governments to the advantages, and securing patents for the invention, having already filed a caveat at the patent office in his own country. His mission was a failure. England refused to grand him a patent, and France gave him only a useless *brevet d'invention,* which did not secure for him any special privilege. So he returned home, disappointed but not discouraged, and waited

patiently four years longer, before he again attempted to interest Congress in his invention.

The year before he went to Europe, Professor Morse suffered a severe disappointment in the way of his profession. He was an unsuccessful applicant for a commission to paint one of the pictures for the eight panels in the Rotunda of the national Capitol, which a law of Congress had authorized.

Morse was greatly disappointed. His artist friends showed their sympathy in the practical way of giving him an order to paint a historical picture, raising funds for the payment for it in shares of $50 each. The first intimation the Professor had of their generous design, was when two of his professional brethren called upon him and gave the order, and at the same time informed him that $3,000 had already been subscribed. "Never have I read or known of such an act of professional generosity," exclaimed Morse. He agreed to paint for them the picture he had projected for the Government—"The Signing of the First Compact on board the Mayflower"—and addressed himself to the task. But the telegraph soon absorbed his attention, and so won him from painting that he almost abandoned its practice. In 1841 he returned to the subscribers the amount in full, with interest, which had been paid to him, and so canceled the obligation. "Thus," wrote General Cummings, "while the world won a belt of instantaneous communication, the subscribers lost the pleasure of his triumph as an artist. The artist was absorbed in the electrician."

While Professor Morse was in Paris, in the spring of 1839, he formed an acquaintance with M. Daguerre, who, in connection with M. Niepce, had discovered the method of fixing the image of the camera obscura, which was then creating a great sensation among scientific men. These gentlemen were then considering a proposition from the French government to make their discovery public, on condition of their receiving a suitable pension. Professor Morse was anxious to see the photographic results before leaving for home, and the American Consul (Robert Walsh) made arrangements for an interview between the two discoverers. The inventions of each were shown to the other ; and Daguerre promised to

FAC-SIMILE OF THE FIRST DAGUERREOTYPE OF THE FACE MADE IN AMERICA.

This sentence was written from Washington by me at the Baltimore Terminus at 8ʰ 45 min. A.M. on Friday May 24.ᵗʰ 1844, being the first ever transmitted from Washington to Baltimore, by Telegraph, and was indited by my much loved friend Annie G. Ellsworth.

Samˡ. F. B. Morse,. Superintendent of Elec. Mag. Telegraphs.

send to Morse a copy of the descriptive publication which he intended to make so soon as the pension should be secured. Daguerre kept his promise, and Morse was probably the first recipient of the pamphlet in this country. From the drawings it contained he constructed the first daguerreotype apparatus made in the United States.

From a back window in the New York University Professor Morse obtained a good representation of the tower of the Church of the Messiah, on Broadway, and surrounding buildings, which possesses a historical interest as being the first photograph ever taken in America. It was on a plate the size of a playing card. He experimented with Professor J. W. Draper in a studio built upon the roof of the University, and succeeded in taking likenesses from the living human face. His subjects were compelled to sit fifteen minutes in the bright sunlight, with the eyes closed, of course. Professor Draper shortened the process and was the first to take portraits with the eyes open. Some of the original plates so photographed upon by Professor Morse were presented by him to Vassar College, of which he was a trustee.

On the preceding page will be seen an engraving of part of one of these plates (which originally contained three figures), in which the costumes almost mark the era of its production.

Again Professor Morse appeared before Congress with his telegraph. It was at the session of 1842-3. On the 21st of February, 1843, the late John P. Kennedy of Maryland moved that a bill in committee, appropriating $30,000 to be expended, under the direction of the Secretary of the Treasury, a series of experiments for testing the merits of the telegraph, should be considered. It met with ridicule from the outset. Cave Johnson of Tennessee moved as an amendment, that one-half the sum should be given to a lecturer on Mesmerism, then in Washington, for trying mesmeric experiments under the direction of the Secretary of the Treasury. Mr. Houston thought Millerism ought to be included in the benefits of the appropriation. After the indulgence of much cheap wit,

Mr. S. Mason of Ohio protested against such frivolity as injurious to the character of the House, and asked the chair to rule the amendment out of order. The chair (John White of Kentucky) ruled the amendment in order, because, as he said, " it would require a scientific analysis to determine how far the magnetism of Mesmerism was analogous to that to be employed in telegraphs." His wit was applauded by peals of laughter, when the amendment was voted down and the bill laid aside to be reported. It passed the House on the 23d of February, by the close vote of 89 to 83, and then went to the Senate. The efficient friends of Professor Morse in procuring this result were J. P. Kennedy of Maryland, S. Mason of Ohio, David Wallace of Indiana, C. G. Ferris of New York, and Colonel J. B. Aycrigg of New Jersey.

The bill met with neither sneers nor opposition in the Senate, but the business of that House went on with discouraging slowness. At twilight on the last evening of the session (March 3, 1843) there were 119 bills before it. As it seemed impossible for it to be reached in regular course before the hour of adjournment should arrive, the Professor, who had anxiously watched the tardy movements of business all day from the gallery of the Senate chamber, went with a sad heart to his hotel and prepared to leave for New York at an early hour the next morning. While at breakfast, a servant informed him that a young lady desired to see him in the parlor.

There he met Miss Annie Ellsworth, then a young school girl — the daughter of his intimate friend, Hon. Henry L. Ellsworth, the first Commissioner of Patents — who said, as she extended her hand to him : " I have come to congratulate you."

" Upon what ? " inquired the Professor.

" Upon the passage of your bill," she replied.

" Impossible ! Its fate was sealed at dusk last evening. You must be mistaken."

" Not at all," she responded. " Father sent me to tell you that your bill was passed. He remained until the session closed, and yours was the last bill but one acted upon, and it was passed just five minutes before

the adjournment ; and I am so glad to be the first one to tell you. Mother says, too, that you must come home with me to breakfast."

The invitation was readily accepted, and the joy in the household was unbounded. Both Mr. and Mrs. Ellsworth had fully believed in the project, and the former, in his confidence in it and in his warm friendship for Prof. Morse, had spent all the closing hours of the session in the Senate chamber, doing what he could to help the bill along, and giving it all the influence of his high personal and official position.

Grasping the hand of his young friend, the Professor thanked her again and again for bearing him such pleasant tidings, and assured her that she should send over the wires the first message, as her reward. The matter was talked over in the family, and Mrs. Ellsworth suggested a message which Prof. Morse referred to the daughter, for her approval ; and this was the one which was subsequently sent.

A little more than a year after that time, the line between Washington and Baltimore was completed. Prof. Morse was in the former city, and Mr. Alfred Vail, his assistant, in the latter ; the first in the chamber of the Supreme Court, the last in the Mount Clare dépôt, when the circuit being perfect, Prof. Morse sent to Miss Ellsworth for her message, and it came.

" WHAT HATH GOD WROUGHT ! "

It was sent in triplicate in the dot-and-line language of the instrument to Baltimore, and was the *first message ever transmitted by a recording telegraph.* A fac-simile of that first message, with Professor Morse's indorsement, is here given.

The story of this first message has been often told with many exaggerations. It has roamed about Europe with various romantic material attached to it, originating mainly in the French imagination, and has started up anew from time to time in our own country under fresh forms, but the above story is simply and literally true. An inventor in despair receives the news of his unexpected success from his friend's daughter, and he makes her a promise which he keeps, and

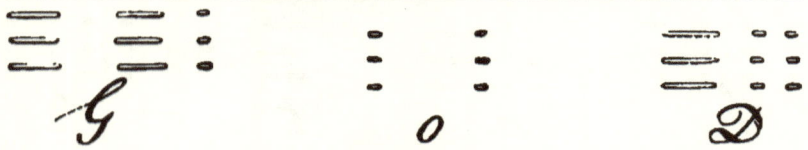

thus links her name with his own, and with an invention which becomes one of the controlling instruments of civilization for all time.

The first public messages sent were a notice to Silas Wright, in Washington, of his nomination for the office of Vice-President of the United States by the Democratic Convention, then (May, 1844) in session in Baltimore, and his response declining it. Hon. Hendrick B. Wright, in a letter to the author of this sketch, says : " As the presiding officer of the body, I read the despatch ; but so incredulous were the members as to the authority of the evidence before them, that the Convention adjourned over to the following day, to await the report of a committee sent over to Washington to get *reliable* information upon the subject."

Such were the circumstances attending the birth of the Electro-Magnetic Recording Telegraph. The ingenuity of man had fashioned a body for it ; but there it lay, with all its perfections undreamed of, excepting by a few prophetic philosophers,—its mighty powers all unknown,—almost as lifeless and useless as a rock in the wilderness, until Morse, divinely inspired, as he always believed, endowed it with intelligence. The poet said concerning the discoveries of Newton, which dispelled so much of the darkness which hung around the truths of science,

"God said, Let Newton live, and all was Light."

With equal truth may Morse be ranked among the creative agencies of God upon the earth.

The infant of his conception, so ridiculed and distrusted, immediately gave signs of its divinity. The doubters were soon ready to bring garlanded bulls to sacrifice to it as a god ; and a prophet wrote :

" What more, presumptuous mortals, will you dare ?
See Franklin seize the Clouds, their bolts to bury ;
The Sun assigns his pencil to Daguerre,
And Morse the lightning makes his secretary ! "

He stood before the world as the peer of Kings and Emperors, for the application of his thought to exquisite mechanism revolutionized the world. And kings and emperors soon delighted to pay homage to his genius by substantial tokens.

The Sultan of Turkey was the first monarch who recognized Professor Morse as a public benefactor, by bestowing upon him the decoration of the *Nishan Iftichar*, or *Order of Glory*. That was in 1848, the same year when his Alma Mater conferred upon him the honorary degree of Doctor of Laws. The Kings of Prussia and Würtemberg and the Emperor of Austria each gave him a *Gold Medal of Scientific Merit*, that of the first named being set in a massive gold snuffbox. In 1856, the Emperor of the French bestowed upon him the *Cross of a Chevalier of the Legion of Honor*. The next year the *Cross of Knight Commander of the First Class in the Order of the Dannebroge* was presented to him by the King of Denmark, and in 1858 the Queen of Spain gave him the *Cross of the Knight Commander* (de numero) *of the Order of Isabella the Catholic.* The King of Italy gave him the *Cross of the Order of SS. Maurice and Lazarus*, and the Sovereign of Portugal presented him with the *Cross of the Order of the Tower and Sword*.

In 1858, a special congress was called by the Emperor of the French to devise a suitable testimonial of the nation to Professor Morse. Representatives from ten sovereignties convened at Paris under the presidency of Count Walewski, then the French Minister for Foreign Affairs, and by a unanimous vote they gave, in the aggregate, four hundred thousand francs ($80,000) as "an honorary gratuity to Professor Morse," a "collective act, to demonstrate the sentiments of public gratitude justly excited by his invention." The States which participated in this testimonial were France, Austria, Russia, Belgium, Holland, Sweden, Piedmont, the Holy See, Tuscany and Turkey.

Like all useful inventions, Morse's recording telegraph found competitors for honors and emoluments. Its own progress in securing public confidence was at first slow. In 1846 House's letter-printing telegraph was brought out, and in 1849 Bain introduced electro-chemical telegraphy. Rival lines were established. Costly litigations ensued, which promised, at one time, to demand more money than the income from the inven-

tion. Finally, in 1851, the rival lines were consolidated, when different companies were formed to operate under the same patent. Since then other consolidations have taken place, and the Western Union Telegraph Company now controls a greater portion of the business in this country. According to a statement made by its able electrician, George B. Prescott, in January, 1871, that company was then operating 56,000 miles of line, 125,000 miles of wire, 4,600 offices, and was transmitting over 10,000,000 messages annually. The remaining companies were then operating about 10,000 miles of line. At about the same time there were in round numbers 175,000 miles of line and 475,000 miles of wire in operation in Great Britain, Ireland, and on the European continent. At the same time also there were over thirty-six thousand miles of submarine lines laid under the waters of the Atlantic and German Oceans; the Baltic, North Mediterranean, Arabian, China, Japan and Red Seas; the Persian Gulf; the Bay of Biscay; the Straits of Gibraltar and Malacca, and the Gulfs of Mexico and the St. Lawrence, by which the civilized world is put into close mental communication.

Of marine telegraphy, Professor Morse was the originator. So early as 1842, he laid the first marine cable across the harbor of New York, which achievement won for him the gold medal of the American Institute; and in a letter to John C. Spencer, then Secretary of the Treasury, in August, 1843, concerning electro-magnetism and its powers, he

MORSE'S RESIDENCE AT LOCUST GROVE.

wrote: "The practical inference from this law is, that a telegraphic communication on the electro-magnetic plan may with certainty be established across the Atlantic Ocean. Startling as this may now seem, I am confident the time will come when this project will be realized." That prophecy was fulfilled in 1858, when Professor Morse had yet fourteen years of life before him, and the most wonderful achievements of his marvelous invention were yet unrevealed. Among these was the long-worked-for result, accomplished only a few weeks before his death, namely; *the transmission of messages both ways over the same wire at the same instant.* This is the last great triumph of electro-magnetic telegraphy.

Very soon the almost sentient electro-magnetic nerve will convey instant intelligence through every ocean to every continent of the globe. May we not liken that nerve, throbbing with its mysterious essence, to the voice of the angel in the Apocalypse, who stood with one foot upon the *land* and the other upon the *sea* and proclaimed that *time* should be no longer?

Professor Morse enjoyed the full fruition of his great discovery, and received during his life the honors and emoluments which were justly his due. In addition to the attentions paid to him by governments, he was made the recipient of public honorary banquets in London, Paris, and New York. At the latter, given at the close of 1868, the Chief Justice of the United States presided, and many of the dignitaries of the republic and the British minister at Washington were in attendance.

In 1871 a statue of Professor Morse was erected in Central Park, New York, at the expense of the telegraph operators of the country. It was unveiled on the 10th of June with the most imposing ceremonies, in which leading men of the nation participated. There were delegates from every State in the Union, and from the British provinces. In the evening a public reception was given to the venerable inventor at the Academy of Music, at which Hon. William Orton, President of the Western Union Telegraph Company, presided, assisted by scores of the

leading public men of the nation as vice-presidents. Impressive speeches were uttered. The last scene was most impressive of all. It was announced that the telegraphic instrument before the audience was then in connection with every other one of the 10,000 instruments in America, when Miss Cornell, a young telegraphic operator, touched its key and sent this message to all: "GREETING AND THANKS TO THE TELEGRAPH FRATERNITY THROUGHOUT THE WORLD. GLORY TO GOD IN THE HIGHEST, ON EARTH PEACE, GOOD-WILL TO MEN." Then the venerable inventor was conducted to the instrument, touched the key, and the sounder struck "S. F. B. MORSE." A storm of enthusiasm swept through the house for some moments, as the audience arose, the ladies waving their handkerchiefs, and old men and young men alike cheering as with one voice.

Professor Morse appeared in public for the last time on the 22d of February, 1872, when he unveiled the statue of Franklin erected in Printing House Square, in New York. After that his health rapidly declined, and on Tuesday, the 2d of April, 1872, his spirit passed out peacefully from its earthly tabernacle to the bosom of God. On the 5th his remains were carried in a casket to the Madison Square Presbyterian Church, when the glorious Anthem, "I heard a voice from Heaven," was sung, a funeral discourse was pronounced by Rev. William Adams, D.D., and a concluding prayer by Rev. B. F. Wheeler, pastor of the church at Poughkeepsie, of which the deceased was a member. Then the remains were taken to Greenwood Cemetery. Just before his death, Professor Morse's physicians, uncertain as to the exact nature of his disease, raised him up and sounded his chest with finger tappings. The Professor roused from the stupor in which he had

been lying, when one of the physicians said, "This is the way *we* telegraph." The dying man comprehended the point, and replied, "Very good—very good." These were his last words.

Professor Morse was twice married. His first wife, as we have seen, died in 1825. His second wife (still living) was Sarah Elizabeth Griswold, a grand-daughter of the late Arthur Breese, of Utica, and Catharine Livingston, of Poughkeepsie, to whom he was married in the summer of 1848.

The Professor's private life was one of almost unalloyed happiness. After his last marriage, his summer home was on the banks of the Hudson just below Poughkeepsie, called "Locust Grove," and his winter residence was in New York City. His presence was always sunshine to his family, and his influence in society was benign. He was, in the highest sense of the term, a Christian gentleman, a faithful disciple of the Redeemer, and a fine exemplar of dutiful obedience to every law in all the relations of life, domestic and social.

The invention of Professor Morse is a gift to mankind of immeasurable value. It has already widened the range of human thought and action, and given to literature a truer catholicity and humanity, whilst more than any other agency it is binding the nations of the earth in a brotherhood which seems like the herald of the millennial era. Its silent forces are working with awful majesty in the realm of mind, reducing the ideals of the old mythologies to practical and beneficent results.

Has inspiration ceased? Have revelations come to an end? Was that first message a chance communication, or a direct inspiration of the Almighty? "WHAT HATH GOD WROUGHT!"

Or all the freaks of the telegraph, the following is one of the most laughable. A young man, when about to start for his new parish, was unexpectedly detained by the incapacity of his Presbytery to ordain him. In order to explain his non-arrival at the appointed time, he sent the following telegram to the deacons of the church:

" Presbytery lack a quorum to ordain."

In the course of its journey the message got strangely metamorphosed, and reached the astonished deacons in this shape:

" Presbytery tacked a worm on to Adam."

The sober church officers were sorely discomposed and mystified, but, after grave consultation, concluded that it was the minister's facetious way of announcing that he had got married, and accordingly proceeded to provide lodgings for two instead of one.

The Song of the Plug.

WITH thumb and fore-finger worn,
  With expression of infernal glee,
A country plug sat in his place of toil
  Plying his dare deviltry.
Break! break! break!
  As contented as cats on the rug.
And, still on a key of excellent make,
  He warbled the song of the plug.

Break! break! break!
  While experts grow mad and profane.
Break! break! break!
  Till they think I'm a terrible bane.
Blaspheme and abuse me and swear,
  Swear at, abuse me, blaspheme,
Till they're forced to refrain since no words remain,
  To build dams for profanity's stream.

Oh, plugs! this vast country o'er!
  Fellow fiends of a calling so dire!
It is not your fingers you're wearing out,
  But the patience of kings of the wire.
Break! break! break!
  As contented as puss on the rug,
Breaking on duplex and single strings too—
  On all kinds considered a " bug."

Break! break! break!
  My toil seems never to cease.
And what are its wages?—a cushioned chair
  And a post of endless lease.
This best of wires, that longest trick,
  And favors so many and great,
That my written thanks would fill all the blanks
  The printers could ever create.

Break! break! break!
  They often wish me dead,
And schemes devise to extirpate
  All plugs that o'er earth are spread!

But 'tis vain to speak of death,
  We never, never die.
'Tis merely a waste of experts' breath,
  They must only endure us and sigh.

Oh! but to break on a wire
  Where rushists are happy and glad!
On a circuit so easy to break,
  Where experts so lightly get mad.
For only one short month
  To break as I used to break,
Before my fingers were stiff and old,
  And my break-thirst so easy to slake.

Oh! but for one short month—
  A month however short!—
(E'en February would suit me well,)
  To increase my wicked sport.
A little practice would serve me much,
  But to get it my work would flag;
And I could not provoke the expert folk—
  No, I can not and will not lag!

You may swear and howl and shout,
  You may shout and howl and swear,
But my tribe will live and thrive and grow.
  (Ah! I see you with horror stare!)
We shall live to ever afflict.
  We shall thrive to perpetuate breaks.
We shall grow—increase; you shall have no peace,
  Until Gabriel's trump the world awakes.

With thumb and fore-finger worn,
  With a look of infernal glee,
A fiendish plug sat in his place of toil
  Plying his dare deviltry.
Break! break! break!
  When currents are weak and when strong,
And still in a style that never knew Morse—
  Would it might know a healthy remorse—
  He merrily warbled his song.

Joseph Christie (Werner)

Was born in Manchester, England, but came to the United States while yet young, making Philadelphia his home. During 1869, '70, '71 he was in Utah, Wyoming, and California. In the latter part of 1871 he visited South America, returning ere long to the United States *via* the West Indies. Until within the past year Mr. Christie has been an attaché of the Western Union Telegraph Company's Philadelphia office, filling various positions, in all of which he served with honor to himself and advantage to his employers. At present he is one of the representatives of the Associated Press in Philadelphia, and apparently a rising man. Mr. Christie is best known to his immediate associates as an operator of unusual expertness and finish; to the remainder of the profession he is best known as the author of the contributions to THE OPERATOR variously signed "Junius," "Beppo," "Werner." His writings are perhaps the best, viewed in a purely literary light, that have yet been offered by a telegrapher for the entertainment of telegraphers. Possessing the rare faculty of perceiving humor wherever it exists, kind-hearted, sympathetic, and keenly appreciative of worth in others, Mr. Christie has a vein of satire withal which has many times and oft stood him in good stead. The unrelenting enemy of all petty abuses and tyrannies calculated to demoralize or degrade his brethren, he has repeatedly subjected such abuses and tyrannies to a round of ridicule at once scathing and polished, which generally resulted in an amelioration of the evil, while those who had been at fault were left as much in the dark as to how and when they received their hurt as the Persian soldier of tradition beheaded with the magic scimeter without knowing it. While Mr. Christie, therefore, has all along disavowed any particular ability as a writer, it must be conceded that he stands in the foremost rank among those of his kind. He is, moreover, a very expert draughtsman, a caricaturist of much cleverness, and, better than all, a painter, who gives promise of future distinction. Added to all these accomplishments, Mr. Christie possesses charms of mind and a sterling worth of character which he does not proclaim from the housetop, but which a long and intimate acquaintance surely reveals, while his familiarity with books, with political and social methods, and the higher arts stamps him as a man of studious instincts, with an inherent taste for everything which is good, noble, and elevating.

A Centennial Telegraphic Romance.—Drawn by Frank Beard.

A Centennial-Telegraphic Romance.

It was New York day at the Centennial. All roads seemed to lead to Philadelphia, and every road, and every train, and every car was crowded. When the 7:45 express train moved slowly, and thirty-five minutes behind time, out of Jersey City depot, it had twenty-three passenger cars attached, and carried—the conductors only know how many thousand passengers.

Mr. Sydney Summerville, a denizen of the Western Union main office, having secured a two days' leave of absence for the purpose of visiting the Centennial city, was one of the passengers. He walked through four several cars before he could find an unoccupied seat. At length in the rear car he found the little sofa at the forward end vacant, and thankfully took possession of it—the solitary occupant.

He had a *Herald* and a *Sun* with him, and read for a short time after the train started. Then he gazed lazily out of the window. It was a delightful morning. The fields, bathed in mellow sunlight, never looked lovelier; nature seemed to have donned her holiday attire for the occasion, and as Summerville closed his eyes, and listened to the monotonous clickety-clack of the wheels, he fell into a delicious reverie. He had already spent a week at the great World's Fair, and so favorably impressed was he with the exhibition, and particularly the Art Gallery, that he felt that he must see it at least once more before it closed forever.

Opening his eyes at last, he looked around upon his fellow-passengers. A few, he could see, were "city folks," but the majority were evidently hardy sons of toil. The garments of many still showed the crease of the ready-made clothing store, and the bright, new neckties and shining shirt-bosoms evidenced that the wearers meant to appear at the Centennial looking their very best.

Every cross seat in the car was occupied, and for fully five minutes Mr. Summerville kept gazing from one to another of the passengers, wondering whether he might not be familiar with the face of some one present. His eyes wandered slowly to the farther end of the car, and then back again, until at length they rested upon the little sofa opposite. It was his first conscious glance in that direction, and a close observer might have noticed a little involuntary start as he caught sight of the—like himself—solitary occupant of the little sofa.

Perhaps the reader will not blame him, however, when I say that the seat was occupied by a fair young girl of not more than eighteen, bright, intelligent, radiant with smiles, and decidedly good looking.

Summerville's heart fairly stood still, and opening his eyes he gazed at

"The lovely apparition sent
To be a moment's ornament,"

for several moments admiringly, and almost spellbound.

It is but fair to mention here that this was a very unusual proceeding on Summerville's part. If there was any one thing upon which that gentleman prided himself more than another it was on not being what the world calls a "ladies' man." He was simply a very sensible, practical person, and had never, so far as any of his friends were aware, been guilty of the little indiscretion of falling in love.

But love sometimes enters a life abruptly and unexpectedly. Love, as somebody has said, is a dear divine passion of the gods. It is the only thing in this world that makes the long interval between fourteen and seventy in any way acceptable. Life without love is an ugly, monotonous song; a low, wearisome, uneducated parrot's song that dolefully rings out in the dreary space, frightening the timorous traveler. To meet an utter stranger, and gaze in the unfamiliar eyes unthinkingly, and suddenly to find ones heart still and cold, while everything in the world underwent a grand, wondrous change, that is love at first sight—the sweetest, most divine and glorious of all love. It is worth life and worth death to love like that. Such was Summerville's love. As he gazed at the sweet, frank countenance of the lady before him, he felt that the ever-changing smile was but the reflex of a pure and innocent heart within, unclouded by sorrow and unsullied by contact with a dissembling world.

As he continued to gaze enraptured upon the fair picture, a sweet sensation crept over him such as he had never felt before. Life seemed literally strewn with roses, and he wondered how he could ever have come to consider it dull, and scarcely worth the having.

The young lady was of a full rounded physique, perhaps about five feet five inches in height. A profusion of golden hair hung in studied carelessness over her shapely shoulders. Her large hazel eyes had a peculiarly hearty, merry twinkle. She was faultless in form and feature, with a complexion where the blended rose and lily seemed to vie for ascendency. With these she carried a bright, joyous, and ever-changing expression, which might well have melted the heart of even the most thorough woman-hater. The following lines seem to suit her so well that it may not be out of place to quote them here :

" Step as light as any fawn ;
   Sweetest eyes, where seem to dawn
Beams of love and every kind of little wile ;
   Figure, like her features, chaste ;
   Oh ! and such a dainty waist ;
And a perfectly intoxicating smile.

   Teeth as white as ocean spray ;
   Lips where lightest fancies play
Like warm sunbeams in and out among the flowers,
   Yet some sober thoughts, I ween,
   Keep their vigils in between,
When the twilight deepens into evening hours."

She was not alone. On the seat immediately behind, and with their faces toward her, sat

" The father and mother, to guard from the whirl
   Of a hollow world this priceless pearl,
   This innocent, loving and lovely girl
   On her way to the great Centennial."

Her father sat next the window. He was a man of perhaps fifty years ; clear, bold, sharply-defined features, a firm mouth and high, intellectual forehead. His countenance indicated great force of character, and Summerville could not but set him down as a stern disciplinarian. The mother was younger, but appeared to have passed through more trials. She was clad in deep mourning. Dark rings around her eyes bore testimony to long, weary hours of patient watching, perhaps by the dying bedside of a loved child. But she had a sweet, pleasant face, and as her countenance was occasionally lit up by a smile of maternal pride as she gazed at her lovely daughter, Summerville saw that she was still a very beautiful woman. She seemed very proud of her daughter, and the latter properly reciprocated the affection. When their eyes met, Summerville saw that the face of each wore a sweet, pleased smile, as if the one were all the world to the other. The father scarcely ever looked toward his daughter. He occasionally turned to speak to his wife, but the greater part of the time he gazed doggedly out of the window.

The more Summerville looked at the young woman, the warmer grew his admiration for her. He could scarcely keep his eyes off her. But so far he had received no encouragement. If she looked at him at all it was merely a momentary glance. All at once, however, those lustrous, handsome dark eyes beamed full upon and almost dazzled him with their brightness. Their eyes met. Each looked at the other steadily, but with perfect modesty for perhaps ten seconds. His heart quickened its pace, and a little blush stole to her cheek. After looking out of the window for a few moments her eyes wandered in his direction once more. Again their eyes met. There was no smile, no sign of any kind. Each simply gazed full in the face of the other. Her mother noticed the direction of the daughter's glance, and, looking that way, met Summerville's eyes. She turned, and looked at her daughter reproachfully, but with a pleasant, maternal smile. Her daughter returned the smile, and leaning back in the corner, blushed and turned away her face, a little ashamed—not, perhaps, so much of having looked at the handsome stranger as at being caught. Then she looked at Summerville with what was evidently intended for a frown, as if she would say: "Now, see the pretty mess those handsome eyes of yours have got me into! You ought to be ashamed of yourself!" But the frown speedily vanished and gave place to a sweet and much more becoming smile, which Summerville promptly and gallantly reciprocated. The lady seemed a little abashed at this, and in her embarrassment caught the little window fastener in her dainty fingers and listlessly thumbed upon it a moment. Presently she clicked, in tolerably fair Morse:

"I, I. That bright smile haunts me still."

Summerville jumped bodily from his seat. It had been a question in his mind all along whether this was all a dream, or whether he had merely taken leave of his senses. Now he was satisfied that it must be both. But if a dream, oh, what a delicious one! If out of his mind, he never desired to be in it again!

She still held the improvised telegraph key in her fingers. A happy thought struck Summerville. He would telegraph to her. Tell her how much he thought of her. In a few hours they would be parted, perhaps forever, but here was a means by which he could tell her that she had at least one admirer.

But how was he to do it? If the window fastener beside him were pressed into service, it might attract attention. He felt in his pockets. His lead pencil! The very thing. He drew it from his pocket carelessly, tapped listlessly for a moment on the window sill, at the same time keeping his eyes intently upon the young lady before him. Finally he caught her eye. She looked over, and he spelled out very slowly in Morse characters:

"Oh, I see you are an operator."

Now it was the lady's turn to be surprised. Had the train been run into and telescoped, the passengers tossed fifty feet in the air, and half their number killed, she could not have been more so. In fact, she had half expected

that all along, but to meet a real live telegrapher, one who could read what she clicked off the little window fastener, and answer her in the same "language," was more than her most vivid imagination could have fancied. It was several moments before she recovered sufficiently to click back:

"Yes, or perhaps you would say a plug."

"If the writing, on a regular, key is as beautiful as the writer—"

"You musn't flatter," with a sweet smile.

"Excuse me; but I—"

At this moment a newsboy interrupted the lovers' telegraph by opening the door and bellowing: "Only authorized guide to Philadelphia and the Centennial, fifty cents!" The father purchased a copy, and while his wife and himself examined it the young people kept up a pleasant telegraphic communication with their eyes. Very little was said, but both their faces wore pleased, contented smiles, and each seemed what might be called "unutterably" happy. He attempted to say something in telegraphic characters with the eye farthest from the passengers, and she essayed a similar feat, but veracity compels me to say that neither effort was entirely successful.

As the lady looked at Summerville, the one side of his face as solemn as a judge's, while with the other he made frantic efforts to "send firm," the spectacle was so grotesque that, completely forgetting the crowd in the car, she gave vent to the heartiest kind of a little giggle. Her father looked up with a frown and said, severely:

"What are you laughing at, Eva?"

She blushed, but did not reply.

Her mother looked at her, and probably divining that the handsome stranger was at the bottom of it, smiled. Summerville was so pleased that he felt like throwing his arms around the mother's neck and kissing her for not interrupting their little flirtation.

They were now passing a small station. Summerville consulted his watch and the time-table, and found that the train was an hour and thirty-five minutes late. In less than thirty minutes more they would probably reach the Centennial. How he wished that it might be thirty hours, instead of thirty minutes, or, in fact, that " time might at a standstill be forever." He wanted a chance to telegraph to the young lady again, and every turn of the wheel brought the train a little nearer the point where they must part forever. In an hour they would be separated as effectually as if they never had seen each other. Their paths in life would diverge, and she would never know the favorable impression she had created on his mind. Although the train was so much behind time, the journey had seemed a very short one to Summerville. " How swiftly falls the foot of time that only treads on flowers."

But alas! how rarely do we poor mortals enjoy perfectly unalloyed happiness. Like a dark pall, some unwelcome thought is sure to intrude ever upon our most delicious moments, casting a gloomy shadow over the sunshine, and tinging our joy with sadness. Although Summerville felt how delightful it would be if, instead of coming home to a cold, cheerless boarding-house, he should be every evening welcomed by the pleasant countenance and genial smile of the lady before him ; and if the entire day were one gigantic struggle with " crosses," " breaks," and " grounds," how pleasantly he could lay his head in her lap at night, forgetting his business perplexities, and feel, in that little circle where nobody was above him and nobody unsympathetic, as if he were in a heaven of ease and reparation—notwithstanding this, and even in the midst of the pleasant thoughts occasioned by what had just transpired, Summerville could not dispell others of a more unwelcome character, which arose unbidden, and would not be kept down, despite his assiduous endeavors to turn his thoughts into other channels.

The train was heavily loaded, and progressed slowly. When it got into a kind of " dog trot," Summerville could not persuade himself but that the wheels were repeating the injunction of Mrs. Norton:

> " Love not, love not, ye hapless sons of clay !
>   Hope's gayest wreaths are made of earthly flowers—
> Things that are made to fade and fall away
>   When they have blossomed but a few short hours.
> " Love not, love not, the thing you love may change,
>   The rosy lips may cease to smile on you;
> The kindly beaming eye grow cold and strange,
>   The heart still warmly beat, yet not be true."

Then he would laugh at himself for feeling annoyed because these particular lines happened to occur to him at that instant. He felt that she was too good, too innocent, and too beautiful to be other than a whole-souled, sweet-tempered, constant and true woman.

But as the engineer, finding the train getting farther and farther behind schedule time, had the fire replenished, and put on more steam, the quicker whirl of the wheels seemed to flaunt back in his face the words of Mrs. Osgood :

> , " Beautiful, yes ! but the blush will fade,
>   The light grow dim which the blue eyes wear;
> The gloss will vanish from curl and braid,
>   And the sunbeams die in the waving hair."

Still the young lady sat there as graceful as a queen, occasionally smiling as she looked at Summerville, " like moonlight on a troubled sea brightening the storm it cannot calm." Summerville made several efforts to reopen telegraphic communication with her, but on only one occasion was he successful. After attracting her attention he drummed with his pencil:

" Eva, of thee I'm fondly dreaming."

She bowed her head a little and smiled. They had now reached the junction. Two trains were on the track ahead of them, but after a slight delay, they proceeded. The flag-bedecked buildings were soon in sight, and every one was on *qui vive* to get a glance of them. Summerville felt that the moments to be spent in her company were now fast waning. He took out his note-book and pencil and wrote.

" I wonder if it would be proper to hand her this ? " he mused. " I don't want to give her my correct name just yet, but I shall surely do so if she answers."

After a moment's pause he continued: " Although I may never see the young lady again, I wouldn't offend her sensitive nature for the world, but I don't think there can be any harm in handing her the note, or endeavoring to make her acquaintance:

> 'She is lovely, therefore to be wooed,
> She is woman, therefore to be won.'

And then there's the noble motto of the gallant Montrose:—

> 'He either fears his fate too much,
> Or his deserts are small,
> Who dares not put it to the touch,
> And gain or lose it all.'"

Having thus logically argued the matter out to his own entire satisfaction, he folded the paper and waited, wondering whether he would have an opportunity of handing it to her.

Presently the train moved slowly up in front of the Atlas Hotel, where it stopped. There was a grand rush for the doors. Summerville alighted quickly, and remained at one side, awaiting an opportunity to present the little note to the lady in whom he already felt so much interest. In a few moments the trio approached—the mother a few steps in advance, the daughter next, and the father bringing up the rear. Summerville found no opportunity of handing her the note, however, for the father, immediately behind, watched her every movement. All Summerville could do was to look once more into those sweet eyes. She simply returned the gaze—all she could do under the circumstances.

Summerville's heart sank within him. Oh! the conventional rules of etiquette that prevented his making known his regard for his beautiful fellow passenger. He watched her as she gracefully moved with the rest of the crowd toward the admission gate. "It is too bad," he muttered, "that after I had almost come to love her, we should be thus ruthlessly parted. Well might Byron say, 'There's not a joy the world can give, like that it takes away.'"

He stood almost dazed for several moments. He had lost all interest in the Centennial, and felt that the Art Gallery could not interest him now. However, he would go within the grounds. Perhaps he might

3

meet her there. He felt that at least it was possible, though by no means probable.

At length he reached the gate. He had a fifty cent stamp in his hand, and was stepping forward to pass through the turnstile, when he noticed that but few of his fellow passengers had yet gone in, nearly all requiring to procure the necessary change. At the window stood Eva's father. Summerville looked around for the young lady herself; at last he saw her, and catching her eye, she smiled. There was a considerable crowd, the father had just procured change, and motioned his wife and daughter to follow him. But progress was slow. The mother was again in front, and the daughter a short distance behind. Summerville approached the young lady. He wanted to at least speak to her. "Excuse me, Miss, but do you remain long in Philadelphia?" he said, trying to speak naturally, and without trepidation.

"Until next Tuesday," she replied, pleasantly and unaffectedly.

"Please read that when you reach your hotel to-night," and he blushingly handed her the note.

They had now reached the turnstile. She stepped inside, and he followed. Her father, mother, and herself walked slowly toward the House of Public Comfort, and Summerville toward where the large bell was ringing out a noonday chime. Summerville saw her place the scrap of paper in the pocket of her handsomely fitting jacket. As they separated she looked toward him, and once more smiled. All the sunshine of his life returned, and he walked off, humming:

> They may rail at this life, from the hour I began it,
> I've found it a life full of comfort and bliss;
> And until they can show me some happier planet,
> More social and bright, I'll content me with this."

At the House of Public Comfort our three friends partook of some refreshments, and the younger member of the family, with the curiosity of her sex, glanced surreptitiously at Summerville's note. It read:

"If not asking too much, it would afford me great pleasure to receive a note from you at your convenience. Please address C. S. St. John, care P. O. Box, 3,393, New York."

Box 3,393, be it known, is the Post Office box of the Western Union Telegraph Company, at the New York General Post Office.

CHAPTER II.

"Charles Mailagent Holmes, I presume?"

"At your service."

It was Sunday morning. The genial mail agent, who acts as floor manager, so to speak, of the Western Union general office on the Christian Sabbath, sat near the window beside the stock indicator, in the receiving department.

"Havn't you received a letter for C. S. St. John, yet?"

"No, I've been on the lookout ever since you spoke about it, but so far it has not made its *debut.*"

"Two weeks ago, last Thursday. It seems like two years. She was to have left Philadelphia last Tuesday week. Suppose she reached home on Wednesday, she has had ten days to write, and yet no letter. 'Out of sight, out of mind,' I suppose, and, yet, if she only knew how honestly and devotedly I already love her, she would have written; but women have always been an enigma to me, I never could understand them; I did think, however, that she was an exception. Oh, Charlie, if you could only have seen her."

"What! Summerville, are you at last a victim of the tender passion?"

"Yes, madly, irrevocably, hopelessly—and I don't even know the name of the lady in the case. But, Charlie, you wouldn't blame me if you could only see her. Oh, that face! 'so lovely, yet so arch, the overflowing of an innocent heart.'"

"More than painting can express, or youthful poets fancy when they love, eh?"

"Yes, I could not begin to tell you how lovely that young lady was. There are not words enough in the entire English language. She was like a dream of poetry that may not be written or told—exceedingly beautiful."

"Well, Summerville, you're the last man in the building I'd have accused of falling in love with a pretty face without knowing one iota about the lady herself or her folks."

"I can't say that I positively know anything particularly to the lady's credit, but I certainly know nothing to her discredit, and surely she deserves the benefit of the doubt. She has already become the central figure in many of my bright castles in the air, and I prefer to consider her all perfection until she shall have been proved otherwise. Perhaps she has faults—there are few perfect, especially of her sex—but as Pope says:

'If to her share some female errors fall,
Look to her face and you'll forget them all.'"

"Which Pope said that, — Ralph or Frank?"

"I'm in no humor for jesting this morning, Mr. Holmes. I want a letter from Eva."

"Is that her name?"

"Yes; but I don't know her surname."

"Did you Eva!"

"By the way, do you ever examine the Post-Office box on Sunday, Mr. Holmes?"

"Sometimes."

"I have a presentiment that there is a letter there from my little Centennial beauty. Won't you come up and see?"

Charlie being the best natured and most accommodating person in the world, acquiesced, and they went.

Sure enough, there was the letter, addressed in a neat, lady-like hand, on a rich cream-colored fancy envelope, postmarked Glen Cove, L. I. Summerville clutched it eagerly, immediately broke it open, and, while his heart beat a wild tattoo of ecstatic bliss, read as follows:

GLEN COVE, L. L., October 7th, 1876.
MR. C. S. ST. JOHN—DEAR SIR:—Presuming that you have arrived home in safety ere this, I will now write you. Perhaps you don't know who I am. Girl who attracted your attention on the train going to the Centennial, and to whom you "telegraphed" with your lead pencil. That note which you handed me was quite a little surprise. I supposed that when we "parted at the gate" the line was down, and all further communication between us at an end, but it appears that you wish to "switch in on another wire," as it were, and continue the matter, and I don't know that I am altogether unwilling. I was very favorably impressed with your appearance, and don't think I should object to becoming personally acquainted with you. Father, mother, and myself remained in Philadelphia until

September 26th, and were all much pleased with the exhibition. I particularly liked the Art Gallery, though I was quite interested in Machinery Hall. Isn't Tiffany's display splendid, especially that elegant diamond set? But perhaps you will never receive this letter. If you do, please answer soon, and send me your photo.
Your would-be friend,
EVA C. MARSHALL,
—— —— Street, Glen Cove, L. I.

P. S.—I would like to have an answer as soon as possible, if convenient.—EVA.

"It must be a very entertaining letter to make you smile so sweetly," ventured the mail agent, after a pause.

"It is. It's a delightful letter from a delightful woman."

"I see she's not like the one I once met at a ball. I was young and gay then, and 'buzzed' this one considerably that evening. After awhile I bent over gracefully, handed her my address, and remarked benignly that I should like to receive a note from her sometime. But oh, my! didn't she get on her dignity, though! She looked at me in wild astonishment and perfect horror, and said, witheringly, 'No, sir! I never write to gentlemen. I think it's against the rules of impropriety!'"

"You might have told her that you were no gentleman," suggested Summerville, quizzingly.

He seemed to have dodged abruptly enough, but it took him near the terminus of the spinal column all the same.

"Does she add a postscript to that letter," asked the mail agent, after another pause.

"She does," answered Summerville.

"Oh, of course! I never knew a woman yet to write a letter without a postscript, unless by accident. She seems to consider a postscript her inalienable write, as it were. I remember when I was young and in my prime my girl once went off on a visit. She said she would write every alternate day, sure. 'Do,' I replied, 'and for the love of goodness do not add to every letter 'please excuse writing and spelling,' and above all, don't add a postscript; most women do, and if there is any one thing I detest more than another, it's a postscript.' She said she wouldn't. The first letter came at last, and

after very sensibly and exhaustively touching on every point of interest, and signing her name, she added : 'P. S.—Now you see I can write a letter without a postscript!'"

Summerville thought that Charlie manifested entirely too much disposition to severely criticize the gentler sex, and gallantly came to the rescue by remarking :

"And, yet, with all their little shortcomings, what would we do were it not for woman :

'Without the smile from partial beauty won,
Oh! what were man—a world without a sun!'"

"I don't know, I'm sure," replied the mail agent, "how we would get along without

'Dear woman! who divides our joys,
And trebles our expenses,'

"But I know one lady that I think the great American people could manage to dispense with. She is immortalized in a little poetic gem I have in my pocket," and he hunted for some time, and finally produced a Western Union blank with something scrawled on the back, which after assuming a dramatic posture, he read as follows :

"'He stood on his head on the wild seashore,
And joy was the cause of the act,
For he felt as he never had felt before,
Insanely glad in fact.
And why? In that vessel that left the bay,
His mother-in-law had sailed,
To a tropical country far away,
Where tigers and snakes prevailed.'"

"You would change your mind on the subject of woman, I think, if you only enjoyed the acquaintance of such persons as Eva—Miss Marshall—that's her name," suggested Summerville, at a loss exactly what to say next.

"I havn't the slightest doubt," replied Charlie, "but that Miss Marshall is like the rest of her sex—after marriage she'll think that two and two will come to make five, if she only cries and bothers enough about it, and I dare say she'll turn out as proverbially obstinate as the rest of them.

'I will,' when I am made a bride,
'I won't,' through all my life beside.

"I have my own opinion, moreover, of girls who carry their 'hearts' in their sleeve on

Centennial trains, and part with them so very easily, as Miss Marshall appears to have done."

Summerville felt that he was losing ground. His face flushed scarlet, and he replied pettishly:

"You may not, perhaps, be aware that there is a period in the early life of every true woman when moral and intellectual growth seems for a time to cease. The vacant heart seeks for an occupant—"

"Always of the opposite sex, too, interrupted Mr. Holmes.

'Men disunite and differ in their plan
But women are for union—to a man.'"

"The intellect," continued Summerville, without appearing to notice the interruption, "seems to feel the necessity of more intimate companionship with the masculine mind. Here, at this point, some stand for years, without making a step in advance—"

"True as gospel," broke in the mail agent again. "I knew one woman who stuck right there for twenty-three years to my own knowledge, and the cream of the joke is, that she was always just twenty-four years of age!"

"Others," continued Summerville, looking disdainfully down upon the mail agent, but without noticing what he said, "marry, and astonish in a few brief years, by their sweet temper, their new beauty, their high accomplishments, and their noble womanhood, those whose blindness led them to suppose women devoid of such traits."

"Summerville! you've been drinking!" ejaculated the mail agent, excitedly. "But," he continued, in a lower key, "if you'd only get off such a speech as that to Miss—what did you say her name was?—country swains, even with two pounds of candy in one pocket, and a dozen sticks of chewing gum in the other, would sink into utter insignificance in her eyes before you. When you go down you must choose a moonlight night, and serenade her. How I'd like to be there to hear you bellowing forth : 'When the mo-oon is shi-hi-hi-ning o'er the lake, Oh,

the-hen I'll thi-hink of thee-he-he-hee! Oh, the-hen, Oh! the-hen, I'll thi-hink of thee!' Serenading is delightful recreation, especially when the old gentleman gets up and hurls endearing epithets, brickbats and other miscellaneous articles at you. But these things should not discourage you. The greater the difficulty, the more glory there is in surmounting it. You can quietly wait until the enraged, stern parient retires, and then step up under the window, and sing:

'If Eva I cease to love,
May Jay Gould become President of the W. U. T.,
If Eva I cease to love.'

"And when the angelic creature herself appears at the window and tenderly lisps that magic word, "Uradarling," or starts a dog the size of a flour barrel after you, you can then properly appreciate the fact that women were sent into this wicked world of ours 'to fling golden gleamings over the sombre tints of life.'"

Summerville saw that the mail agent was incorrigible. "I have an engagement up town, Mr. Holmes, which calls me away," he said, "but at some more convenient season I will call at the office, and we'll talk the whole matter over." And as they reached the door, he added: "In the meantime, I'm ever so much obliged for the letter—thrice thousand thanks, my friend. Good morning."

To give Summerville's reply and the subsequent letters, which followed thick and fast between the two young people, would occupy too much space, and it is questionable if they would interest the general reader. Such correspondence, interesting as it is to the parties · immediately concerned, is stale and dry to the world at large. Summerville, however, in his third letter inclosed his photograph—one that he had taken specially for herself—and she reciprocated by sending him her very latest in return. In a subsequent letter Miss Marshall said that herself and her friend Miss Parker had been contemplating a two days' visit to some friends in the city, and had finally concluded to start the following Thursday. Nobody was to meet them in the city, and she thought it would be "so nice" if Mr. St. John would meet them on the Long Island side. Of course "Mr. St. John" did. He was introduced to Miss Parker, a young lady of about sixteen, and whom 'twere base flattery to call handsome. This fact, however, only enhanced Miss Marshall's beauty in his eyes, and of course, in the latter's company, he scarcely even noticed Miss P.

Summerville saw the ladies to their friend's house, called for them in the evening, and escorted them, one on each arm, to Gilmore's Garden. The next morning the Plymouth Rock went on an excursion to New Haven, and among the passengers were our three friends, bright and joyous as three birds.

It is a trite saying that it never rains but it pours. Summerville found it so. For years he had wandered comparatively friendless and forlorn in a cold, unsympathetic world, feeling the lack of a kindred spirit to whom he might pour out his soul in love, and who would love him in return, and now when the kindred spirit did come, it came double!

As they drew three camp-stools into an eligible position and sat down, Summerville could not help muttering to himself:

"How happy I could be with Eva,
Were 'tother dear charmer away."

As he pondered how he was honorably to rid himself for a time of Miss Parker, a co-laborer in the Western Union main office passing, stumbled upon him."

"Hello! Summerville; glad to see you; going to New Haven?"

"Summerville?" Miss Marshall looked at him inquiringly.

"My middle name," he explained, while a guilty blush suffused his face—"Charles Summerville St. John."

The main office man had passed "aft," and of course did not hear the fib.

"Oh!" thought Summerville, "I wish I had told her my real name, and I would, too, had she been alone."

This little incident annoyed him so much that he determined to tell Miss Marshall

his real name at once, but of course they must be alone. He must rid himself of Miss Parker in some manner. Excusing himself a moment, he followed the denizen of the main office, and addressed him thusly:

"Say, Marvin, I should like to introduce you to a very intelligent young lady. You are alone, I see, while I have two, and as I am not at all selfish, I thought I would like to make you happy for the day. Come along!"

Marvin went, and an introduction followed. Summerville is a rather bashful person, but no such accusation can be brought against Marvin. The latter, moreover, appreciates good looks in the gentler sex, and it did not take him long to get into pleasant conversation with the ladies, honoring Miss Marshall with many an approving smile. But that wasn't the worst of it. In a few minutes he remarked, persuasively, "P'raps the ladies would like a promenade around the boat;" and the great, selfish, blundering, heartless idiot actually offered his arm to Eva, and left Summerville to bring up the rear with the homely Miss Parker!

Although a man who seldom, if ever, indulged in an oath, Summerville felt that about two dozen good enthusiastic ones on this occasion would be a positive relief. I am happy to say, however, that his early Sunday school education triumphed. He merely began repeating something about "Heaven's etherial blue," but stopped after the first word. Some would, perhaps, have called it swearing, but they don't know Summerville as well as I do. He was simply a little frustrated—that was all.

Although Summerville spent a miserable day in consequence of being compelled to dance attendance upon a lady he did not care for, while another basked in the sunny smile of the seraphic being he adored, Miss Marshall considerably relieved his mind before they parted that night by assuring him, with womanly tact and sweetness, of her gratitude for his many kindnesses during her brief stay, and so on. She was to return to her Long

Island home the following afternoon, and promised to speedily write.

Marvin, delightfully unconscious that he had so nearly succeeded in severing two loving hearts, had stuck to Miss Marshall persistently all day, but Summerville could not blame him. It only showed his good taste. He vowed, however, that if ever Miss Marshall visited the city again, he should make a point of not introducing her to Marvin " or any other fellow."

On Monday evening business was dull on Summerville's wire, and he stepped over to the Glen Cove desk to speak to the operator. Miss Marshall, he had already learned, was not a regular operator, but had merely taken a fancy to telegraphy, and often came to the office to practice. Her father was well off in the world's goods, being the proprietor of an extensive manufactory, and she never expected to be under the necessity of earning her own living, either by wafting lightning or otherwise, but the mysterious art interested her, and so she learned it.

He had just succeeded in attracting Glen Cove's attention, when that lady said, " Here is a message for you—please take it," and went on :

" No. 5.   GLEN COVE, L. L, 23d.
To J. S. Marvin, W. U. Tel. Office, New York:
    Arrived an hour ago. A little tired, but quite well. Will write you to-night.   EVA.
    14.   D. H.

Summerville finished the message, gave O. K., and left the wire without speaking to the Glen Cove operator, as he had intended. The fact is, he was too much thunderstruck at Miss Marshall's conduct, in the light of the message he had just received, to take much interest in anything her friend the Glen Cove operator might say about her.

He could see the whole thing distinctly— Miss Marshall had not gone home on Saturday, but remained in the city until after Sunday. Marvin had called upon her, and she had agreed to open a correspondence with him.

" What a precious jackass I have been to think so muc'. of one who has proved herself so utterly unworthy of honest affection," Summerville muttered, as he sadly wended his way back to his own wire. " I thought I had found an angel, but she turns out to be a very ordinary mortal—in fact a full-fledged flirt. I can now truthfully say with Tom Moore:

> ' Away, away—you're all the same,¶
>   A fluttering, smiling, jilting throng !
> Oh, by my soul, I burn with shame
>   To think I've been your slave so long ! ' "

It was late ere Summerville reached his room that night, but he could not sleep until he had written Miss Marshall. His letter ran as follows, and to him was perhaps one of the saddest he had ever penned :

NEW YORK, October 23, 1876.
DEAR MISS MARSHALL:—You don't know how pained I was this evening to read your telegram to Mr. Marvin, which I happened to receive. I have been extremely disappointed in you. I suppose there is no use now in denying that since our rather romantic meeting on the way to the Centennial, I had already learned to—may I say it?—love you—honestly, devotedly, tenderly. I fondly hoped that you might in time reciprocate that love, but in the face of your message to Mr. Marvin I now see the utter madness of such a hope. Would that we had never met! If you could only know the pang that you have caused one who, since he has known you, has been happy only in your smile, and who even now would almost, as somebody says, " rather die than live without you," you would at least pity me. I should like to hear from you just once more—literally your farewell letter. After that I shall never trouble you again. In the meantime, please excuse the show of feeling in this letter. I had come to regard you as one woman picked out of ten thousand, and this sudden and very unexpected blow stuns me. I, however, cordially and sincerely wish you every happiness through life, and pray that your future may be always bright and full of sunshine. As Erin's bard says:

" Well, peace to thy heart, though another's it be,
And health to thy cheek, though it bloom not for me."

And now, as nothing remains on my part but to say farewell, perhaps the sooner it is said the better:

> " Adieu, adieu, our dream of love
>   Was far too sweet to linger long;
> Such hopes may bloom in bowers above,
>   But here they mock the fond and young.
> We met in hope; we part in tears!
>   Yet oh! 'tis sadly sweet to know
> That life in all its future years
>   Can reach us with no heavier blow."

Disconsolately, but still your friend,
        C. S. ST. JOHN.

Time dragged its weary length along, very drearily to Summerville, until the following Thursday, when he was handed a letter postmarked Glen Cove, and in Miss Marshall's handwriting. He opened it nervously, and read :

GLEN COVE, October 25, 1876.

DEAR MR. ST. JOHN:—Yours of 23d surprised me so much that I went straightway to the telegraph office to investigate the case. It turns out that on Monday Mr. Marvin's sister, a namesake of mine, came on a visit to some friends in Glen Cove, and desiring to notify her brother, who was on duty at the New York main office, of her arrival, Miss —— (the operator) sent a message to him D. H. . That's the whole matter. Ha! ha! it's a good joke. And to think that you gave me credit for being the Eva!

Believe me, I should be very sorry indeed if your letters stopped. I enjoy them very much, and don't think I can ever forget one who has shown me so many kindnesses. I mentioned to papa yesterday that I was going to invite a gentleman I had met in New York to come down and spend a Sunday with us. I asked him if he would consider it bold of me, and he said not if I were well enough acquainted with the gentleman. Papa likes New Yorkers. I wish you would come down some Sunday. We will try and make your visit pleasant. Please answer soon, and say when you think you can come.

Very truly your friend,   EVA.

It is needless to say that this letter completely dispelled any doubts Summerville had ever entertained in regard to the state of the young lady's feelings toward him. Of course he was overjoyed to know that she was not the Eva who had sent the message, and gratified beyond measure to receive so welcome an invitation to visit her.

In his next letter Summerville fully explained why he had assumed the name of St. John—not knowing anything of Miss Marshall, he did not care to give his correct cognomen until he should hear from her, and afterward kept putting it off from letter to letter. He now begged her pardon for the deception, well knowing that it would be promptly granted.

When Summerville visited Glen Cove, he was treated with great politeness, Mr. and Mrs. Marshall hoping he would come to see them often. He found the former much more genial and less distant and austere than he had at first given him credit for; the latter sweeter and more pleasant than ever. Mrs. Marshall evidently remembered him in connection with the trip to the Centennial, but her husband did not appear to think he had ever seen him before.

Of course the young people have grown more and more attached to each other every day. He often remarks that with "New York day" is associated the most important event of his life, and if Miss Marshall were questioned I have no doubt she would say the same thing.

I am looking every week for the announcement of their marriage in the telegraphic papers—regretfully, too, for I know that immediately after that event the fraternity will lose an expert operator and genial gentleman, as Mr. Marshall is to be succeeded in the active supervision of his manufactory by his son-in-law, Mr. Sydney Summerville.

By Telegraph.

Click! click! click! and the clattering tongue of brass
Seems alive as I listen and hear the signals pass;
Many a wonderful message goes flashing along the wire [dire.
With words of joyful greeting or a tale of calamity

Travels the spark electric over mountain, and valley, and hill,
Under the deep-flowing river, over the rippling rill.
Hark to the message flashing through the crystal air of morn,
"Unto us a son is given, an immortal soul is born."

Click! click! click! and the mystical wires again
Are telling another story unto the children of men;
"Masseltof, greeting we send you, may your happiness lasting be,
Your wedded life be joyful, your path from care be free."

And yet another message is mournfully flashing by
As only the lightning travels or evil tidings fly;
Imagine the heart's emotion as the sorrowful missive is read,
"A soul has returned to its Maker, your darling mother is dead."

An Evening Reverie.

KIND reader, did you ever steal away from everybody and everything, and, seeking your library, sit down in the coming twilight before a glowing grate? If you have, you will sympathize fully with me in that sweet inertia that comes over one as he sits thus and puffs the much abused but ever soothing weed, of which his Satanic majesty is said to have sown the germ. If you have never done so, listen, and you may sit by me. The cheerful fire awakens pleasant memories, and the fragrant tobacco induces a mellowness of mind almost ecstatic. When the moon's soft beams fall beside you, as the evening advances, as was the case with me last night, there is little else attainable in this world worth wishing for. You may not see the pictures on the wall, but you feel their presence. You realize that Beatrice Cenci regards you kindly as you puff the smoke rings upward. And though Washington and his small band of followers are crossing the Delaware—in a steel engraving—over behind you, are invisible as you gaze into the fire, you know that they are dividing their attention between the guidance of their frail craft on its perilous journey and your airy musings. There are many other pictures adorning the walls, and you experience that quiet satisfaction inseparable from being in delightful company. On your right sit Washington Irving and his friends, and on your left Shakspeare and his contemporaries, both groups indulging in a chat, which you would give half your life—possibly that half you are done with—to have heard. The busts of Burns, of Scott, and Byron surmount the mantelpiece; a pair of Rogers' groups are near at hand, and, finally, there are those wonderful entertainers, the books on your library shelves. And if Washington and his followers are mute; if Beatrice is content to entrance the eye without adding the music of her voice; if Irving, Shakspeare, and their respective associates say nothing to you, and

Burns, Scott and Byron deign not to relax their set features for your instruction, what recks it? The books will talk to you as men can never speak. You sit within an enchanted circle and have only to rise, step forward two strides, and, *mirabile dictu*, you may commune with Charles Lamb, with Goethe, Shakspeare, Plutarch, Balzac, or any of the others who have contributed their wisdom for the benefit of mankind, from wise Confucius to quaint, bewitching Charles Dudley Warner.

I was sitting thus last evening, when I heard a voice so wondrously modulated and sweet that I fancied for the instant which it required for me to emerge from my reverie, that Beatrice had surely spoken, and the voice inquired, "May I come in?" Before I could say "Yes," this practical observation followed, "Why, John, you great goose, why don't you light the gas? It is as dark as a pocket here;" saying which, my bonny wife approached me and brushed back my hair with the same lingering tenderness with which she fondled me ten good years ago, when we were in the heyday of our honeymoon. We are lovers still, Mary and I—we must always be. Adapted to each other by temperament, education, and general tendencies, our love has grown with our years and strengthened with our strength. Behold in us the happiest couple in Christendom. Not that we are by any means alike; oh, no. Mary is shrewd, practical—in fact she is common sense personified. She makes good bargains, takes a wholesome view of life, and does good to all about her as naturally and easily as the sun shines or the wind blows. I am a bit of a dreamer; I am given to the advocacy of ideas which I am so often convinced are impracticable that I have but little faith in my own views; I am easily imposed upon in numerous ways, and, except at rare intervals, I go about my business feeling, with Meredith, that life is not altogether what we planned it out. As you may judge, Mary is a perfect balance for me. Without her I should be as nothing, but together we are a steady going couple, who admire each other's qualities, and fall more and more deeply in love as we grow older, for in spite of our differing views we sympathize fully on all matters of importance to our own and the well being of those near and dear to us.

I regret that I have not time to tell you all about ourselves, and give an episode here and there in our married life. Suffice it that we were friends at first, lovers betimes, and "married folk" at last. I would like, moreover, to tell you what we were talking about last evening, but Mary would not approve of it, and as usual I yield to her better judgment. I am so happy under circumstances peculiarly adapted to my eccentric though not altogether sunless nature, that I would communicate my thoughts and the pretty things my wife and I say to each other to the whole world. But Mary says the world would laugh at us, and very likely she is right, so I shall spare you a report of our conversation.

But I may safely tell you what was occupying my mind when Mary came to sit by me. I was thinking of our early love; of how we were associated together in a pretty Massachusetts village, and of our increasing fondness for each other as we approached that period which by a polite fiction is called years of discretion. She grew to be delicate in health as she attained her eighteenth year, and fears were entertained that she would die of consumption, as her mother had done. Her physician prescribed a change of air, and her father took her abroad. Our parting was very sad, for she was ill and strangely whimsical. "I shall die in some strange land, John," she said, "and shall never see you again." And then she wept softly, and my own eyes were not wholly dry. I had just graduated at the bar, and went to Boston to practice my profession in her absence. During the two years which followed I was mod-

erately successful, but I must confess that I was not happy. Mary's letters and those from her father were not encouraging, but I was young and brave hearted. So I hoped for the best, and, if sometimes I lost interest in my law books, and my mind wandered to the sequestered village where I had met my love, and I fell to thinking fondly of green lanes and of her who used to be my companion amid scenes of quiet loveliness, I came back to myself shortly and resumed the duties of my work-a-day life. I cannot say that I thought of the country with a feeling of regret. I only dwelt on it because it suggested the happiest hours of my life— my three years as a student in Judge Bascom's office. I was a town man by birth and instinct, and admired the country something after the manner in which that very funny man admired the sea, who, after sailing around Cape Horn ejaculated in homely rhyme:

"Oh! I love the sea, as I've said before,
But I love it best when seen from shore."

Well, Mary came home at last and we were married. How well I remember that golden August day—the seventeenth. She had entirely recovered her health, and oh, how beautiful she was! I remember that she seemed to me as an angel, and even at the altar my better nature rebelled at the idea of linking her pure life with my imperfect one, and I had serious intentions of forbidding the bans. But I was selfish, as all men are, and, ignoring my own unworthiness, I permitted the ceremony to be consummated. As we emerged from the church, followed by the worthy villagers, the birds sang joyously, and I was very, very happy. I felt that God had indeed blessed me beyond my deserts, but I kept my emotions to myself. A week later, deferring to my whimsical tendencies, and intuitively fathoming my unfitness for the country, Mary announced one morning her preference for the town, and asked me as a favor to her that we go at once to Boston. Her father accompanied us, but he passed away after a few years. He blessed us with his dying breath, and smilingly went forth into the great hereafter. How the past came back to me last night as I sat dreaming my day dreams in the mingled moon and fire light! I was almost a poet then, and if a diviner hand had not swept the lyre to the same purpose, I believe I could have written something beautiful on "The Pleasures of Memory."

"Will I let the children come up?" inquired Biddy, from the dining-room.

The children finally come up. There are three of them—John, nine years old; Henry, seven, and Mamie, three. I object to having the gas lighted when Mary urges its ignition. Behold me victorious in the dimly lighted room. On a low stool at my side sits Mary, fairer, sweeter than the flowers—those voiceless, yet earnest and convincing preachers. On one knee sits John, on the other Henry, while Mamie clings to my neck, and nestles her sunny head upon my shoulder. Verily I would do without the gaslight always, if only to have the children sit so closely and seem to place themselves under my protection without reserve—to have them look up to me with that aspect of perfect trust, which never characterizes my children except when darkness is around us. Of course we must tell them stories, so Mary and I alternate as the inventors of little romances, such as children like. She relates tales of knights and great achievements, and I tell them of the grotesque and fanciful. And how silent the little ones are, as Mary weaves her pretty tales of chivalrous men and deeds! How merrily they laugh when I narrate the mythical adventures of impossible boys and girls. We are very happy, I can tell you. Then follows song after song, with very perfect result, for Mary's voice, like her every other attribute, is sweet and winning, and the boys are making good headway with their music. Mamie and I are the only weak ones in our home quintette, she being too young to learn the songs the boys are taught at school, and I, being ambitious to sing the right words

to the wrong tune, without making a discord, and always failing.

As the evening drew on we purposed to close our delightful session with "Hold the Fort," something perfectly familiar to all of us, even to Mamie. The first verse seemed to limp a little, and I looked inquiringly at Mary, but her glance of encouragement reassured me, and I sang on right sturdily thenceforward. It was during the progress of the second stanza that we discovered the cause of the inharmony—Mamie was singing "Little Brown Jug, You and Me." At this we laughed heartily, and as our voices died away a sort of blindness stole upon me. My wife's sweet face seemed to fade from sight, then the children began to recede from view, at last dissolving altogether, and, starting up, I stood alone. The fire was nearly dead, there were no pictures on the wall, there were no copies of Shakspeare, Plutarch, Goethe—nor of anybody except Coke and Blackstone, and other legal lights on the single shelf above the fireplace. My vision had passed away, and again I was an old bachelor lawyer—the self-same gray old man whom my brethren who congregate at the court-house know so well, and, no doubt, depreciate, were the truth known. I walked stiffly to the window, for my limbs are no longer young, and looking out I beheld the sleeping city bathed in radiant light. The cathedral bells had just rung out the midnight hour. Turning, I marked that the moon's soft beams fell across the oaken floor, as I had seen them rest upon the richly tinted carpet of my library, and a pain like an unexpected twinge from an old sprain shook me, for I knew that the moonbeams lighting my dingy room rested also on a grave in a country church yard not far remote. They have rested there through thirty years—above my Mary's dust. John and Henry and Mamie—God bless you my dream children—were never born, but since God willed it so, I thank Him as I brush away an old man's foolish tears.

Edward O. Chase (*Nuf Ced*)

Was born in Philadelphia. He first turned his attention to telegraphy while employed on the engineer corps of the Pennsylvania Railroad in 1865. In the summer of '67 he joined a party of United States engineers, and with them went to Nebraska to make a geological survey of that Territory. Returning home the following winter he then began the actual business of telegraphing, securing a position as operator and clerk for the Pennsylvania Steel Company at their works at Baldwin Station near Harrisburg, Pa. He remained at this place during the winter months, but in the early summer of '68 a recurrence of the fever and ague, contracted the previous season in the region of the head waters of the Missouri, compelled his resignation and obliged him to go north. He next turns up as operator in Portsmouth, N. H., on the line of the now defunct International Telegraph Company, which was absorbed by the Western Union in 1872. At the close of the year he was promoted to the main office of the same company in Portland, Maine, and next went to Augusta as report operator, engaged in transmitting to Portland and Boston the reports of the State Legislature.

Returning to Portland at the end of the session, he soon after resigned his position and accepted the managership of the summer office of the W. U. at Crawford House, White Mountains. At the close of the season he was ordered to Portland W. U. office, and late in the fall of '68 was sent to Bangor, Maine, as night manager and press receiver, which position he filled to the satisfaction of all concerned until July 5th, 1872, when night work having resulted in failing health, his resignation took effect and he left the business to return home and accept the assistant secretaryship of the American Iron and Steel Association of Philadelphia, where his duties consisted chiefly in the editorship of the bulletin of the association during the absence of the secretary. In the spring of '73 he had a relapse of the old uneasiness and returned to his first love, this time as operator at the Ocean House summer office of the Western Union at Newport, R. I. At the close of the season he entered into the manufactory of machinists' tools and light machinery, as manager of his father's factory in Newark, N. J., which position he still occupies, only having left it to assume the position of chief operator at Saratoga Springs, N. Y., Western Union office during the seasons of 1874 and '75. In '76 he declined many telegraphic offers to attend the Centennial as exhibitor in Machinery Hall and correspondent of THE OPERATOR.

Mr. Chase is widely known among the fraternity as an amiable gentleman of much culture of mind, and possessing social and literary talents of a high order. As a telegrapher he is recognized as a first-class man in every respect. May his original and humorous articles long continue to grace the columns of THE OPERATOR, and may his shadow never be less.

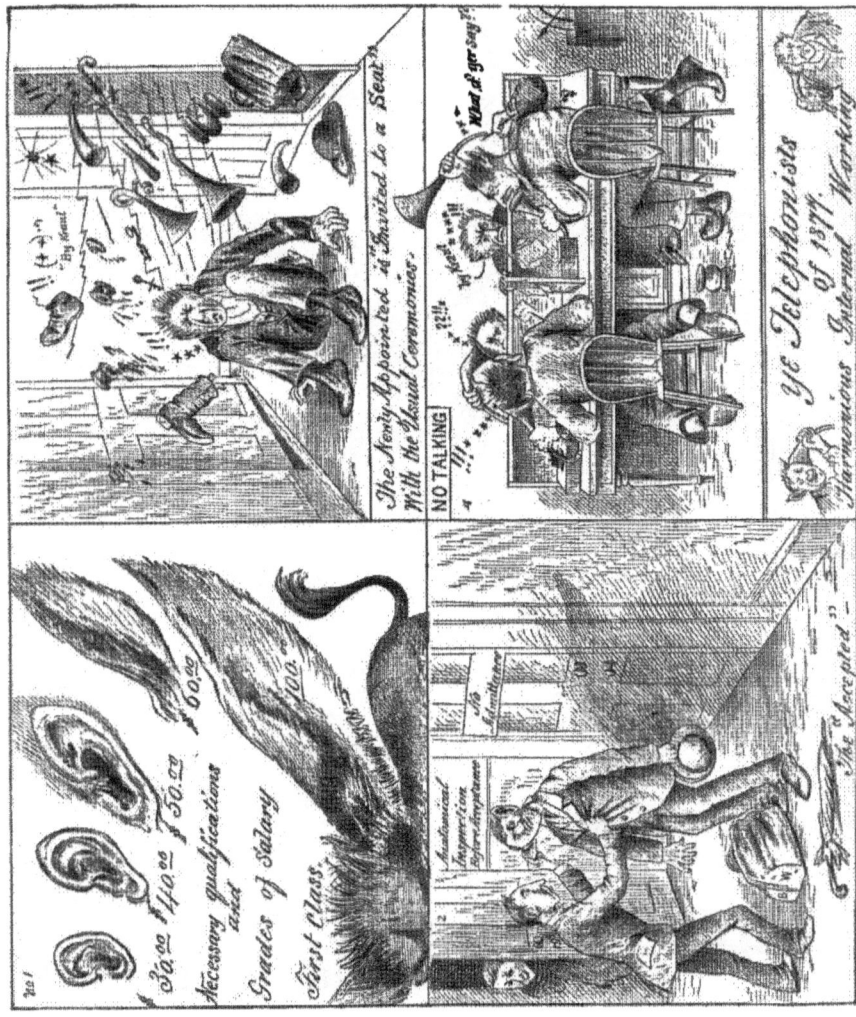

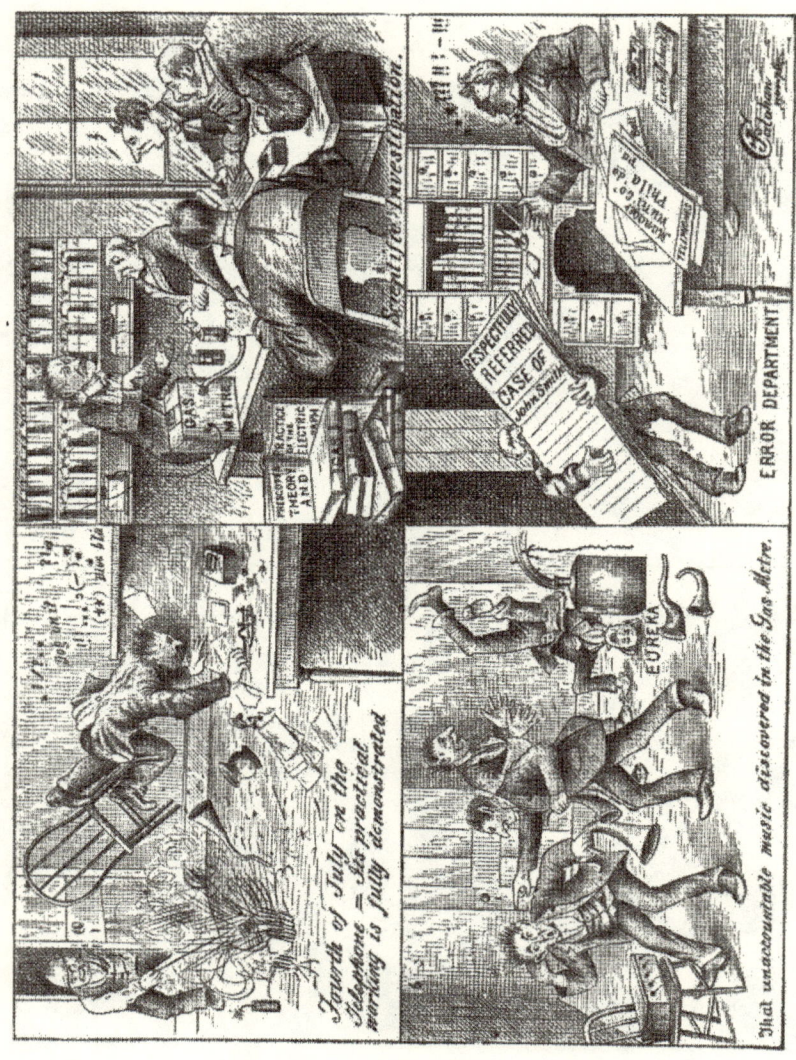

A Leaf of Autobiography.

"If you will come over and see Sanderson right away," wrote my friend, the managing editor of *The Plantation Harbinger*, "I think you can obtain the position of local editor. Gregory has lit out." Sanderson was the proprietor of *The Harbinger*, and I was a new comer in the journalistic field who wanted work, so I went in pursuit of him. I met Gregory on my way over and asked him what was the trouble. and where he was going.

"To Boston," he answered. "Sanderson does not pay his help."

"Why," I returned, "his managing editor, Mr. Fenceslat, has just written me a note asking me to go and see Sanderson about the situation you have vacated. He said nothing about bad pay, simply stating that you had 'lit out.'"

"Fenceslat is in the ring," observed Gregory, significantly, and he hastened in the direction of the Boston depot.

It was with my enthusiasm considerably abated that I entered the presence of Mr. Sanderson. I knew him slightly; his rotund form and genial face, in connection with a stub-tailed horse and Concord wagon being familiar to about every man woman and child in town. He was a person who never wholly lost his *aplomb* under the most discouraging circumstances, as I afterward learned, and who, under ordinary conditions, was a perfect Chesterfield. It will be a good many years into the future before I shall have forgotten the cordial grasp he gave my hand and the benignant smile which played upon his lips as he said:

"Mr. Fenceslat's heart is set upon having you come on our paper as local editor. I have studied with great care such occasional work as you have done for us. It is exceedingly good. I am a man of few words, Mr. Phillips. I like you. I want you to like me. I do business on the square. I will pay you twenty dollars per week, and you get

your cash every Saturday." Afterward I learned that Sanderson never read a line in his paper unless his attention was called to something, and he read it then under protest. I learned a great deal during the next year, but of that hereafter.

"Mr. Gregory said—"

"One moment," interrupted Sanderson, "see you again in a second," and he went to his desk and making a note for thirty days sent it to the bank. Before I could resume my story about Gregory, Sanderson said:

"I never like to talk about a man behind his back. But here are the facts in a nutshell: Mr. Gregory is a good fellow, sharp writer and all that, but he is extravagant. He has drawn his salary in advance ever since he came here from New Haven. Yesterday he wanted me to advance him a hundred dollars. I declined, and he is gone, thank fortune. It is a good paymaster who pays when the work is done. I do that. I am willing to pay one or two weeks' salary in advance, but I can't furnish money to everybody who comes along in quantities to suit—like to accommodate, you know, but it isn't business, and I am not in a position to do it without cramping myself. Another thing," he went on glibly, "Gregory's wife is afraid of thunder and lightning, and every time a shower comes along off he goes home—no matter if it's only eight o'clock. Now, the local editor of a morning paper can't go home at eight o'clock in the evening and do justice to the city department. I tolerated this because I wished the man well, but you know how 'tis yourself. There comes a straw one day that breaks the camel's back, and Gregory's constant hypothecation of his salary and his attempts to browbeat me into lending him large sums have done the business for him."

After a great number of compliments on my lively way of writing, and no end of assurances that if a man did not "impose on him unreasonably it was all right," I left the mighty presence with a very high regard for Sanderson and a very seriously changed heart toward my avaricious predecessor. And if Gregory's rapacity in seeking to do a sort of free banking with his employer hadn't settled him in my estimation, his habit of going home "in the midst of a murder," as Sanderson said, "if a thunderstorm came up," would have done the business for him of itself. I had engaged myself for one year at twenty dollars per week, and began work the next day. As I had only worked half a week when pay-day came I thought it wiser to let the amount lie until the next Saturday, and I did so. As my hours were from seven P. M. to two or three A. M., and as Sanderson seldom, if ever, visited the editorial rooms at night, I did not see him from one end of the week to the other. Occasionally I visited the counting room to find it in charge of a supremely saucy boy, who sat on a high stool and shrilly whistled, and who invariably answered the question, "When will Sanderson be in?" with a grunt, which the practiced ear recognized as "give it up." But though I saw him not, Sanderson sent me numerous kind messages during the week, and finally, at the bottom of one of his pleasant notes, he wrote: "Didn't see you Saturday; money waiting for you." On receipt of that missive so great was my confidence in his integrity I would have lent him a thousand dollars could I have raised it. When Saturday arrived I went to the counting room and ran upstairs with a light step. Sanderson was not in, and several persons with anxious faces were in waiting. To my question as to when Mr. Sanderson would be in, the shrill whistler grunted as usual, and as I seemed at a loss what to say, he volunteered the remark: "Don't pay off till two o'clock." The city clock struck eleven as I passed down stairs and out upon the busy street. I felt very sure about Sanderson, but I had my doubts about the boy, Creeks. He was becoming a thorn in my side with his stereotyped "give it up," and his disturbing remarks. I was positive he misrepresented Mr.

Sanderson, and took advantage of his absence to snub and render uncomfortable not only employes, but also patrons of the paper. I determined to speak to Mr. Sanderson about him and have him admonished—annihilated, if possible.

I returned to the office at five minutes past two o'clock to find the little counting room crowded with compositors, pressmen, reporters, editors, route boys, bootblacks, and a great many others. As I peered over the sea of shoulders my eyes caught those of Sanderson, and he shouted, "Make room there for Mr. Phillips." As I approached the desk Sanderson dipped a pen, put his chubby finger where he wished me to sign, and before I had scarcely finished my name he placed thirty dollars before me. I stepped aside to make room for Dr. Flowers, our foreman, who had just came in, but I did not retire, as I wished to consult Sanderson about several matters which struck me as being of vital importance to *The Harbinger's* welfare. As I stood waiting I observed that Dr. Flowers' youthful face wore an expression much graver than I had ever seen there before. I was surprised that no pen was dipped for him to sign with, and that Sanderson requested no one to "make room for Dr. Flowers." The doctor was admitted behind the counter after a few seconds and Sanderson whispered with him earnestly. Then a ten dollar note was handed him, and he walked out looking very severe. I saw it all. Dr. Flowers had been drawing his salary in advance, and Sanderson would only be imposed upon within reasonable bounds. He had given the doctor ten dollars, which was generous under the circumstances. My heart warmed toward him for his liberality. Next came Henry Child, the news editor.

"What can I do for you, Henry?" inquired Sanderson.

"Let me have twenty, said Child, "rent due."

"Sorry, but I can't do it, Henry," returned Sanderson, in the blandest tones imaginable. "Here," he added, "is two dollars in pennies.

Now git." I had no doubt Henry Child had overdrawn *his* salary by several hundred dollars, and his assurance in coming to ask for money at all surprised and pained me. The next Saturday Mr. Sanderson paid me with less alacrity, and I noticed that he addressed me by my given name. A week later he said " Wally, old boy, here's fifteen dollars for you, can't make change any nearer. Hand you the other five Monday," and upon my third appearance he simply handed me a ten dollar note with the observation: "Here you go, Phil, hang up the other ten with that five I owe you on last week."

"But what kind of a way to do business is this?" I asked.

"Oh, run along, sonny," said Sanderson, with a smile; "no time to 'yawp' on the day preceding the peaceful Sabbath. Come in any day but Saturday and we will talk matters up."

I walked out considerably down in the mouth. " Come in any day but Saturday " was refreshing in the extreme. As if I hadn't visited his office day after day to talk about the feasibility of having another reporter added to our force, and been met by that incorrigible whistler whose " give it up " had become a perfect nightmare. Mr. Sanderson was seldom in, though I found during my periods of watching and waiting that very few men were in greater demand.

On making my fifth appearance as I reached for a pen my employer said : " You needn't sign that book, Phil."

"Not sign ! " I ejaculated, thoroughly nonplussed.

"No; money about all gone. Have to pay the compositors or they won't go to work Sunday night—have no paper Monday. You and Child and Flowers get three dollars apiece to-day, and that settles your hash. Members of the intellectual department are supposed to work for fame, not money." He handed me three dollars, and inquired if I would like to go to the Theodore Thomas concert that evening. Replying in the affirmative, he passed me two complimentary tickets, and

dashed down stairs. A moment later he was gathering up the reins which had fallen under the feet of the stub-tailed horse, and I sat watching him as one in a trance.

"Creeks ! Creeks ! " called Sanderson. Creeks made a break in the tune he had been whistling ever since I knew him, and going to the window responded, " Aye, aye." "Charge Phillips with six dollars—three cash, and three for those Thomas concert tickets," said Sanderson. And then he drove away.

To say that I was enraged as I tore up street, but feebly expresses the intemperate frame of mind in which I found myself after all this. I soon met Flowers and Child and began my tale of woe. They stopped me at once and said: " So he's landed *you* too, eh? Give us your hand." I felt that congratulations were not by any means in order, but I mechanically put forth my hand and both shook it warmly. They knew that I had "joined the band."

I staid on *The Harbinger* a whole year, and with the exception of such payments as I have mentioned, I never received a dollar in cash. Why I remained I can not explain. Fenceslat, who had once visited Sanderson with the determination of squeezing fifty dollars out of him, was assuaged with an " order " for a grindstone; but in the face of this asking for money and receiving a stone, Fenceslat still stuck to the paper, and " salivated the Republican party," as he expressed it, months and months after his labor had ceased to bring shekles. Flowers and Child, the ancient and precise ship news reporter— God bless you all—and many others were doing the same thing and wondering at it. There was something in the atmosphere of *The Harbinger* office which had a mollifying effect on everybody who entered Sanderson's service, and at the end of two months I found myself very well contented with my lot, a popular man around town, and the possessor of more furniture, curtains, cooking stoves, etc., which I had taken from Sanderson or purchased on his "orders," than I knew what to do with. When I had been with him six months, I was one day in sore need of money and sought his office. Luckily I found him in, and I stated my case with an eloquence that ought to have moved him. But it didn't. He listened patiently until I had closed, and then replied: "Haven't a dollar, but," pointing to a corner, "there are two hundred and fifty feet of galvanized iron clothes line that I took on an advertisement which I'll sell you cheap." I retired, heart-broken.

Mr. Sanderson was a man of "orders." There was nothing under the canopy "from a rotten apple to a locomotive," as he phrased it, which he could not furnish on call or give an "order" for. "I get a man to advertise in *The Harbinger* as a general thing," he explained, "on the strength of my offering to take my pay out in trade. Then I send you or Child or Flowers or Fenceslat and buy about fifty dollars worth, and I keep buying so that I am always ahead of that man. He wants to take his advertisement out at the end of three months, but he can not do it because I am owing him. Had men in this paper several years in just that way. Once in a while a man gets mad and I have to square up with him in cash and let him take his advertisement out, but that don't often happen."

It happened sometimes, however, when I was present, and it was then that Sanderson's abilities shone resplendent. The reader must have surmised that Sanderson was always short of ready money. He was. So when one of these troublesome advertisers came along and demanded a settlement, Sanderson would meet him something as follows:

"I owe you a balance of $79.85. I have no money, but I'll give you my note for thirty days. Put it in your bank, get her discounted, and I'll pay the discount. Just as good as cash."

To this the party of the other part would assent, and Sanderson would draw up a note in very pretty shape, and bringing it over would say:

"I've made this note for a hundred and fifty dollars because I make all my notes for a round sum. You get it discounted and send me your check for the balance. Here, Creeks, go down with Mr. Blank and bring back a check." And before the astonished recipient of the note could recover his equipoise, Sanderson would have bowed him out of the room.

Sometimes the men who accepted these promises to pay, and gave checks which could be used immediately, found themselves in a rather embarrassed situation when the notes matured. Sanderson was one of those men who imagined that it added dignity and character to a promissory note to let it go to protest. Thus it would often happen that after the disaffected advertiser had enjoyed the felicity of paying Sanderson's note, and had visited the whistler fifteen or twenty times without even getting a sight of the object of his search, I would receive a letter from Sanderson instructing me to write a third of a column notice puffing the business of the man to whom the note had been given. When this appeared, Sanderson would drive to the store of his whilom customer, and laying *The Harbinger* before him would say:

"It's the biggest kind of a shame that I haven't taken up that note, but I have not had the money. I haven't it now, but if it would give you any satisfaction to kick me you are at liberty to do it," and he would present himself for chastisement.

I believe, however, that he was never kicked. After this the editorial notice, which I had written the night before, would be read as Sanderson's own production, and in nine cases out of ten that hundred and fifty dollars would eventually be taken out in advertising. And the men thus won over never deserted him. They had met the enemy and they were his.

Many years have passed since I wrote my last line for *The Harbinger*, but sometimes, sitting in the twilight, the remembrance of those old days comes back with such startling force that it seems as if the atmosphere of that dingy editorial room was still around me, and I half imagine I see Child and Flowers and all the rest filing up the narrow stairway thankful for the little Sanderson has for them. I know that things are changed now. I know they are all scattered, that the thundering press whose clangor was as music to my youthful ears is stilled forever, and that *The Harbinger's* precarious existence is ended. Still, I remember it kindly, for with its life are associated some of the pleasantest episodes in mine.

Kate.

AN ELECTRO-MECHANICAL ROMANCE.

CHAPTER I.

THE ENGINE.

SHE was a beauty. From head-light to buffer-casting, from spark-arrester to air-brake coupling, she shone resplendent. A thing of grace and power, she seemed instinct with life as she paused upon her breathless flight. Even while resting quietly upon the track, she trembled with the pulsations of her mighty heart. Small wonder that the passengers waiting upon the platform came down to gaze upon the great express engine, No. 59. She seemed long and slender like a greyhound, and her glistening sides, delicate forefeet, and uplifted head were suggestive of speed and power.

The engineer stepped down from his high throne with his long nickel-plated oiler in hand, and the fireman clambered over the glistening heap of coal and swung round the great copper water-pipe that the magnificent creature might have a drink of pure spring water. The engineer looked eagerly up and down the platform as if in search of some one. Two or three tourists of the usual type and a stray idler were all to be seen. A group of big fellows were unloading mail bags, and beyond them the busy throng down the platform was lost to view. How lovingly he touched the shining arms of his great pet with the smooth clear oil, golden and limpid. Here her great cylinder, seventeen inches wide, and with a stroke of twenty-four, safely rested behind the sturdy buttress that held her forefoot so daintily thrust out in front. The head-light gleamed in all the sparkle of plate glass, and her shapely rods fairly glowed in polished beauty. On one side lay her boiler-feed pump, a finished bit of mechanism, and on the other was hung a steam-injector for forcing water into the boiler without the aid of the pump. How perfect everything! Even the driving-wheels were works of art. From balanced throttle-valves to air-brake she had every device that American skill had produced, or that such an engine could demand, and her thirty-five tons of chained-up energy seemed the perfect expression of the highest mechanic art.

With a loud roar her safety-valve yielded to her pent-up vitality and filled all the air

"A HANDKERCHIEF IS QUICKLY FLIRTED IN THE AIR."

with clouds of steam. The engineer gazed proudly upon his noble steed, and then looked anxiously down the platform to see if any came whose presence would be welcome.

The fireman swung back the great copper pipe, and the idlers suddenly withdrew. The last trunk was thrown in, and the engineer climbed slowly up into his house. He looked anxiously about the long platform. It was nearly clear, and he could see the gold band on the conductor's hat glistening in the sun.

Where can she linger? Why does she

not come? 59 is here, and still she comes not. The gold-banded cap is lifted in the air. With one hand on the throttle-valve, the engineer glances down the long empty platform. The bell rings; there is a hissing sound beneath the giant's feet; the house trembles slightly; the water-tank seems to move backward; the roar of the safety-valve suddenly stops; the fury of the great iron monster vents itself in short deep gasps; clouds of smoke pour down on everything. They almost hide the platform from view.

Ah! A dress fluttering in the door-way. Some one appears abruptly upon the platform. With both hands on the throttle-valve, the engineer leans out the window. A handkerchief is quickly flirted in the air. He nods, smiles, and then turns grimly away, and stares out ahead with a fixed look as if the world had suddenly grown very dark, and life was an iron road with dangers everywhere. The fireman shovels coal into the fiery cavern at the engineer's feet, and then stirs up the glowing mass till it roars and flames with fury. The steam-gauge trembles at 120°, and quickly rises to 125°. The vast engine trembles and throbs as it leaps forward. The landscape—woods, houses and fields seem to take wings in a wild Titanic waltz. The engineer gazes ahead with tight-set lips, but his heart can outrun his locomotive, and lingers behind at the deserted way-station.

CHAPTER II.

THE TELEGRAPH OPERATOR.

WITH that perversity for which railroads are famous, the line did not enter the town, but passed along its outermost edge, among the farms and woodlands. This affected the life of the place curiously. At one hour the station was animated and thronged with people; at another it was dull, quiet and deserted by all save the station-master and his daughter. She it was who guarded the little telegraph office, received and sent the telegrams of the town, and did anything else that pertained to her position. She had a little box of a place portioned off in one corner of the ladies' waiting-room, where there was a sunny window that looked far up the line, and a little opening where she received the messages. She viewed life through this scant outlook, and thought it very queer. Were people always in a state of excitement? Did everybody have trouble in the family that demanded such breathless,

heart-rending messages? Was it in every life to have these awful, sudden things happen? Life from her point of view was more tragic than joyful, and she sometimes thought it a relief to receive a prosy order to "tell Jones bring back boots and have mower mended." Sometimes between the trains the station was quite deserted, and were it not for the ticking of the clock, and the incessant rattle of the fretful machine on her desk, it would be as still as a church on Monday. At first she amused herself by listening to the strange language of the wires, and she even made the acquaintance of the other operators. With one exception they all failed to interest her. They were a frivolous set, and their chatter seemed as empty as the rattle of a brass sounder. One girl she knew must be a lady. Her style of touch, and the general manner of her work, showed that plainly, and between the two a friendship sprang up, though they lived a hundred miles apart, and had never met. Finally, she took wisely to reading books, and the sounder chattered in vain, except on business.

Then there was John. She saw him for one hurried moment every day, and the thinking of it filled many a weary hour. He was the engineer of the express, and stopped at the station every afternoon at five and just before daylight every morning. She met him at the water-tank by day, and by night she awoke to hear his train thunder through the valley. She heard it whistle as it passed the grade crossing, a mile up the line, and as it pulled up at the station. If the night was calm, she heard the faint rumble as it flew over the resounding iron bridge at the river. Then she slept again. He would soon reach the city, and on the morrow she would see him again.

The happy morrow always found her at her post, busy and cheerful as the long day crept away, and the time drew near for his train. Oh! if her window only looked out the other way, that she might see No. 59 come round the curve in the woods! The station was always full at that hour, and messages were sure to come in just as she wanted to close her little office and go out to the water-tank, where John waited, oiler in hand, to see her. Strange, that he should always be oiling up just there.

This time, she waited with calm face and beating heart to see if any stupid passenger had forgotten anything, that he must telegraph home. Fortunately, none came, and as the engine rolled past her window, she hastily put on her pretty hat and ample cloak and went out on the platform A few quick steps, and she was beside the noble 59.

The fireman smiled a grimy smile, and, while he swung the water-pipe over the tender, he gave a lively whistle. The engineer tipped up his oiler with a sudden jerk, as if the piston-rod had quite enough, and then climbed hastily into the cab. There she sat on the fireman's perch, radiant, blushing, and winsome.

"She's a beauty—perfectly lovely, and a Westinghouse, too! I tried to see you yesterday, and aren't you very proud of her?"

John thought he was rather proud of 59. She was perfect. Ran her one hundred and fifty miles yesterday, for the first time, The little electrician was charmed. To think that John should be appointed master over the Company's new express engine. Dear fellow, he had run that old 13, till she was ready to rattle to pieces. And now, what a magnificent machine he had beneath him!

"And everything is so bright and handsome. I know you're proud of her."

John thought he was also proud of somebody else. Then they smiled, and the fireman whistled softly as he pushed back the water-spout. How brief the precious moments!

John pulled out a little blank-book and began hastily to tell her about the new prize the Directors had offered to the engineer who should travel five thousand miles with the least expenditure of coal and oil. It would take about twenty-seven days to decide the matter, and then the books would be all handed in, and the records examined, and the prize awarded.

"And if we could get it!"

"It would come in very convenient for——"

She blushed a rosy blush, and, clasping his arm, she laughed softly, and said:

"My dear, you must win it. We shall want it for—our——"

"Lively, now! Here comes the Conduc." What a friendly fireman! How sharp he watched for the lovers! The girl prepared to spring down from the engine when the gold-banded cap of the conductor came in sight.

"Run up to the siding, Mills, and bring down that extra car."

"Aye, aye, sir. Cast off the couplings, Dick." Then, in a whisper: "Wait a bit, Kate. Ride up to the siding with us."

The girl needed no invitation.

4

"Oh! I intended to. Here, let me tend the bell."

"Good! Do. Dick must tend the couplings."

With a hiss and a jar the monster started forward, while the girl sat on the fireman's high seat with her hand on the bell-rope and one little foot steadied against the boiler. Suddenly, John turned the valve for the air-brake and reversed his lever, and the monster stopped. A deafening blast from the whistle.

"Where is that signal man? Why don't he show his flag?"

Again the whistle roared in short, quick blasts.

"Oh! Why didn't I think of it before?"

"Think of what?"

"That whistle. You could use it to call me."

"When?"

"Why, you see, I never exactly know when you are coming. I cannot tell your whistle from any other, and so, I sometimes miss seeing you."

"I—have—noticed—that——"said John, pulling at the throttle valve. "But, what can I do? If I gave two whistles or three, they would think it meant some signal, and it would make trouble."

"Yes, but if you did this, I should know you were coming, and nobody would think anything of it."

So saying, she stood up, leaned over the boiler, and grasping the iron rod that moved the whistle, made it speak in long and short blasts, that may be represented as follows:

"— — —— - —— —— -"

"I see. Like a sounder. Morse's alphabet. But what does it spell?"

"K —— - —— A- —— T —— E -"

"Oh! Let me learn that by heart."

"You must, John. And will it not be amusing to hear the folks talk? What on earth can that engineer be roaring about with his '— - —— - —— —— -'"

The signal-man looked indignant as 59 rolled past him. What was the good of such a din on the whistle! Was the man crazy!

"You must write it down, Kate. It won't do to practice now. See how the people stare on—the—platform."

The sentence was broken up by John's efforts over the reversing bar, and the deep-toned gasps of the engine drowned further conversation. The monster backed into the siding, where Dick stood ready to couple on the extra car. Then he climbed up into the cab, and the lovers were silenced. The engine, with the three, rolled out upon the main line, stopped, and then backed up to the train. Kate, with a pencil wrote some marks on the edge of the window-frame, and with a bright smile she shook hands with the

"THE GIRL SAT ON THE FIREMAN'S HIGH SEAT."

burly engineer, nodded to the fireman, and then sprang lightly to the ground.

The safety-valve burst out with a deafening roar. The smoke belched forth in clouds, and while fairy rings of steam shot into the air, the train moved slowly away.

Presently, the girl stood alone upon the deserted platform, with the ruddy glow of the setting sun gilding her bright face.

The roar of the train melted away on the air. Still, she stood listening intently. She would wait till she heard him whistle at the next crossing. Then, like a mellow horn softened by the distance, came this strange rhythmic song:

A smile and a blush lit up her winsome face.

How quickly love can learn!

That night, the waning moon sank cold and white in the purple west, while the morning star came out to see the sleeping world. Kate awoke suddenly and listened. Was that the roar of his train?

"How soft and sweet the notes so far away! There! He has crossed the bridge. Dear John!"

Then she slept again.

CHAPTER III.

THE OTHER OPERATOR.

THE last local train to the city left the station. The gray old station-master put out the lamps on the platform, rolled the baggage-trucks into the freight-house, and, having made the tour of the switches to see that all was clear for the main-line night mail, he returned to his little ticket den.

His daughter still sat reading like a demure cat in her little corner. The old man remarked that it was ten o'clock, and time to go home.

"Leave the key, father; I'll lock up and return home as soon as I have finished this chapter."

The old fellow silently laid a bunch of keys on her desk and went his way. The moment he departed she finished her chapter in a flash, and laying the book down, began to operate her telegraphic apparatus.

— — — —   — —.

No reply. Middleboro had evidently gone to bed, and that office was closed.

— —   — — —   — — —.

No response. Dawson City refused to reply. Good. Now, if the operator at the junction failed to reply, she and Mary would have the line to themselves with none to overhear.

— —   — — —   — — —   — —.

Allston Junction paid no heed. Good. Now for:

— — —   — — —   — — —   — —.

Mary replied instantly, and at once the two girl friends were in close conversation with one hundred miles of land and water between them. The conversation was by sound in a series of long and short notes—nervous and staccato for the bright one in the little station; smooth, legato and placid for the city girl.

Translated, it ran as follows:

Kate—"I taught him my name in Morse's alphabet, and he sounds it on his whistle as he comes up to the station; but I am in daily terror lest some impertinent operator should hear it, and, catching its meaning, tell of it."

The other operator was all sympathy, and replied:

"I see the danger. At the same time, my dear, I think the idea is worthy of your bright self. It is perfectly jolly. Think of hearing one's name for miles over the country on a steam-whistle. I never heard of anything so romantic in my life."

Kate—"And when he passes in the night he sounds my name all through the valley, and I can hear it for miles. How people would laugh if they knew what it meant."

Mary—"They would, I'm sure, and it would be very unpleasant to be found out. Why don't you fix up some kind of open circuit and let him telegraph to you from the line as he approaches your station?"

Kate—"My love, your idea is divine. If I only had a wire."

Mary—"It would take two wires, you know, and a small battery. At the same time, it would not cost much, and would be perfectly safe."

Kate—"Would not some one find it out and be ringing the bell out of mischief?"

Mary—"No. You could hide the connections in the bushes or trees by the road, and his engine could touch it as it passed."

Kate—"Yes, but wouldn't every engine touch it?"

Mary—"Then you could fix it so that a stick, or something secured to the engine, would brush it as it passed. No other engine would be provided with the stick, and they would all pass in silence."

The idea was almost too brilliant for contemplation, and the two friends, one in her deserted and lonely station in the far country, and the other in the fifth story of a city block, held close converse over it for an hour or more, and then they bid each other good night, and the wires were at rest for a time.

About five one afternoon shortly after, Kate sat in her office waiting for 59 to sound its Titanic love-signal. Presently it came in loud-mouthed notes:

"— — — — — — — — —"

She closed her little office hastily, and went out on the platform. As she opened the door, two young men laughed immoderately, and one said aloud:

"Kate! Who's Kate?"

Found out! She hastily turned away to hide the blush that mounted to her temples and walked rapidly up the platform to the water-tank.

59 rolled up to the spot, and the lovers met. With one hand on the iron front of his great engine, she stood waiting him, and at once began to talk rapidly.

"It will never do, John! They have found it all out."

"Oh! I was afraid they would. Now, what are we to do? If I could only telegraph you from the station below."

"It wouldn't do. It is too far away. Besides, it would be costly, and somebody would suspect."

"Conduc!" shouted the fireman, as he swung back the great water-pipe.

"Good-bye, dear. I'm sorry we must give it up."

"So am I. And, John, come and spend next Sunday with us."

"Yes, I will. Good-bye, Good-bye."

59 hissed out her indignation in clouds of steam from her cylinders, and moved slowly forward. Then Kate stood alone again on the platform. The sun sunk in angry clouds, and the wind sighed in the telegraph wires with a low moaning sound, fitful, sad and dreary.

"KATE UNROLLED THE WIRE AS HE TOOK IT UP."

The next morning the express tore savagely through the driving rain, and thundered over the iron bridge till it roared again. The whistle screamed, but love no longer charmed its iron voice.

The electrician listened in silence, and then, after a tear or two, slept again.

CHAPTER IV.

LOVE AND LIGHTNING.

It was a lovely autumnal afternoon, and the lovers went out to walk in the glorious weather.

To escape observing eyes, they wandered down the railroad track toward the woods, where the line made a great curve to avoid a bend in the river.

After a while they reached a shady dell in the woods, and, taking down a bar in the fence, they entered its depths. Just here the various telegraph wires hung in long festoons from their poles. With a sudden cry of delight, she seized his arm and cried:

"Look, John. Just the thing. An abandoned wire."

"Well; what of it?"

"My dear, can't we use it? Come, let us follow it and see where it goes. Perhaps we may make it useful."

John failed to see how that might be. Kate was all eagerness to follow the wire, and returned to the track, and began to trace the wire up and down the line as far as it was visible. John replaced the fence rail and joined her. Then she began to talk in that rapid manner that was so becoming to her. He was fairly dazzled by the brilliancy and audacity of her ideas. They both walked on the sleepers toward the bridge over the river. The wire was still continuous, but after walking about half a mile, they found it was broken, and apparently abandoned. Then she laid down her plan. This wire had been put up by a certain company some years since, but as the company had failed, the wire had been abandoned, and here for perhaps a mile it was still hanging on its insulators. At the bridge it came to a sudden end.

"Now, if we can manage to rig up another wire from here to our station we can make an open circuit, and as you pass this point you can join it and——ring a bell in my office!"

The two sat down on the iron bridge and fairly laughed at the splendor of the idea. Suddenly she looked very grave.

"The expense!"

"Ah! yes. Well, I'm willing to pay something for the advantage of seeing you every day. It's worth——"

"How much?"

"About $5,000,000."

"John!"

Two days after, a package came by express from the city, and Kate stowed it away in her telegraphic den till the evening. Then, when the day had passed, and she had some leisure, she carefully opened it and found a neat little wooden box with a small brass gong or bell attached to the bottom. A slender hammer hung beside it, and there were places for securing the connecting wires, an electric bell and 3,000 feet of insulated wire and a bill for the same. Eleven dollars.

"Not half so bad as I expected. As for the battery, I fancy I can make one myself. A pickle jar, some zinc and copper and a little acid will answer, and John can arrange the rest. Fortunately I selected insulated wire, as we shall have to carry our line through the woods to cut off that bend in the road."

Thus talking and planning to herself, she examined her purchase, and then carefully placing the bell and the wire in a closet under her desk, she closed up the station and went demurely home, conscious of the innocence of all her dark plottings.

The third day after seemed like the Sabbath, and was not. It was Thanksgiving Day, and all the very good people went soberly to church. The good people like Kate and her lover did nothing of the kind. John Mills, engineer, did not ride on No. 59 that day. He had a holiday, and came to see Kate quite early in the morning. She proposed a walk in the woods, as the day was fine.

"Did you bring the boots?"

"I did, my love, spikes and all. I tried 'em on an apple-tree, and I found I could walk up the stem as nicely as a fly on the ceiling."

"That is good; for, on the whole, I think we must shorten the line, and cut off that great bend in the road."

"And save battery power?"

"Yes. My pickle-jar battery works well, but I find that it is not particularly powerful. It rings the bell furiously when I close the circuit, but the circuit is not two yards long. What it will do when the line is up, remains to be seen."

"Where did you place the bell?"

"Oh, I hung it up in the cupboard under my desk. I can hear it, and no one will be likely to look for it there. But that is not the great difficulty. How are we to hide the wires that enter the station?"

"I wouldn't try. Let them stand in plain sight. Not a soul will ever notice them among the crowd of wires that pass the station."

By this time the two had reached the railroad station, and, opening her little office, they both went in. Presently they reappeared, each with a brown paper parcel, and, with the utmost gravity, walked away down the line toward the woods.

In a few moments they were lost to view round a curve in the road, and they turned off toward the bank and sat down on a large, flat stone.

"The boots, Kate."

She opened the bundle she had in her hand, and displayed a pair of iron stirrups having an iron rod on one side, and a sharp steel point on the bottom. There were also leather straps and buckles, and John, laying aside his burden, proceeded to strap them to his feet. When ready, the iron rods or bars reached nearly to the knee, and the steel points were just below the instep. Kate meanwhile took a pair of stout shears from her pocket and began to open the other bundle. It contained a large roll of insulated copper wire, some tacks, and a hammer.

Then they started down the track, with sharp eyes on the abandoned wire hanging in long festoons from its insulators. All right so far. Ah! a break; they must repair it. Like a nimble cat John mounted the pole, and Kate unrolled the wire as he took it up. In a moment or two he had it secured to the old wire. Then up the next pole, and while Kate pulled it tight he secured it, and the line was reunited.

Then on and on they walked, watching the wire, and still finding it whole. At last they reached the great iron bridge, and anxiously scanned the dozen or more wires, to see if their particular thread was still continuous.

"We must cross the river, John. The line seems to be whole, and we can take our new line through the woods on the other shore till we reach the town bridge."

It was a relief to leave the dizzy open sleepers of the bridge and stand once more on firm ground.

"This must be the limit of our circuit. I wish it was larger, for it will not give me more than three minutes time. Now, if you'll break the line on that pole, John."

There was a sound of falling glass, and then the new insulated line was secured to the old line; the broken end fell to the ground and was abandoned. For half an hour or more the two were busy over their work, and then it was finished. It was a queer-looking affair, and no one would ever guess where it was or what it was designed to do. A slender maple-tree beside the track had a bit of bare copper wire (insulated at the ends), hung upright, in its branches. Near by stood a large oak-tree, also having a few feet of wire secured horizontally to its branches. From the slender maple a wire ran to the old telegraph line. From the old oak our young people quickly ran a new line through the woods by simply tacking it up out of sight in the trees.

Then they came to the wooden bridge where the town road crossed the stream. It took but a few moments to tack the insulated wire to the under side of one of the string-pieces well out of sight, and then they struck off into the deep woods again.

Three hours later they struck the railroad, and found the old wire some distance beyond the station up the line. Again the two-legged cat ran up the pole, and there was a sound of breaking glass. The old wire fell down among the bushes, and the new one was joined to the piece still on the line. A short time after, two young people with rather light bundles and very light hearts gravely walked into the station and then soberly went to their dinner. That night two mysterious figures flitted about the platform of the deserted station. One like a cat ran up the dusky poles, and the other unrolled a bit of copper wire. There was a sound of boring, and two minute wires were pushed through a hole in the window frame. The great scientific enterprise was finished.

CHAPTER V.

ALMOST TELESCOPED.

IT was very singular how absent-minded and inattentive the operator was that day. She sent that order for flowers to the butcher, and Mrs. Robinson's message about the baby's croup went to old Mr. Stimmins, the bachelor lodger at the gambrel-roofed house.

No wonder she was disturbed. Would the new line work? Would her pickle-jar battery be strong enough for such a great circuit? Would John be able to close it? The people began to assemble for the train. The clock pointed to the hour for its arrival.

"He cometh not," she said. Then she began to be a little tearful. The people all left the waiting-room and went out on the platform, and the place was deserted and silent. She listened intently. There was nothing, save the murmur of the voices outside, and the irritating tick of the clock.

Suddenly, with startling distinctness, the bell rang clear and loud in the echoing room. With a little cry of delight she put on her dainty hat and ran in haste out upon the platform. The idle people stared at her flushed and rosy face, and she turned away and walked toward the water-tank. Not a thing in sight? What did it mean?

Ah! The whistle broke loud and clear on the cool, crisp air, and 59 appeared round the curve in the woods. The splendid monster slid swiftly up to her feet and paused.

"Perfect, John! Perfect! It works to a charm."

With a spring she reached the cab and sat down on the fireman's seat.

"Blessed if I could tell what he was going to do," said Dick. "He told me about it. Awful bright idea! You see, he laid the poker on the tender brake there, and it hit the tree slam, and I saw the wires touch. It was just prime!"

The happy moments sped, and 59 groaned and slowly departed, while Kate stood on the platform, her face wreathed in smiles and white steam.

So the lovers met each day, and none knew how she was made aware of his approach with such absolute certainty. Science applied to love, or rather love applied to science, can move the world.

Two whole weeks passed, and then there suddenly arrived at the station, late one evening, a special with the directors' car attached. The honorable directors were hungry—they always are—and would pause on their journey and take a cup of tea and a bit of supper. The honorables and their wives and children filled the station, and the place put on quite a gala aspect. As for Kate, she demurely sat in her den, book in hand, and over its unread pages admired the gay party in the brightly lighted waiting-room.

Suddenly, with furious rattle her electric bell sprang into noisy life. Every spark of color left her face, and her book fell with a dusty slam to the floor. What was it? What did it mean? Who rang it?

With affrighted face she burst from her office and brushed through the astonished people and out upon the snow-covered plat-

form. There stood the directors' train upon the track of the on-coming engine.

"The conductor! Where is he? Oh! sir! Start! Start! Get to the siding. The express! The express is coming!"

With a cry she snatched a lantern from a brakeman's hand, and in a flash was gone. They saw her light pitching and dancing through the darkness, and they were lost in wonder and amazement. The girl is crazy! No train is due now! There can be no danger. She must be ——

Ah! that horrible whistle. Such a wild shriek on the winter's night! The men sprang to the train, and the women and children fled in frantic terror in every direction.

"Run for your lives," screamed the conductor. "There's a smash-up coming!"

A short, sharp scream from the whistle. The head-light gleamed on the snow-covered track, and there was a mad rush of sliding wheels and the gigantic engine roared like a demon. The great 59 slowly drew near and stopped in the woods. A hundred heads looked out, and a stalwart figure leaped down from the engine and ran on into the bright glow of the head-light.

"Kate!"

"Oh! John, I ——"

She fell into his arms senseless and white, and the lantern dropped from her nerveless hand.

They took her up tenderly and bore her into the station-house and laid her upon the sofa in the "ladies' room." With hushed voices they gathered round to offer aid and comfort. Who was she? How did she save the train? How did she know of its approach?

"She is my daughter," said the old station-master. "She tends the telegraph."

The President of the Railroad, in his gold-bowed spectacles, drew near. One grand lady in silk and satin pillowed Kate's head on her breast. They all gathered near to see if she revived. She opened her eyes and gazed about dreamily, as if in search of something.

"Do you wish anything, my dear?" said the President, taking her hand.

"Some water, if you please, sir; and I want—I want——"

They handed her some wine in a silver goblet. She sipped a little, and then looked among the strange faces as if in search of some one.

"Are you looking for any one, Miss?"

"Yes—no—it is no matter. Thank you,

ma'am, I feel better. I sprained my foot on the sleepers when I ran down the track. It is not severe, and I'll sit up."

"SHE FELL INTO HIS ARMS SENSELESS AND WHITE."

They were greatly pleased to see her recover, and a quiet buzz of conversation filled the room. How did she know it? How could she tell the special was chasing us? Good Heavens! if she had not known it, what an awful loss of life there would have been; it was very careless in the superintendent to follow our train in such a reckless manner.

"You feel better, my dear," said the President.

"Yes, sir, thank you. I'm sure I'm thankful. I knew John—I mean the engine was coming."

"You cannot be more grateful than we are to you for averting such a disastrous collision."

"I'm sure, I am pleased, sir. I never thought the telegraph——"

She paused abruptly.

"What telegraph?"

"I'd rather not tell, sir."

"But you will tell us how you knew the engine was coming?"

"Must you know?"

"We ought to know in order to reward you properly."

She put up her hand in a gesture of refusal, and was silent. The President and directors consulted together, and two of them came to her and briefly said that they would be glad to know how she had been made aware of the approaching danger.

"Well, sir, if John is willing, I will tell you all."

John Mills, engineer, was called, and he came in, cap in hand, and the entire company gathered round in the greatest eagerness.

Without the slightest affectation, she put her hand on John's grimy arm, and said:

"Shall I tell them, John? They wish to know about it. It saved their lives, they say."

"And mine, too," said John, reverently. "You had best tell them, or let me."

She sat down again, and then and there John explained how the open circuit line had been built, how it was used, and frankly told why it had been erected.

Never did story create profounder sensation. The gentlemen shook hands with him, and the President actually kissed her for the Company. A real Corporation kiss, loud and hearty. The ladies fell upon her neck, and actually cried over the splendid girl. Even the children pulled her dress, and put their arms about her neck, and kissed away the happy tears that covered her cheeks.

Poor child! She was covered with confusion, and knew not what to say or do, and looked imploringly to John. He drew near, and proudly took her hand in his, and she brushed away the tears and smiled.

The gentlemen suddenly seemed to have found something vastly interesting to talk about, for they gathered in a knot in the corner of the room. Presently the President said aloud:

"Gentlemen and Directors, you must pardon me, and I trust the ladies will do the same, if I call you to order for a brief matter of business."

There was a sudden hush, and the room, now packed to suffocation, was painfully quiet.

"The Secretary will please take minutes of this meeting."

The Secretary sat down at Kate's desk, and then there was a little pause.

"Mr. President!"

Every eye was turned to a corner where a gray-haired gentleman had mounted a chair.

"Mr. President."

"Mr. Graves, director for the State, gentlemen."

"I beg leave, sir, to offer a resolution."

Then he began to read from a slip of paper.

"Whereas, John Mills, engineer of engine Number 59, of this railway line, erected a private telegraph; and, whereas he, with the assistance of the telegraph operator of this station (I leave a blank for her name), used the said line without the consent of this Company, and for other than railway business: "It is resolved that he be suspended permanently from his position as engineer, and that the said operator be requested to resign——"

A murmur of disapprobation filled the room, but the President commanded silence, and the State Director went on.

"——resign her place.

"It is further resolved, and is hereby ordered, that the said John Mills be and is appointed chief engineer of the new repair shops at Slawson."

A tremendous cheer broke from the assembled company, and the resolution was passed with a shout of assent.

How it all ended they never knew. It seemed like a dream, and they could not believe it true till they stood alone in the winter's night on the track beside that glorious 59. The few cars the engine had brought up had been joined to the train, and 59 had been rolled out on the siding. With many hand-shakings for John, and hearty kisses for Kate, and a round of parting cheers for the two, the train had sped away. The idlers had dispersed, and none lingered about the abandoned station save the lovers. 59 would stay that night on the siding, and they had walked up the track to bid it a long farewell.

For a few moments they stood in the glow of the great lamp, and then he quietly put it out, and left the giant to breathe away its fiery life in gentle clouds of white steam. As for the lovers, they had no need of its light. The winter's stars shone upon them, and the calm cold night seemed a paradise below.

Out of Adjustment.

A TELEGRAPH office, plain and simple,
  Furnished poorly and scant in space;
A youthful maiden with smile and dimple,
  Adorning a delicate, winning face.
A single window to light the room,
  Its view obstructed by cars of freight;
A depot dreary, nor thrift nor bloom,
  But all around a desolate state.

Now working her key with might and main,
  As though the current were feeble and weak,
Now closing the same again and again,
  As if to let Patience whisper and speak.
Adjusting the relay with hope in her heart,
  Once more she strives to accomplish the deed,
But failing, the tears from her eyes quickly
    start,   [freed.
And flow unrestrained till her great grief is

"Sweet maid, why labor here?" said I,
  While with pity my throbbing heart stood
    still;
"Why stay out here to languish and die,
  When you can know content if you will.
Go to the city and merry be!
  Go where the currents and wires are good!
Seek thou an office where thou canst see
  The beauties of nature, of river and wood,
The busy motion of toil and pleasure,
  And of life's many joys find a comforting
    measure."

Thus did I speak to that fair gentle maid,
  As I loitered one day near the rural depot,
Awaiting the steam-horse to come down the
    grade,
  Which was now behind time an hour or so,

Watching her face through the little soiled pane,
  I saw her despair and her tears gently flow,
And sympathy strong that I could not restrain
  Led me into the office my comfort to show.

For I was a knight of the telegraph key,
  And knowing that currents when terribly
    weak
Beget a fell anguish, a dire misery
  That pen can't portray nor human voice
    speak,
My heart urged me forward; go in there I
    must,
  And do what I can to offer relief;
Perchance I could teach how to gently adjust,
  And, if this were the trouble, dispel all her
    grief.

"Pray dry thy sad tears, my dear little friend,
  And let not harsh sorrow be stamped on thy
    face;
Invoke the bright angels from heaven to send
  Pure smiles of bright joy thy sweet visage
    to grace;
Courage is thine if patient you'll be,
  For patience is courage, and courage is power,
Before it despair will instantly flee,
  And your mind over sadness triumphant
    shall tower."

The words were scarce said when a smile most
    serene
Appeared on her face, and illumined it o'er
Like a beautiful rainbow that's oftentimes seen
  Succeeding the rain drops which come with
    the shower;

And the sweet glance she gave me of gratitude's
trust,
As she raised up her eyes and gazed softly
in mine,
Was so tempting and winsome that kiss her I
must,
And our lips met together on love's holy shrine.

This tribute to love had scarcely been paid—
We still stood together in ardent embrace—
When puffing and screeching down over the grade
The steam-horse rushed in in a moment of space;
A ruddy cheeked brakeman leaped out from the
car,
His eyes flashing anger, a cane in his hand,
And, quick as the flash of a twinkling star,
Right there in the office before us did stand; ·

Then speaking to me in a loud angry tone,
His cane raised aloft just over my head.
" What brought you in here with my girl all alone,
Embracing and kissing, and loving?" he said.
" This girl and myself have long been engaged;
And for so heinous an insult I'll have your vile
life;"
Ye gods! that young brakeman was greatly en-
raged,
For I had been kissing his dear future wife.

As for me, there I stood, not a word could I
speak
To explain a perplexing position like this;
I acted dejected—exceedingly meek.
But my fears quickly fled when that fair gentle
Miss,

Addressing her lover with faltering tone
Said, " Harry, my love, pray let me explain
The reason this youth was with me alone,
Embracing and loving again and again.

" You remember I told you a short time ago,
Of a darling young cousin I had in the West? "
" Why yes," he replied, " you did tell me so,"
" Well, this is the one," said she, laughing with
zest,
" And now on the way to his old native town,
He stopped here to see me an hour or so.
Now, Harry, my love, take your horrid cane
down,
This youth is my cousin, but you are my beau."

His anger had vanished, his cane had come down,
But not on my head as I tremblingly feared;
A smile had supplanted the harsh angry frown,
And instead of abuse a kind greeting appeared,
He grasped my hand quickly, and shook it with
zeal,   [side;
While the fair maid most lovingly stood by his
I was saved from a caning, but could not help feel
That the angel beside him had fearfully lied."

As we parted that day she whisperingly said,
" You adjusted my relay, assauging my tears,
And I in return have reciprocated,
For I soon " adjusted " your troubles and fears.
Your work was performed by the rules of the *lins*
I copied from you with the best of success,
My work, too, was done by the rules of the *lyin'*,
And saved you and me from great trouble I
guess."

George Washington Cribbs' Telegram.

It was a small messenger boy that took out the midnight signal reports that night, and they told him to hurry, to run and deliver them at the Observer's office at No. — South Second Street. The promising little fellow *did* run, ran all the way—with the exception of a slight deviation in the direction of his home to partake of a little lunch—but, true to his undying aspirations as the telegrapher of the future, he ran to the wrong place, and brought up at No. — South Street—the correct number but the wrong street. This place, instead of being a Government weather office, proved to be a cellar occupied by a colored gentleman of some 114 years, or less, by the name of George Washington Cribbs. That proud aristocrat being temporarily absent, together with the other dusky members of his subterranean household—probably on a nocturnal foraging expedition—and everyone thereabouts assuring the small boy that that was undoubtedly the proper place, he pushed the weather reports—which, as all operators know, are written in a most outlandish cipher—under the aged George Washington Cribbs'

door, and looking again at the number thereof to satisfy his conscience, departed.

Now, if there is any one thing which pleases a colored man more than another, next to carrying a tin watch with a California brass chain attached, it is the receipt of a letter. It will thus be understood that when George Washington Cribbs, aged 114 years or less, returned home at 2 A.M., with a recently deceased chicken slung over his shoulder, that he was exceedingly gratified to find the United States Signal Service official weather reports awaiting him; and it was only after many an ineffectual attempt to decipher the same that the broad grin vanished from his face and made way for a very forlorn expression, as his natural suspicions of a horrible fate in store for him dawned upon his mind. Could it be the bull-dozers?

It was just previous to the election, and George Washington Cribbs not only belonged to a colored political club, but was also president thereof, and despite his advanced age, had registered a public vow that, should Tilden be elected, on the morn which followed such a night Mrs. Martha Washington Cribbs should wear the widow's weeds. Although George was a very humble individual to the world at large, he appeared before his political friends at the club in his official capacity as " The Grand Exasperated Quadrilateral (the Chair")—quadrilateral being peculiarly symbolic of his eminent position as " the chair," and exasperated doing duty as a standing menace to all inquisitive members of the club who might take issue with their exalted Grand Exasperated Quadrilateral on the subject of official finances.

At the first blush one would hardly suppose that a vigorous nigger of such prominence, whose head had successfully withstood many an uncompromising bombardment of bludgeons and cobble-stones, could be frightened with a paltry cipher message; but, it must be remembered, that the man who was born not for war but to hoe the corn and hunt the 'possum, who would scoff at a judicial warrant for his arrest for hen-roost depredations, or who would gaze with cynical disdain on a written summons to pay his tithing to the church, or a tailor's bill, or any other document which he could understand and point at with the finger of scorn with impunity, is totally annihilated by an ominous cipher message bearing all the evidence of the bull-dozer's high art and fell determination.

The more George Washington Cribbs tried to make sense out of that Signal report, the more dispirited did he become, for he felt that although there might possibly be a misunderstanding somewhere, there was still something extremely evanescent, something unutterably diaphanous—something too subtle for a mind of purely Simian origin to grapple with—in a communication containing obscure references to the chief " Signal " office, etc., and surreptitiously injected into his domicile at midnight. He felt that a rational colored man, aged 114 or less, with a tender regard for his own personal welfare, ought in these troublesome times to draw the line of war risks somewhere; and, therefore, with wonderful sagacity he concluded to draw it at such obscure and anonymous communications as:

" Savannah, Noiseful, Alias, Budge,
Cabin, Gimlet, Earnest, Glance,"

written in the form of blank verse, and thrust under his door by unseen hands at unseasonable hours. No conscientious colored man, aged 114 or less, staggering under such an official title as the Grand Exasperated Quadrilateral (the Chair), could be reasonably expected to keep cool with a White Leaguer's communication awaiting him at 2 A.M., since the merit of an undecipherable note—considered in a political sense, and pushed under a nigger's door about election time—suggests to that " gemman "

the imperative necessity of an immediate trip westward—and, in most cases, a-foot.

Under this view of the case, at daybreak, while a cracked hand-organ outside was playing the Dead March in Saul, and other dirges, fancying that he already heard the tat-too of Watterson's drums and the spontaneous roar of a hundred thousand (unarmed) men, George resolved to commence his westward journey at once ; and for the purpose of exciting no undue attention among the higher classes of the occidental regions — California, Oregon, and other foreign shores—he gave himself a coat of whitewash, donned a cheap red shirt with pockets, and painted his nose with a brilliant vermilion pigment, that he might still more resemble the aborigines of those arid wastes. With scalding tears trickling o'er his calcimined cheeks, he bade farewell to his pail of lime and artist's brush ; his wife put up his lunch for the last time, and, muffled in his linen duster to keep out the wintry blasts, he crept in silence toward the region of sundown; but, on second thought, concluded to confine his operations to groping through the trackless forests of the 24th Ward, rather than brave an intolerable existence amid the monstrous growing carrots, the colossal radishes, and the Herculean turnips of the Pacific coast.

Sorrows—even the outcrop of bulled Signal Service reports—after the first shock always purify us and make us bolder and nobler; and the sweeping flood which threatens to overwhelm us frequently brings down on the breast of its own irresistible torrent the floating log which we clutch to save us. It was so, at least, with George Washington Cribbs, aged 114 or less, the fugitive Grand Exasperated Quadrilateral (the Chair). He carried the dreaded " threatening letter " in his pocket, and, one day, in a fit of reckless courage, took it to a police station. The Mayor, who was somewhat of a municipal plug, thereupon issued a call for a large force of special police, and summoned an extra session of City Councils; and it was only after the document had been lithographed for Forney's *Press* that it was by chance discovered to be a telegraphic weather report, and delivered to its proper destination.

And now, George Washington Cribbs, aged 114 or less, having resigned his position as the Grand Exasperated Quadrilateral (the Chair), is back at his old civil post, filling an important office as janitor in a Walnut Street commercial house. He never talks very much about the bull-dozers, although he missed getting in his vote for Hayes, but when questioned on the subject he goes right on sweeping out the vestibule, and, without raising his head, merely remarks that it was a tolerably funny affair, but that " those telegraph folks do everlastingly mix things up."

Scenes on a Jersey Railroad.—Drawn by J. Christie.

"Two plugs with but a single thought—Two keys that beat as one."——*Ingomar Altered.*

Telegraphy—Ancient and Modern.

Thoughts for Serious Moments.

Friendship is full of dregs.

Youth holds no society with grief.

So sad, so fresh, the days that are no more.

Some are too wise, or too difficult, to be pleased.

Reading without reflection will never make a man wise.

We darken our own lot, then call our sorrows destiny.

Passions are as easily evaded as impossible to moderate.

From the follies of youth usually spring many of life's after sorrows.

Man creates more discontent to himself than ever is occasioned by others.

The higher the rank the less the pretence, because there is less to pretend to.

A habit of sincerity in acknowledging faults, is a guard against committing them.

Be reserved in discourse; it never can be hurtful, and it may prevent much mischief.

He who cannot conceal his vexation, makes himself a laughing-stock for his enemies.

The surest and most speedy road to distinction is the diligent cultivation of natural tact.

We should accustom the mind to keep the best company by introducing it only to the best books.

Men are seldom struck with incongruities in their own appearance any more than in their own conduct.

The heart that has something to love, and is loved in return, can never be utterly and remedilessly wretched.

Good breeding is benevolence in trifles, or the preference of others to ourselves in the little daily occurrences of life.

Scorn not the advice of an inferior; the underling of fortune may be, in merit, your superior. Situation never determines ability.

Our enemies deserve our greatest attention always, sometimes our extreme respect; from them comes amendment and correction.

Nothing is greater than to bestow favors upon those who have failed in their duty to us; nothing meaner than to receive any from them.

National progress is the sum of individual industry, energy, and uprightness, as national decay is of individual idleness, selfishness, and vice.

A restless mind, like a rolling stone, gathers nothing but dirt and mire. Little or no good will cleave to it; and it is sure to leave peace and quietness behind it.

The Athenians erected a large statue of Æsop, and placed him, though a slave, on a lasting pedestal, to show that the way to honor lies open indifferently to all.

Genius is only great patience.

Peace is rarely denied to the peaceful.

Things past may be repented, but not recalled.

As if you could kill time without injuring eternity!

Moments sometimes make the hues in which years are colored.

Politeness has been well defined as benevolence in small things.

That man lives greatly, whatever his fate or fame, who greatly dies.

He who assumes to be what he is not, will inevitably become nothing at all.

As charity covers a multitude of sins before God, so does politeness before men.

Conscience, when once hushed to sleep, may rise to torture, but will wake no more to save.

I love such mirth as does not make friends ashamed to look upon one another next morning.

Gentleman is a term which does not apply to any station, but to the mind and feelings in every station.

Talent lying in the understanding is often inherited; genius, being the action of reason or imagination, rarely or never.

Those who will not condescend, as they term it, should be extremely careful not to assume any sort of deportment indicative of superiority.

Prayer among men is supposed to change the person to whom we pray; but prayer to God doth not change Him, but fits us to receive the thing prayed for.

I give it as my deliberate and solemn conviction that the individual who is habitually tardy in meeting an appointment will never be respected or successful in life.

The poor man who envies not the rich, who pities his companions of poverty, and can spare something for him that is still poorer, is, in the realms of humanity, a king of kings.

Garments that have one rent in them are subject to be torn on every nail, and glasses that are once cracked are soon broken; so is man's good name once tainted with just reproach.

Great characters are seldom known; great merit is as seldom understood. Greatness is, in fact, only a term of comparison, though it is not always allowed to see what is greater than itself.

A fair reputation is a plant delicate in its nature, and by no means rapid in its growth. It will shoot up in a night like the gourd of the prophet; but like that gourd, it may perish in a night.

The immortal God
Accepts the meanest altars that are raised
By pure devotions; and sometimes prefers
An ounce of frankincense, honey, or milk,
Before whole hecatombs, or Sæbean gems,
Offer'd in ostentation.

PRIOR to the introduction of patent brakes the brakeman on a passenger train was an individual calculated to command respect. He cultivated his muscle assiduously, and the man who could give the brake an extra twist after his fellows had done their best, and who could slide the wheels under his coach, was regarded as the king bee in the profession.

In those days, when a dead-beat attempted to evade his fare, and the conductor called in the brakeman, the delinquent took in the situation at once, and came down with the fare without more ado.

Full of conscious strength, the breakman indulged in "chin music" without stint, and brave must be the man who combatted his opinion when publicly expressed. Alas! that Westinghouse has substituted another kind of wind for what was once so useful an article.

The want of exercise has brought on an effeminacy which on many roads has stilled the brakeman's voice forever, and when he still attempts the announcement of stations it is with so indistinct an utterance as to be unintelligible. Bashful in his new nature, he shoots out of the car door with his words half uttered, lest the glance of some fair maiden might overcome him. If he attempts to announce Laphark, for instance, it sounds like whang-bang, and in his hasty retreat he slams the door so vigorously that the voice, mingling with the rattle of the window-panes, becomes incoherence itself. Woe to that passenger who depends on the brakeman for the knowledge that he has reached his destination.

There tarries in New York, not far from the post-office building, during business hours, a legal gentleman, in the prime of life, who has given much sage counsel to men older and younger than himself. All his tact and wisdom did not keep him, however, on one occasion from falling a victim to the brakeman's degeneracy.

Following Greeley's injunction to "go west," he started on a business trip in that direction. When within a hundred miles of his destination a junction was reached where the train divided, but no announcement being made, he went into supper with others in blissful ignorance of the fact. Sauntering out after the meal, he stepped on what appeared the last car in the train, and passed to the rear end, where he found the door locked, and a lady whom he had noticed during the day sitting not far from himself.

Just then her husband, looking anxiously, passed by on the platform, and she tried to attract his attention, fearing he would be left.

Our legal friend assured her there was no danger, as the train had only been separated to do some switching, but when the husband stepped on a distant and receding car, and it continued to move from the depot, the mistake dawned upon him. Rushing to the forward end of the car, he sprang to the platform and gave chase to the fast disappearing train. His hat flew off, his gray locks fluttered in the breeze, and as the depot was long and full of people, they paused to enjoy the race. He was greeted with plentiful advice, such as, "Go it, old man!" "Two to one you win!" "If you don't catch him come back in five days!" "Take her along on your coat-tail," etc. Having made an unprecedented time, but in vain, to a point outside the depot, he drew up against a lamp-post to recover his breath and repair damages.

Presently he was joined by his new lady acquaintance, bearing the missing hat. She had fallen in attempting to recover it, and was now crying in heartrending tones, "Oh, my husband! My husband! My husband!"

Full of conscious guilt, our legal friend still determined at once to put his foot on her histerics, and so he calmly said:

"My dear madame, I am *not* your husband. Please do not address me in that way."

By degrees he calmed her into self-possession, and they finally walked arm in arm to the waiting-room. A telegram was soon dispatched to the missing husband, and in due time an answer came that he would stop at the second station beyond and await the arrival of his wife, who was ordered peremptorily to take the first train.

She was a sensitive little woman, with the misfortune to be linked to a morose and tyrannical companion, but under the genial influence of our learned friend the pent up vivacity of her nature returned, and the hours of waiting were passed in pleasure and almost forgetfulness of the mishap.

Shortly before train time a young couple came into the depot, bringing with them a babe. This they placed in a seat near by our friends, where it slept quietly. Presently the mother said she would like to step out into the air with her husband a moment, and asked our lady acquaintance to look after the child, to which she readily assented. The moments flew by and the couple did not return, but the train was announced, and something must be done. At this juncture an old lady, who had watched the proceedings, spoke up in a sharp voice, and said: "Yew needn't think that woman's comin' back—she's runned away from her child."

At this our friend drew back the vail and kissed the innocent face beneath. In a fit of desperation she wondered what her husband would say at her bringing the baby home, and then declared she would take it anyway. In spite of expostulations, she kept her courageous determination, and the train sped on its way with the legal representative and his two companions. To say that moments seemed hours to him would be a faint expression of his anxiety, but the baby was good, and all things have an end.

At last the station where the husband was to be met was reached, and our friend bounded out of the front door to find him. At the same moment the husband bounced into the rear door, and discovered his wife, but when he saw the infant upbraided her in a shocking manner.

Matters were not helped when our legal friend came in, for the wife, remembering his kindness, and the car being full, she told her husband that the seat he occupied belonged to the stranger. The husband had a dark complexion, black hair and a fierce eye. At this information he swore a fearful oath, and with a bound bolted for the smoking-car. Our legal friend, in much trepidation, but full of determination not to encourage any further marital infelicity, followed close at his heels. By dint of much plain talk he induced the husband to return to his wife, and for himself smoked away the time till his destination was reached, little dreaming of the other events which were transpiring. Those who sat near the reunited husband and wife say that he scolded her savagely, the baby screamed, and the lady cried heartily till they were overtaken by an unexpected incident.

In the meanwhile the young husband and wife had returned to the depot, and finding the young fledgling gone, the father swore eternal vengeance on the guilty heads, and the mother, in heart-broken accents, bewailed her child.

The old lady was still on hand with her sympathy. "She knew sumthin' was wrong with that old sinner. She heered him talk. He had runned away with another man's wife, and now had stoled the bairn."

This added fuel to the flames, and the young husband fairly foamed with rage.

It was now midnight, and most of the telegraph offices were closed, but from the first one reached a telegram was sent ordering the arrest of the man and woman with the stolen babe. The constable was promptly on hand to execute his orders, and no amount of explanation or threats could prevent him from locking up the desperate husband and his innocent wife.

In the morning on came the young couple, and the two ladies soon became sympathetic —the one in joy at the recovery of her child, and the other in satisfaction at the mother's happiness. The two husbands had a stormy scene. The younger sued the older for damages on account of the theft of his babe. The fierce gentleman pursued our legal friend and brought action for depriving him of his wife and consequent damages. Our representative of the New York bar would have sued the railroad company for damages for not keeping a brakeman to announce the stations and changes, but he knew it would take his life-time to get judgment, and that his posterity would not live long enough to collect it. Reason prevailed at last, however, explanations were made, and the suits were withdrawn amid general harmony.

Our legal representative was anxious to keep his adventure quiet, but Dame Rumor travels fast, and on returning home he had hard work to prevent a divorce case in his own domestic circle. To this day, when he starts on a trip, as his wife puts her arms around his neck and kisses him good-bye, she says, " Do, my dear, keep out of scrapes ! " As he leaves the house the spinster over the way, peeking through the blinds, remarks: " There goes Mr. —— on another tower ! He'll get into another woman scrape ! *My*

husband shall never leave the house alone, if I know myself ! "

Thus our deeds do follow us. And now for the several morals of the story :

First. Beware of the modern brakeman, for he has long since ceased to be worthy of your confidence.

Second. Never restrain a lady from fleeing to her husband when he is in sight, but rather hasten such a consummation, lest disaster befall you.

Third. Beware of small responsibilities, for they frequently cause much mischief.

Fourth and lastly. When traveling look out for No. 1, and be not too officious with advice till sure of your own ground.

Do you, like the children, ask if this is a true story ? The Father of our Country has always been the greatest object of my admiration. It is not likely he would prevaricate about so small an apple of discord as whether a story should be spoiled by too close an adhesion to the truth, and no more can I. As the novelists say, " This romance is founded upon fact."

A Reminiscence.

THE average Philadelphia operator, who is seldom seen in anything but an agitated frame of mind, finds himself in a state of fermentation on the first and fifteenth of each month, those being the two happy days when the ghost walks through the office doling out the much coveted dollars. The boys, who for the previous ten days have been " spacing it," (a process by which those living on the European plan make at least one meal a day for economy's sake on nothing more substantial than vapor), find themselves at boiling heat, consumed by the undying thirst for lucre; and cases have been known where they have met the cashier at his down town residence in the early morning, and accompanied him in a body to the office. All their numerous outstanding notes go to protest on

these particular days, and the variation of ten cents against them in their account with the cashier necessitates the " spacing " of an extra meal time.

Fully understanding this arrangement, the reader, who has not been there himself, can understand something of the panic which succeeded the announcement, made in December, 1875, of the company's very reluctant resolution to reduce salaries. One has only to reflect on the close calculations which are made on a certain amount, and the sudden depreciation of that amount of from four to ten dollars, to realize the fact that many a poor fellow wilted and floated away on a gentle east wind. Everybody leered askance at his neighbor, but we all doubted the rumor. There was every reason to doubt it—

the good Centennial time a-coming, the instinct of hopeful ambition and consciousness of guiltless conduct, the suddenness and universality of the calamity, and the thoughts of "all the little (tailors') hearts that would ache" bewildered us, and even made us incredulous; but when the "notices" *did* come, printed forms filled in with horrible official scribbling, and heralded by official proclamations and such mottoes as "Order 164," "Sliding Scale," etc., we sat down prepared to believe any story which might be told us hereafter, how wild soever it might be.

But it's an ill sliding scale that blows no one any good, and in addition to those fortunate ones who got more after the reduction than they did previously, some of the fun-loving members of the force derived much satisfaction from the scenes of weeping, wailing, and *smashing* of teeth. When the great unreasoning crowd had gone home to make wry faces in a looking glass, some sacriligious miscreant, who was probably as little affected by the shock as a millionaire would be, took out a notice addressed to the lamb-like Johnny Volrath, changed his reduction notice so as to read from $60 to $33, and carefully sealed it with the manager's inscription on the back.

When the nervous John arrived at the office in the state of mind which I have just described—that is, prepared to believe any story, how wild soever it might be—a dozen willing hands offered him his "letter." Now, although the reverend gentleman on whom this joke was perpetrated has always been a shining light in our intellectual department, and his deep baritone voice (veritably a Cave of the Winds), has been loudest around their council fires; although he was forever exhorting them to remember what Moody and Sankey observed about loving your neighbor, he got about as much consideration or sympathy in that corner as would a young cat in a kennel of Scotch terriers. His office

life, which was then drawing to a close, had been one continued tumult—a whole "ragged edge" in itself—and although one day's experience had been fraught with danger to his spectacles and flowing looks, he had an unfortunate but uproariously funny faculty of getting into new dilemmas on the next day. It will thus be seen why a dozen willing hands offered him his "document." He opened and read it, which was, as far as I know, his last official act on earth. *I can never forget* "the tablet of unutterable thoughts" that flitted over his face, and as he glided toward the door, we made a jovial response to his cold and sickly good night.

He has only been seen once since, and that was on the stairway shortly afterward. He was shaking the brawny hand of old Owen, the janitor, who had been reduced too, while tears flowed down both their cheeks as they mutually declaimed:

My old friend Joe,
It's little I know
Of the ways of this companee;
But I'll eat my hand
If I understand
How these are things can be.

CONTRARY to rule, I had transferred my attention from the click, click, click of the instrument to "Paradise Lost," and was accompanying the Arch Fiend through the boundless realms of space, in search of new worlds, all unconscious of the furious repetition of my "call." The whistling of an approaching engine broke my reverie; the familiar sound of B, B, B, next greeted my ears; I answered, and received the following: "'D,' 10th. To Conductor Kutting, train No. 7: B. Put Poor Dick in the cradle. A."

A singular message, I thought, to a freight conductor. "D" was first telegraph station west of me. "A" was the lady operator's private "sig." I delivered the message to the conductor, he read it, smiled, but said nothing. This would probably have been the last of Poor Dick, so far as I ever was concerned, had I not chanced to hear the following the next day: "'H.,' 11th. Miss A., 'D.' Poor Dick is dead. Kutting."

To which Miss A. feelingly replied: "Bury him 'neath the weeping willows, down by the bank of the rippling brook, where the music of the waters and the rustling of the leaves will ever chant a requiem to his tear-embalmed memory."

This excited my curiosity to its highest pitch, and I said I would solve this mystery if it took all winter. When the conductor passed on his return trip, I incidentally remarked: "Poor Dick is dead!"

"Yes," he replied, "and that is all you will ever know about it."

"Don't be too sure," I said.

"There are only two persons that know it, beside myself, and they will never reveal it," he confidently answered.

I knew those two persons, and knew that their veracity could not be questioned, in so far as their natures would permit. They were ladies; women, if you please. Upon this fact I based my hope of success, and was content to bide my opportunity.

I had not long to wait. In less than a fortnight I heard Miss A. at "D" get permission to be off duty from Saturday until Monday, and that Miss G., her sister, would fill her place. I involuntarily exclaimed: "Now is the winter of my discontent made glorious summer by the going of this daughter of lightning," and immediately set about accomplishing it. I indited a letter to Miss G., as follows:

"'B.' 19th. To Miss G., 'D'—Burn's immortal lines:

' Man's inhumanity to man
Makes countless thousands mourn ;'

have occupied my mind for the past few days, to the exclusion of every ray of sunshine. I am not given to grief, nor prone to seek sorrow; but for some reason beyond my conception, the death of Poor Dick has struck a chord in my anatomy that has set the battery of my soul on fire, and though the whole fountain of my nature plays upon it continually, it increases in intensity and threatens my entire destruction at no distant day. It is not so much the demise of Poor Dick that grieves me, as the uncertainty of his earthly nature, the animal kingdom in which he reigned. I have appealed to Mr. Kutting with all the power and tenderness of an afflicted soul, but he turns a deaf ear to all my entreaties. In my extremity I cry:

' Oh, Death ! the poor man's dearest friend,
The kindest and the best !
Welcome the hour my palsied limbs
Are laid with thee at rest.'

"My only hope of relief is in you. I know the injunction of secrecy that seals your lips, and I would not, for any consideration, ask you to break it, did I not sincerely believe that there is a *higher* law governing the actions of women than of men. The saying that a woman cannot keep a secret seems to run back to the beginning of time, and as time was before all things, therefore secretiveness is not an organ of her nature. She could not be confiding, trusting, loving with it. You can readily see that though you are morally bound to keep Mr. Kutting's secret, you are released by a higher law from doing so. I would cast no reflection upon you or your sex, but believing that what is to be, will be, shall anxiously look for immediate light upon the subject nearest my heart — Poor Dick! Yours in trouble,

              SAMSON."

By return mail I received an answer as follows:

"'D.' 20.   To Samson—'B:'

"Your lamentable and inflammatory epistle is at hand. Its first strains awoke within me feelings of sadness and sympathy, and, like a summer night's gentle dew that settles on all around — seemingly tears of the sky for the loss of the sun—first caused a sigh and then a groan to escape me, and ere I knew it, my eyes were bubbling over like boiling springs, and their briny effusion falling upon your letter almost made it illegible. To add to my commotion, I could not see my way clear to help you out of your dilemma. I had faithfully promised Mr. Kutting not to discover Poor Dick's 'incog.' to any one, but refer all inquiries to him. These reflections made me feel gloomy indeed; but relief came in a manner entirely unexpected, which lifted the cloud and dispelled it with as great acrimony as that with which a boy sends a brick through the air at a mewing cat on the roof of the house, that has been disturbing his repose.

"A woman can't keep a secret. I know *one* that can. Weep, miserable wretch, for daring to harbor such a belief! I'll not expose Poor Dick to thee while a drop of moisture remains in thy distrusting body. What generous souls, what noble natures you men possess! It is not our fault that we will talk and 'blab,' but a 'higher' cause. Oh, perverting, dissembling creatures, I wonder that 'higher' power does not blast as with a simoon the minds that dare conceive such ideas! But then, I suppose, like everything else, He considers the source, and pities more than censures you. Indeed, now that I reflect that in Adam all men (not women) sinned, I am half inclined to bury the hatchet which I have resurrected, and pardon you for your lack of faith. I will not say what Poor Dick was or was not, but if

     A 'higher' law excuses woman fibbing,
     Then Poor Dick is not—the epizoo took him.

"Hoping your grief will be assuaged, I extend you the hand of peace.   G."

Miss G.'s reply, though equivocal, I was satisfied contained the clue tо Poor Dick's character, and I was consequently elated.

Mr. Kutting's first salutation, for some time past, on meeting me, had been: "How is Poor Dick?" to which I could make no reply but that of continued hope of finally being able to answer it.

The first time he passed after I had heard from Miss G., I made answer to his query, "How is Poor Dick?" that I knew all about him.

"I will wager twenty dollars you do not," he replied, and so sanguine was he that it was impossible for me to arrive at Poor Dick's pedigree, that he would have staked any amount on the result.

I could not accept this challenge without abusing Miss G.'s confidence, but I made the proposition, that as Christmas was approaching, whoever lost should supply the ladies with a goodly supply of sweetmeats. This was agreed to.

Thinking to entrap Miss A. into a voluntary confession of the secret, I made the drawing below, and composed the lines beneath it.

Poor Dick, that good old horse, is dead;
They've put him in his little bed.
Unintentionally he caught the epizoo,
And notwithstanding all his skillful friends could do,
His spirit went where the woodbine twineth,
And now Miss A. and Kutting repineth.

I also inclosed a report of the post mortem examination of the body by three learned doctors, which contained so many medical terms that it was "confusion worse confounded." And also the decision of the coroner's jury that sat upon his remains. I received the following racy reply:

" ' D.' 21 : Friend Samson—artist, poet, etc., etc. (Ahem !)

"Words fail me! I cannot, in the English language, find sentiments adequate to express my aroused and excited feelings! The paintings of all the old masters combined, or the ghost of my great grandfather turned into an elephant, would fail to arouse such feelings of deep emotion as those which assailed me when I perused what the transmigration of souls had effected, when the spirit of Poor Dick departed from this ' frail tenement of clay.' Why, my friend, oh, why, didst thou imagine my pet was a poor old epizootic? Better far to have given him the form of a whale, ' rocked in the cradle of the deep.' "Let us pause a moment that I may let fall a few of those briny tears so touchingly depicted by your pencil. "Most faithfully have I perused and reperused the decision of that coroner's jury, but I fear, that, to my dying day, I shall never know what made Poor Dick die.

"Ah well!
'Of all sad words of tongue or pen, The saddest these, it might have been— a horse, a dog, a cat, a sheep, or a rat, who knows? But if you really wish to know, just ask Mr. Kutting. 73. A."

I gained nothing here. However, when Christmas arrived Mr. Kutting admitted that I had solved the riddle, and fulfilled his agreement, and all were happy.

The facts to this incident are that a sick horse and a cradle were both loaded into the same car at "D.," by Mr. Kutting. Miss A. sent the message—to put Poor Dick in the cradle—for a joke. The horse dying next day, Mr. Kutting jokingly apprised Miss A. of the sad event by telegraph, and thereby hangs the tale. But neither of them know to this day how I found out that Poor Dick was a horse.

The Telephone.

Och, Biddy, ashtore! d'ye know what they tell
Of a foin grand invinshun of one Misthur Bell?
They say it can shpake, it can cry, and can sing,
Though its only a wiare like a long pace of string;
You jist titch your tongue to a wire all curled,
An' it shpakes all at once all over the worruld!
If you were in Ireland, and jist gave a laff,
I'd hear it right here by this new tilegraph.
An' they say it's all thrue, an' before a long time
We'll hear cannons firin, an' Pariah bells chime.
An' thin wid the gintry they'll be grand affairs,
For they'll hear Queen Victoree repaytin' her
    prayers;

An' whin its complayted they'll be a new era,
For them that are far thin will spake to us nearer!
An' the Queen will spake plisant to Prisident
    Hayes, [if you plase."
Who'll spake back, like Grant, " Let's have pace
An' more they cud do wid this wiare, galore,
They cud sink it down deeper and hear Satin roar
But of Satin they wants to be quite indepindent,
For science must iver be in the ascindant;
An' so they'll ascind in a foin big balloon,
An' jist give the ind to the man in the moon,
Who'll spake of the weather more thruely, ochone,
Nor Vennor or Probs, wid this grand telephone.

CABLING ACROSS THE ATLANTIC. — How long does it take to transmit a message through the Atlantic cable? The New York *Journal of Commerce* has been investigating this question, and simple as it looks at first sight, there are many singular and interesting points in the answer. When the electricity is applied to the cable at one end, two-tenths of a second pass before any effect is felt at the other end, and three seconds are consumed before the full force of the current is in action. The first signal is felt in four-fourteenths of a second, but the following ones go through more rapidly. As many as eighteen words have been sent over the Atlantic cable in one minute; fifteen can usually be sent under pressure, and twelve words a minute is a good working rate. In May, 1876, 891 messages were sent over the Direct Cable in 24 hours. Messages of twelve words have been sent all the way from New York to London in two minutes. A fact not yet explained by the scientists is that the electricity does not move as rapidly from New York to London as in the opposite direction.

The Vow of the Six Telegraph Operators.

CHAPTER I.

It was twenty-five years ago—long before the City of Hartford, Conn., had acquired the great commercial importance and lofty prominence that the business interests, horse-races, and base-ball matches of the present day have given it—long before it ranked with the first of the centers of our Republic in the encouragement of healthful out-door sports and gay festivities—that a horse-race occurred there with which the succeeding incidents of this narrative are closely connected.

The telegraph business of the city, and, indeed, of the entire country, was very meager, and the office itself, located in an obscure part of Asylum Street, furnished with extreme modesty, suggested that economy of management was the paramount consideration of the then struggling company. One operator was fully competent to perform all the limited business which the public, but slightly appreciating the benefits of the wondrous art, offered. Yet he did not enjoy much leisure time, for, in addition to his duties as operator, he was required to perform the entire work of the office. He delivered his messages, cleaned the batteries, acted as his own accountant, and, in a word, was the embodiment of all the titles in which a score of proud telegraphers glory in any first-class office of the present day. Reading by sound was then comparatively unknown, and William White, the manager of Hartford office, was constrained, from lack of other methods, to trace out the mystic symbols, as one by one they were recorded by the register on the now almost discarded ribbon. In these advanced days of telegraphy, White, with so scant a knowledge of the science, would unquestionably be assigned to that infamous phalanx known by the expressive title, plugs; but in that day he was considered an expert, and ranked among the best telegraphic knights of which the State boasted.

I have said that White in his day was as competent as the best, but, my amiable critic, if you consult your own experience, you will agree that there is a time in the career of every operator when he merits the stigma of that odious appellation—plug. A day when his bungling and undexterous manipulation of the key justifies the application of the title with all the galling opprobrium and shame-bearing humiliation that the word conveys—a day when the word so far fails to express the being to whom it is applied that necessity demands that the contemptuous curl of the lip and passionate flash of the eye be seen, and the profane adjective that accompanies it heard ere it can be fully realized in its intense and bitter significance, and be said to fittingly apply to the one at whom it is hurled.

White would have readily admitted this fact if he were engaged to-day as we find him at the opening of this chapter, leaning over his register, and with deep scrutiny deciphering the words that were flashed to him from Waterbury, Conn.

"Say, Billy, I am going up to Hartford to-morrow to see the horse-race."

"Good enough!" exclaimed White, "good enough! So Fred Green, operator at Waterbury, is coming up. Well, old boy, come along. We'll try to make your visit a pleasant one, and Billy White won't stint himself in extending to you the hospitalities of the city as far as lies in his power. Good enough!" and White slapped his right thigh vigorously.

Another call and White, momentarily restraining his glee, rushes to the key to answer. The words are recorded slowly and plainly, and with a space between each letter that defied economy in register-paper and operators' time. It was Augustus Ballou, of New Haven, writing.

"Frank Gray, of New London, and myself will be in your city to-morrow to see the fun."

White, after expressing himself to Ballou as happy to know it, shouts out, "Good again! Even better! My old friend Gus Ballou, one of the primest lads that ever broke bad sending, is coming up to see me; and with him Frank Gray, the New London operator. I don't know this Gray, but as long as he's a friend of Gus, he's a friend of mine. Good again! Even better! And he attempted to kick the office ceiling in the effort to give vent to his joy. He failed to reach it, and before he was able to repeat the effort another call had arrested his sportiveness, and he again copied from the ribbon, and read as follows:

"Tom Brown, operator at Norwich, Conn., and I are to be at the Hartford races to-morrow."

White's happiness was now nothing short of ecstatic, and after giving "O. K." to the announcement, he closed his key, opened his mouth, and shouted vociferously, "Good enough! Good again! Continual goodness! So Harry Black, of Bridgeport, is coming, too, and with him—let's see—oh yes, Tom Brown, of Norwich. I don't ever remember to have met Brown or Gray. They hail from the great whaling ports. Old salts, I reckon. And then with a triumphant shout he went to the spot of his failure of a few minutes previous and reattempted to kick the ceiling. The effort was successful to a degree beyond his most sanguine expectations. His foot reached the ceiling, but losing his balance, over he went backward, striking his head squarely into a pail of water, his heels coming into violent contact with six glass jars which he had but a moment before filled with battery preparation, shattering them into a thousand fragments. As has been seen, White was a youth of very merry disposition. He was much addicted to puns and witticisms, in which he found great amusement, and which frequently proved, as in the present instance, a salutary balm for his afflictions. The average operator would have indulged in profanity and indignation. Not so with White. He carefully arose, with the water dripping from his head in a stream, and gazing at the chaos, said:

"*Water* misfortune this is! How refreshing these baths are! I love to take them, but this was rather too sudden and unwarned. I love swimming, but the width of that bucket and the depth of the water are too circumscribed to allow activity and expansion—two things most desirable in the practice of bathing. Well," he continued, after a pause, "I have lost six jars and—let me see—have I gained any? Yes; jarred my head, one; both legs, two; right shoulder, one; left side, one; whole body, one; total, six jars; therefore I gain all I have lost;" and he gazed smilingly at the broken objects, gathered them up, lighted a cheap cigar, and coursed his way homeward to provide for the coming of his friends on the morrow to witness the great horse-race of July 4th, 1851.

CHAPTER II.

As William White walked leisurely toward his humble home that evening he revolved many plans in his mind for making the visit

of his friends agreeable. He thought first of entertaining them at his residence, but immediately abandoned this idea on account of his limited accommodations. He had several beds, but lacked bed-clothes. "To be sure," said he, "I might get a few soft sheets at the office, but warm as this July weather is, these would be an insufficient protection from the nocturnal chill. I could fill each couch with monthly-report blanks, and thus amply *blank it*, but that would not do either," and he speedily banished the mental suggestion. He could not permit them to repose in the office, as they would be in danger from the rats that made their abode there, and which, in their famished state, he suspected of subsisting upon his blue vitriol and other supplies. It would not be exactly in accordance with manliness to keep them walking all night, but, he soliloquised, "I have many, many times roamed the village all night myself, though, to be sure, I was too full of invigorating beverages to be either responsible for the deed or conscious of weariness."

Thus did White practice his inveterate habit of punning, even while, as in the present instance, he was serious in his thoughts. It was his nature to give them an expression of levity, deriving, as he did, a complacent merriment by so doing.

But suddenly settling his mind to a sober train of thought, he ceased to view the plans of entertainment lightly, and began to gravely consider what his mode of operation should be. He was not abundantly favored with worldly goods, and the prospect of becoming so on a salary of thirty-eight dollars a month was not very cheering. His heart was large, his impulses generous and sincere, and his devotion to friends and acquaintances always of the most sterling and noble character. He was so overjoyed at the prospect of the pleasure that the visit of his five friends would create that he had not given the subject of the manner of their entertainment the least reflection. He was just now without money, and wending his way homeward the consciousness of this fact presented itself vividly before him, creating a feeling of depression and despair, which contrasted strongly with his naturally jocund nature. "What shall I do?" he asked of himself, destitute of hope and little surmising that the question would be answered so suddenly, and the seemingly insurmountable obstacle of penury removed. As he propounded this query to himself he involuntarily raised his eyes, and a sign

above a store which he was at that instant
passing, arrested his attention. It read
"ABRAHAM ISRAEL, Pawnbroker." In his vest
pocket he carried a beautiful gold watch, be-
queathed to him by his dying father three
years before, who, in handing his boy the
precious relic, said: "William, my son, this
watch I leave you. Keep it, guard it well.
In future times its presence will recall the
memory of happy days spent ere I met the
adversity that deprived me of fortune and
courage."

William stopped outside the store. "How
easily" he thought, "I can pawn my watch
and raise the necessary cash!" He drew forth
the beautiful gold emblem from its repository.
It was just as bright and perfect as when
taken from the parental hand three years ago.
His father's injunction came up vividly before
him, "Keep it; guard it well," and the
words seemed written upon his burning
brain in letters of fire, standing out clear and
lurid. He restored the treasured souvenir
to his vest pocket. Then casting hurried,
searching glances up and down the street, at
the housetops, and, lastly, at the twinkling
stars above, he quickly opened the door,
entered the pawnbroker's shop, and stepped
up to the counter. The contents of the place
were such as are ordinarily seen in shops of
this character—a profusion of clothing of all
kinds, children's garments, gentlemen's apparel, ladies' habiliments, fine silk dresses,
costly furs, elegant camel's hair shawls, rich
jewelry of all values and patterns, magnificent
diamonds, gold and silver watches, sets of
furniture, unique in design and of rare material, piled about in graceless confusion, and
speaking of the dire distress into which ad-
verse circumstances had plunged those who
had left them here. What misery and agony,
tears and sighs of regret the loss of these
articles must have caused. What a pitiful
history must be contained in them. What
happy days and scenes were known by their
original possessors ere the stern and inexorable decree of necessity wrested them away,
and consigned them to the flinty-hearted and
unnatural being who now claimed them!
These thoughts rushed through White's
mind in rapid succession as he gazed around
the shop, and his heart experienced a violent
throb as the possibility of his soon becoming
a patron of this miserable place occurred to
him with startling suddenness. "I must
not give way to such thoughts," he whispered,
and forthwith he administered three rapid and
vigorous thumps upon the counter, at the

same time exclaiming, "Who works this circuit? Answer quick for business." Whether
this specimen of telegraphic parlance was
comprehended by the Jew or not, it is quite
certain that it had the desired effect, for
from out the folds of the silk dresses came a
decrepit old man, whose bent form and
wizzened features betokened extreme old
age. Everything about him, except his eyes,
which shone with a shrewd and dazzling
freshness, and his general facial expression
of unbounded greed, indicated physical
decay. He approached, rubbing his bloodless hands together, while on his face he
wore that bland and dangerous smile that a
spider is supposed to have preparatory to
entrapping a harmless fly. As he opened his
mouth to speak the fact was revealed of his
having but two teeth, one upon the upper
jaw, the other on the lower, the latter being
exactly beneath the former, so that with the
mouth closed they rested upon each other,
precisely as the two small pieces of platinum
in a telegraph key rest with a closed circuit.
"Goot eefning, my frent, goot eefning.
Nice vedder oud. Vot can I do to pleas dee
yoong shentlemens? Speak avay. Speak
avay. Doo you vant some gold to borrow?"

Thus he spoke, and White stood in silent
meditation. And now, gentle reader, were
you ever in a situation similar to that of
White? Poor and needy, to have money
was imperative, to get it, difficult. Would
you blame him if he took his father's parting
gift from his pocket, and, with the sincerest
intentions of redeeming it at some more
prosperous time, entrusted it to the person
who now stood before him? In view of the
pressing circumstances of the youth, would
you censure the action and condemn the
young man as faithless to a dying parent's
admonition? I see you hesitate—a wavering
doubt controls you, and you scarcely know
what reply to give. Well, it was not so with
our hero. He had not the slightest idea of
parting with his gold watch, and if he had
for a moment seriously entertained the
thought of committing such a deed, he would
have accused himself of base ingratitude, and
stigmatized himself as dishonorable and un-
grateful. Oh, no! Such a thought was far
from his mind from the very first. But he
had a cheap silver watch in another pocket,
and a plain gold ring on his finger, and it
was to pawn these that he entered the shop
of the three pendant balls, in which we find
him negotiating a loan.

"Ah! good evening, Jim. Rather compact and cozy here. I believe this is a money order office?" said White, in reply to the Jew's salutation.

"Mooney orter office! Vat you mean? I'm see man vot gif mooney on dee ardickles, but I don't vas gif mooney orters. Wrong blace, young veller—wrong blace."

"No, Jim; your copy above the door reads plain. This is the right place. What I came here for was to have some cash advanced on these trinkets. Now, do you '13?'" asked White, producing the silver watch and ring.

"Ha! ha! ha!" laughed the Jew. "I see now, young vellar. Right at home on dees little madders."

"Now, then; how much can you let me have on these? I hate to part with 'em, but the law of necessity is strict and pressing, and I must. Name a good round sum, old man."

"Vell, young veller," replied the Jew, "a goot round zum is O," and he raised his hand with his thumb and forefinger together, describing a circle, "but dot would be doo mean. I'll gif you ten dollars for six days. If you don't vas cum back on the exshpectoration of six days you vorfeit die ardicles. If you do cum back you can haf die ardicles on the bayment of fifteen tollus, right avay; or, in udder vords, you allow boor Israel fife tollus inderest money. And now, young veller, to use your own vords, Do you '13?'"

White felt like laughing, but he restrained the desire, and seriously said: "That is rather a large sum, Israel; fifty per cent interest is enormous for a week's use of money. It is usury of the most marked kind."

"Vell, young veller, you know my derms. If you don't like 'em you can go somevare else. I can't shtop to make barguns mit a man who don't vant to drade," and he started from the counter.

Now, White had no intention of allowing such a glorious opportunity to pass by unimproved, so he said:

"Very well, Jim, I'm hard up and will take the money."

But Israel, with a cunning peculiar to his race and profession, was not unmindful of the fact that when a man confesses that he is "hard up," he is then only the more susceptible of being mercilessly imposed upon by taking advantage of his necessities.

"Led me inshpect die ardicles a leedle closer," said he.

White handed them to him, and, after a moment's deliberation, the Jew returned them, saying, "The meddle of the watch is vorn out—cases too thin. I take back my offer of ten tollus, young veller; can't gif but eight."

"Only eight?" said White, greatly taken aback by the change affairs had assumed. "Why, you extortionate old fraud, I—" but he restrained his rising indignation, realizing that he might blast his hopes if he yielded to the temptation to tell the Jew how much he loved him. "Well, give me the eight dollars, and let's have no more words about it. I suppose you want me to sign documents of agreement?"

"Yes, yes; dis way, young veller," said Israel, leading White toward a dilapidated old-fashioned writing-desk just beyond the end of the counter. The desk had evidently seen long service, and besides being scratched and soiled with time, one of its legs was gone, and the place supplied by a small dry-goods box, which, to all appearances, was used for no other earthly purpose.

By way of explanation of what is to follow, it may be well to inform the reader that White had an inveterate habit of kicking out with his right leg whenever he seated himself at a desk or table. The result of this practice was not unfrequently very painful to the shins of those who happened to be in close proximity to the ungovernable member, and though the howls of rage and agony that followed the action were frequent and unmistakably genuine, yet they failed in breaking White of the obnoxious habit, and the motion was still common to him. He perched himself upon a high stool that the Jew had provided, and, after an instant's delay, as if to assure himself of the security of his position, he launched out his leg, striking the dry-goods box that propped the table, upsetting the box, writing-desk, and himself, and strewing the floor with articles of various characters.

"Hell und ten tousend blazes!" screamed the Jew. "Vat are you up to?"

"What am I up to?" repeated White. "Well, I don't know, but I feel as if I was up to my neck in dirt!" "But," he went on, laughingly rising out of the *debris*, "I beg your pardon for the offense, and will help you restore things to their proper places."

This apology seemed to satisfy the old man, and together they set to work to replace things. In gathering up the scattered effects, what was White's surprise to discover four registers and relays entirely new, six rolls of register paper, three pairs of lineman's pliers, several small coils of fine office-wire, and many other things incidental to a telegraph office.

The discovery was very agreeable to him. It was only three months previous that his office had been burglariously entered and robbed of a large quantity of telegraph material of this description, which he had only received from headquarters a few days before. Diligent search by detectives had availed nothing, and the matter reposed in mystery, and was now almost entirely forgotten. How strange that it should be brought to light in this manner at last, when no thought was given to such a contingency. Surely all that we do is the result of some unseen power. We must recognize this fact in the face of such testimony as this.

"Luck enough for one day," said White to himself. "I will use the means that Fate has placed at my disposal, and besides restoring the articles to the company, will make the incident be profitable to myself."

"Look here, old man," said he aloud, "this collection of telegraph instruments, wire, and tools is stolen property. It belongs to the company of which I am an agent. These things now scattered on your floor were taken from the office on Asylum Street three months ago, and you, sir, are in my power."

"Oh, vat you giffin' us, roosder? You can't schgare me in my own house. Vat you take me for, right avay?" and Israel endeavored to display the greatest amount of nonchalance possible—a sentiment, however, that he did not feel—for he realized intensely his hazardous position, and sought, by assuming an indifference on the subject, to force White to abandon his suspicions.

White was not to be thwarted thus, and looking sternly at the Jew, said, "O. K., my aged fraud, I will see what the police can do to change your tune." He hurried to the door, but ere he could reach it the voice of the Jew forced him to stop, and presently the old man, seizing him by the coat-tails, fell upon his knees, and in tones of pitiful entreaty supplicated. him to proceed no further.

"Don't exscpose me, young veller. My drade will be ruined and I will be arrested and imprisoned, and will die in jail—die in jail—die in jail!" and he repeated the words each time more sadly and slowly than before. His fears were of the most powerful nature. His body was all of a tremor. The bland smile of a few minutes ago had gone, and in its place an altered expression of misery and

horror which the dread of exposure had created. For once, at least, the Jew was sincere in his motives. Artifice and deceit were now impotent, and he appreciated the importance of candor in every action.

"Oh, young veller, don't gif me avay. Don't egschpose me. I am a miserable olt man. My life will be short in jail. Oh, don't gif me avay. Don't betray me." And he wept piteously. "Led me seddle dee madder in sum vay, young veller. I will gif you back dee ardicles and a goot rount sum of mooney. Say, young veller, vill you gonsent? Oh, say yes! say yes! for I am a miserable olt man."

"Look here, Israel," said White, "I don't want to ruin you—neither do I wish to protect a thief, and thus sanction roguery. It is evident that you stole these goods from my office, and—"

"Oh, no, no, young veller, I didn't shteel 'em. I burchased dee ardicles from two vellers who brought 'em here, overing 'em vor leedle or nodding. Dee brice vas so schmall, and dee ardicles so nice, I vorgot my brudence and bought 'em for fife tollus," said he, still weeping.

"Even so," replied White, "you are a receiver of stolen goods, and the law—just and impartial—will not make your offense and its punishment the less."

These words only caused the tears of Israel to flow with renewed vigor. Clutching with his skinny, bloodless fingers the few straggling locks of hair that Time had left him, with his attenuated body rocking rapidly to and fro, he ran rapidly across the shop, exclaiming:

"Woe, woe, woe! Miserable olt man! Woe, woe, woe! Don't egschpose me, young veller. Woe, woe, woe!"

White, much as he felt for the old man's grief, could not, with his great love for a joke, suppress, even here, the merriment that this scene prompted. The galloping appearance of the old man, coupled with his exclamations of "Woe, woe, woe!" which, with the Hebrew accent given, it sounded like Whoa, whoa, whoa! caused White to laugh vociferously. Grasping the old pawnbroker by the shoulders, he held him securely, at the same time shouting with hearty emphasis, "Now, whoa! whoa! whoa!" This action had a two-fold effect. First, of restoring the Jew to presence of mind, and secondly, of putting White into a state of good humor and amiability. The Jew suddenly recollected that White was in need of money, and concluded that the most effective means of exacting a promise of secrecy was to pander to his cupidity rather than to his sympathy. "Say, young veller," said he, "You vant mooney unt I vant safety. I vill gif you a hundred tollus, gif back dee shtolen goods, and do you vavor venever I gan, if you vill say nodding aboud dis leedle avair. Vot do you say, young veller?"

White hesitated a few moments lost in thought, revolving in his mind the question of right and wrong. He would not wittingly be a party to a nefarious contract, but his necessities were so pressing that he might make very little distinction between a nefarious contract and a just one. "After all," thought he, "the Jew may have bought these things without intending to receive stolen goods, and perhaps he is an innocent man." Then turning to the pawnbroker, he said: "Give me the hundred, old man, give me the hundred, and I promise to guard your secret as sacredly as I would the contents of a message. Return the stolen articles to my office on Asylum Street, label them carefully, "Remorse and Restitution," I will acquaint my officers of their restoration, and no one will ever know anything about the affair."

The Jew was delighted at the success of his proposition, and willingly presented the cash, saying, "Don't gif me avay. Don't egschpose me. I am somedimes a miserable olt man, and somedimes a habby olt rooster. Remember, young veller."

Our hero, now well furnished with money for the morrow, left the pawn-shop with a light heart, little dreaming that the hundred dollars was counterfeit, which, let me say, in justice to Israel, was given without intention, the old man having, in his perturbation, taken it from the wrong side of his plethoric wallet.

The evening was now considerably advanced. White quickened his footsteps and kept on his course, never stopping, except now and then to reply to a friendly salutation from the by-standers, who admired him with that intensity that children possess for a magician, for in that day telegraphy was an art of deep and sacred mystery to the outside world, and its followers were looked upon with wonder. Having reached his unpretentious domicile, he was welcomed by his mother, who expressed surprise at his long detention.

"Of course you know, mother, that in our business we quite often have special reports for the papers, which, coming at no particular hour, are apt to detain us."

"Yes," she replied.

"Well, it is owing to 'special' business that I am late to-night," said he, and dismissing the matter, he commenced eating his supper. He ate very voraciously, and having finished, he lay down upon a lounge, and, after perusing for two hours a favorite book of his, entitled, "How to Clean Batteries Without Swearing," he retired to his couch and peacefully slept.

CHAPTER III.

The bright rays of a summer sun shone brilliantly upon Hartford, Conn., on the morn of July 4th, 1851, and augured a propitious day for the great horse-race. The entire population of the city was early astir, and the streets exhibited an animation as rare as it was pleasing. Gaudy decorations were visible on all of the public buildings, vari-colored streamers danced from the mast-heads of the vessels at the wharves, the roar of cannonry was heard coming from different quarters of the city, and many other demonstrations combined to prove that the day was to be fittingly observed. The citizens, with commendable zeal, had left nothing undone in their desire to have a celebration eminently worthy of the great event which it commemorated. All citizens, irrespective of nationality, were replete with fervent enthusiasm; and no less so were the five young operators whom we find approaching Hartford by train, eager to reach their destination. As they are en route to the city, and while we await their arrival, it may be excusable to give a short description of the youths, preparatory to a more formal introduction.

Fred Green, of Waterbury, is a youth of twenty, rather short in stature, with hair of a bright, glossy red, cut extremely short, and as he never permits his moustache to grow, the belief is engendered that he dislikes that too common hue so much as to discourage its development.

Coming in another direction, but with the same object in view, were the four others. They had all met in New Haven, to go thence to Hartford, and having procured free-trip passes without difficulty, secured seats together on the train, and were passing the time pleasantly together to their journey's end. With what pride and joy their young eyes followed the delicate thread-like telegraph lines upon the poles, as if they might read the words that were flashing along, and when, ever and anon, their sharp glances discovered an insulator missing, they would fain stop the train and supply the loss.

Augustus Ballou, of New Haven, and Frank Gray, of New London, sat together. The former is a true type of manly beauty. An abundance of dark ringlets nestles upon a classically-formed head; eyes dark as night and full of expression compare well with the firmly set lips beneath them, indicative of a thoroughly courageous and dauntless spirit. A dark, curling moustache adorns his face. Tall and erect, with a physique perfect in symmetrical beauty, he bears unmistakable signs of a leader. His immediate associate, Frank Gray, is cast in an entirely different mold. Of average height and build, features delicate, but not effeminate; hair of a rich, dark brown color; eyes of blue, and with expression mild and gentle; complexion light, but ruddy with health. He was well suited to converse with Ballou, whose spirit, strong and impulsive, required a soothing, placating nature like that of Gray to hold it in check.

In the opposite seat sat Tom Brown, of Norwich, and Harry Black, of Bridgeport; both of medium stature and of light complexion. The only difference between their appearance—indeed a very marked one—was that Black was fat and corpulent, while Brown was lean and emaciated, the former's voice being deep, deliberate, and sonorous, the latter's sharp and rapid.

None of the party exceeded twenty years of age, and they were as noisy and jocose as youthful spirits are wont to be—particularly when in pursuit of pleasure—and as they were all securely fortified against the emergencies of travel by the possession of snug sums of money, varying from forty to one hundred dollars, it is presumed they were proportionately happy. Along the route the conversation of the four youths was of the most animated and sparkling character, as the continuous peals of laughter attested, the subjects of their conversation being themselves and the young ladies throughout the State with whom they were severally intimate. Notwithstanding their hilarity, a person listening to the talk would have observed that many serious and quite natural facts were developed, and that the youths were much more in earnest than they pretended. The disclosures were made that Ballou had a strong admiration, not to say love, for a certain Miss Lilly Gregory, of Meriden, Conn., whom he had been introduced to over the line by the Meriden operator. He was a regular and esteemed cor-

respondent, and had progressed so far in her favor as to have called upon her at the Meriden telegraph office, where he was received with unmistakable pleasure.

Miss Gregory was but sixteen. Her father had accumulated great wealth in the manufacture of cotton fabrics, and still continued the business, controlling several large mills. Lilly was his only child, accomplished, the idol of her parents, and possessed a disposition as winning as it was frank and unassuming. She loved Ballou devotedly, and upon his making two or three visits to her father's elegant residence, he was received by them with that marked hospitality that is ever extended to a person on a mission similar to that of Ballou, viz.: introducing a private telegraph line from Mr. Gregory's mansion to his distant mills. The affection existing between the two was wholly unknown to the father, and hence he found no opposition from that quarter.

Gray's affection was centered in a young lady of Middletown, a Miss Rose Beverly, whom he had met at the house of a friend at New London. From the time of his introduction his friendship had gradually, but unconsciously, ripened into love—a sentiment that the young lady returned with visible ardor. He intended to make her his wife on the attainment of her nineteenth birthday, for which he had one year to wait.

Green was less fortunate in his efforts in this direction than those already described. His red hair was an insuperable obstacle to his progress with the gentler sex. He even despaired of ever having the good fortune to secure a helpmate through life, and as he had vowed to remain single rather than marry a telegraph operator, his chances were indeed slim, for even at that early day, as at the present time, there were few marriageable feminines outside the pale of its motherly protection.

Black, of Bridgeport, and Brown, of Norwich, had very little familiarity with the opposite sex, and in both cases it was attributable to bashfulness, or, as we now classically term it, a lack of "cheek"—something, however, that no operator in the profession lacks now-a-days, for if they did the myriads of plugs would never receive the constant and varied abuse that every operator feels it his duty to shower upon them. The bashfulness of Black and Brown was of an entirely opposite character, however. Brown would not speak to a young lady for all the old zincs and porous cups owned by the company; and if, when working with a distant station, the lady operator should ask, "Is that you, Tommie?" a nervous tremor would seize him, and he would break and break all day upon the circuit just like an accomplished and full-fledged plug.

Bashfulness affected Black in a different manner, however, and would show itself only when he was face to face with the cause of it. He daily conversed over the line with a young female operator a few miles from his office, and manifested a coolness and *sang froid* on such occasions that was perfectly refreshing. One day the young lady said, "Harry, I am to be in Bridgeport this afternoon," and Black made arrangements accordingly to avoid seeing her. To speak over the wire was bliss, but to speak face to face, misery. Engaging an unemployed operator for the afternoon, he hurried away from the office and sought the country hills, where he might look down upon the verdant fields and be at peace with the whole world. Thus he whiled away the hours until assured of her departure to her native village, when he rambled back to his office and resumed the reins of government.

Having thus introduced them, we will now return to our friend White, who was on his way to the depot to meet his expected guests. He had not as yet discovered that the hundred dollars was spurious, and nothing else had occurred to depress his mirthful disposition. He had not long to wait ere the arrival of Green, which was soon followed by that of the others. The necessary ceremony of introduction having been performed, the party repaired to the nearest saloon to drink a social glass of wine together—a custom now entirely obsolete with operators, whisky being the standard beverage. In paying for the fluid the bar-keeper remarked to White that his bill was a bad one, and added, "If you think you can palm off such stuff as that on me you must be fresh."

"That's a word you can't apply to your wine," retorted White. "It's as old and as sour as yourself. Don't take me for a beat; I've got plenty of stuff, my friend," and he produced another note—a ten.

"That is as bad as the other," remarked the barkeeper. "I guess you have struck the wrong man to get rid of that article."

White was now indignant, and feeling the humiliation that such insinuations placed him in before his friends, he called the barkeeper a "lying plug."

"Look here, you counterfeiting fraud, it's

bad enough to offer a man bad money, without offering your whelpish spleen."

White, with a courage characteristic of the craft, struck at him, but his arm was stopped by Ballou, who said, "Come, come, old man, no fighting for circuit. It delays business, chum."

Gray spoke advisingly to the barkeeper, and pacified him by paying for the wine and refusing the change due him.

The words of Ballou prevented what threatened to be a bad beginning of the day's sport. A coachman was hailed, the party passed out, and they were driven to the race-course. White had the presence of mind to stop on the way and adjust money matters with Israel, receiving twenty-five dollars additional for the trouble the mistake had caused him. His words with the Jew were in his usual strain.

"Jim, I have returned here to adjust something, and I demand that you just add something," and it was fixed at twenty-five dollars.

Arriving at the course, the party secured seats located so as to afford a good view of the field, and having, in their telegraphic enthusiasm, deposited twenty-five dollars each in the pools upon a horse named "Telegraph," they awaited the beginning of the sport. At length the horses, eight in number, were led forth by their drivers amid great excitement, hurrahing and waving of hats and handkerchiefs. Our young friends were very anxious to see the horse upon which they had hazarded their coupons, and upon inquiry the favorite, "Telegraph," was pointed out to them.

"Why," remarked White, "he is an *old* plug, and I'll bet five dollars his teeth are as long as a plug's life—endless. And, do you see, fellows, the reins are made of telegraph wire, and the harness-leather is taken from lineman's climbers."

"Yes," said Ballou, "and I think that the driver is our New Haven line-repairer. Yes, it is. I recognize him now."

"Well, that's the winning horse," said Gray. "My money is on him."

"Yes, and so is mine, and the others, too. If 'Telegraph' succeeds, we succeed; if he fails, we fail," remarked Green.

"Quite right, Greeny, quite right," said White. "Your words are just as true of our profession as they are of the horse. Our business is now on trial and our interests are with it."

At the word "Go," the horses made a

beautiful start, and flew around the course urged to their greatest speed. The eager eyes of the multitude followed their every motion, and ejaculations that could not be repressed broke forth on every side. "Telegraph" had up to the present maintained the lead, but as he was on the last quarter he became apparently nervous and unmanageable, and fell to the rear.

"Curse the plug!" ejaculated White, in wild excitement. "See him 'break,' see him 'break!'"

"But look," said Ballou, in the happiest of tones. "Look, boys, they are taking him from the circuit;" and, sure enough, the driver had stopped the horse and was leading him from the course toward the stable. "I feel well repaid for my journey," said Brown, "and I would willingly come here again—nay, go around the world even—to see justice so well administered—to see a breaking plug taken instantly from a circuit!"

"What a hang-dog look the beast has got," said Black. "That is, perhaps, the only difference between him and the telegraph plug—the latter, instead of being ashamed, rather delights in breaking."

"Yes, I always noticed that when I had any messages to send you," said White, playfully, causing Brown to be the object of laughter.

"I was about to mention your name as a specimen," said Black, "but as usual you broke me before I had finished."

The laugh was now on White, but he quickly rejoined: "It is quite impossible that I broke you—the horse did that pretty effectually a few moments ago."

No one felt like laughing at this reminder of their ill-luck, and as they thought of their losses the race course suddenly seemed too uncongenial to their tastes, and Gray proposed that they repair to the office, where they could find more pleasure.

"Agreed," said White, and they directed their course back to the office. Having reached there, and being politely ushered in by White, what was the surprise of the visitors to find that a pleasant transformation had taken place during their absence. In the center of the office stood a large, plain table, improvised for the occasion, and bending under the weight of tempting viands, fruits, cake, boned turkey, and delicately cooked oysters worthy of the sumptuous hospitality of a prince. Six little urchins, arrayed in suits made entirely of the various blanks then used by the company, noiselessly moved about the table. Having arranged his guests at the table, and filled six goblets with champagne, he went to the nearest key, and writing slowly and distinctly so as to obviate breaks, said: "Here is success to our glorious profession. Long life to operators—short life to plugs."

"Amen, to that sentiment," responded the guests, emptying their glasses, which were instantly refilled by the watchful urchins.

"A health to our noble host," said Ballou. "May he never run short of message blanks and have to borrow report blanks for his monthly statement." Again the glasses were drained, and the party were feeling as merry as an operator on pay-day.

"Say, fellows," said White, "look at our names, Brown, Gray, Black, Ballou, Green, and White. In name we are not 'birds of a feather,' but we are in trade, and we will flock together. Behold the gaudy plumes—excuse me, plumage—that the association of six such colors will make! Chums, what bird do we most resemble?"

"The jail bird," replied Green.

"Yes, your short hair resembles him," said White.

These repartees were so good that the champagne was again passed around. None of the party refused, and having finished the banquet and lighted cigars the party gave their attention to White, who asked their serious consideration of an idea that suggested itself to him just at that moment.

"Boys," said he, "we have all been employed at operating more than two years. As far as I can learn, none of your positions are so desirable but that they can be relinquished without regret. My proposition is this: that we all resign our present situations, leave our native towns, and seek positions elsewhere; continue telegraphing or espouse another occupation, as your taste may dictate, then meet again at some future day which we shall name, and recount to each other the course of our travels."

"The proposition is a startling one," said Ballou, "but I agree to do it. Suppose we make the period of separation twenty-five years from to-day—the reunion to be July 4th, 1876."

"Yes," said Black, "and let us agree not to inquire about each other during the whole time, nor listen to others if they allude to the subject."

"I have with me," said Green, "a dozen rings that I fashioned in my leisure time at home. Suppose each of us take one, wear it during our separation, and guard it as a memento of our vow." He produced the rings and handed them to White for distribution to the party. Much ingenuity was displayed in the making of the rings. The metallic part consisted of ordinary telegraph line wire, niched at different points throughout its entire circumference diamond shaped, the niches being filled with small fragments of a broken insulator very neatly inserted, and much resembling emeralds. Between each setting was engraved a miniature telegraph pole with two cross-arms thereon. Connecting the cross-arms of each pole were two delicate film-like wires running entirely around the ring and making two complete circuits.

The party all having agreed to White's proposition, each one selected a ring to fit his little finger, and Ballou wrote the following poetic vow, to which the whole party subscribed their names:

We who sign our names below,
With our senses clear and sound,
Pledge to leave our homes and go
Where our hearts' desires are found.
Of each other ne'er inquiring,
To return not e'er desiring
Till old Time presents the day,
Proving that there's passed away
Five and twenty complete years,
With their laughter, sighs, and tears.
Then, and only then, return,
To this village once again,
Tell the tales both sweet and stern
Of our journey o'er the main,
And to keep the ring and vow
That we take in earnest now.

Five o'clock p. m., July 4th, 1851.

After the understanding had been established that they should meet at the telegraph office at Hartford at the expiration of the twenty-five years, the party left the office and returned to their respective homes throughout the State.

CHAPTER IV.

Years rolled on. Progressive changes occurred in every branch of industry. New inventions appeared, startling the world with their wondrous powers of utility and artistic mechanism, the people of the country manifestly increased in intelligence, and everything savored of an earnest effort to improve upon the past. Telegraphy advanced with immeasurable strides. Various new companies sprang into existence, and the old one extended its facilities, by the erection of new lines, with an energy indicative of present prosperity and an auspicious future. The events recorded in the preceding chapters had become mere phantoms of the past to all except the six operators, who, scattered around our wide land, were faithfully accomplishing the obligations of their vow. Ten years had elapsed, and nothing had ever been heard of them, when one day the mail brought to the manager of the Hartford office a large package containing a letter addressed to him, enclosing one hundred dollars and a sealed letter marked, "To be called for July 4th, 1876." The letter to the manager was opened, and read as follows:

NEW YORK, July 15, 1861.

DEAR SIR—In a few days will be forwarded to you for interment the ashes of one who occupied, ten years ago, the position now filled by you. It was his dying request that his remains be sent to you to be consigned to a spot in his native city, where the trees, 'neath which, in his boyhood, when heated with exertion, he often sought a cooling shade, may spread their friendly branches o'er his grave. This place is near the graves of his parents, James and Julia White, whose resting place can be found at the eastern section of the third burial ground. Let the funeral cortege be participated in by all persons connected with the telegraph business of your city, and otherwise have it as simple as possible. I inclose the sum of one hundred dollars, which he gave me for the purpose, and with deep sorrow for unfortunate William White, I remain,

Fraternally yours,
FREDERICK STEVENS,
Telegraph Operator.

The lapse of a few days was followed by the arrival of the body. The manager of the office, whose heartiest sympathies had been awakened by the perusal of the sad letter, left nothing incomplete in making arrangements in compliance with the wishes of White, and the corpse was placed in their last resting place in the presence of all the representatives of the telegraphic fraternity that could be spared from duty. The mysterious package was deposited in a vault of one of the city banks for safe keeping, and, though its strangeness provoked various conjectures as to its contents, yet its sanctity was religiously respected, and in time it had ceased to awaken curiosity, and was almost forgotten. The grass and herbage of the cemetery grew vigorously upon the little mound 'neath which White reposed, the world's noisy machinery moved incessantly, telegraphic improvements were developed from day to day, and the wheels of time rolled onward toward eternity—never pausing, ever constant, regular, and tireless.

And now, dear reader, we must take an abrupt leave of these scenes, and seek our friends in their different fields of labor.

It is June 28th, 1876. Standing in a crowd in the city of Chicago on that day was a man upon whom the good fortunes of life had not perched. On his fourth finger he wore the peculiar ring that he had placed there twenty-five years before, at the Hartford telegraph office, and as he heard one lawyer beside him remark to another that he had business in Hartford July 4th, he appeared greatly agitated, and hurriedly bending his footsteps toward the Chicago telegraph office, rapidly pursued his course onward, as if on a mission of life and death. Arriving there he entered, and, breathing hard from the fatigue of his rapid walk, told the manager that he would be unable to attend to his duties as line-repairer for a month or more. He hoped that his position would be retained for him until his return. "Whether it is or not," said he, "I must start immediately for Connecticut. I am forced to go." The manager saw that expostulations would be of no avail, so he promised to do his best to restore the position when he returned. Having obtained from a railroad superintendent, for whom he had performed many favors, a pass to New York, together with a letter of introduction, to be shown to conductors and others in position, Harry Black, formerly of Bridgeport, Conn., took a train going east, and was soon on his way to Hartford.

About the same time the good old ship "Iceland," with a full cargo of whale-oil and seal-skins, was three hundred miles out at sea on its homeward voyage from Greenland. The hearts of the sailors were throbbing with the delightful expectations of setting foot once again upon their native land, and folding to their breasts the dear ones they had left three years before. But with one of the crew these bright hopes were tinged with sadness, for he feared that he might not be able to accomplish a desire that controlled his spirit.

"What ails you, mate? Cheer up! Our voyage is nearly ended. We have been prosperous in our cargo and health, and now that we are so near our port that the gulls can be seen skimming along the water, Frank Gray ought to be as jolly as an Esquimau in a snow-storm, and not heavy and down in the mouth like a lot of whale's blubber."

"True, Jack, true; but as I look at this ring it reminds me of a promise I made many years ago, and the thought of not being able to keep the promise weighs me down. I must be in Hartford July 4th if it's in the good old bulk to help me do it."

"Well, mate, it *is* in her. And you will be there as sure as the compass points to the

north. If we don't furl sails and weigh anchor in New London harbor by July 3d, you can cut adrift from my advice forever."

"I never knew your judgment to fail yet, Jack, and I will not doubt it now. You have given me hope, and I thank you."

"Don't mention it, mate. I am only glad to make you feel like yourself again;" and he went forward whistling "A Life on the Ocean Wave."

Gray gazed affectionately at the ring for a moment, sighed deeply as he noticed several of the glass settings gone from their places. "I wonder if the other lads have been so careless with theirs," said he. "Well, if they yet live that is enough, whatever becomes of the rings." A tear coursed its way down his cheek as he conjured up the remembrance of the past, and rather than give way further he shouted for the crew to take in sail and coil the cable, hoping by being occupied to forget the possibility of disappointment to his hopes.

CHAPTER V.

What a change the city of Hartford has undergone in twenty-five years! The population and industries have increased with surprising rapidity, placing the city among the first of the business centers of the country, and giving it an enviable name throughout the world. Edifices elegant in design and costly to a degree almost without estimate, have arisen in the places once occupied by squatty shanties. The imposing insurance buildings, the State capitol building, the colleges and magnificent private residences are the subject of wonderment to visitors and of justifiable pride to the citizens, giving as they do an air of splendor to the city, contrasting strikingly with its humility in 1851. The telegraphic business of the place displays signs of a similar, and even greater, prosperity. The old office of Asylum Street has been surrendered in favor of the present commodious one on State Street. The duties of the office, formerly performed by White alone, now demand the services of a score of employés, and, indeed, in any respect the Hartford of 1851 would not be recognized in that of 1876.

It is now July 4th. At an early hour four men, apparently about forty-five years of age, are standing on the steps of the Hartford telegraph office earnestly shaking hands and uttering fervent ejaculations of greeting. Three of them were very plainly, but neatly dressed, their apparel indicating them to be persons of comfortable circumstances in life, rather than of wealth and refinement. The fourth was attired in garments which suggested the most abject poverty. Tatters and patches were visible everywhere. An old beaver hat, faded and broken and much too large for the wearer, rested upon his head, reaching down to his ears. A large rubber boot on his right foot illy compared with the leather shoe on his left, and indeed the only genuine article to be seen about him was the mirthful expression that his face wore—as strange as it was constant. And this is Augustus Ballou. This is the man whose courageous bearing and noble qualities evoked our admiration twenty-five years ago. How comes he thus? Why this strange and unexpected change? But I will not anticipate —he is to relate the causes of his condition, and I shall be silent thereon. The remaining three are Tom Brown, formerly of Norwich, Harry Black, whom we left on the train at Chicago, and Frank Gray, whose fears about reaching Hartford were not realized. Fred Green, the old Waterbury operator, has not yet come. They are chatting gaily together upon the present days, congratulating each other upon life having been spared them, and kindred matters of conversation, but eschew all allusion to their lives and adventures during the long and memorable separation—that being reserved for the time when all shall have assembled. As they thus stand together they are startled by a voice, and looking up, behold a man rugged, ragged, and abandoned—a tramp of the most confirmed and irreclaimable stamp; worse looking even than Ballou, for the latter showed no signs of dissipation. And this is Fred Green! On his hand the admonitory ring was visible through the dirt and scars thereon, and though his hair was disordered, and manifested a long freedom from the labors of the comb, still the red hue of early days was unmistakably there. His beard had grown abundantly, nearly covering his face, and was fierce and fearful in its bristling, red appearance. His nose, from constant and indiscriminate imbibings, had developed a hue appropriate to his beard, yet rivaling it in its fiery nature. He was welcomed as heartily by the others as his sad state would permit, and little passed in the way of conversation for some time after his arrival.

"I wonder where can White be," said Gray, breaking the silence. "Of course none of you have ever heard of his whereabouts—that would be contrary to the vow."

"I for one have never tried to find any of you," said Ballou.

The others stated they had never sought to, either, and the remark of Gray elicited no information.

"But," said Green, who, like all tramps, was never loth in addressing strangers familiarly, "'spose we ask the proprietor of this bar—I mean the manager of the office—if he knows anything about White." Then walking boldly up to the office counter and rapping thereon he said:

"Say, boss, can you tell us if there's a chap working here by the name of Billy White? Used to run the old ranche on Asylum Street, below here, twenty-five years ago. A jolly rooster as ever lived. Must be about five and forty now. He promised to meet some of his old comrades here to-day, and we don't find him. Do you know him?"

At this question the manager murmured to himself, "It must be for these men that the mysterious package was intended," and then replying to Green, said:

"I can't say that the William White I have in my mind is the one you seek for, but a package was received at this office fifteen years ago superscribed, 'To be called for July 4th, 1876.' It was sent here with a letter announcing the death of a William White, whose corpse came a few days later, and now repose side by side with those of his parents in the third burial ground, which is just beyond the suburbs of the city."

The whole party had followed Green into the office and heard the sorrowful information.

"Poor Billy," said Black. "It is he. The best lad of the whole lot of us is gone. Heaven grant that he is happy!" and his tears flowed silently as he spoke. The others were similarly affected, and bent their heads while they yielded to the deep and heartfelt emotion that controlled them.

Gray asked that the package be obtained for them, and the manager hastily dispatched one of the telegraph messengers to the bank with a written request that it be sent to the office. The messenger was not long in performing his errand; and now the package being in their hands, the party, at Gray's suggestion, made the manager acquainted with the facts of their early life, and having thanked him for his kindness in regard to the package, and also his expressions of sympathy, they set out to seek the grave of White, and there open the package. As they sauntered along through the city Black recounted his adventures, which were, in brief, that he had steadily and persistently pursued the telegraph business for five years, but as promotions to better positions did not follow in accordance with his abilities, he lost ambition to become high in the profession, and that from that time forward he had worked along without making an effort at improvement, and, in fact, lost expertness in performing telegraphic work. The result was, that as time advanced better operators appeared in the field and supplanted him. Rather than accept a lesser position at operating, he had sought for and obtained a position as line-repairer at Chicago, which position he now held. He had worked in San Francisco, St. Louis, Richmond, Boston, and many other places around the country. He had never married, and, as he said, "I walk this dreary world alone, finding a happiness in watching for 'crosses' and 'breaks,' which is sufficient for me. I never thought that the breaks that used to make me swear long ago would at last be the means of giving me a subsistence, but so it is."

Green related that he had been employed in nearly every office in the State during the first five years of his vow, and had saved considerable money, with the intention of marrying at some future day, if he could find any one to accept him—red hair and all. He had by prayer and patience overcome his innate objections to marrying a female operator, but even with this obstacle removed, he found, as years glided by, that he had nothing on which to base hopes. Even they (strange as it may seem, in view of the fact of their usual willingness to participate in the nuptial ceremony) rejected his overtures with contempt and rebuffs, which completely discouraging him, he had abandoned the telegraphic profession and followed other pursuits. Five years he had spent discharging coal vessels, the remainder of the time being equally divided in serving out a long imprisonment at Sing Sing Penitentiary and roaming the country over as a vagrant. "It would take hours to tell of the tramp operators I have met in my travels," said he, in closing, "and I will not tire you by attempting it." The party accepted what he had told as sufficient to show his adventures, and called upon Brown, who said:

"I have never left Connecticut. After parting with you twenty-five years ago I obtained a situation as station agent at ——, on the Hartford, Providence, and Fishkill Railroad. My life has been uneventful, except the fact of my marriage, which occurred twenty years ago. My wife I first met in Norwalk, Conn. She was employed at telegraphing at the time in the New York office, and was visiting some friends in Norwalk whom I knew, and, calling upon them, was introduced, and found my affinity. She has been always an excellent wife and mother. The eventful part of the affair is not in the marriage so much as in my overcoming life-long prejudices, and finally marrying a telegraph operator. My objections to doing so were as strong as our friend Green's, but I have been happily disappointed, and find that telegraph operators make fully as good wives as others of the sex." His companions made no reply to this startling statement. "And," he continued, "I glory in being the father of five children—all boys. I shall keep them from telegraphing, for, as they are smart, intelligent lads, and likely to become expert, I know that they would never attain to any high position, these being reserved for the less gifted men in the business." His associates admitted this to be too true, and he proceeded: "I would be glad to have you all come down and see me. It would delight you to see my eldest son, William, patiently cleaning batteries and making out monthly reports, never swearing, never getting angry over it, but working with pleasure until the perplexing job is over. I often think how superior he is to his father. I used to kick the glass jars to pieces in my anger, and swear like a trooper." He shrugged his shoulders at the thought that his words conjured up, and ceased speaking.

Frank Gray had started for Canada after taking the vow, and been employed in Montreal office for a year, when he returned to New London, and shortly after married Miss Rosa Beverly. The whaling business, which at that time offered a road to fortune, attracted his attention, and he shipped on a voyage to Greenland. He had followed this life steadily since his first voyage, and had been moderately successful, being now the mate of the good ship "Iceland," which, as previously stated, had just returned with a rich cargo. He described the strange fact of his returning just in time to be with them, and concluded the narrative as follows: "I have a sweet little cottage on the environs of New London, in addition to several acres of productive land, and now intend to abandon the sea and till my land. It is much less hazardous to plow the soil than the waves, and as I have an ample maintenance, I shall find a pleasure in passing the balance of my days training my eight children for the duties of life, which they already know a great deal about from the teachings of their mother."

As Gray finished speaking they had reached the burial ground, and silently entered. After a careful search among the graves, reading the inscriptions thereon, and cautiously treading between the mounds, the grave of William White was at length discovered between those of his parents. No tombstone marked the spot, no kind hand had plucked away the wild vegetation that grew around, but everything spoke of neglect. Standing with uncovered heads near the sacred spot, from which they had removed the weeds and briars, the party waited in silence as Ballou, breaking the seal of the package, prepared to draw forth the letter within. Ere this could be done a ring dropped from the envelope and fell upon the grave. It was quickly picked up by Black, who with a trembling hand exhibited it to the others. The sight of the dear emblem forced the tears from the eyes of all, and the memory of the happy days and scenes long fled with which it was associated rose vividly before them.

"Compose yourselves, my friends, if possible, and listen while I read the letter—the last, probably, that our absent comrade ever penned," said Ballou, and having gained their attention, he read as follows:

ST. MARK'S HOSPITAL,
NEW YORK, July 4th, 1861.

MY DEAR FRIENDS—Lying here on my couch, prostrated with fever, broken in health and spirits, penniless and almost friendless, I realize that my end is fast approaching, and I desire to be represented at your gathering fifteen years hence by this epistle, as I cannot be in person. I have never forgotten the vow taken ten years ago, and have faithfully and honestly observed its obligations ever since. I left Connecticut in the month of August, 1851, and came to New York City. Having secured a position in the telegraph business, I worked on hopefully. With advancing years I improved my abilities, better positions with increased salaries were given me, and my future seemed bright. All went well for two years, when temptations that I had long resisted overpowered me and I fell. I took to drinking. The habit grew upon me, and in its wake came other vices. I yielded to the lowest forms of dissipation, and became a hopeless and abandoned man. Thrice discharged from the office, I was allowed to return to my old position on promises of better behavior, but the wild life I had been leading had gained a power over me that my weak nature could not throw off, and at length I became so negligent of my duties that I lost situation, friends, and honor. I bade farewell to New York in 1859, and took a tour around the country, working in offices as substitute operator wherever I found an opportunity. Earning simply enough to satisfy my most pressing wants, I would seek new quarters every few days, all the time yielding to the craving for drink. After following this life for several years I returned to New York, made firm resolutions of amendment, and was doing much by the uprightness of my course to atone for the errors of the past, when the effects of my unsteady life displayed themselves, and I was stricken down with this fever. My peace is made with my Heavenly Father, and hourly imploring his tender forgiveness, I await his summons. May He grant that your lives have been brighter than mine, and oh, my dear friends, as a last request I ask, if any of you have pursued a course similar to mine, abandon it while you yet have time. May God bless you all. Good-bye.

Affectionately yours,
WILLIAM WHITE.

Green was the first to break the silence after hearing the letter read. Tears streamed down his cheeks, and sobs almost choked his utterance. He exclaimed: "Poor Billy! Beloved friend! Your request shall not be utterly in vain. One of us at least will obey it, and that is myself. Oh, comrades, my life has been a hard one! I have fallen into the follies and vices of the world time and again, and now I promise over the ashes of my best friend resting here to change my ways and be a man. This vow I make today, comrades, and swear to keep it as true as I have kept the old one!" He kneeled upon the grave while speaking, and raising his eyes toward Heaven, his lips moved in prayer. He prayed long and earnestly, an act that perhaps he had not performed for years.

Ballou, upon seeing Green arise at last, reminded the party that he had not told them of his career, and said that he had purposely deferred it from private motives. "I resigned from New Haven office immediately upon my return from our eventful meeting long ago," he began. "Having announced to my love —Miss Gregory, that I would write regularly during my absence, I departed for Boston, where I remained for two years, working at telegraphing. All this time I had continued my correspondence with Miss Gregory, and our affection developing into love, I went to Meriden and solicited her father's consent to our union. At first he treated my request with a polite but firm refusal, stating that my rank was not such as he would desire to have his daughter's husband possess. I argued the case with him steadfastly and clearly, but in vain, and left the house. In the meanwhile his daughter introduced the subject to him, and assuring him that with any one else she would never know happiness, he relented and gave his permission, and we were married. I left the telegraph service and assumed charge of two of his mills in New Britain, where I now reside. Years glided by, my cup of happiness always being full to the brim, and at last my wife's father dying, she succeeded to his vast estate and property, and I have now the entire control of them. I disguised myself in this humble garb knowing that I could in this way best learn the sincerity of your friendship, which, I am glad to say, has been loyal and true. Mr. Green, I offer to you a position in my Meriden mills, and if you will accept it I will be glad to have you accompany me back to New Britain. And you, also, Black, I have something in store for you. As for the rest of you, gentlemen, your circumstances are good, and I congratulate you."

As Ballou finished, each of those present crowded around, and grasping him by the hand warmly congratulated him on his good fortune.

The party then retraced their steps back to the city, and parted with expressions of friendly sorrow, first having arranged for the erection of a tombstone over the grave of White. It can now be seen in Hartford, bearing the following inscription:

WILLIAM WHITE,
Telegraph Operator,
Died in New York City, July 10th, 1861.
Aged 30 years.
This Monument was erected by five Operators
who knew and loved him.

The rings, which were retained through so many trials, disappointments, and joys, and had always kept the vow fresh before them, were placed into small niches upon the monument, forming a cluster, with White's ring in the center. The sight frequently awakens curiosity in the minds of those who see them, which is never gratified, as very few know of the incidents they commemorate.

The remaining five operators are all living now, and find in the practice of upright lives and the pursuit of honest aims a higher pleasure than is enjoyed by hundreds of others who, holding lofty positions in life, are discontented with their lot, and perpetually crave for more exalted and lucrative places.

Some Oxberience Mit a Railroats.

Some beobles ash tondt no zomedings apowet a railroats tondt hat baetter loaf roundt a goot teal. Ven I virst gomes me py der blains I goes mit a railroat office und makes abbligation for a shob. "Vot kan you done?" says der souberoftendent. "Whose your peezness?" I told him I vash a obrader, und I should like to hire me owet, und of I broved him sadisvations I vould advance my salary according ash his meridts varranted. "Vash you a ear obrader?" says him, "kan you ketch lidning py der soundt?" "You pet my life!" I told him. "Und you vash a virst glass mans?" "I usder vash," I told him, und den I hat to sbeak apowet taking some brass ven I vash only dree mondths py der peezness. (I usder took it from der hooks to der brinters, but I diden't mention dot.) Und ven I vash drough he looked surbriced, und said it vash marfellous apowet der apilities ouf zome mens. Den he said: "I subbose you hafe all doze requisites ash pecomes a virst glass mans?" "Who is doze?" I onquired. "Oh, I s'bose," says him, "dot you gan sit roundt all tay, turink viskey und cigares, shews derpacker, und sbit all over der ofvice vurniture, und some forth?" "Don't scmoke, don't turink, don't shews derpacker, don't sbit some all ofer der vurnitures!" I yells mit oxsidement. "Whose shurch you pelong of?" onquires him. Den I dink he vash making foolishment mit me, so I oxglaims, "Goot-tay, mister!" Den him hollers, "Holdt on dare, Tutchy! don't bin of a svveat. Took dis bass (und he hands me vone) und go mit Bodunk Sdation on der virst drain to-nide und rebort vor tooty in der mornink." So I goes me immediately

mit Bodunk, und reborts ash accordingly. I tondt had peen on der tooty more ash flof minnids pefore I kets me a meskage vot reads: "Flag und holdt enchine 'Bulldog' until more orters vash necessary." I vash oxsidet, because I don't vash aggustomed mit railroats peezness, und I askgd dot dispatcher who he means by a flag. "'Vy,'" says der tispatcher, "put out der flag und holdt her; und make tem foolishness, und be quick." Den mine hair sthood owet like some brickers on a gooceperries. Und I runs to mine trunk und gets mine flag, den I gets mine refolver, blants der flack in der middle ouf der drack, und cocks der refolver. Shurst den slonk gomes dot enchine dwice more swift ash lidning. Und, py dunnerwedder! dey don't vould sdop! I heared vone man yell "'Hoald der Vort' schnoozer!" Den I vash schkared all to beices, und toldt dot tispatcher der engine don't vould sdop, und if I shall hold drains I mushdt hafe reinvorcements und more guns. "Vot! you lunadicks, did you try to hoald dot engine mit a kun?" "No, mit a refolver," I told him. Den so hollop mine cracious I nefer heared some svearing like dot pefore. "Diden't you put owet der flack?" onquired der tispatcher. "Yaw," I told him. "Vot kind, a redt or a creen vone?" "No! der American flack!" I rebliet. Vell, vell, I don't shall nefer vorget some of doze remarks ash dot tispatcher made. I coulden't sthandt it some longer, so I cuts me owet, und den I skint owet mineselof, und I don't vash hearet of in doze barts zince. I hafe buildt op my merit ash a railroat mans, I tondt vash some sugcess.

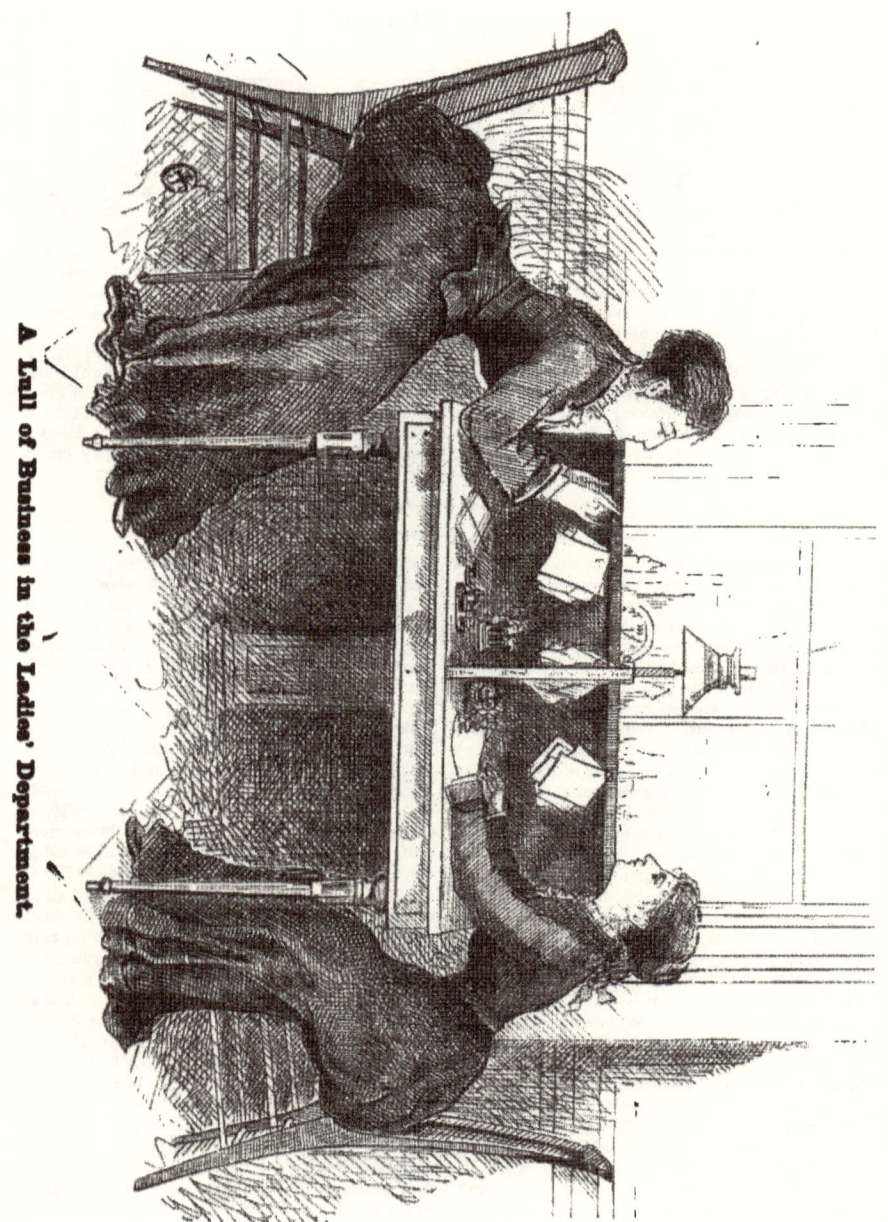

A Lull of Business in the Ladies' Department.

Consulting Electrician Prof. James La Rissey called not long since upon Mons. C. McCarty, Chief Engineer of Electromotive Force, at the latter's laboratory, in the Main Office in this city. A learned discussion ensued in regard to the uses of "ile" in Callaud Cells.—*The Operator*, Sept. 15, 1874. Drawn by J. CHRISTIE.

A GOOD story, if not a true one, was recently reported from London, of a telegram sent by mistake to Lord Dunraven, in Canada, which was meant for Lord Dungarven, both noblemen being members of one club, and Lord Dunraven having left orders that all telegrams received there for him should be forwarded to Canada by cable. The message was in reply to one from Lord Dungarven ordering two boxes at the Gaiety Theatre for Jan. 19. "We can imagine," says a London paper, "the beaming smile of delight over the face of Lord Dunraven, when, comfortably ensconced in a snow-drift, enjoying with guides and trappers a hearty meal of pemmican, he was informed, at about the cost of the national debt, that on Jan. 19 boxes F and G were reserved for him at the Gaiety Theatre, in London !"

"I don't see how any one can write such nonsense, and then get credit for being clever, and understanding human nature?" exclaimed Miss Sunnidale, shutting the book she had been reading with a protesting bang. "I don't believe one word of it! Do you, Dick?"

The question was addressed to her pet canary, and he answered with his usual accommodating chirp, which might be interpreted to mean yes or no, according to the questioner's wishes.

It was "Vanity Fair" she had been reading, and this is the passage which provoked her indignant exclamation: "Old or ugly, it is all the same, and this I state as a positive truth: A woman with fair opportunities, and without an absolute hump, may marry whom she likes."

Now, poor little Miss Sunnidale had reason to doubt this comforting assertion. She had not the shadow of a hump, and if it had been possible for her to marry whom she liked, she would not have been thirty years old and still a spinster. Her idea of Paradise was to have a little home of her own, no matter how humble, with a dear, good husband to love and live for. Long and patiently had she waited for the lord of her life to appear, but still he came not. Love, with all its gladness and grief, with all its sweet tumult and pain, was to her but a beautiful myth—a fairy tale; but none the less did she dream of it, and long for it; for her poor, innocent little heart was as romantic as that of any young school miss. Poor, lonely, little old maid! No wonder, then, that she differed from Thackery in his estimate of woman's power to marry whom she liked.

She did not believe in the modern "Woman's Rights" movement, and although she had been earning her own living, bravely and uncomplainingly, for nearly twelve years, it was not from any desire to be independent that she did so, but simply because she had no one to earn it for her. None of her near relatives were living, and, though naturally of a cheerful and sociable disposition, she had always been very much alone in the world. Most of her life had been spent at school-teaching in a country town, and wearisome enough she found it, trying to train the minds of her rustic pupils. Anxious for a change, she determined to learn telegraphy, and for this purpose made arrangements with the operator, Mr. Wylie, to instruct her in the mysteries of the art, and let her practice in his office after school hours. She had been practicing most perseveringly for over two years, and was now a pretty fair sound operator, but, unfortunately, could not

get a situation. After sending in about half a dozen applications, which always met with the same discouraging reply, "No vacancies at present," she began to despair of ever getting an office, and tried to settle down contentedly to school teaching. But she had no taste for it, and found it irksome. With telegraphy it was different. She felt sure she could succeed at that, for her heart was in it. To her there was an interest—a fascination about it. It was so much pleasanter than going over, day after day, and year after year, the same dull lessons, with duller children. It was the height of her ambition to be put in charge of a nice little office of her own. But she did not expect to get it, for, as she sometimes plaintively declared, Dame Fortune seemed to have a grudge against her, and never would let her have anything she set her heart upon.

However, the fickle goddess at length decided to make a little variety in the programme of Miss Sunnidale's life, by granting her wishes.

The day after that on which this veracious narrative opens, she went down to the office, and told the operator she had decided not to waste any more time practicing, as there seemed to be no hope of getting a situation.

"Well," said he, "I was just going to advise you to apply for this office. I am about to give it up and go back to farming, and will ask the superintendent to let you take my place, if you wish."

Of course she did wish, and he wrote without delay. In a few days the answer came back, authorizing him to transfer the books, etc., to her. She soon found a substitute to take her place at school, and in less than a fortnight was in formal possession of the office.

There were not so many lady operators in those days as there are now, and when it was flashed along the line that a lady had charge of "Sg" office, there was quite a little excitement in most of the other offices over it. Some of the operators signified their approval of it, in telegraph vernacular, by voting it "immense;" others, less gallant, felt that the presence of a lady on the line would be a restraint upon their freedom of (telegraphic) speech, and they would no longer be able to vent their wrath on offending brother artists in their accustomed style, which was often more forcible than elegant.

Tom Gordon was manager of the next office on that line, and when he heard of the appointment he scarcely knew whether to be pleased at the novel idea of having a lady to work with, or to resent the innovation of a woman presuming to engage in what he considered man's work. After due consideration he came to the conclusion that it would not be likely to affect the fact to any great extent whether he resented it or not, so he philosophically resigned himself to fate, determined to make the best of it.

That evening, when Phil Burke, operator on the opposition line, dropped in, as his custom was, to compare accounts, and tell about the wonderful amount of business "our Co." did, Tom cut him short by complacently observing:

"Oh, we know all about that, but we're one ahead of you yet, old man! We can boast of a young lady operator on our line!"

"You don't say so!" exclaimed Phil, with an incredulous air.

"Fact, sir!" said Tom, laconically.

"Is she good looking?" inquired Phil, deeply interested.

"Guess so—she sends well."

"What in the wide world has her sending to do with her looks?" quoth Phil, impatiently.

"Well, perhaps not a great deal, but as I haven't seen her yet it's all I have to judge by. It's one great point in her favor, at all events, for it would set me crazy to listen to her if she handled the key in the nervous, jerky style some girls do."

"She seems to have made a pretty good impression on your tender young heart," remarked Phil, mockingly. "Take my advice, old fellow—be careful you don't get caught. I was reading in a paper, the other day, of a fellow who fell in love with a 'sister operator' whom he had never seen, and only became acquainted with by talking to over the wire. He rashly proposed, she as rashly accepted, and they saw each other for the first time upon the wedding day. Rather risky business, I should think!"

"Well, of course, matrimony is a risky specula-, tion any way, but my opinion is that he stood as good a chance of getting a wife that would suit him under those circumstances as any other. You can form quite as good an estimate of a girl's character and temper by working and talking with her over the line, as by being personally acquainted with her; better, perhaps, for you take her on her merits alone, and are not prejudiced by her appearance. Now, it is a well known fact that a pretty girl's beauty blinds us to her intellectual deficiencies and faults of temper, while, on the other hand, we are too apt to do homely women injustice by taking it for granted that their characters are as unattractive as their faces. I have a theory of my own——"

"Oh, bother your theories!" broke in Phil, irreverently. "You are the prosiest old preacher I ever knew. Every time a fellow asks you a simple question you trot out a perfect legion of facts, fancies,

and theories, promiscuously mixed up, in a way that is fearful to contemplate. Better cut the matter short, and put your theory into practice, by persuading the fair unknown to change her name to Mrs. Tom Gordon."

"I might think seriously of doing so," answered Tom, with imperturbable good nature, "only the trouble is, the cash valuation the company puts on my services is barely enough to keep me in cigars, much less enable me to indulge in the luxury of a wife."

"Economize, my boy, economize! You might have been a wealthy man by this time if you had not indulged in so many extravagant habits."

Which, indeed, was partly true, for Tom's salary was good enough, if only he had not been so careless about money matters. Handsome, generous, pleasure-loving, and with no one but himself to think of, he never took the trouble to save, having, as he said, no object for so doing. This "having no object," had been the great drawback to Tom's success in life all along. He was clever enough to have made his way in the world, if he could only have been brought to feel that it was worth while trying. But he allowed himself to drift along, carelessly, aimlessly, making little use of the splendid talents nature had given him. The ability was there, but the stimulant was lacking. In short, he was a man who needed to have a good, loving wife dependent upon him, in order to develop the noblest part of his nature, and keep him from degenerating into a selfish, lazy "good-for-nothing."

Little Miss Sunnidale has been in possession of her office about a week, and already the place wears a tidier and more cheerful aspect than it used to under the old masculine regime. It isn't much of an office, to be sure—only a little corner of a book-store, partitioned off, but it is pleasant and cosy. On the floor is a bit of pretty, fresh-looking carpet. The ugly, ink-stained counter, and the equally ugly desk on which the instruments stand, are neatly covered with green baize. At the window stands a mammoth geranium, perfectly gorgeous in its array of scarlet blossoms. Dick's cage hangs beside it, and Dick's sweet voice answers cheerily back to the monotonous click, click of the sounder.

There has not been much doing all day, and the busy little woman, who cannot bear to sit idle, is wishing, for the fiftieth time, that somebody would come in with a message to send, or that one of the other offices would call her up to receive one. Her wish seems likely to be granted, for presently she hears the instrument tick off her office call, "8g, 8g." Thinking some one had a message for her, she made haste to answer, but instead of a message comes the rather abrupt inquiry:

"What is your name, please?"

With her usual simple frankness, she answers: "Mildred Sunnidale."

"Odd name, but pretty," remarks her unknown querist. "How do you like your new office?"

"Oh, very much, now that it is cleaned up, and re-furnished, and is no longer redolent of cigars," she replies. "What office are you in?"

"In 'Cn' office," is the answer. "My name is Tom Gordon."

Before she has time to make a fitting response to this interesting piece of information, an ill-natured fellow, away down the line, rudely breaks in, and without even taking the trouble to say, "Excuse me," as telegraph etiquette demands, jerks out, "To Sg. Here, take this," and begins sending a message in his usual rapid, unintelligible style. Now, this operator is the one drawback to Mildred's satisfaction with her new occupation. It always makes her nervous to have to copy from him. He "sends" so fast, and gets so cross if she fails to catch it.

She strains every nerve in her anxiety to get the message correctly, and having got as far as the sig-nature without a "break," is beginning to congrat-ulate herself, when bang! goes the door, effectually drowning the sound of the instrument, and causing her to lose a word. She asks him to repeat the sig-nature, and after a series of impatient "Oh's!" he condescends to do so. She makes frantic efforts to catch it, but fails, and is obliged to ask him to repeat it, whereupon he becomes abusive, and savagely snaps out:

"Oh, get away, and let an operator take your place who can copy a message without 'breaking' at every word."

The poor little spinster is terribly frightened, and meekly replies:

"Please repeat it again, and I will try to get it this time."

But, as is the nature of bullies, her very meekness emboldens him to be still more tyranical and im-pertinent.

"No, I'll be hanged if I will," he replies. "I'll re-port you to the superintendent, and get him to send some one to relieve you."

Tom Gordon is listening to it all, his handsome face flushed with generous indignation at the unman-ly display of tyrannical ill-nature. He now thinks it time to interfere.

"See here, Pugh, you mean coward," he says hot-ly, "Do you know it is a lady you are working with? Don't let us have any more of that nonsense, or I'll report you for using insulting language and willfully delaying business.

"Who asked you to interfere?" retorts the irate Pugh, defiantly. But still he evidently thinks it best

to heed the warning, for he repeats the signature, so that Miss Sunnidale gets it without further trouble.

And when she begins to express her gratitude to her self-elected champion for so kindly taking her part, Mr. Gordon cut short her thanks by saying simply:

"It makes me feel ashamed of my sex to hear a man speak roughly to a woman. If any of these op-erators do so again, it won't be my fault if they are not punished for it."

And from that day kind-hearted Tom makes it his business to see that she is respectfully treated by every one on the line. He seems to consider her un-der his especial protection, and she—well, she thinks him a perfect hero, and worships him from afar. They fall into a daily habit of wishing each other "good morning" and "good night," and sometimes, when the line is not busy, their friendly greetings lengthen out into pleasant little chats.

And so it comes to pass that they gradually learn a great deal about each other's habits, tastes, and opinions, and begin to feel acquainted.

Although he, like most of his sex, is not at all in the habit of under-estimating his own importance, it would surprise him to know what a large portion of Miss Sunnidale's thoughts are devoted to him.

And the poor little old maid, who has never been made much of by anybody since those far-away days before her mother died, would scarcely credit, should any one tell her, how much he speculates about her, and how often he wonders whether she is as nice as she seems to be over the wire. For he finds her very interesting—so different from any of the rest of his rather numerous lady acquaintances. She has so many quaint little ideas, and odd, original ways of expressing them. To him there is a certain fasci-nation about her old-fashioned simplicity, which would seem almost childish but for the sound com-mon sense she displays along with it. He knows she is a lady—no one could work with her long without discovering that. And when, as sometimes, she has occasion to speak seriously on serious subjects, she does it so earnestly and bravely, yet so unassuming-ly, withal, that he feels a sort of involuntary rever-ence for her simple faith and pure childlike nature, and is conscious of a dim longing to lead a better, loftier life than he has been doing.

Ah! if all women were but brave enough to use the mighty influence they possess over men to good purpose, by helping them cultivate the good that is in them, instead of encouraging them, actively or passively, in their follies and wrong-doings, how much better the world would become.

And so the days pass by, quietly and peacefully, as some people's days have a way of doing. The winter melts into spring, the spring into summer, and, little by little, Tom and Mildred grow very friendly with each other.

He often wonders if she is pretty, and if she has a pleasing voice, for Tom is rather sensitive about voice. It makes him shudder to hear some girls talk. Is she fair or dark? Tall or *petite?* And what kind of eyes has she? At last a happy thought comes to him. He will get her to exchange photographs.

So one day, when there is a lull on the line, he calls her up and artfully remarks:

"I have been getting some new pictures taken."

"Are they good?" asks Mildred.

"Yes, splendid," he modestly replies. "Best I've ever had."

And then he waits, expecting her to say she would like to see one. But she only asks:

"When did you have them taken, and how did you manage to leave the office long enough to sit for them?"

Tom is covered with confusion and feels himself a swindler, for the pictures have been lying in his desk since last Christmas, and she would naturally suppose, from the way he spoke, that they had only just been sent home from the artist's. In order to get out of the dilemma gracefully, he ingeniously ignores the first part of her question, and answers the second:

"Oh, I got Phil Burke to run the office for a few hours. He is able to manage two offices when he likes to exert himself, you know."

He has not time to say more, for some one is waiting to get business off. But he does not give up the notion—it is not his way to do that. He begins casting about in his mind for some other way of accomplishing it. By-and-bye he forms a bold resolution.

"That's it," he exclaims. "I'll send her my photo, and ask her to return me her's."

He is not afraid she will refuse—no one ever does refuse Tom anything he sees fit to ask.

Next day Miss Sunnidale receives a letter, with the picture of a very handsome man enclosed, together with a little note. The note is beautifully written, but carelessly worded.

"I take the liberty of sending you my photo," it runs. "Please return the compliment by first mail."

She is surprised and perplexed. What does it mean? It is something new for her to receive a note from a gentleman, still more a picture. She scarcely knows whether to be pleased or offended. He is very nice looking, but the note sounds cool and conceited. What right has he to send his picture without asking permission?

Then the spirit of mischief enters in and takes possession of the little lady.

She gets a dainty sheet of note paper, and demurely writes thereon: "Many thanks for the compliment. I return it by first mail, as requested."

This she encloses in an envelope, together with the picture he sent, addressed it to him, and drops it in the post-office without delay.

He only lives ten miles away, and it is now nine o'clock—it will reach him by noon. So she quietly sits down to await developments.

Tom is furious when he receives it—just at first. He is not used to being snubbed, you see.

But presently the humor of the affair forces itself upon him, and he laughs heartily.

"It just serves me right," he reflects. "It was rather impudent of me to send it. Well, she knows how to hold her own, at all events, for all she seems so simple."

But still Tom feels rather sore about it, and never speaks a word to her all day. When evening comes, instead of wishing her good-night, as usual, he goes off without a word.

In the meantime Mildred is waiting and wondering what he will say. She expects him to take it good-humoredly, and perhaps make some half laughing apology. But as the day passes away, and he gives no sign, she grows anxious, and wonders if he is very angry about it. However, he will be sure to call her up to say good-night, and then they can have a little laugh over it.

When night comes and she finds that he has gone away without calling her, her foolish little heart sinks within her. She closes up the office, and walks slowly to her boarding house, feeling very wretched.

She doesn't want any tea, she says, when her landlady knocks at her bedroom door to announce that it is ready. During the hot summer night that follows she tosses up and down restlessly, sorrowfully, and finally cries herself to sleep.

Of course it wasn't right—it was very undignified and silly; but don't be hard on the poor little creature. Her's was such a lonely life—her heart was so hungry for friendship, and Tom had been very kind to her. How could she help feeling sorry she had offended him?

Next day Tom relents—he bids her good-morning. She answers quietly, pleasantly, just as usual. Not for worlds would she have him think that she had noticed last night's neglect and been troubled by it.

Then Tom says, "I owe you an apology for sending that note yesterday, but I did not think you would be so hard-hearted as to snub me quite so unmercifully."

"Oh, I'm sure I never thought of snubbing you," she protests, very earnestly, "I only meant——"

But she finds a difficulty in explaining what she did mean, so naively adds, " I simply obeyed orders. You told me to return it, you know."

" But you knew well enough what I meant," says Tom. " I've a great notion to send it back to you again. Would you think me very presumptuous if I did ? "

No, she would not think him presumptuous. And her heart flutters strangely.

" Would you send me back one of yours ? " continues Tom, craftily following up his advantage.

But to this she answers not a word. She is thinking, " Would he want it if he knew I was thirty years old, and so dreadfully plain ? "

Next day the handsome picture comes back to her again. She does not return it this time. She takes it home, instead, and dreams over it.

But Tom has hard work to persuade her to send him her's. And, at length, when she does so, she tells him very honestly that he must not think it is like her, for her pictures are always a grand improvement on the original.

It is true that she makes a very good picture. The large brown eyes show off to full advantage, the " tip-tilted " nose takes a more classic outline, and you would never suspect that her hair was red. But, on the other hand, her gentle, womanly expression is not enhanced by the photographer's art, and you miss the wondrous sweetness of her smile.

He has an album full of pretty girls' pictures at home, but none of them ever received so much attention from him as this. He looks at it again and again, studying every point of view, and at last, when no one else is in the office, consistent Tom, who has a great contempt for " softness," and was never known to act the " spooney " in his life, casts a furtive glance around, as if afraid of being seen, and actually raises the poor little spinster's picture to his lips ! After which he blushes furiously, calls himself a soft head, and tries to make believe he is only stroking his moustache with the card.

Presently he calls Miss Sunnidale, and asks her if she will remain a little while after office hours, as he has something to tell her.

She consents, and during the rest of the day keeps wondering what it can be.

And at night, when business is over, and the line is quiet and still, he cautiously cuts off all the offices on the other side of him, by putting on the ground wire, so as to guard against listeners, calls " Sg," and begins to tell it.

It is only the old, old story over again—the story of heartfelt respect, of undying love. But to Mildred it sounds strangely new, and strangely sweet.

It is hard—oh, so hard ! to put it away from her, but she does it bravely, firmly.

When he vows to love her, and be true to her all life long, and asks her to plight her troth to him in return, she answers :

" No, it is not me you love, but some ideal assemblage of virtues of your own creation, which you fancy I resemble. When you saw me, and discovered your mistake, you would repent your bargain. Why, I'm an old maid, with red hair !

She makes the announcement slowly, as though conscious that she is thereby demolishing every vestige of romance connected with her in Tom's imagination, and feeling sadly reluctant to do it.

Tom laughs. It is so funny of her to think it such a dreadful thing to have red hair !

He solemnly declares that red is his favorite color in hair, and as for her being an old maid—well, the more aged she is the more sense she is likely to have. He tells her he doesn't set much value on a pretty face. It is her good qualities he is in love with—her purity of heart, her nobility of mind, her sweet, unselfish disposition. With her to help him he could lead a better, nobler life than he could ever hope to do alone. She would be his good genius, his guardian angel—restraining him from evil, encouraging him in good.

But the little woman is inexorable. She holds steadfastly to her point, and refuses to engage herself to a man whom she has never seen, and she won't tell him whether she likes him or not.

Tom is in despair and at last asks if he may drive over on Sunday and see her.

She agrees to that, and hastily bids him good night, half suspecting that it is all a wild dream, out of which she will presently awaken, and laugh at her own folly.

It is three whole days till Sunday, and Tom and Mildred both think that days never dragged themselves out to such an interminable length before since the world began.

It comes at last, the longed for, yet dreaded Sunday. Mildred rises early, though she knows he cannot be here for some hours yet. She is too restless to lie still.

Very anxiously she gazes into the glass and sees a wee face, with a feverish flush on the cheeks and eyes glowing like stars.

The day is going to be intensely hot, and she arrays herself in a fresh white muslin, cool and dainty looking, with pale blue ribbons at the throat.

Again she stares earnestly into the glass, sees that her dress is very becoming, feels conscious that she is looking her best, and is glad. Then comes the re-action. Something tells her it is not quite fair to make herself look better than usual. So she takes off the pretty white dress a little sadly, and dons a quiet dove colored silk, that makes her look like a little Quakeress.

A perfect simpleton !

Well, perhaps so. But she knows very little of the ways of the world, and is true to her own idea of honesty. After all, there are many things worse than being a simpleton.

She fastens a bunch of pansies and mignonnette in her bosom, and, book in hand, descends to the parlor to await his coming.

About an hour afterward she hears a knock at the door, and then a tall, fine looking man, with wavy brown hair, and eyes of the deepest, darkest blue, is shown in.

He stands before her, clasping her little hand in his, respectfully, yet tenderly.

And this is Tom? She looks up to him without a word, wondering wistfully if he is very much disappointed in her.

If he is he does not show it. He picks up the book she let fall on his entrance and passes some remark about it. Soon they are engaged in an animated discussion of books and authors. After awhile he skillfully managed to bring the conversation around to the point where they dropped it the other evening. He wants her to tell him if she thinks she could learn to love him, now that she has seen him.

The tell-tale flush spreads swiftly over her cheeks and brow, and she begins to tremble. But she willfully refuses to answer just yet. She will see—she will tell him some other time—she must get ready for church now—the bells are ringing.

So they go to church together, and mingle their voices in prayer and praise. After that they take a quiet, pleasant ramble through the cool shady lanes, then go home and have lunch, and another delightful long chat in the quaint old parlor. The kind hearted landlady, with whom Mildred has boarded for years, is "glad that Miss Sunnidale has got a beau at last—and such a likely looking gentleman, too. But if she should get married and go away, the place will seem very lonesome without her."

It seems quite probable that she will get married, too, for when Tom leaves for home there is a tiny ring gleaming on the little old maid's finger, and a bright, happy look in her face, which makes her seem ten years younger, and almost pretty.

Some weeks afterward, when Phil Burke rushes into the office, and excitedly demands if it is true that he is going to marry the operator at "Sg" office, he calmly answers, "Yes, I have taken your sensible advice, and put my theory into practice by asking her to become Mrs. Tom Gordon. It may be a very risky way of choosing a wife, but I'm satisfied I've made a good hit of it. She is as good as gold—the best little woman that ever lived; and I don't believe that I would ever have found it out except by working with her over the line."

Phil congratulates his old friend very heartily, but is still rather doubtful of the advisability of "Wooing by Wire."

As for Mildred, she no longer disputes Thackeray's assertion that a woman may marry whom she likes. Her prince has come at last.

A Lady Telegrapher's Interesting Reminiscences of a Summer in the Country.

I DIDN'T feel very well last spring. Close confinement, the doctor said, and suggested that I try and spend a few months in the revivifying asmosphere of the country. A friend who keeps a summer hotel offered me the situation of operator. I accepted, and, telling my friends that I was "going in the country for the summer," packed my trunk, shook the dust of the great, bustling city from my feet, and hied me away to the shores of the clear and sparkling Silver Lake, on which the hotel is built.

Oh! what a delightful change that was from the ceaseless hum and dull routine of the office! As I sat near the edge of the lake, from whence a grateful breeze arose and fanned my forehead, I used to close my eyes, and imagine that I was soaring away through endless space to a far brighter and more enchanting world than this. And as the trees gave a lazy rustle, and I could feel the genial warmth of the sun for a moment upon my cheek, or hear the trinkling of the water at my side, I tried to close my eyes still firmer, and say, in the words of the song, "Ah! do not wake me, let me dream again."

My salary at the office was small, but so was the volume of business. I suppose it is hardly my place to criticise, but there were one or two as poor operators on that wire as I ever want to have anything to do with. The one at Sandy Hill positively broke so often that I never for the life of me could tell whether he was sending or receiving! By the way, he invariably dated his messages as coming from "Handy Pill," and it was better than a circus to hear the encounters he sometimes had when new men came on the wire. "Handy Pill?" they would repeat; "Handy Pill!" he would rejoin, good-naturedly enough, "you don't seem to be able to take me very well." "No," they would reply, "you are decidedly the worst pill I ever attempted to take." Then he would make a few dots and try once more. Again the same old "Handy Pill," and the receiving operator would break in with a provoking "?" At this point he generally lost his temper, and remarked, petulantly, "I guess you are not familiar with that name;" to which the other would respond, "I am not familiar with that kind of sending." But although where regular business was concerned his sending and receiving were slow and painful, in conversation he managed to acquit himself remarkably well—probably doing some pretty tall guessing. He seemed to be very fond of poetry and poetic language—and also of your humble servant. Why he thought so much of me I'm sure I don't know, for he never even saw me, but the avowals of undying affection he used to send over that senseless wire were both frequent and fervent. It was too funny for anything. I told him, for a joke, that I belonged to Germany, had only been in the country four months, and could talk but little English. He said he always liked the Germans; alluded incidentally to his own sweet nature and loving disposition, and declared that he "knew we would get along first rate together." Then he told me he was coming up to see me—if he could get a pass; and I lived for several days in abject terror lest he might come and dispel that German illusion. One night Deanville called me, and said that Mr. Ross, of "Handy Pill," was there. I recognized the sending, and replied, "Well, what of that?" Although he had traveled seventeen miles, and was now within four of my office, he didn't come on, but took the next train back to Sandy Hill. I felt immensely relieved, especially as he treated me so very coolly ever after.

The Deanville operator had the finest temper I think I have ever seen—for a telegrapher. He was very interesting in conversation, too, and so polite and nice that I asked him to come down and show me how to make out my monthly statement. Well, I wish you had seen him! In he walked that evening as stiff as a poker, and as awkward as an elephant. He had fiery red hair, a rough, harsh blotched face, and clothes that fitted him decidedly too much. He never attempted to remove his hat, sat down with a thud on the seat that I offered him, and scarcely uttered three words all the time he was there. I was horribly disappointed in him, but tried to draw him into conversation. It was no use. He only answered in monosyllables, or stared vacantly at me, "ears agog and eyes set open wide." Finally I asked him if he had ever seen THE OPERATOR. He gave a start that quite frightened me, and eagerly inquired, "Who's he?" I told him, and showed him a copy, and he was quite delighted with it. That rigid manner didn't wear off until he rose and got hold of the key. Then he seemed quite at home. Calling the other offices he informed them, with evident pride, that he was in my office. He was the queerest person I think I have ever seen.

One of the Boston men spent a few days at the hotel. He was a magnificent operator, and insisted upon sending and receiving all the business while he was present. I thought a great deal of him. He is engaged to be married to a very handsome, and I doubt not loving and amiable, young lady; and for one, I hope that when their tiny bark is launched upon the great untried sea of matrimony, sunny skies and genial weather may ever attend them.

Another gentleman stopped at the hotel who a few years ago left the business and went in partnership in an extensive hardware store. Rumor says that the world has prospered with him, and he is reputed wealthy.

One Sunday I wandered off after dinner toward a cozy nook on the edge of the lake that I greatly admired. Before reaching the spot I found the above ex-telegrapher—whom I had already met once or twice before—sitting on the trunk of a fallen tree, smoking a cigar with evident relish, but apparently completely lost in thought. I tripped up to him lightly, and awaited a recognition. But he only kept his eyes intently fixed upon the ground. His face wore a look as hard and cold as steel, utterly devoid of warmth or expression. His brows were contracted in sharp, deeply-set lines, and as the smoke from his cigar ascended in lazy wreaths over his head, he raised his eyes and seemed perfectly unconscious of everything around him in watching the blue rings as they expanded to their greatest extent, and finally burst and became lost in the surrounding air.

I felt that I was intruding, and attempted to retreat, and leave him alone with his thoughts. But something bade me stay. I waited a few moments, and then said, softly:

"Are your thoughts of so very pleasing a character that you cannot afford to interrupt them by recognizing a friend?"

He looked up with a startled, frightened expression, as if he had just been discovered in the act of committing some heinous crime, and said, apologetically:

"I beg your pardon, Miss ——, but I was thinking of the past, and quite forgot myself."

"I did wrong to disturb you," I said, sympathetically. "Perhaps you prefer to be alone."

"Oh, no! not at all," he replied, sadly. "To me recalling the past possesses an unaccountable fascination, but is nevertheless extremely unpleasant, as the picture presents little save a few faded flowers—dry, dead, withered remains of rosebuds that once bloomed, oh! so sweetly, and shattered remnants of many once bright air castles which have crumbled into ashes among my fingers. But there, there! I must not cast a cloud over your bright nature by talking upon this disagreeable subject. Tell me something about yourself, and dispel this fit of the blues."

"Believe me, I sincerely feel for you," I said, in a tone of as great tenderness as I could utter the words. "So far as my own experience goes, I have often found great relief in telling my troubles to another whom I knew would sympathize with and perchance be able to aid me. I should like to ask you to make a confident of me—speak as freely to me as you would to a sister, if you can, and tell me precisely what the trouble is. I promise that if I can in any way be of service to you, I shall render that service willingly."

He looked at me steadily for several moments, seemingly absorbed in thought, and at length said:

"Thank you. I think you are right, and if you will take that seat I shall make you acquainted with a little of my history."

He whirled his cigar into the lake, turned around, and, looking squarely into my face, went on:

"I am a man with whom business has prospered, upon whom the fickle goddess Fortune has smiled, and who is even secretly envied by the world for what it is pleased to call my success in worldly affairs. Yet I feel as I sit here to-day that in the only thing in this world worth striving for my life has been an utter and complete failure.

"Two years ago to-day a life went out in which was bound up my entire existence. A heart ceased to beat which had never before failed to quicken its pulsation at my coming; feet were stilled forever that had often lightly run to welcome me; eyes became cold and glassy and meaningless that so recently were wont to light up with joy at my approach, and a voice—the sweetest, to my mind, in the whole world—was hushed forever. Two years ago to-day the woman whom I had chosen of all the world to be wife lay dead! Is it any wonder that I feel sad on this the anniversary of perhaps one of the greatest calamities that can ever happen to a man of a highly sensitive and loving nature?

"She was not my first love. Four years ago I had charge of the office at Sedalia, Mo. Regularly every morning and afternoon a young girl of about seventeen passed the office on her way to school. I knew the time, and always managed to be at the window when she passed. I don't know how it was, but any morning that she happened to pass without looking in or smiling I was sure to feel out of sorts all day, and when I caught that sweet, modest, lady-like smile in the morning, it remained with me like a genial ray of sunshine throughout the day, illumining my pathway — thorny enough it was, too, sometimes, God knows!—and cheering me as nothing else seemed capable of doing. After a while I used to go to the door and greet her with a pleasant nod, and finally I even went so far

as to raise my hat and say 'Good morning,' and 'Good afternoon.' I used to imagine that she walked more slowly as she passed the office, and one afternoon I spoke to her—just a few words. After that she generally stopped a few seconds on her way home every afternoon to ask me something about electricity and the like. Then we managed to meet pretty often, kind of "accidentally on purpose." The more I saw of her the more I liked her, and in due time we had come to love each other with that sweet, pure, guileless affection which the world too often sneeringly designates schoolboy's infatuation. I loved her with all the warmth of my enthusiastic nature, and to be in her company always gave me a feeling of exquisite pleasure. It did not matter whether I spoke to her or not, to be near her seemed to be all that was necessary to render me completely happy. The great, cold, suspicious, matter-of-fact world would doubtless find fault with us, and say that a few years and a little more experience would show us that we did not really care for each other. I don't know what she thinks, but for my part, the recollection of those delightful moments spent with her will ever be looked back upon as one of the greenest spots in my existence.

"But she was the only daughter of an eminent physician of the place, a man too rich and haughty and proud to hear of her marriage with a poor, obscure telegraph operator. She was forbidden to speak to me. My character was even assailed, and an effort made to induce the superintendent to have me transferred. Although smarting under this injustice, I showed her father that I was at least a gentleman. I loved his daughter too dearly to stand in her way, and I knew that I was not worthy of her, and on my meagre salary could not offer her as good a home as she had been accustomed to under the paternal roof. I therefore made up my mind to bow to the father's wishes and—difficult as I knew the task would be—try and forget her. When I saw her and announced my determination, she said she felt prouder of me than ever before, and as the time came to say farewell—a long, last farewell—I thought her heart would break. Leaning her head confidingly and with absolute helplessness upon my breast, she sobbed so piteously that my courage almost failed me, and I had to literally tear myself away. The next morning I forwarded my resignation to the superintendent. I could not stay any longer in the place.

"I went to New York and obtained employment at 145 Broadway. I thought that amid the excitements and confusion of a great city I might forget her. But I couldn't. That gentle, loving face, and sweet, frank smile ever haunted me. At a busy wire all day I was at least partially successful; but in the evening I felt so lonely and desolate, and utterly forlorn, that to drown my sorrows and deaden my feelings I had recourse to the intoxicating cup. But oh, what a hollow mockery that is! Byron uttered a truism when he said:

'Though gay companions o'er the bowl
Dispel awhile the sense of ill,
Though pleasure stir the madd'ning soul—
The heart, the heart is lonely still.'

"About this time a daughter of the lady with whom I boarded displayed a very kind interest in me. She asked me if I knew what my present course would inevitably lead to—certain ruin of both body and soul. She not only warned me of intemperance, but spoke earnestly and feelingly of God and Heaven. Her sympathy touched a chord in my heart long dormant, and in all probability rescued me from being now classed among the great army of drunkards. My heart yearned after sympathy, and I needed pleasant conversation to make me forget the past. These I got from her, and you will not perhaps be surprised to learn that my gratitude soon ripened into deep respect, and finally by degrees into sweet, pure, manly affection. My heart had been bruised and crushed, and there was a great void there which only a woman's love could fill.

"As time wore on I discovered new beauties in her character, grew to love her more dearly every day, and at length proposed for her hand, and had the satisfaction of becoming her accepted lover. A friend having offered me a half interest in his hardware establishment, my father advanced what money I required, and I left the telegraph business to engage in the new pursuit. The business was remunerative, everything seemed to go well with me again, and as I saw the sun bursting forth in all its splendor from behind the cloud that had obscured its genial rays so long, I felt very happy. It is only the man who has experienced such a calamity as I had that really understands the full meaning of the word happiness. 'Spring,' you know, 'would be but gloomy weather if we'd nothing else but spring.'

"We were to have been married in November. But on the 21st of July, while travelling on the Long Island Railroad, on her way to visit some friends there, the train came into collision with a freight train. Several of the passengers were killed, and herself so seriously injured that she died the following morning, July 22d—just two years ago to-day. What a terrible shock the message announcing her

death gave me! I shall never forget it, and, indeed, question whether I shall ever be entirely myself again. The thought struck me that it was a direct dispensation of Providence; that I had not thanked Him as I should when He sent prosperity to me, and that He in his wisdom considered it necessary to speak to me thus harshly by making me once more drink deep of life's dregs. But I rebelled against the decree, and said, 'If He speak to me thus, I shall never hear!' I have since come to look at it differently, however, and tried in all faith to say, 'Thy will be done.' Since then I have had little inclination for pleasure or amusement of any kind. I feel that my lot has been an exceptionally hard one. Few know how wretched and miserable, how cold and dreary and desolate is a life such as mine. Disraeli truly says that life without love is worse than death. Without this essential and pervading charm how vain and void, how flat and fruitless appear all those splendid accidents of existence for which men struggle. Yes! without this transcendent sympathy, riches and rank and even power and fame are at best but jewels set in a coronet of lead.

"I remember once reading an article which spoke of the future as being always a fairy land to the young, and so it is. At first Life is like a beautiful winding lane, on either side bright flowers and beautiful butterflies and tempting fruits, which we scarcely pause to admire, so eager are we to hasten to an opening which we imagine will be more beautiful still. But, by and by, as the trials of life thicken, and the dreams of other days fade one by one in the deep vista of disappointed hope, the heart grows weary of the struggle, and by degrees as we advance the trees grow bleak, the flowers and butterflies fail, the fruits disappear, and we find that we have arrived to reach a desert waste. At least such, I am sorry to say, my life has been."

"I beg your pardon," I said, as he paused, "but what about the Sedalia young lady? Did you ever hear of her?"

"Yes," he replied. "I saw the announcement of her marriage to Judge Wilson, about a year and a half ago."

As we walked back to the hotel I was so much absorbed in this wonderful romance of real life, and he seemed so completely occupied with his own thoughts, that not a single word passed between us

The Telephone.

WE'VE often heard and often read
About a conversation's thread;
But now-a-days it may be seen—
The one I saw to-day was green;

It carried many a word and tone
From telephone to telephone.
Ah! Science give us one more link,
That we may hear our neighbors think.

"STILL SO GENTLY O'ER ME STEALING."

"MEMORY OFT BRINGS BACK THE FEELING."

A "Shocking" Affair.

The Telegraph Dispatch.

A STORY OF TELEGRAPHY IN THE EARLY DAYS.

CHAPTER I.

The mystic wire is in the air,
It winds from shore to shore,
By dark Missouri's turbid tide,
By deep Niagara's roar.

Bear along the lightning song,
Down the Ohio;
A thousand miles are already up,
And thousands more to go.

It was late one Saturday evening in December, 1847, that after finishing some engrossing correspondence, I arose with the intention of immediately proceeding to my quiet lodgings in Chestnut Street, there to take the welcome rest that ushers in the day of sacred repose. It had been a busy day and a toilsome one. I had been alone in care of the two registers connecting with Baltimore and New York, the day cold and rainy, and both lines working with a fitful uncertainty, corresponding well with the weather. Slowly and tediously had the new wonder performed her office. The perfection to which telegraphic structures have since arrived was then unknown. It was the nursing of a rickety child, the guiding of a keelless craft. Yet the constant suspicion of my own ignorance had made me patient. Hour after hour I repeated and repeated—aye, to the seventh time—each dispatch to my patient associate at the other terminus. I sighed and longed for dinner, but sighed in vain. A cup of coffee from a neighboring restaurant gave new patience to my troubled spirit. Yet nine o'clock found me with my files all clear and letters all written, a wearied martyr to a new and unpromising pursuit.

Before rising from the hard stool on which I had performed my martyrdom (we had no stuffed chairs in those days), I moralized a moment. The revolutions I had innocently caused on Wall Street gave me no concern. Bull Bridges had been a steady attendant at the pine railing which kept the inquisitive public from overflowing me; and the size of his quid and the magnitude of his "stream" indicated the agitation of the "fancies."

Busy Sylvester and grim Riddle, too, were anxious and inquiring. Yet Wall Street affairs had no lodgement in my anxieties, and they had come and gone, as had the ill-tempered winds without, free from sympathy with me.

Otherwise, however, the day had been eventful. Joy and sorrow had found in me an interested medium. I had seen some of the few phases of eventful life just beginning to be intrusted to the new messenger which the kind-hearted and ingenious student of Poughkeepsie had given to his country. It had identified me with my race. I was a necessity. Love had opened her heart to me, and in my faithful hands had her secret been held. Agony had forced me to a partnership. Jealousy had made me hear the uneasy gritting of her teeth. Joy had rung his merry laugh in my ears, and sorrow had wet my hands with tears that met my own.

How various had been my mission! How many vibrating chords had been sounded that day by my instrumentality! I had learned a lesson of human sorrow which succeeding years have only widened and deepened. I learned to prepare my own heart for the storms of life and the anguish of the years to come. It was well. Some of these have already come. There are others still to follow. 'Tis pleasant to know that amid life's sunshine as in its darkness, when the stars are cloudless as when they have one by one hid behind the gathering gloom of clouds, that the Great Pilot is at the helm, and the war-ship of life, careening upon a thousand waves, is still steady on her course, safe in His hands.

And now for home. My little room in the third story with its modest furniture, but clean white bed linen, and cheerful fire, held out new charms to me. Already I was within its clean, warm blankets, thankful for its sweet and quiet repose, and dreaming of the coming day, when man and beast were alike to enjoy the blessedness of the week's grand holiday.

Before turning off the gas, however, I went to the messenger's table, to see whether that worthy had performed his duties, and properly delivered his dispatches. One only remained on his table; and, supposing it to have been one not deliverable at so late an hour, I was on the point of leaving, when a vague suspicion of its import crossed my memory, and I returned to its examination.

Late in the afternoon, a little after sunset, I had received from Wilmington, Delaware, a brief dispatch to "James Mornington, Kensington," which had excited my keen interest. Its language was terse, yet touching. It uttered a name dear to me. I had asked its quick delivery. The unfaithful hound had gone home, chary of the rain. Here it lay undelivered. I opened it. It read as follows:

"Poor Mary will die to-night; she asks to see you. Come quick. .

REBECCA WARRINGTON."

It was now half-past nine. The cars left at eleven. By great activity I could deliver it in time to secure its purpose. With an indignant malediction of the lazy subordinate, and an indefinite resolution to commence the week by an act of summary decapitation, I placed the missive securely in the breast-pocket of my coat, buttoned myself to the throat, tucked up my nether garments, and sallied out into the storm.

CHAPTER II.

" There is, indeed, one crowning joy,
A pleasure that can never cloy,
The bliss of doing good;
And to it a reward is given,
Most precious in the sight of heaven,
The tear of gratitude."

I turn aside from this relation to have a

talk with messengers. I have become, con amore, a messenger boy. They are, therefore, my associates. The occasion is a suitable one. We must see if we cannot realize our position. What part do we bear in the great system of communication now developing itself?

Here, for example, I carry a message from the house of death, dictated by the absorbing circumstance of the decline of an affectionate sister, longing to see her only brother before her trembling spirit says farewell to earth. The telegraph to her is the minister of heaven. But for it, no message could have reached her brother's home, and fresh and bitter tears would have wet the pillow of death. But its power has become known to her; with trembling hope it is carried to the office; a kind, attentive operator received and sent it to me; it came in good season to secure to that dying girl her heart's desire. Ah! boys, there is not one of you but would have run like a mercury to deliver it. And yet here am I doing what a mean exception to the corps should have done hours before! His name is known to me. I will not give it. But in some dark hour, if he yet lives, he will sigh for comfort he cannot procure.

Boys, one word more! Electricity is very fast—very. It compasses the earth in a second. But it needs you at the end. It cannot do without you. You are, in many important respects, the life, the energy, the soul of the system. The postboy is a mere piece of baggage compared to you. Remember that in your hands is committed an important trust. Day by day, human happiness and commercial success depend on your promptness and integrity. You are watched closely. No boy has a surer passport to a prosperous and honorable manhood than the faithful telegraph messenger boy.

A few years ago I saw one such. Quiet, but ever at his post, he seemed to comprehend that on him devolved an important duty. His neat, clean attire showed that he was well-bred and cared for; while his respectful address and love of truth revealed the impress of the heart and counsel of a pious mother. All knew the telegraph boy, and many an encouraging word was spoken to him by the merchants, as he delivered to them their telegrams from his dispatch-book, unsoiled by finger-mark or rain, and took their receipts. Years have passed since then. He is still young. Yet his course has been onward and upward.

Early in the long summer mornings, he used to rise with the day, put on the local battery, and, while all else were asleep, be struggling to learn how to operate. This he did for some time unknown. With genuine modesty he struggled alone. He succeeded, and became a beautiful writer. The manager of the office was taken suddenly ill, but his messenger boy conducted his business for him until restored. He distinguished himself by an indefatigable industry in the delivery of dispatches. No rain or storm could stop him. These only quickened his gait. He is now manager of a respectable office, with an excellent salary, and no one has better prospects of promotion than he. The two Durfees were examples; both, alas! now passed away, but bearing with them the cherished remembrance of all who knew them.

In the prosecution of my duties as superintendent, I loved to meet the messengers. The shake of their young hands was ever gladsome to me. I saw in them the embryo managers of our offices. I liked to cheer them in the prosecution of their arduous duties, and as, one by one, they were promoted to more remunerative, although not more important stations, I seemed to enjoy their success with more than a personal pleasure. Their own hopes and mine united.

But for the reprobate who sent me out in that dreary rain, already weary with the multitudinous duties of the day, I have, even now, a most punishing recollection. Well, I ought to forgive him for the experience of which he was the cause. My contact with sorrow had been slight. I was young, and my day had, so far, been one of sunshine and delight. I was to be initiated into the shadows of life, to feel and witness its gloom. Many are the tears these cheeks have borne since then. I can almost excuse the lazy hound who, to save himself from a tedious walk, had cheated a dying girl of the solace of a brother's affection, but who had, unwittingly, lifted up one fold of the curtain which hid me from the realities of life.

CHAPTER III.

"Oh, death, what art thou!—A husbandman that reapeth always,
Out of season as in season, with the sickle in his hand."

The communication of sorrowful tidings is in itself a sorrowful task. To a sensitive mind it produces all the agitation of personal grief. The tear is ready to mingle with the tear expected. The heart throbs with a painful consciousness of the possession of a secret, which, discovered, must agonize; which the possessor would gladly have die with him; but which he must convey with delicate sympathy lest another, less moved by sympathy, might, with indelicate haste, send, like an arrow doubly barbed, to the bosom it most concerns.

So, as through the storm I wended my way to a home I might render desolate, before me ever appeared the image of a suffering girl, moaning, in her agony, for her distant brother. Long before I reached my destination, I had marked, in imagination, all her features, pencilled her sorrowful eye, and enshrined her in my heart as a sister, whose pillow I should have rejoiced to smooth, and whose ebbing spirit I should have loved to solace with the hopes of a better land than this.

A single light illumined a room of the house where Mornington resided, which seemed, from its locality and appearance, to be occupied by one in the middle walks of life. No plate on the door indicated the occupant, but the number, 64, painted in plain figures over it, and lighted by a lamp near by, satisfied me that I had reached the place.

Knocking gently at the door, it was opened by an elderly lady, who, with a politeness I scarcely expected, invited me to walk in and await her son's return.

"This is his birthday," she said. "and he and part of the family have gone to a little merry-making near by, whence I expect them every moment. They promised to return by ten, and it is now a few minutes beyond."

"It is somewhat important I should see him soon," I replied; "I have a message from his sister, to which I would be glad to carry a reply."

"From my daughter Mary?"

"I believe it must be from her."

"From Wilmington?"

"Yes, I received it from there this evening."

"You did not, then, come from Wilmington? I was in hopes you might have seen my daughter, and brought us news of her health. Poor child; we sent her there to see if change of scene would restore her to health again. But—she is a tender plant, and needed a mother's care. But her brother proposed the change, and to her his wish is her guide."

"The dispatch I bear would indicate her ill health, and, fearing that it might be important to be delivered soon, I came thus late to deliver it."

I said this in a tone of voice I intended should be easy and unagitated; yet, having absorbed my mind with the subject of it, my speech was tremulous, and I saw at once that the perceptions of a mother's heart were aroused. The knitting-kneedle dropped from her hand, and, with a hurried, anxious voice, she replied—

"Has anything happened, sir—is my daughter worse? You seem to regard your errand here as urgent. Something must be wrong! What keeps my son? He seldom disappoints me; I am aged and infirm, and could not join them in their gathering." Then, lowering her head, she said, sorrowfully, "My poor Mary, I fear thou wilt soon leave us." And I saw the tears coursing each other down her aged cheeks, as, shaking her head sorrowfully, she went to the window to see if there were indications of her son's return.

There was no time to lose. I might have handed my message to that aged mother; I rose twice to do so. Had I done so, I would have hurried from the house. I know, and none knows more deeply, the power of a mother's love; the clinging, living grasp with which it encompasses her children, and I dared not give her the chalice, which would surely induce the ebullitions of a grief I could not bear; and yet I must accomplish my errand. That dying girl seemed following me with tears and low expostulating entreaties to grant her request. Fail I must not, and I was just about to propose to find the object of my search amid his festivities, when a rapid sound of footsteps at the door, and the ring of merry voices, assured me of his return. "Ah," thought I, "what a mission is mine!" I began to hate my avocation. I felt myself to be a miserable raven coming to croak a note of woe, where all was happiness, and hilarity, and hope.

The party who thus came in upon us were, first, a young, gentlemanly-looking man of thirty, with a gentle, benignant countenance, deeply expressive of inward sensitiveness and delicacy; a little lady of twenty-five, with a bright, cheerful countenance—the token of a trusting and open heart within—whose merry voice and evident sweetness of disposition recalled to mind the pretty Spanish song, which we must give you, kind reader, if only to show how strangely thoughts mix themselves up in this sensitive heart of ours, as well as to break up, in some degree, the heaviness of our story, but which, in the object before us, seemed to have so true an application:

"In a little precious diamond,
　What splendor meets the eyes!
In a little lump of sugar,
　How much of sweetness lies!
So, in a little woman,
　Love grows and multiplies;
You recollect, the proverb says—
　'A word unto the wise.'

"A pepper-corn is very small,
　But seasons every dinner
More than all other condiments,
　Although 'tis sprinkled thinner.
Just so a little woman is,
　If love will let you win her;
There's not a joy in all the world
　You would not find within her.

"And, as within the little rose,
 You'll find the richest dyes,
And in a little grain of gold
 Much price and value lies;
As from a little balsam
 Much odor does arise,
So, in a little woman,
 There's a taste of paradise.

"The skylark and the nightingale,
 Though small and light of wing,
Yet warble sweeter in the grove
 Than all the birds that sing.
And so a little woman,
 Though a very little thing,
Is sweeter than all other sweets,
 Even flowers that bloom in spring."

The third was a bright little girl of five summers, a merry, prattling child, with little round cheeks and chin, who, with her hands full of confections, was struggling between the sleepiness of so late an hour and the hilarity of the festive occasion from which she had returned. It was an interesting scene to see the beautiful tokens of affection pass between them and the aged lady, as she kissed, with true maternal warmth, her children and little granddaughter, wishing her boy many a returning birthday and a long and happy union with his companion—tokens which, in their delicacy and touching affectionateness, I fear are too rapidly passing away from our households. This greeting, however, was soon terminated by the conscious presence of a stranger.

It was in vain to endeavor to prepare this loving circle for the message of death. I essayed to do it. Kind words were welling from my heart, but they refused arrangement in the preface work of consolation. I handed my message, took my hat, hoping to escape the burst of emotion which I felt was to follow, when I was paralyzed by a moan so deep and agonized that threescore years and ten shall pass in fruitless effort to efface it from my memory. In a moment that little group were crowded together in a most touching attitude of mortal grief. The aged mother, with her trembling hands clasped, her eyes closed, and her furrowed features livid, as if in death, could only exclaim, in agonized accents, "My poor child!" and sank back motionless upon her chair.

It was thus I left them unnoticed. I doubt-

ed not Mr. Mornington would make immediate preparation to leave by the train at eleven P. M., and my mind was relieved of a load of anxiety. Such duties, since then, have, alas! been too frequent to affect me thus deeply; but the performance of this was accompanied by even deeper anxiety than the language of my narrative might seem to indicate. I was like a sailor boy looking with awe on the billows he sees for the first time, but which, afterward, he rides without the thought of their magnitude or danger.

During my return, my mind dwelt much on the responsibilities the telegraph, as a great agent of humanity as well as a medium of commerce, was to bear in its future history. The world had, as yet, learned little of its power. It was a giant, the mighty energies of whose sinews had not been tried for any extended purpose of human use. Entering alike into the social as into the commercial necessities of society, its destiny was evidently general, and of the most multiform application. To my mind, it had already become a sure warning to the universe, in whose beams every clime might rejoice, making mankind, the world over, a common brotherhood, and associating earthly governments into a close community of common interests. I saw it guiding or accomplishing the diplomacy of courts, the adjudicator of national disputes, the sail of fleets, the march of armies, the fiscal arrangements of national treasuries, the exchanges of commerce, the defenses of extended seaports, municipal regulations, and every public want in which communication by voice, or sign, or courier, has hitherto borne their tardy parts. But after all these uses of its wondrous power had passed like a panorama before my mind, I saw that on the minor arrangements, by which these capacities were made useful, must depend its great usefulness and acceptability. Science had shown its power to annihilate distance and time; it had enabled man to sit in his arm-chair and listen, as it were, to the roar of all of earth's oceans breaking upon her many shores, and hear the jubilee of her countless tongues. It had placed the avenues and opportunities of commerce and social convenience within human reach, a bell-pull in the chambers of the world; but there it ceased, and the play of minor agencies commenced. The receiving operator, the transcribing and recording clerk, and, above all, the faithful messenger, had to complete the work of an agency thus otherwise almost omniscient and omnipresent. My position as superintendent of the first line built by private enterprise in America, became one of deeper anxiety to me. The twig seemed in my hands. Others, it is true, were skilled and interested spectators. I was subordinate to controlling minds; yet their presence and influence were hidden amid the appeals which my own mind urged to watch its growth, and bend it into forms of beauty. It came upon me like the birth of a first-born, whose future I was to watch, and into whose expanding mind I was to pour the genial milk of human kindness, and thoughts suggestive of pure and elevated purpose. It was then I resolved to give the new enterprise all the best services of my head and heart.

CHAPTER IV.

"Gird thee, and do thy watching well,
Duty's faithful sentinel!"

Instead of going direct to my lodgings, I returned to the office to assure myself that the machinery was carefully cut off from connection with the wires outside, in case of danger from lightning during the night. This I found I had neglected to do when the business of the day had closed, and I was surprised to notice, on examining the magnet, that some distant operator was endeavoring to call me. Relighting the gas, I found the operator at Wilmington assiduously endeavoring to arouse me, hopeless as must have been his task. The English reviewer who described a telegraph operator as a taciturn, suspicious-looking individual, never say Joseph Beatty, who, with his ample rotundity, carried within him the blessedness of most

fat men, much goodness of heart. As evidence of this, here was he indefatigably calling with a patience characteristic of him, P P P P—77. P P P—77. which the click of my register brought to me with a certain slowness of sound, as if hope was beginning to wane within him. These characters, be it known, are the signals by which an office is called, and mean "Philadelphia! Philadelphia! Philadelphia! Are you ready to take a message from me?" Replying immediately to his call, I found that the friends of the dying girl, moved by her constant wailing for a brother, who, by some peculiar sympathies, had become especially dear to her, and who, not receiving any reply to her message, had shown signs of deep despondency, had come to the office and besought Mr. Beatty to make the effort, thus apparently so providentially successful. Gladdened by the singular coincidence, I immediately gave information of my delivery of the message, and my belief that the request of the sufferer would be answered by the speedy arrival of her brother in the night train.

And do you think we took no pleasure in our work, ye sellers of tape and sugar? Was there not, good Joseph, a kind streak of peculiar sunshine pass athwart that generous paunch of thine in thus ministering to the relief of human sorrow, especially when the subject of it was young and beautiful? Even over our lean and cadaverous features a smile of warm complacency, and a certain gentleness and approvingness about the heart, richly repaid me for my weary and stormy journey; nor did I seek to repress an uprising prayer to Him who smoothes the couch of earthly sorrow and gilds it with the luster of the better land, that life might be prolonged until the longed-for union of those loving hearts.

Oh! how sweet came sleep that night! Did it not come to thee, kind Joe, like gentle rain upon the tender herb, albeit thine herbage numbered so many years? Did not the smile, the kind, grateful smile of that pretty child close gently thine eyelids even as the summer's breath at eve closes the corolla of the gentle flowers—those delicate eyes of thine, Joe, that love so much to have the smile of beauty rest thereon? And those thankful, loving orbs, pictured to our imagination by a busy though fanciful pencil, closed ours also, and we sunk to rest at night's silent noon as if the sounds of softest music, heard from afar o'er Borneo's smoothest bosom was lulling us to repose.

CHAPTER V.

"Atoms and thoughts are used again, mixing in varied combinations;
And though, by molding them anew thou makest them thine own,
Yet have they served thousands, and all their merit is of God."—*Tupper.*

MANY months after all this had occurred, and other things had excluded it from my memory, I was walking on Chestnut Street, Philadelphia, accompanied by a friend, in the mutual enjoyment of an evening of peculiar tranquillity, when my eye fell upon the features of a lady and gentleman slowly approaching us, with whom my mind endeavored, but in vain, to associate some recollection of a past acquaintance.

They seemed engrossed in a quiet, meditative conversation, their eyes looking downward, but both countenances glowing with an unspeakable calmness and repose, as if heaven dwelt within, and conveying the impression of the meaning of those beautiful words which speak of the possession of a "peace which passeth all understanding." The features of the gentleman were especially familiar to me. Yet I racked the dusty corners of my memory in vain to assure myself of an acquaintance. He was dressed with much plainness but true elegance; his costume, however, bearing a very subordinate part in my observation. After resting upon the strongly-marked yet delicately defined lines of sympathy around his eyes, forehead, and the corners of the mouth, my heart bounded to him as to a brother; and as they passed me, and I could but just hear him say: "Yes, Mary, that was a dark night to us all," the

occurrence to which I have before alluded broke at once upon me, and I remembered the night in which I became a messenger-boy, and saw for the first time James Mornington, his pretty little wife, and mother. It was certainly he—I could not be mistaken.

But who was she who thus so closely resembled him in the winsomeness of her pale features, the interesting gentleness of whose countenance had, even more than his own, riveted my attention, and caused a momentary throb of deep personal interest, as if some kindred spirit had magnetized me with its presence.

Mary! That was the name of my first-born, the most beautiful name given to womankind—a name associated with woman's sincerity and purity—with childhood's loveliness and affection. It was the name of that sister, too, whose dying request had so excited my interest and roused my sympathies. Was this that sister restored from the very ebbings of the tide of life? All the power of a woman's curiosity was upon me, and so much engrossed had I become, that I had paid no notice to the request of my friend to enlighten him as to the cause of my silence and abstraction.

We continued our walk away to the Schuylkill, enjoying the cheerful, elegant quiet that pervaded that part of the city, and the weather, which was most delightful, our conversation dwelling much on the circumstances which I had just narrated, and which had awakened within the highly religious and intelligent sympathies of my friend the source of much elevated thought and comment, to which I became a pleased and gratified listener.

"Every day's experience," said Wardlaw, "induces me to note an overruling Providence in the most minor events of life. The thought which induces a charity is a whisper of the spirit to my heart. The reception of that charity is, mayhap, an era in the life of the beneficiary, a rainbow on his pathway, brightening his future and kindling an undying hope. When, also, in the performance of accustomed duty, untoward circumstances arrest the hand, and render futile the best-laid designs, I have seen the imagined evil so often the precursor of unexpected pleasure, that God seems to guide the very cup from which I drink, even as He seems to guide the trickling waters that the dew-drops form in the valley and flow onward to the great ocean, where all the world's streams unite."

"Yes," replied I, "and I have often thought how strangely a passing thought, arrested, leads to the most wondrous results. The falling of an apple leading Newton to the gigantic truth of scientific discovery, on which are based the pillars of the world; the boiling of a kettle leading to the surprising appliances of steam. And the idea that a thought like that which passed through Morse's mind, perhaps in some lonely hour, when no human voice was near him, or away out on the deep sea, tossed about upon its billows, should be now the promising sustenance of so many families, with the prospect of thousands feeding by its mechanical use, aside from the conveniences it is introducing into society, fills me, at times, with emotions of awe at the contemplation of the hidden agencies around me."

"Well, Reid," replied Wardlaw, "your business interests me more than anything on which my mind has recently dwelt. Morse's application of the magnetic force is certainly a most simple one, and for that reason likely to be useful. I should glory in being the possessor of such a thought; but I regard him honored, chiefly, as the medium by which one of the grand providences by which the condition of our race is elevated has been introduced. If he is a right-minded man, he will feel so, and the influence of a mind so impressed will add much to the luster which its future use will reflect upon him."

"I am inclined to believe," I replied, "that Morse so regards it, and I am also impressed with the dignity of its uses and the pleasure of its extension, if confided to suitable hands, who will guard its development from the abuses to which it must be peculiarly subject.

Already the great advantage those who use it have over those who do not is remarkable. Sales are now made in distant places in an hour, involving large and quick profits; and in what I have been telling you of the couple who passed us, you see how wonderfully it is to affect social life."

"I want you to learn the result of that circumstance," eagerly rejoined Wardlaw; "your connection with it will easily place you in the way to learn all its details. Be assured there is a spring of pleasure there in which I would be glad to be a sharer, but which I have a keen curiosity to know."

"That is my determination," I replied, "and I feel assured that my curiosity will be met with respect and kindness, or I much mistake the parties concerned in it. After supper this evening I will call, and with as little intrusiveness as possible divulge my object, and to-morrow we will meet again, and you will know all."

On returning, thus deeply and pleasantly engaged, and just as we were about to turn the corner at Thirteenth Street, we saw the object of our conversation coming up Chestnut Street, and, what was particularly pleasing to me, Mornington had evidently recognized me, and seemed to be speaking of me to his companion. Their eyes were both directed toward me, and Wardlaw and I agreed to keep on toward them.

On approaching, Mornington's face smiled in recognition, and I at once advanced with outstretched hand to join him in salutation.

"I am very pleased to see you," Mornington said; "your visit to us on that stormy night is associated with very pleasant recollections. Sister Mary, dear," he added, "this is the gentleman who delivered that message of which we have spoken so much," and we were thus introduced to each other in a manner leading directly to the object of my curiosity. My friend Wardlaw was also introduced, and at once a circle of sympathy seemed established.

It would please me very much," Miss Mornington replied, "to meet one who has, unconsciously, perhaps, saved my life, and restored me to this kind brother of mine, and to my dear mother. We are now near home; if you will accept our invitation to a simple supper with us, we will be delighted to have you and your friend join us, and we can also then express our gratitude more fully. Come."

This was said with so much frankness and sincerity, that we accepted the unexpected request, and were soon ushered into a beautiful residence not far from where the welcome invitation was given.

CHAPTER VI.

" 'Twas to thy hearth, domestic happiness,
  Where, in the sunshine of a peaceful home,
  Love's choicest roses bud, and burst, and bloom."

THE circumstances of the family had much changed since I first saw them. A large legacy had fallen to young Mornington, which justified the purchase of the beautiful mansion into which we were now introduced. It was furnished with simple but elegant furniture. All the arrangements indicated a refinement which made prosperity come to the Morningtons with a quiet pleasure and adaptation to their new condition. Such only enjoy the elegancies of life. The unrefined, uneducated, who come suddenly upon wealth, often find these elegancies sources of sorrow. Home is filled with expensive ornaments, but the mind has no unison or congeniality with them. In this case it was otherwise. Affluence found the Morningtons a family adapted to the unexcited indulgence of their new circumstances. Everything was suitable, and well arranged, and beautiful. As I entered I saw that same bright-eyed little wife arranging late flowers in a vase near the window, the beauty of whose tints were nothing lovelier than those which bloomed upon her own sweet face.

To both her and the aged mother of Mornington we were kindly introduced, the old lady at once remembering me. and entering into the details of my visit with a gratified recollection, which promised a quick solution of the matter. She immediately related to us as follows:

"My daughter Mary here, dear child, was the same who lay so ill at Wilmington, and who so anxiously asked to see her brother. We knew how delicate she was, and little expected to see her pleasant face again. One remembrance only sustained us. We knew she was ready to blossom in that better land where sorrow comes no more. She trusted in the Redeemer. That hope united us. This was a pleasant consciousness, even amid the agony of parting. Yet it was very hard to think of her being so far from us, with none of us present to cheer the last hours. She felt so too, and this rendered the expected approach of death less tranquil.

"After the message was sent she seemed calm, but receiving no reply, and having no assurance of the coming of any of the family, she yielded to despondency, from which she was, late in the evening, partially aroused by a communication you sent after seeing us, and which was deemed by the friends at Wilmington an act of very unexpected kindness, both on your part and on that of the gentleman there.

"The hours wore gradually away, but no train arrived at the time expected. The cars ran off the track near Darby, detaining them an hour and a half. The delay threw Mary into a deeper melancholy than before, and death seemed very near. In the half delirious state this found her, she gave way to the sorrow of her heart, and exclaimed:

"'No, no, no! I will see them no more; they are all gone—gone;' and her head sunk in death-like stillness upon her pillow. It was thought that a few moments would close the scene, when James arrived, greatly excited by his delay.

"Seeing the friends weeping around, and supposing that all was really over, he rushed to the bed, and exclaiming, in great agony of mind, 'My poor, poor sister,' kissed her fervently, and gazed on her pale features with all the passionate affection with which he regarded her.

"That agony saved her life. She started from the death-like stupor into which she had fallen, recalled, as it were, to life by the sound of a voice so dear to her, clasped her arms for a moment wildly around his neck, and, murmuring his name, fell back again, exhausted, on her pillow.

"The attending physician arrived just as this occurred, and intimated that this excitement might, with great care, be productive of happy results. He advised the withdrawal of all the friends except her brother, who sat by her bedside, watching with intense emotion every variation of the features of the sufferer.

"By morning the crisis had passed. The poor child opened her eyes, and found her brother holding her hand in his, and from that moment the work of restoration began. Her recovery was very slow, but there she sits, spared to us, we trust, for many years to come. In our conversations respecting her sickness, we often ascribe her recovery, under Him who holds human destiny in the hollow of His hand, to the use of the telegraph. It must be a deep source of gratification to you, sir, to have been thus instrumental in securing us this great happiness, and for which, we assure you, you have our deep gratitude."

I replied expressive of the happiness I felt in having thus unconsciously contributed to the happiness of so loving a family, and in the restoration of one so worthy of life. It added a new tie to the business I had chosen, and I trusted that it might be the means of enlarging the amount of human happiness. I trembled when I thought how nearly an unfaithful messenger had plunged an amiable circle into sorrows which might have robbed it of its chief charms, and left it desolate.

After a pleasant supper and a delightful hour spent with this affectionate family, to whom I had become thus singularly attached, we bade them, amid many kind words, and a cordial invitation to call again, a kind farewell, and retired to our apartments to dream over the telegraph in its new vocation as the restorer to life of sweet Mary Mornington.

"'Tis Better to have Loved and Lost."

SUCH a sweet, little darling she was. Those large lustrous eyes, and that beautiful golden hair were fast laying their weight on my susceptible heart, and when she stepped up to the counter and "desired to send a telegram" I swallowed a nickel's worth of masticated cavendish, fell over the message boy's three legged stool, and—handed her a blank. It was only a few words to her friend at Beeville, "Am tired. Will be there to night." Oh! that such an angel should suffer and be tired. It was too bad, but—"How much is it?" recalled me to earth. "Forty cents," I muttered, with a dim idea that filthy lucre was out of place in connection with this innocent, artless being. "The telegraph is a wonderful thing," she said, "I should like so much to see it work," and, transported to the seventh heaven at the opportunity to form her acquaintance, I offered to initiate her as far as possible into the mysteries of the art. Everything was so strange, so new to her. It was beyond her comprehension, and *four* wires! How *could* a person look after so many! I explained it all, the use of each key, each button, each wire, and when with a fond, grateful look she withdrew to the passengers' waiting room, I felt that I had conquered, made a deep impression, and touched the secret spring of her heart.

I was brushing the soil from my No. 10's preparatory to asking her address and permission to call, when one of the boys came in. "Has that girl been talking to you?" "She has," I replied, with dignity. "What about?" I told him. He rolled over, and for five minutes I supposed him crazy. Then I could understand amid his peals of laughter, "Why, you blamed fool! That's Mrs. D's cousin. She's an old telegrapher from down east." In the agony of the next half hour I received the following: "Sulphur Springs, 18th, to J. B. Dellwood, Cherokee. The odor smothers health. Improving none. Water rising, (signed) Jim." Mr. Dellwood wanted a better version, and I tried it again. It came, "Theodore's mother's health improving. No new arrivals, [signed] Jim." Frailty thy name is woman.

THE discipline of railroad, steamboat, and telegraph companies is not calculated to inspire much reverence for the Sabbath among their employés. It was on Sunday that the events which I am about to narrate transpired.

It was in the spring time. The balmy southern breeze had driven away winter's frost and snows. The fresh grass, the buds and blossoms, and the opening leaves hinted at the wealth which Nature had in store, so soon to be revealed. The birds sang their sweetest anthem song, and, above all, the bright, warm sun, so refreshing after a winter of dreary length, lured to the open air.

It was in the year when the Chicago and Northwestern was the only railway running into Council Bluffs, and the Union Pacific Road, still uncompleted, was being pushed with astonishing vigor toward the Golden State.

To those familiar with the rich, black soil of Western Iowa, which borders on the Missouri River, it will be a relief to know that the genial rays of the sun had dissipated the moisture of the rainy season, and made prairie navigation possible.

The big Missouri, however, in response to the mountain freshets thousands of miles away, was overflowing its banks, and threatened a universal flood on the bottom lands. That swift-running, muddy, mighty and fickle stream was transferring hundreds of acres of land from the Iowa to the Nebraska shore without so much as a "by your leave" to the former occupants.

A few months before, the Union Pacific people had put down a telegraph cable diagonally across the Missouri River, for the purpose of maintaining communication between their terminus in Nebraska and the Chicago and Northwestern Railway in Iowa, where they had a large accumulation of materials and stores.

The river, true to its antecedents, had buried one end of this cable beneath a sand-bar, and, by means of snags and wash-outs had destroyed the other.

In hopes that something could be done to regain the cable, and in any event to decide what to do, the writer was in hasty route for the scene of disaster.

In his company was a gentleman so full of energy as to constitute a whole town in himself, and whether dispatching trains, managing a telegraph circuit, running a hotel, or driving a team, he always wanted to handle the reins.

It was well into the morning when the train reached Council Bluffs, and without delay we hastened to a livery stable to secure a buggy and span for an expedition a few miles up the river.

As the location was unknown, the necessity of a guide presented itself, and none better could be thought of than the manager of the city telegraph office.

· He bore the same name as the inventor of the American telegraph system, and was the manager both for the express and telegraph companies. His ability and enterprise have since been recognized by a prominent Western railroad, which made him its general Western agent, and his future career is well assured.

It did not take long to drive to his house, but he had gone to church, where we soon followed. As the matter was urgent, we coaxed the sexton to call him out, and after a hurried consultation with his wife, he appeared in a fine broad-cloth suit, as handsome a man as could be found in the State of Iowa. On explaining our mission, he promptly consented to go, and jumped in with us.

It was suggested that the new-comer had better drive, on account of his familiarity with the scene of action, but our friend, who was fond of holding the reins, persisted in his ability to do the right thing, and was finally permitted, much to our future discomfort. While the road continued on the prairie no obstacles were encountered, but when we were obliged to go on the bottom lands the progress was slow and difficult. The road proper had been washed away, and a path must be picked as best it could from the most favorable ground some distance back from the river.

We at length came to a little knoll, from the top of which our destination could be seen.

While our attention was taken away the horses started down hill on a trot, and in a moment we found ourselves mired to the hub in a horrible hole.

We sprang out instantly, jack-knives in hand, to cut brush and throw under the horses to keep them from miring beyond help, and, after two hours' hard work, rescued the team from its predicament.

But what a spectacle did the three young men present, who prided themselves on their personal toilet, and who started out so recently with so gay a rig?

Besmeared from head to foot with mud, fatigued and disgusted, we nevertheless commenced a faithful, though unsuccessful, search for the missing cable.

As we were about turning away the city manager determined to make one last attempt, and started on a short cut for a sand-bar, which promised a favorable out-look.

Suddenly the baked-clay crust on which he ran gave way, and left him floundering waist deep in Missouri River mud.

Dear reader, did you ever walk with a friend who suddenly sat down in a public place without premeditation, and not laugh at his misfortune?

Did you ever see a silk hat blown along by a ten-knot breeze, followed by its owner in close pursuit, and not laugh at the sight?

Did you ever witness the comical side of a misfortune to any human being and not give way temporarily to hilarity?

Then pardon the writer and his companion, for when they saw the ludicrous situation of their comrade they roared with laughter, and, had his life depended on it, could have rendered no assistance.

A madder man never issued from the slough of despond, but he was not to be disturbed in his self-possession.

Calmly viewing the sky above, the river beneath, and his own condition, he remarked

> Earth hath no charms
> To lure me to her breast;
> Lest we meet further harm,
> We'll let the cable rest.

At this unexpected outburst there was a general hand-shaking, and when composure was regained we mounted into the vehicle, homeward bound.

To return by the way of entrance was impracticable, and an attempt was made to pass through the river timber, in which we soon became entangled.

Fortunately a gentleman, who is now general superintendent of a Texas railway, was near at hand, superintending a gang of men who were clearing a new landing for the Union Pacific transfer boats.

On learning our predicament he sent a force to extricate our team and escort us to terra-firma, for which he received our everlasting thanks and gratitude.

It was at dusk when our forlorn expedition, with its jaded horses, wrecked buggy, and disconsolate passengers approached the limits of Council Bluffs.

In the darkness it was difficult to discern our exact whereabouts, and, drawing up in a favorable spot, the welcome approach of strangers was awaited to acquire information.

Presently two travelers were hailed. They drew near, and having closely inspected our condition, the spokesman said:

"Hic, hic. We're drunk; but—hic, hic—not so drunk as you be!"

This was the crowning climax of the day's proceedings.

That this trio, who boasted of their temperate habits, should be charged with beastly intoxication, was the last straw which broke the camel's back.

We proceeded on in sadness, and, after much preambulation, deposited our friend at his own door. What his reception was has ever remained a secret.

Whether his wife upbraided him for the desertion of the morning, and reviled him for his present state, or whether she soothed and comforted him till self-respect returned, is not for us to know.

Who carries the talisman with which to unlock the domestic drama to open view?

Memory recalls a lady, reared in luxury, suddenly deprived of friends and money, who nobly earned her own and her sister's livelihood. She afterward married the husband of her choice.

He became prosperous, but with success there came neglect, fretfulness, and sometimes scorn.

Though he returned at all hours and in all moods, she ever met him with a smile and the tenderest sympathy for weeks and months and years.

At length misfortune overtook him, and he learned that a woman's love is worth more than all the world beside. Thus did she triumph, and the sweetest joy reigned where might have been the blackest woe.

May blessings ever throng upon her pathway—but pardon the digression.

The Western Union master withstood the freshet, and by the magnanimity of that company a wire across the Missouri was speedily secured for railroad use, so that, in spite of the disastrous expedition, the final success atoned in a measure for its misfortunes.

Since that memorable occasion, however, our faith in the old adage that "the better the day the better the deed," has been much shaken, and old and young are advised to consider well their ways, for you know not when to expect a snag.

How a Signal Service Man Lost his Sweetheart.

THE following rather romantic episode, connected with the life of one of the most prominent officials of the Signal Service Bureau, is another of the instances of education completely subduing the natural propensities of man. This officer, our informant states, was at one time engaged to be married to a beautiful young lady, and the evening before that set for their marriage called on her. They were seated on the sofa in the parlor, the gas was turned down to a twilight strength, and they were talking in the usually low tones peculiar to lovers before marriage of the future, which seemed to be " all so bright" before them. Suddenly the young lady said—

" Albert, dearest, there is one thing I wish you to do when we are married."

" Name it, pet," he replied, in his most encouraging tones, and at the same time giving her such a squeeze that she imagined her corsets were a mile too large for her.

"Well, my darling, I wish to have no rain on Mondays; because, you know, my dearest, that on Mondays we cleanse our linen, and if our things are not washed and dried on those days one entire week's work is so fearfully set back. You will grant me this one request? "

" Maud," he replied, gazing into the depths of her dark blue eyes, and dallying with her golden ringlets, " Maud, dearest, my duty to my country imperatively demands that I shall ' whoop-em-up,' so to speak, the precise sort of weather that heaven will probably send impartially during the succeeding twenty-four hours, upon the just as well as the unjust, without regard to age, sex, or previous condition of servitude. If an area of low barometer exists in the Northwestern States on Monday, how can I, consistently with my duty, declare that the indications favor clear weather, with light winds from the southeast? No, angel; ask me anything but that. I love thee, dear, so much, but I love my honor more."

" Then you don't love me; no, not a single bit," she replied, between her sobs, and the tears fell thick and fast as she pleaded with him to change his stern resolve. The struggle between love and duty was a fearful one, but his military teaching left him but one path to pursue, and he chose his duty. It is easy to imagine the results—a sudden coolness, quarrel, breaking off of the engagement and the meteorologist heart. She returned his numerous presents, letters, etc., and is now lecturing on woman's rights; while he, a confirmed misogynist, sits up, and on Sunday nights at the Signal Office with fiendish glee makes up the indications for Monday. He takes especial pleasure in announcing for that day falling barometer, atmospheric disturbances, heavy rains in the lower lake region, high winds from the northwest, and so on through the entire category of unfavorable meteorological nomenclature.

Manager's Out.

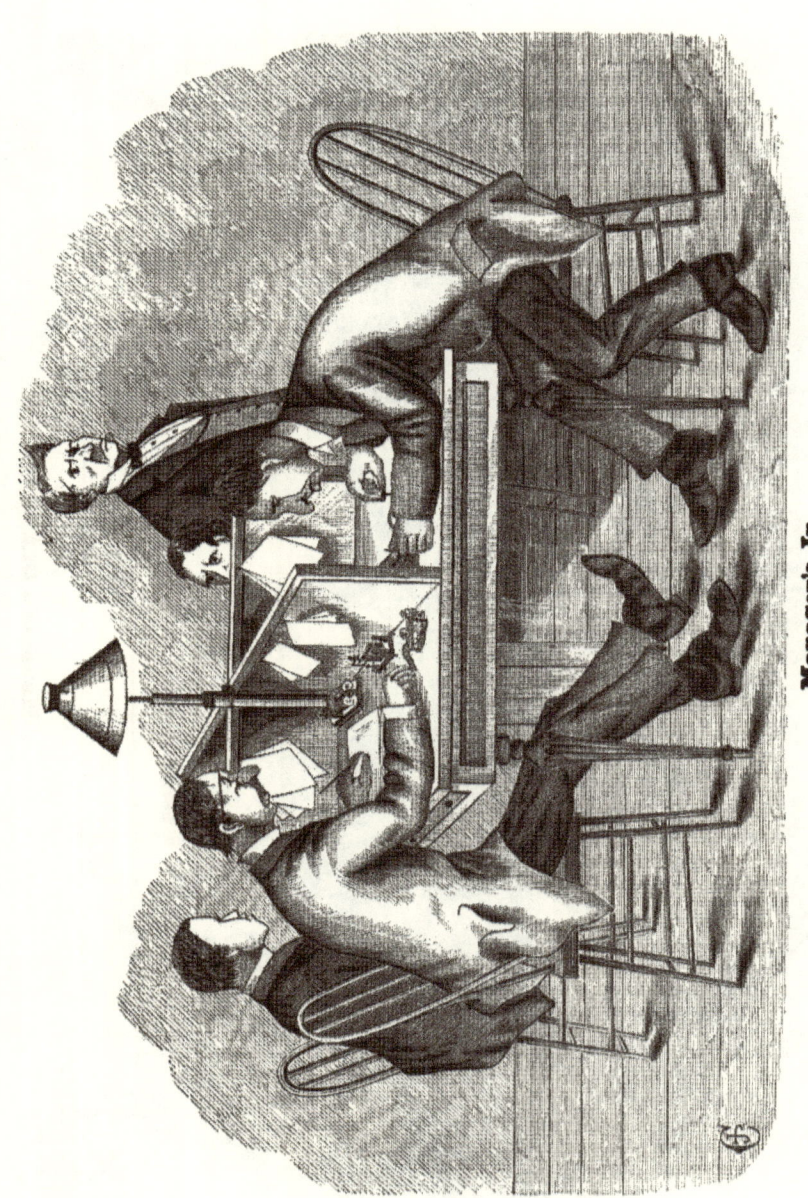

Manager's In.

Into the Jaws of Death.

A TELEGRAPH OPERATOR'S STORY.

"Want a yarn, eh?" said my friend, Erhardt, as he tipped his chair back and deposited his number sixes upon my operating table. "Well, I am afraid you have applied at the wrong window, young man. There never was a much worse hand at telling stories. I have had in my life but one experience which was at all remarkable, and I think I have told you of that."

"Your adventure with the highwaymen in the depot here? No, you have never told me about it. I have heard the station agent speak of the affair once, but that is all. Tell me the whole story."

Erhardt was an ex-operator and the cashier of the H— bank, a solid, substantial institution, the repository of the savings of the farmers for miles around, and which, in its way, transacted more business than many of its more pretentious city prototypes.

He was waiting at the depot to meet a friend expected on the milk train, which, as usual, was a trifle over four hours late. He had expressed a proper amount of disgust on the receipt of this information, and finally took a chair in my office to wait. It was a cold, blustering night; the wind howled without, and my fire (of old railroad ties) roared and leaped in its cast-iron prison.

"If I *must* wait here for that confounded slow coach, I might as well spend the time in that way as any. I like to hear myself talk pretty well." And he settled himself in his chair and lighted a cigar.

"It was some seven or eight years ago, 1867, I think, that I was sent to open the office here. I remember a little interview I had with the superintendent just before I started. I was a little wild in those days, and had just returned from a week's fun.

"'Erhardt,' he said, 'I will give you just one more chance. I am going to send you down to H—. If you behave yourself there, and show that you have any of the true stuff in you, I will give you a better position in time. If not, I shall wash my hands of you, and you will receive no more employment from this company.'

"He looked after me somewhat regretfully, I imagined, as I went out. I think he was inclined to like me, but my conduct made it impossible for him to show me much favor.

"Well, I came down here and opened this office. Telegraphing was more of a curiosity then than it is now, and I found myself regarded as a sort of lion by the people here. I was then a first-classer, and could take my forty words a minute as easily as any one. Had it not been for my frisky habits I would probably at that time have graced some large office.

"I now tried hard to be steady and sober, and really succeeded very well. I struck up an acquaintance with the station agent here, who was a steady, thorough-going young fellow and an excellent companion. He was greatly taken with the mysteries of telegraphy. Very much to his delight, I offered to teach him, and had soon transformed him into a very tolerable plug. He read very well—much better than he could write. I very quickly saw that Mason had in him the material for an excellent operator. He had a keen sense of humor, and we were eternally playing jokes on each other, which were always taken in good part.

"About fifty miles further down the road was a small office in charge of a Miss Annie L—. I introduced Mason to her over the wire, and they practiced together a great deal. Mason was a little the best receiver, and somehow managed to spend very much of his time retailing to her that ineffable nonsense which is so interesting to the participants, and such idiotic bosh to outsiders.

"I looked upon all this with considerable amusement, not, perhaps, unmixed with a spice of envy. They took so much pleasure in conversing with each other that I felt called upon to interfere. But how?

"One day I fell into a brown study—determined to do *something*. The result of my cogitations was that I rummaged in my 'local' closet and produced an old antiquated Morse key which I had brought to H— with me, thinking, perhaps, it might be of use. This I proceeded to fix up in a corner under my table, connecting it to the main line precisely as my other key was connected. My table stood against the wall, directly under a window, and it was so dark underneath that there was absolutely no danger of discovery. Then, at odd times, when Mason was not around, I practiced sending *with my foot*. I found the process of writing in that manner not half so difficult as one would suppose. I had bent the circuit closer so that I could move it easily, and the rest was merely a matter of practice. I persevered until I grew quite proficient in this novel method of transmission. My foot-writing, so to speak, sounded remarkably like Miss L—'s style!

"It was not more than a day or two after I had decided that my foot was sufficiently versed in the new art to commence business, that an opportunity presented itself. It was after supper. The last train but one had passed. There were in those days very few passengers by the milk train, and H— was not a milk station, so Mason did not wait for it. He slammed his ticket window down, shut up his safe, and then came to my desk, leaned over, saw that the wire was quiet, opened the key, and commenced calling 'Ax, Ax, Ax—M.' Her private call. Now was my chance!

"'I, I, Ax,' answered my pedal extremity.

"'G. E. Isn't it a beautiful evening?—M.'

"'Good eve. Yes, delightful. I am going to take a walk after I have closed up the office.—Ax,' I answered.

"'What are you doing this evening?—M.'

"'I have just finished my book, and have nothing to do until I close.—Ax.'

"It must be remembered that my mischievous foot took the part of 'Ax' in this conversation.

"'Good.' (Draws up a chair.) 'Then we will have a little chat. What have you been reading to-day?—M.'

"'The Moonstone. Do you know, I believe I have the gift of second sight! I fancy I see you. Yes, I can see you! You are leaning upon a table; now you have arisen. You have on a blue suit, with a black necktie, and gold watch chain. You had a straw hat on your head, but have just taken it off.'

"At these details, which were, of course, exactly correct, Mason's face assumed a look of extreme astonishment, mouth and eyes wide open, resembling nothing so much as an exaggerated exclamation point.

"'Now you have taken out your handkerchief and wiped your forehead. Your personal appearance would be much improved by closing your mouth.'

"Mason shut it with a snap, then tried to say something and failed.

"'Yes, that is better. If you only would not stare so —'

"Mason siezed his hat and dashed out of the office as if the evil one were after him, not even bidding me good night.

"I laid back in my chair and laughed until I was weak. My attention was attracted to the sounder by hearing 'R' (the largest city on the line, thirty miles, above H—), calling furiously. I answered and was rewarded by—

"'I wish to Heaven you would stop that nonsense and attend to business. Ahr, 21.—R.

'To J. R. C—, Pres. H— Bank:

'The bullion has arrived. Do you wish it sent by milk train to-night? I shall not send it unless I receive direct orders at once.   Wm. K—.
'25 paid, 95.   Cashier R— Bank.'

"I copied the message, inclosed it in an envelope, directed it, and called the freight-house porter who was in the outer room.

"'Be sure and get an answer, William,' I said.

"'Faith, I will,' he replied.

"I followed him to the door. The moon had gone down, and it had grown very dark. The station was about half a mile from the village, and I could just see the lights of the nearest house nearly that distance away. It was not built up then as it is now. The situation was certainly a very lonesome one, but I did not feel at all afraid though now alone in the station.

"In about half an hour William returned.

"'Rather a lonely walk, William,' I said.

"'Yis, sur,' he answered. 'I came back across the fields and so shortened it.'

"Which, in all human probability, saved his life!

"I tore the envelope containing the answer open and read it.

"'You can go home now, William,' I said. The message read:

'To Wm. K—, Cashier R— Bank:
'No; do not send the bullion to-night. I will give you further orders to-morrow as to its disposition.   J. R. C—, Pres.'

"I had checked the message, and, standing by the table, had stretched out my hand to the key to call 'R,' when an arm was roughly thrown around me, pinning my hands to my sides, and I felt the pressure of cold steel on my temple.

"'Move, shout, or speak but a single word and I will blow your brains out,' said a harsh, determined voice in a low tone.

"I am as brave, perhaps, as most men, yet I confess I was thoroughly frightened—scared almost to death.

"I could hear the muffled tramp of men in the room. One of them blew out my kerosene lamp, and turned a dark lantern so that it shone in my eyes and almost blinded me. Another man, low in statue, but short and thick set, with a long beard, and a mask over the upper part of his face, placed himself directly in front of me and produced a pair of handcuffs which he secured upon my wrists. My arms were then released by the man who had held them. He with the beard, who seemed to be the leader of the gang, then, by the light of the lantern, hunted over the table until he found the message, which he read and carefully placed in his breast pocket.

"'You are sure this message has not been sent?' he said, addressing another of the gang.

"'I know it has not,' was the answer. 'He was just getting ready to send it when we entered.'

"'Very good. Now,' he said, turning to me, 'I want you to understand that we are going to secure the treasure which was to have been sent down from R— to-night, and you will help us. If you have any objections this little persuader will silence them.' As he spoke he tapped the butt of a revolver which projected from his pocket.

"He took up a pencil and proceeded to write a message on a soft sheet. While he was thus employed I took occasion to glance around. There were eight men in the room, all of whom wore masks similar to that worn by their leader. I could just make out their forms in the dim light. A hand dropped upon my shoulder showed me that even the turning of my head had been observed.

"'There,' the leader said, 'you will send that instead of the other message.'

"He held the sheet up before me. It read:

'To WM. K—, CASHIER R— BANK:
'Yes, send the bullion by the milk train to-night without fail. My cashier with a guard will be at the station to receive it.   J. R. C—, Pres.'

"I looked down at my manacled wrists. The irons were heavy, and the chain connecting the two rings not more than three inches long.

"'I can't send it with these on,' I muttered.

"'You *must!*' said the chief, grimly.

"I meekly resolved to try. Taking up a pencil I managed to count the words and scrawl the check on the message with some difficulty. I was going to remark, from force of habit, that it should be written on a message blank under the conditions, but bethought myself in time.

"'Stop—what is that?' said the chief, pointing to the check.

"'The number of words and the amount paid,' I answered.

"'Is this necessary?' he asked of the man to whom he had spoken before.

"'Yes, sir. It is all right. They call it the check, and put it on every message.'

"'Very well then, go ahead. This man is an operator; he will watch you closely, and at the first sign of treachery I will put a bullet through your head. Smith, stand out of range, or you may get a taste of it, too.'

"I sat down at the table—he pushing the chair closer. Opening the key I commenced calling 'R.' I again felt the cold barrel of the revolver on my forehead, and it made me so nervous that I could hardly manipulate the key. 'R' answered.

"'That is good,' said the man addressed as Smith, who was the operator.

"'Send slow. I can't read fast writing,' he added. I proceeded very slowly, and Smith pronounced each word as I made it. The leader glanced alternately at Smith and myself uneasily. It was evi-

dent that this was the crisis of their bold conspiracy. 'R' broke me in the middle of the message, wanting to know why the deuce I sent so slowly. I closed the key and took my hand away nervously.

"'What did he say,' demanded the leader.

"'He wanted to know why I did not send faster,' I said.

"'Tell him you have a sore finger,' said Smith. I spelt this lie out slowly, Smith reading it aloud, then went on and finished the message. 'R' gave a sharp and distinct 'O K,' which the renegade operator read aloud. The leader gave a sigh of relief, which I promptly echoed as he removed the pistol barrel from my head. He then unlocked one of the handcuffs, removed it, placed my hands behind my back and reclasped the ring around my wrist, thus rendering me perfectly helpless.

"There was nothing to be done now except to wait. The men disposed themselves on the chairs around the room, the leader still guarding me, revolver in hand.

"As I thought over the events of the last half hour I was filled with rage at the dastardly deed I had been compelled to commit. This money, which would now fall into the hands of these miscreants, was the property of honest farmers, widows, and orphans. And I had assisted to rob them! Better far to have sacrificed my life, if unharmed, how could I ever hold up my head again? Oh, that I had refused to be their tool! Was there no way to undo what I had done?

"Stop! *The key under the table!* Why had I not thought of it before? I opened it with my foot and made a few dots.

"'What is that?' said the leader.

"'Only some one practicing,' I answered, readily. He looked at Smith, who nodded.

"I called 'R' rapidly.

"'What did he say then?'

"'Pacticing the letter 'O,' sir,' I answered, glibly. 'Do you wish me to read aloud all that passes over the wire?'

"'No, it is not necessary,' said the chief.

"'I can read most of it,' said Smith, giving me a penetrative glance.

"I had my own reasons for doubting this statement. 'R' answered. I said, writing as rapidly as I could under the circumstances;

"'Has that message been delivered yet?'

"'Yes—long ago.'

"'Then go after it and stop it. *That bullion must not be sent to-night.*'

"His key opened and remained so for nearly five minutes; then it closed, and he said:

"'All right—the bullion will not go. What is the matter?'

"'The matter is that this office is full of armed highwaymen. I was forced to send that message with a loaded revolver at my forehead.'

"'Good Heavens! Wait a minute.'

"I turned and met the eye of the robber chief. I could not help smiling sarcastically.

"He was on his feet in an instant.

"'By G—d,' he said, 'if you have played us any trick, young fellow, you will pay for it with your life.'

"'He has not said a word,' remarked Smith.

"'It is well for him,' said the leader. 'If that bullion arrives all right you will be released uninjured. If it fails to come, or if there is a sign of treachery, your corpse will be found on the floor to-morrow morning with your brains spattered on that wall.' I shudered at this picture, which was beginning to loom up as a black reality before me.

"'The chief of police is here,' ticked out the sounder, 'and wants to know how you are situated.'

"'My hands are handcuffed behind me, and a man sits at my side with a loaded and cocked revolver,' I answered.

"'Thunder! Then how can you send?'

"'I am sending with my foot on a concealed key under the table, which was rigged up to play a joke on Mason.'

"'What can be done to save you?'

"'Nothing; but capture these robbers if possible. When does the train leave?'

"'In ten minutes.'

"'Then hold it. There are eight heavily armed burglars here. Better have twenty-five or thirty well armed men on the train. Let it stop just above, on the curve, and have them walk down and surround the station.'

"'R's' key opened a moment, then he said: 'It will be done. What will they do to you?'

"'I am doomed—will probably be shot the very first thing. But some one will swing for it.'

"'Good God!' said 'R.' 'Is there no help?'

"'No—none. I would like to have you bid Mr. —— (the Superintendent) good-by for me. Tell him I had resolved to live a better life. And tell Mason in the morning of the trick I played on him.'

"'I will—I will. Is there nothing else?'

"'No. I had better stop now or I may arouse suspicion. Good-bye.'

"'What is all this about?' demanded the leader of the highwaymen.

"'A couple of students practicing,' I said wearily.

"A deep silence followed, broken at last by the sounder ticking out: 'The train has just left with twenty-eight policemen and citizens aboard.'

"'O K,' I answered.

"It would make the run in forty or forty-five minutes.

"A distant church bell chimed out eleven o'clock. Where would I be at twelve?

"The time wore heavily away. I reviewed my past life. So far as I knew I had never harmed any one. Surely the manner of my death would atone for some at least of my sins. Whatever was before me I was prepared for.

"I had not a relative living. No one, excepting, perhaps, Mason, would mourn me. Well perhaps it was best so.

"'The train is due in ten minutes,' said Smith.

"Just at that moment I caught a sound which escaped the less practiced ears of my companions. The train had arrived and stopped at the curve!

"My blood coursed like wild-fire through my veins; my heart thumped against my side as though it would force its way out. Every nerve was alive with anticipation.

"It came at last. Both doors of the station were burst in with a tremendous crash—a wild rush was made for the inside office—a loud voice exclaimed:

"'Surrender, in the name of the law!'

"'Betrayed!' shouted the leader. He placed the barrel of the revolver to my ear—the hammer fell with a dull thud. It had missed fire! With a curse he raised it in the air and brought it down upon my head—a bright flash passed before my eyes, the room sank away from me, and all was oblivion.

* * * * * * *

"'I think he looks a little better, Dr. Thorne,' said a sweet voice. I opened my eyes.

"'Where am I?' I said. My voice was feeble and weak.

"'You must not talk. You are in the hands of friends, and all is well.'

"I soon found that I was in the house of the president of the bank, and that the young lady was his daughter, Miss Marion C—.

"Nursed by such hands my recovery was rapid. When able to get around I was provided with a clerkship in the bank, whence I have risen to my present position.

"The eight highwaymen were all captured, tried, and sentenced to various terms in the State prison. The ringleader received a life sentence, and is there still. We never found out how they obtained intelligence of the proposed shipment of the bullion.

"I do not consider that I did anything extraordinary, and I think almost any other operator would have done the same.

"Miss C—? Oh, she is Mrs. Erhardt now.

"Well, there comes the train, and I must bid you good-night."

I clasped his hand with a firm grip. He was the first ℏℏℏo I had ever met.

"That was a noble deed of Erhardt's," I observed to Mason, now a railroad superintendent, as I met him the next morning.

"Yes; did you get him to tell you about it? He does not usually like to speak of it. I consider him the bravest man I ever heard of."

Which were my own sentiments exactly.

Hamilton Doless.

THE soothsayers of the village in which Hamilton Doless was born were wont to say of him that "he was a boy bound to make his mark in the world." Fortunately, however, for Hammie, as he was familiarly called, and unfortunately for the predictions of the old soothsayers, the village dominie was an expert in handling the birch rod, and taught the youthful Doless to read and write, much against that worthy's will.

How he came to learn the art of telegraphy I am unable to say. Only on one point am I positive. He began at the lowest round of the ladder and was destined never to reach the top. While working in a small branch office he was in the habit of sending by his messenger many very amusing and tender *billet doux*, with particular instructions to deliver them at the main office "only to the lady with the golden hair who works X1 wire." One morning, with heart and soul thrown into the work of fashioning a grotesque little man out of a cork and four matches, and being at his wit's end to find out how he would put a head upon it prior to presenting it to his fair *inamorata*, a stock broker, who done his telegraphing through Hammie's hands, entered the little office, laid two messages upon the counter, and told him to rush them. Alas! Poor Hammie, after successfully putting a head on his little man, in a fit of abstraction took up the two stock messages, wrapped them around it, gave the parcel to the messenger with the usual instructions to deliver it "to the young lady with the golden hair," etc., sat down and impatiently awaited results. Nor had he long to wait. The messages were found to be mislaid somewhere, and there was an investigation. They were found, and the affair ended in Hammie's dismissal.

I lost track of him for some years after that. It was vaguely rumored that he had entered a well known express company and only left when his practical joking and fits of abstraction nearly precipitated the company in insolvency. I believe he tried his hand as a paripetitic vender of prize packages and light refreshments on a railroad car. The business not proving remunerative, he turned his attention once more to telegraphy, this time as a railroad operator. He never caused any frightful railway collision, because he was not allowed to try his hand at train dispatching. His forte was receiving and dispatching D. H. business from and to the head office of the city in which he resided. Here he became the unwilling victim of innumerable jokes, as well as the author of innumerable bulls. At least his office chums—rather a smart set—tell me so. When a young man sits down and copies a message thus : "Train leaves at nine P. M. with thirteen men on it and going west," and said message should read, "Train leaves at nine P. M.; thirteen Mennonites going west," no one should laugh at him. Such sublime efforts should be above ridicule.

Hammie bade adieu to telegraphy under circumstances in perfect keeping with his well known character. One day while sending a batch of D. H. messages to the head office he discovered the receiver to be a young lady who had already made sad work with his too susceptible heart. After finishing his work he entered into a wire flirtation in total ignorance of the fact that the young lady after copying a few messages had given the seat to a wag named Jent. After some conversation, in which Jent acted in the usual feminine manner by ejaculating the usual quantities of oh ! oh's ! oh ! my's, etc, Hammie was delighted to receive an invitation from Miss Stickem to call on her Sunday at 7:30 P. M., sure. Jent impatiently awaited the *denouement*.

Faithful to the hour appointed, Hammie sallied forth, and people who saw him on that eventful evening say they never saw such whiskers, so immaculate a shirt front, or such shiny boots. His very cane cut victorious characters through the gentle summer air as he waived it aloft in his feeling of exultation. Arrived at the fateful portal, he pulled the bell. Old Mrs. S. answered his summons. To his inquiry "if Miss Stickem was in," she tartly replied that she was not—she had just left the house with an operator from the main office for a drive. Poor Hammie! The wax departed from his whiskers, the starch from his bosom, and the shine from his boots. The joke was circulated near and far. He died a few months after, another victim to the "tender passion."

Scenes and Incidents in a Superintendent's Office.

One pleasant autumn afternoon as the superintendent of a western road was lamenting the scarcity of business; dispatchers and operators were lazily yawning with their feet perched upon the desks, while the instruments had, for the nonce, ceased their everlasting clickety-click, there strolled into the office a perfect specimen of the genus Granger, with a new suit of home spun, heavy stogies, paper collar, and red cravat; evidently got up for the occasion, and doubtless to make a stunning sensation.

Boldly advancing to the nearest operator, he bellowed with an incomparable nasal twang, " Which of you chaps is the superintendent?" On being informed that "that air chap by the window was the gent," he crossed over, coolly took the chief's chair, and opened on the superintendent something after this style—

" Arternoon, boss, I cum in to see about getting a job; have left the farm, and am going to railroading; and if you need a likely chap on the road, just try me."

"Well," says Mr. R., "I have the names of a dozen "likely chaps" on my list, waiting for a situation, so I am afraid your show is poor."

"But," replies the persistent countryman, "I will make a bully railroader, dad says so."

The superintendent looked at verdant a moment, and queried : "What branch of railroading is your specialty?"

Country looked puzzled for an instant.

"Oh, you mean what kin I do best? Most anything; run a train, sell tickets, travel. In fact, anything." And the applicant straightened back, and calmly awaited the expected offer.

Mr. R. turned to his desk with a smile, and after apparently looking at some statistics, made our hero an offer, which not only startled, but started him.

"It has been two days now," remarked the superintendent quietly, "since we have killed a brakeman, and the consequence is that business is very dull; but if you would like to brake on the sand train down in the Pogash pit, and will bind yourself to lose an arm or leg the first day, and thereby revive business, I will—"

But the ambitious Granger, looking wildly around the office, made a sudden bolt for the door, followed by the hysterical laughter and shouts of the amused spectators.

The next caller was a young lady. Timidly rapping at the half open door, she was bade to enter, and as Mr. R. was busy, was asked to be seated. She was a charming looking girl, with eyes and hair as black as midnight, teeth like pearls, cheeks and lips like red, ripe cherries. The operators eyed her askance, with side long glances and evident admiration. But she was apparently unconsciousness. The wires were quiet, dispatchers and operators busy with their own thoughts, or admiring the handsome stranger, when suddenly, Charley opened the circuit, and ticked, "ain't she a stunner, Peaches, fine bird, eh! Jim?"

Jim, a fellow usher, being thus appealed to, edged over to his key, and replied: "Pshaw, can scrape the paint off, false teeth in upside down, and she has on King Calico's coat!" (She wore a beautiful corded jacket.)

A general smile pervaded the office, and the chief scowled fiercely as Charley resumed, "notice her skates, No. 8's at least," meaning her tiny boots, peeping so cunningly from under her dress.

"That hand," rejoins Jim, " reminds me of a whale's ear."

The Chief here seized the key, and remarked, "That lady is a book agent, and she will soon have her revenge." The Chief smiled grimly as a look of blank horror and dismay settled upon the faces of his listeners. By this time the superintendent was at leisure, and politely saluting the young lady, she advanced to his desk, and said: "Mr. Rose, I believe?"   "Yes, madam," he replied, " at your service."

"I have called," she went on, "to obtain any necessary instruction in regard to my duties at Meadow Junction; I am Miss Mattie Dunlap, whom the superintendent of telegraph has kindly appointed operator at that station, with orders to report to you." She here flashed a glance at the embarrassed operators, and they suddenly seized their hats and bounded down stairs.

The superintendent looked inquiringly around, as he noticed their abrupt departure, but a merry twinkle in Miss D.'s eyes was all the explanation vouchsafed that functionary, as the chief swallowed his handkerchief, and the dispatchers concealed their laughter in a violent fit of coughing.

Miss Mattie commenced work the next day, and proved to be a fine telegrapher and a perfect lady; and as Charley and Jim sent ample apologies by train soon after, which were accepted, the three soon became fast friends. But any allusion to "skates," "whales' ears, etc., made to either of the gentlemen by wire or otherwise, is sure to be followed by an explosion. Two years have passed, pregnant with many changes. Jim is now working in the general office of an eastern road. Mrs. Charley F., neé Dunlap, has "gone into other business," and Charley is chief dispatcher, rather austere, but as full of fun as ever.

Our Night Car.

THERE is a large class of disdainful and luxurious aristocrats in this world who pay so little attention to the manner in which they are served by we poor mortals, that they imagine that every man who works after nightfall is necessarily a "watchman" of some kind. They do not, it is true, devote much thought to the matter, but on general reasoning they become possessed of the "ide-yah," you know, that all the professional loafing necessary to make your employers happy is performed during the days, and that any solitary job which necessitates a man's absence from home during the night must, perforce, be in the nature of keeping a watchful eye on the piles of money coined and stowed away in the broad light of heaven during seasonable hours. This class of persons, together with the professional day men, have much to learn of the vast and varied amount of work which is done by telegraphers at night, and some of the thankless duties entailed therewith which are unknown to the freshly polished and intellectual day man. The latter gentleman may form some idea of the amount of labor well and faithfully performed by the night man by looking at the number sheets next morning, or by reading the "specials" as they appear column after column in the morning paper which he invariably borrows; but he can never know of the side scenes —of the drivelling lunatics and rampant madmen who, in large cities, wander about the streets at night, and who are attracted into the office, like moths, by the lights in your window. At one time it is "Old Bradford" who drops in toward midnight merely to give you a striking illustration of his dramatic attitude when the Judge last sentenced him to the lunatic asylum; at another time it is a forlorn and boozy outcast, calling in on general principles — dismal and drenched, with "Led Astray" painted on the back of his coat (an explanation of which he is in blissful ignorance); still again it is the political fiend, mad from too much cipher message, who brings you forty foolscap sheets of bad manuscript which he wants telegraphed at once to the Secretary of War; and the occasions are by no means infrequent when your visitor betrays a lurking curiosity and conveys to you a general impression painfully expressive of the slung-shot, the bludgeon, and the pistol. Clubbing these old clowns out of the office, however, is a very small item in the extra work of a night man for which he never draws any extra pay.

It is in going home, about day-break, freezing in the night car, where you pay double fare for half accommodation, that the night man stores up an experience which will be forever a dark mystery to the professional quacks and botches who cobble up the public business and cook the company's accounts by day, and ride home in luxurious cars in the evening. Everbody knows that when a locomotive has collided with a day car, riddled it through the side with the cow-catcher, and left its head-light and a pair of decayed elk horns sticking in the roof, it would be against any general superintendent's ideas of economy to have it repaired. They simply transfer the wrecked conveyance to the night line, and the extra elk horns in the roof make an excellent hat-rack, while such foreign substances as broken cow-catchers and greasy head-lights afford cheap ornamentation, as well as avoiding the expense of repairing the vehicle. And so when great holes have been worn in the flooring, and some of the passengers fall through, their feet are on the pavement, but the major part of their bodies are in the car. They have to run like fury to keep up with their fellow passengers who, where the floor is solid, are comfortably sitting beside them. As a general thing a man would object to paying full fare for the privilege of running all the way home with the very thin delusion of being inside the car; but, since the pace is rarely a forced one, he falls to reflecting on what a noble work he is engaged in—saving a gigantic corporation the price of a new floor. It is only once in a while, when the horses, upon a sudden recollection

of better days, make a spurt and "force" the running, as it were, that the breathless passenger will get mad and attempt to crawl up on the solid part of the floor where there is not standing room for another man. It is a standing rule of economy at the manufactories—they are all alike—that nothing at all shall be wasted. Wild extravagance and dire necessity occasionally compel the frugal officials to build new cars; and wheels for new day cars, cast in defective molds by cheap workmen—wheels comprising octagon and oval shapes—are reserved for the night line. No wheel on a night car was ever known to be positively round, or if one that had once been round is taken from a day car for night use, by some spendthrift of a roadmaster, it is one of those technically known as a "flat wheel."

Frank drives our night car—Frank Myers. We call him "the two forty-five," that being his starting time. But like a first-class operator he is always late, though he tries to drive very fast. All the night telegraphers entertain a kind of fellow feeling for Frank, for, besides being a robust, cheerful, good, honest fellow, who never knocked down a penny in his life, he is a "night man"—not a vassal, but a peer—just as thoroughly as we are; and we are all classed under the generic title of "owls"—probably from the day men's keen appreciation of our superior wisdom.

Frank, although rarely demonstrative, shows himself to best advantage when, holding his lines well in hand, he is presiding with judicial dignity and undisputed horsemanship over what is known to his profession as a "standing load" of passengers (which includes those who are running, owing to their feet protruding through the floor). It must be borne in mind that Philadelphia night cars, for economy's sake, carry no conductors, so that a standing load is very satisfactory to Frank, as it fills his patent Slawson box with cash.

Although a very muscular man, Frank is generally disposed to be urbane, as the general run of his passengers—newspaper men, telegraph men, and benighted tipplers—are usually very feeble, very tired, or very crestfallen. No tempest can ruffle his demeanor. No winter's snows, nor midsummer night's heat, nor rain, nor hail pelting him in the bronzed face can change the official bearing of Frank. Only when, where there is a double track, he is going up with a standing load and meets a plug of a driver coming down with one passenger does a contemptuous smile play upon his lips as he drives triumphantly past, and marks the dissimulating nonchalance with which the downward bound driver strives to whistle gayly in a vain endeavor to display his total unconcern and supreme indifference.

An episode like this will "draw him out." Holding his lines with one hand, his two emaciated, wheezy, and rheumatic steeds jogging on in chronic despair, he makes excited gesticulations with the other as he relates how, in his golden youth, he drove the Liberty Engine, and how he invariably secured the fire plug nearest the conflagration, although he would achieve that enviable position only by furiously driving for a mile on three wheels, owing to the base machinations of the Reliance Hook and Ladder that purposely run into him. He refers with much pathos to the " mettle " of the two old rips now drawing his car. When one of them lies down to enjoy an extra sound sleep, which is often, he excuses the animal in the most soothing terms to the irate passengers. He will insist that the mettle is there, and that they are unmatchable when " in trim;" but the misfortune is manifest that they never happen to be in trim at one and the same time. When his " chestnut colt "—which can not be less than seventy-five years old—comes out of the stable professedly full of steam and speed, its mate, the " bay mare," is disposed to lie down and reflect on life in general. On another night, when the bay mare—which is worth about two dollars, delivered at the pork packing establishment—is feeling skittish, the chestnut colt will be laboring with the rheumatism. But these crushing facts never melt Frank's faith in the unfortunate quadrupeds. He will keep up the thread of a political argument in the most adroit manner, without a break, even when the jolting of the caboose tumbles him back among the passengers, or when the unexpected stoppage of his cattle—'twere base flattery to call them horses—pitches him headlong over the dash-board.

While engaged in these multifarious duties, Frank can drive a very Shylock's bargain with a fishwoman who proposes to carry her market stall, two baskets of questionable herrings, and her corpulent self all for one fare. Of course, there are times—state occasions—when Frank's temper is ruffled ; for instance, when one of the city authorities, a belated chief operator, or some other pompous individual enters the car, dumps a number of pennies into the Slawson box on top of a fare just previously deposited, and then volunteers to wage mortal combat with Frank rather than admit that he only put nine cents in the box. He would be a base slave who would pay tribute of a single extra cent to a grasping corporation, while on a night car even behind two alleged fiery steeds, would be but a desert waste to Frank if he were bull-dozed into carrying passengers for nine cents. When factious opposition has done its worst, the passengers all stand on the seats to give them room ; Frank coolly hands his reins to me, and it is only after they have

clinched and rolled each other in the straw on the floor, with the regular riders to " trebly thundering swell the gale," that the refractory city authority, belated chief operator, or other pompus individual bows to the great corporation and the gods of war and puts another cent in the box.

When the car stops to pick up a fresh passenger all eyes are, as everybody knows, turned toward the door to see who it is. If the newcomer chances to be intoxicated, all the other intoxicated men in the car consider it incumbent upon themselves to fall down in the straw or to jab their elbows through the window glass, merely to attest their frenzied eagerness to get up and assist the unfortunate stranger. They all shake hands with him cordially, from pure human sympathy. His zig-zag progress from the rear door to the Slawson box in front is one vast tumultuous ovation ; and, while fumbling in his pockets for the fare, he is generously bolstered up with an improvised scaffold—a very forest of walking canes, umbrellas, and other handy props. He is then expected to tread on four men's toes on his way to a proffered seat, where he must deliver a kind of inaugural address, lean over on somebody more stupid than himself, and go to sleep.

Then on a winter night, when the drifting snow nearly blinds Frank, they make all kinds of riotous demonstrations, and get him so worried that in going round a sharp curve he gets off the track. Now, if the large-hearted passengers would only let him alone he could soon get on again all right, but with that unbounded liberality characteristic of inebriated Philadelphians, they emerge with the avowed purpose of lifting the car upon the track again. A very simple calculation will demonstrate that, under ordinary circumstances, forty men can lift a street car, and if they are sober and display a certain degree of unanimity they can carry the same from the gutter and deposit it squarely on the track without much trouble. But, while forty drunken men are quite capable of lifting a car—including a man asleep and a fat woman inside, and the driver on the dash-board—they are, owing to a lack of unanimity, only able to stagger about in the snow, objectless, but enthusiastic and undaunted, embellishing the performance with fiendish screams of encouragement to each other, frantically yelling to " hold her up," " away she goes," etc. Frank gets too mad for anything, and threatens to run a-muck among the fuming crowd, which, after describing numerous eccentric circles with its unnatural load, deposits the same, back end foremost, nearer to the gutter, and suddenly melts into a snow-bank. In spite of Frank's vehement remonstrances they come at it once more, shake hands all round, each congratulating his neighbor on his wonderful prowess, and they sieze it again. Then ensues a terrific racket; the three-ton car is again hoisted into the air, the same pushing and staggering and shouting recommences, Frank's animals rear with affright, the rattling of lamps and window glass awakens the man inside who has been dreaming that he was on a French steamship in a storm. The willing throng, amid a tremendous noise, wander all over the street with their immense load until by a stroke of good luck they let it drop in the proper place on the track. Then comes the pantomine. Frank starts his team at a gallop, and knowing that a second stoppage would stick him again in the snow, he lashes the beasts nto a furious pace. Of course, this proceeding obliges his volunteer aids to mount the car while it is in rapid motion; and it is no easy matter for forty inebriated men to board a rapidly moving car all at one time. By dint of wonderful feats of agility, however, and amid Indianlike whooping and yelling, about twenty-two of them get in through the windows or over the dash-board, while the remaining eighteen go home afoot or fall asleep in the snow.

The lucky ones who have thus got aboard un-scathed generally slumber peacefully after their self-imposed task; but up-town, when Frank wakes them up and disembarks them in squads, the fun recommences. Men who on entering the car were utter strangers to each other congregate under the nearest lamp-post, issue to each other unlimited invitations to dine, and rend the air with fervid protestations of undying friendship. And as I nes-tle up in a vacant corner for a quiet nap I hear our late passengers in the distance extolling, in sup-posed musical meterthe natural and acquired abil-ities of that admirable genius, "Muldoon, the solid man."

Lightning Anecdotes.

COLONEL WILSON, the Chicago superintendent, maintains that the method of reading by sound is a sort of Western institution. It happened that when the Prince of Wales visited this country sound read-ing was a thing entirely new to him, and he and his escort never ceased commenting on the fact that they should come to the wilds of the Mississippi Valley to become familiar with one of the marvels of the world.

Colonel Wilson was the telegrapher accompany-ing the Prince and his suite while traveling in the West, and he has a rich fund of anecdotes concern-ing that period. While traveling through Illinois the party took frequent occasions to indulge in hunt-ing excursions. To this end the most sparsely set-tled regions were selected. At one time, after a protracted hunt, the party had occasion to cross a railway track, and the sight of the telegraph poles and wire excited in the Prince and several members of the suite a desire to place themselves in commu-nication with civilization once more. The Colonel adjusted his pocket instrument, but soon found that in one direction the wires were down, and, casting his eye along the track he noticed the source of the trouble, by means of a field telescope, about half a mile beyond.

"I guess I'll mend that break," said the Colonel, in the presence of the Duke of Newcastle.

"Have you the wire to do it with?" inquired his grace.

"No," answered the Colonel, "but I guess I'll send for some."

"But, sir," said the Duke, somewhat alarmed, "we can't do without you, and I'm sure we can't wait here a day or two while you send to the near-est station, which I understand is ten miles away, for the repairing material."

"I'll repair the break and not detain you longer than the time you will require to dispatch your lunch," returned the imperturbable Colonel, and while he was still talking to the credulous Duke—to whom, however, he had given no hint how the repair was to be effected—a train came in sight. In a twinkling it was upon them and, as it passed the spot where the party was congregated, at a tremend-ous burst of speed, a coil of wire was thrown from the baggage car, and in half an hour the break was repaired.

The Duke after referred to the fact as a most strik-ing example of what was known as "fast" America, and even after the simple explanation of the "trick," he still thought it marvelous and could only have been performed in America. The case was simply this: As soon as Colonel Wilson found the wire broken, and while in communication with the near-est station in the direction in which the wire was not broken, he had given orders to put a coil of wire on the next train, with instructions to throw it off at the point where the company would be found mak-ing a halt. Even while he was giving this order the answer was returned, "The train is now in sight," and hence he could calculate that it would reach the point at which they were camped in less than half an hour. It was about twenty minutes later that he had the conversation with the Duke, and hence it was that while they were still talking over the matter the train came in sight.

At one time, in the early winter months, one of the company's cables crossing the Mississippi was broken. As bad luck never comes singly it so happened at the time that the river was wild with ice, and it was literally impossible for those on one side to communicate with those on the other by the ordinary methods. In this dilemma it occurred to Colonel Wilson to bring a locomotive into requisition. As quickly as possible he submitted himself to a short but comprehensive course of instruction with reference to working the whistle of his new contrivance, and, having acquired the art, the iron

horse was pranced to a point near the river's side, and then the Colonel began to "blow his horn" as he never blew it before nor since. People in the town on the opposite side wondered for a long time what had got into that locomotive, but all of a sudden a telegraph operator over yonder began to pick his ears and exclaim, "Why, that darned locomotive is calling this station; it is giving our signal!" Then it occurred to the operator what was wanted, and, engaging a locomotive on his own side of the river, he ran to a convenient point, and then ensued what must ever be regarded as one of the loudest intelligible conversations on record. The method of confab proved perfectly satisfactory to all concerned.

A.D. 1900.

ANCIENT KNIGHT, PROUDLY—"Yes, Tommy, I was for many years an operator, and in my time transmitted many messages over the wires."

TOMMY, INTERESTED—"What did you sign?"

1. Entrée.

2. Placed—"That familiar sound."

A Deep, Dire, Dreadful Tragedy,

3. HA! HA! I HOPE HE'LL RUSH ME!"

4. RUSHED!

In Four Acts.

$1,000 Reward—My Foot Race with a Telegram.

It was one of the brightest of early spring days—the last Sabbath in April. Too early for the first green foliage of the new-born season, but following closely as it did upon the long, dreary winter months, the warm rays of the sun were so tempting, the artificial heat within doors so oppressive, that the temptations for a long ramble were simply irresistible.

I lived on the border—not exactly the frontier of civilization, but just outside the limits of the city of E——, N. J. South of of me were the pavements, street lamps, modern architecture, and all the accompaniments of city life. To the north stretched the Morris turnpike—sparsely settled, with here and there a weather-beaten, low-roofed farm-house, which may have been at one time the headquarters either of Washington or some of his subordinates. It is, at least, classic ground, for this was the direct route during the Revolutionary War from the American camp at Morristown to either Philadelphia or tide-water. A stroll for pleasure instinctively led myself and companion in the direction of these rural scenes. First across the creek to a saw-mill, the quaint machinery of which was always a source of wonderment, not that its finish was remarkable, or its mechanical complication beyond solution, but that so insignificant a turbine wheel should have sufficient power to move such a conglomerate mass of eccentric gearings, saw-dust, bark, and cobwebs. The details of our ramble were, in the main, like those enjoyed by all who commune with nature. Leaving behind us the ancient saw-mill, the dam, and pond, crossing the highway, scaling the moss-covered fence, built in "those good old days," we plunged into the outskirts of the woods, and were soon threading the underbrush on the lookout for anything that might be of interest. Suddenly my companion halted. I glanced quickly ahead in the direction he pointed, and was startled for the moment upon seeing the prostrate form of a man perhaps fifty yards ahead of us. We approached cautiously, thinking he was asleep, but upon reaching him we saw at once that he must have been dead several days. Having in view the coroner's inquest, I noted the time of day—eleven o'clock—and with due regard for the requirements of the law, we left everything undisturbed and hastened to the city to notify the proper authorities of our discovery. Half an hour's walk brought us before the chief of police, to whom we gave a brief narrative of our morning adventure. He displayed little interest in our story, however, merely remarking that it was probably some tramp who had strayed out of his route and died in a fit. Being out of the city limits, he seemed little inclined to bother with the matter until I remarked that the clothes upon the body were sufficient evidence that the wearer did not belong in the ranks of the traveling poor.

My statement was not without effect. A prospective reward seemed to infuse activity into the corpulent form of the chief, and he at once ordered a carriage, and inviting us to join him, we drove as near the spot as possible, alighted, and were soon again standing around the unknown corpse, with no little curiosity to learn more particulars than we yet knew regarding the apparently violent death. The chief, like most of his class, was a man of few words, but a wise look, as if his waking hours were spent in the fabrication of theories. By virtue of his office and familiarity with scenes of this kind, he did not hesitate to turn the body over as soon as he had made a brief inspection of the surroundings. The face was decomposed to such an extent that recognition would have been impossible even had it not been the face of a stranger. He had been a man of medium height, heavily built, dressed in a dark business suit, with brown spring overcoat and a silk hat, which had fallen from his head as he fell forward, and lay upon the ground six feet from the body. Upon his sleeve buttons was the single initial "R" in the old English letter, which was the only clue to his identity that could be found about his clothing. Underneath the body was a Colt's revolver, with one chamber empty, and upon the right temple of the victim the dark purple spot which marked the entrance of the death dealing bullet.

"Suicide," was the general exclamation, as these developments were brought to light, and, strange to say, the chief had no theory to bring up in opposition to this spontaneous verdict. A further search brought to light among the leaves by the side of the body two dollars and eighty cents in currency; on the other side a pocket knife, a night key, and a few other trifles. The pockets were turned inside out, which at first glance seemed to indicate robbery and murder, but there was no other evidence to support this view of the case, so it was the general impression that the man while sitting at the foot of a tree emptied his pockets of their contents and then deliberately shot himself.

Meantime, the chief had been pondering over a copy of the New York *Sun*, which he found in a side pocket of the overcoat. The paper was folded in such a manner as to expose but a single column on the first page, which seemed at once to throw new light on the mystery. The following was the article:

THE MISSING CONTRACTOR.

"An advertisement appeared in the *Herald* a few days since, offering one thousand dollars reward for information that would lead to the discovery of the whereabouts of Henry Roberts, a wealthy contractor residing in Williamsport, Pennsylvania. At the time of his disappearance he was engaged on a heavy contract at Easton, Pa., and was supposed to have in his possession about five thousand dollars, with which to pay the wages of his hands employed on the job. His friends can not account for his sudden disappearance excepting on the theory that he has been foully dealt with. He is a man of dark complexion, black hair, and wears a heavy moustache. He is five feet ten inches in height, and was dressed in a dark business suit and silk hat. Any information regarding him should be sent to Detective Tully, at Police Headquarters, New York City.

A flutter ran through the little knot of bystanders, and it was plain to be seen that it was the general impression that on the ground before us lay the body of the missing contractor.

Nothing further remained to be done excepting to deliver the body to the undertaker to be prepared for burial, so the little assemblage broke up. I nudged my companion, Charlie, and told him to walk home with me as I wished to talk with him. The other people, including the chief of police and the coroner, rode down in the carriage. After all had gone, I told Charlie what I suspected, and the plans I had formed, based on the following line of reasoning: I was satisfied that the chief intended to get the reward, or a large share of it, provided there was any to be obtained. All the circumstances seemed to indicate that the body was that of the missing contractor, and if so, we were clearly entitled to the reward of one thousand dollars. The person who is first to give this information to Detective Tully will claim the money. Certainly none can show a better title than ourselves, but we must be quick, as the chief is wide-awake. It is now one o'clock. The last train for New York left at twelve. The telegraph office will not be open until five o'clock. If the chief sends a telegram at that hour it will not reach police headquarters much before six o'clock. I propose that we foot it to New York. It is thirteen miles to Jersey City. We can do that in four hours, and if we are prompt in starting we shall have an hour left in which to reach headquarters on Mulberry Street, with a fair chance of being ahead of the telegram. As I was older than Charlie, and well versed in all the details of my proposed plan, he did not hesitate to indorse it, especially as there was a prospect of securing a good sum of money if we were quick enough.

Stopping at our homes only a sufficient time to partake of a hasty lunch, and apprise our friends of our probable absence for the night, we started on our journey. We thought it possible that we might connect with a stage at Newark, which makes occasional trips to Jersey City on Sunday, and this would shorten our walk by seven miles. In this we were disappointed, however, and the only lift we secured was a ride on a horse car through Newark, a distance of about two miles. We reached Jersey City at about five o'clock, as I had calculated, and after a few minutes' detention at the ferry, crossed the North River, and at half-past five started from the New York side, making the best time we could to the Mulberry Street police station. Upon entering the building we were directed to the detectives' room, where we inquired for Mr. Tully. The officer in charge replied that he was not in, but gave us his address on Ninth Street. We were about conversing in regard to our business when a Western Union Telegraph messenger entered the room, and as he stepped up to the the desk and opened his book I glanced hastily at the address of the dispatch he was about to deliver, and read the name "Detective Tully." I darted quickly through the door, followed closely by my companion, and as we reached the street I told him we had no time to lose, that the message just brought in was for Mr. Tully, and the boy would be directed to his house. Our only chance was a foot race to his residence, and as we had a good start, I thought we might beat the messenger, he being one of a class who, although very nimble walkers, seldom break into a run. We reached the house in good time, found Mr. Tully at home and at leisure. He received us very pleasantly, and listened patiently to our story. He seemed to relish our distancing the chief, and said that if we were on the right track we were entitled to the reward. He showed us a photograph of the missing contractor, but we could not determine whether it bore any resemblance to the corpse in the woods. Suddenly our conversation was interrupted by a ring at the door bell. Mr. Tully answered it, and returned with the telegram in his hand.

"You were just in time, gentleman, here is the dispatch from your chief of police," and he handed it to me for my information. I read as follows:

"E——, APRIL 29th.
"Detective Tully, Police Headquarters:
"Body found in woods to-day. Think it is missing man, Roberts, you advertise; come and identify.   JOHN KENO,
"16 paid.   Chief of Police.

We enjoyed a hearty laugh at his expense, and leaving our new friend apparently imbued with profound admiration of our enterprise, we started on the return trip, doubting the possibility of reaching home before breakfast the next morning, but highly elated with the success of our journey, and the corresponding discomfiture of the chief. On our way to the ferry we made arrangements as to the division of our prospective reward and its permanent investment. Inquiries at respective offices of the Pennsylvania and Central Railroads seemed to banish all hope of our leaving the city before morning. Having been recently employed on the Central Railroad, however, I remembered that there was a milk train which ran down Sunday night, and returned from Jersey City as a fast freight with a passenger car attached. This train was largely patronized by deadheads — mostly railroad men returning to their posts of duty after a Sunday's absence. Although not supposed to stop at E——, I concluded to take the risk, so we waited at the ferry gate until the arrival of the boat from the milk train, and returned with it to Jersey City. My whole plan seemed to have been especially favored, as we not only secured our passage, but my face was recognized as a title to a free trip.

The car we had entered was pretty well filled with passengers, the majority of them being railroad men, with many of whom I was acquainted. Our conversation drifted to railroad matters, and it would have been evident to any listener, judging from the criticisms exchanged, that we were thoroughly posted on all the details of the road and its management. One of the passengers, wishing to avail himself of the opportunity to acquire information, casually inquired if that train ran through to Easton, and if it made a close connection with the morning train for Williamsport. He seemed rather disappointed on learning that he would be obliged to wait three hours at Easton. My thoughts being occupied with the adventures of the day, I could not refrain from asking him if he lived in Williamsport. He replied that he did, that being his native place.

"Do you know of a man named Roberts?"

"There are several of that name in Williamsport. I am personally acquainted with some of them."

"The gentleman I refer to is a contractor."

I intended to say more, but a sudden change flashed over the countenance of my fellow passenger, and on the instant my thoughts reverted to the description of the missing contractor and the strange circumstances that had welded it to my memory.

There was no reason for my supposing that this was the man Roberts, although the description seemed to fit him in every particular. So, too, it agreed with the corpse in the woods. When we can almost grasp a long sought object, be it wealth, honor, or position, the attainment of which has long dangled before our eyes, hundreds of imaginary obstacles seem to intervene, dooming us to bitter disappointment. Like the intricacies of a dream, in which we ask ourselves is this merely visionary or is it real? and in our dream we indorse it with a tinge of reality. At last we awake, and it is gone forever, leaving a shadowy imprint of tantalizing joy or unspeakable terror, which lives in our memory for a day and is then filed away, a blank leaf in the archives of our life.

All day I had been reaching for my prospective reward. Every circumstance had favored me; every incident seemed to confirm the fact that it had been honestly offered and fairly earned. Yet, even as I thought, I

would warn myself that there might be some mistake, and here was the first evidence of it which I felt, but could not bring myself to believe.

The next day the New York *Sun* contained a full account of the discovery of the body, with a description of the articles found near it.

On Tuesday there arrived from New York a German lady, who had read the article in the *Sun*, and believed it to be the solution of the mystery attending the disappearance of her husband, A. K. Ritch, two weeks before. Inquiring for the chief of police, she was accompanied by him to the undertaker's room, where she identified the body as that of her husband, and substantiated her belief by a description of the articles which had been taken possession of by the proper authorities. There now seemed little doubt that all difficulties regarding the investment of our reward had been removed, especially as further developments indicated that financial embarrassment had been the incentive to suicide.

The following item, which appeared in the New York papers during the week, completes the history of this strange coincidence so far as I am concerned:

THE WANDERER RETURNED.

"Mr. Henry Roberts, of Williamsport, Pa., whose disappearance a few days since caused so much apprehension among his friends, returned to his home on Monday last. Beyond the fact that he has been in New York city, no explanation of his absence has been made public."

Whether the missing contractor was our traveling companion on the return trip Sunday night, I have never ascertained. I soon lost all interest in the affair, but have since felt considerable sympathy for the police officials who invent theories to fit their mysterious cases, and subsequently see them demolished by actual facts.

"Paul Riverson, are you deaf or crazy? "Hd" has been calling you for at least ten minutes, and here you sit like a stone and never make a move to answer."

Paul quickly placed his fingers on the key, saying, as he did so:

"Is that so? By Jove! I didn't notice that any one was calling me. Just step over here, Fred, and after I receive this message I'll tell you what makes me so absent-minded, for of course you have noticed that I am so."

Business was rather dull in X office that day, so Fred soon found time to go over to Riverson's table. As soon as he was seated his friend began:

"I believe, Fred, I've met my fate. You know I took a trip down to L. the other day. Well, while I was waiting for the train to leave, the operator came into the gentleman's room to bring a message to the station agent, and my heart was lost at once. She is loveliness personified. Talk about Hebe and Juno, and all the rest as much as you choose! I don't believe any of them could compare with my peerless little operator."

"Did you learn her name?" asked Fred, in an interested tone.

"Not then," was the answer, "but I have since. You see, Fred, I thought of nothing but her sweet face after I came back, and called her every time I could get the wire. She chatted very freely with me, and at last I sent her a letter, merely directing to telegraph office, as I did not know her name, but she answered the very next day, and signed Flossie Bates. Pretty name, isn't it? I imagined her name would be something like that. Well, since that I've written to her every morning and received an answer every evening. The last mail isn't opened until ten o'clock, and then I have to go nearly a mile out of my way to get my letter, but I'd rather walk a dozen miles than miss getting it. I told the postmaster not to send them to the office, for the fellows might make remarks if they saw the same handwriting so often. You are the only person I have trusted with my secret, so mind you keep still, old fellow."

Just then Fred was called away, and Paul was left to dream of his charmer undisturbed, for the other operators were out to dinner.

The weeks passed rapidly away until two months had gone by since Paul first spoke with Miss Bates on the wire, when one morning he asked Fred Lawson if he could perform his (Paul's) duties for a day or two as well as his own, as he wished to visit L.

"What! Has it got as far along as that?" asked Fred, in astonishment.

"Yes," answered Paul, "I have come to that pass when I must speak or die. I must know my fate. If she refuses, don't be surprised to find my name among the list of suicides."

A young gentleman could scarcely look more stylish than did Paul as he stepped off the train at L. His new seventy-five dollar suit fitted him to a charm, and the bootblack who gave his ten-dollar shoes their "shine" assuredly understood his business. His eight-dollar hat sat with jaunty grace on his perfumed hair, and in his hand he carried a very pretty little cane.

The telegraph office door was opened in answer to Paul's very genteel rap by a woman of about fifty, with a decidedly stout figure and a profusion of gray hair, the latter frizzled and puffed in every imaginable manner. She was clad in a wine-colored dress, with many small blue bows in front, and a green necktie, the latter tied around a linen collar which came up high in the neck.

What was Paul's surprise when this person threw her arms around his neck and exclaimed:

"Paul, dear Paul, you have come at last! Oh, how impatiently I have waited for this hour!"

"There is some mistake, madame, I assure you," cried Paul, as soon as he could disengage himself from her embrace. He entered the office and sank down on a chair as he said:

"I came to see Miss Flossie Bates. Can you tell me where she can be found?"

There was a world of reproach in the woman's tone as she replied:

"Paul, I am Flossie Bates—your own Flossie, as you have so often called me in your letters."

"But I came to visit the operator," persisted Paul.

"And I am the operator," replied Miss Bates, with dignity.

"For heaven's sake, is there no other operator here?" frantically questioned Paul.

"And if there were, sir, I am the girl you have called at least a dozen times a day for nearly two months, and written to every day for more than four weeks; and after declaring so many times that you saw me when you were here before, and fell in love with my beautiful face, you now behave as if you had never set eyes upon me in the world."

Just then a lady passed by the window beside which Paul stood.

"There," he almost shouted, "that is the girl I came to see. Who is she?"

"That speaks volumes for you, young man," replied the irate operator in a freezing tone. "It is a good sign in a man to be running after other men's wives."

"Is she *married?*" faintly asked Paul.

"Of course she's married. She's the station agent's wife."

Then he understood it all. The lady had been in Miss Bates' office on the day of his former visit to L., and had handed the message which he saw in her hand to her husband. Paul hardly knew how he reached home, and I will not try to tell you. He is now employed under an assumed name in a distant State. He never speaks to any one on the wire now unless the conversation is purely of a business nature, and he is often heard to declare that the best of people will sometimes make mistakes.

The Telegrapher's Song.

From every corner of the earth
  The startling news we bring ;
We weave a girdle round the globe
  And guide the lightning's wing.

Far as the distant thunder rolls
  O'er stream and rock and sea,
We join the nations in one clasp
  Of friendly unity.

We touch our key, and, quick as thought,
  The message onward flies—
For every point within the world
  Right at our elbow lies.

Ours is the greatest boon to man
  That genius yet has given—
To make a messenger of thought,
  The lightning bolts of Heaven.

THE TE-LEG-RAPHER

Walking, although a most exhilirating exercise, is an occupation which of all others imposes the very gravest responsibilities on those who have the hardihood to brave its difficulties, and, like entering upon the telegraphic "profession," when you have once got fairly on the great highway, and all the fair prospects have been left far behind, and all the bad ones are visibly before you, and the well known uncongeniality of the wicked world toward the average telegrapher appears in all its significance, it is very difficult to retrace your steps, and just as discouraging to go on. Even the most sensitive college professor will not deny that telegraphers are assiduous walkers, and that they have been known to travel afoot from Omaha to the sea, east or west, in quest of a chance to salt somebody at a high salary. Indeed, it is well known that the lexicographers have changed the pronunciation of our designating title on this account—" tele-*graph*-er " having been appropriately reaccented, in view of our numerous pedestrian expeditions, and we are now called " te-*leg*-raphers," with the accent placed sarcastically on the "

Wives for Two; or, Joe's Little Joke.

YES, those were halcyon days when we worked old "One East," Joe and I, and jolly times we had of it—even if the hours were longer and the pay less than now—and if it were not for a knowledge of the uselessness of such a wish I should often be tempted to long for the old days back again. Just think of it, boys! There, from Boston to Calais, were Lynn, Salem, Newburyport, Portsmouth, and Portand; then Bath, Damariscotta, Rockland, Belfast, and Bangor— the important points—with a host of smaller towns between, and all on one wire, where we worked as quiety and contentedly as a veritable "happy family," only barring an occasional breeze between rival offices who each thought their claim to the circuit of paramount importance, which served to give spice to life, clear the horizon, and impress us—after the return of the accustomed calm—with the amount of solid comfort we were enjoying!

Well, I suppose that by this time things have changed, and probably even Damariscotta revels in the magnificence of its importance over half a dozen or more wires; but I doubt if there is more real business done than that poor old "Maine" line used to stand without breaking. In the winter it was ice orders for the Kennebec, and reports of the depth of snow from Bangor. In summer all the coastwise towns and cities woke up to attend to their shipping, and long and bothersome charter messages kept the long hours busy, and the wire fairly overflowed with work; and then, all the year round, whenever an ocean steamer arrived at Halifax or St. Johns, every office was closed to customers, no matter how urgent their business might be, and the wire given up to foreign news, which went pounding along hour after hour, cipher, parliamentary, and government, till the long budget was exhausted, and we had a chance at ordinary work again; for that was long before the cable was laid, you know, and everything had to give way

before foreign news, no matter what it might be, and woe to him who broke or grounded on "steamer day!" But the long winter evenings, those were the times when one and all took solid comfort, and they are what I regret the most after all this change that time has brought. You see business slackened up at about six, and then, till "G N." at eight, the wire was given up to what you young chaps now term "buzzing;" the word would have been very applicable then, moreover, as it was more like a hive of bees than anything else, and the amount of good-natured fun and banter that passed between us, not to mention more serious and even "spooney" talk—but of that more anon—was a caution to outsiders! Two of the girls would start it, perhaps, with talk of dress and furbelows, sly hints at village beaux and gentle rivalry, then Joe, who was always on the alert for such chances, would snatch the circuit from one of the fair ones, and send a different and perhaps startling answer to the last question. A moment's silence, and after it a bit of sharp repartee or banter, and in a few seconds more all hands would join in the fun and keep it up till Boston gave "good-night," and one by one we dropped out and left the line to the owls for report.

Practical jokes were not few, and many were so good, and withal so innocent and harmless, as to bind us more closely together, rather than make ruptures in the "happy family;" and whether he deserved it all or not, Joe usually had the credit of most of them. Poor Joe! he is laid away beyond the reach of sounders or even error-sheets now. And if some of his fun did occasionally hit harder than he intended, I hope there is no malice laid up against his account by any of the "victims." You remember Peabody? "Little Fred" Peabody we used to call him; good fellow, good operator, and one of your "copperplates" on his copy; "graduated" now into the dry goods trade, or something equally prosaic. I don't know just what or where he is, but he has disappeared from the ranks for many a year, and been gradually lost sight of by his old friends. Well, *he* got it pretty badly one night, and forever after refused to join in a "buzz." You see, he had just one weak spot, and we knew it. He *would* always "spoon" on every new girl he met, and used to count his conquests by the score.

Well, one night, when work was slack, we heard Fred call Portland—the wire was cut, you know, and Fred had a new flame in Portsmouth under cultivation—and ask for the rest of the wire. Soon we heard it cut on again, and after the end of a Boston message Fred goes for Portsmouth and starts a lively confab on his own account. By-and-bye she remarks: "By the way, Mr. Peabody, I have a new student—Miss Stone—whom I would be glad to introduce to you." "Delighted, I'm sure," says Fred. And then the introduction followed, and the student took the key and made a fluttering attempt at some pretty speech which she managed to make plain enough for us to decipher.

Then Fred began: "Miss Stone, I am charmed, I assure you. Allow me to —" congratulate you on your proficiency, he was probably going to say had not Joe stepped in from his office between them, and, mimicking Fred's style to perfection, completed the sentence with— "hug you and kiss you the next time I come down." Well, boys, you should have heard the roar of laughter that went up in our office, at least, and seen Fred's face as he gradually realized the sell. But on the wire all was as still as the grave, and although others no doubt saw the joke, no one broke the spell, and Fred's buzz was for once and for all completely spoiled. He would have given his boots to know who did the trick, but he never discovered, and she, the fair student, no doubt thinks to this day—that is, if she survived the shock at all — that Mr. Peabody at least had a novel and original way of begin-

ning an acquaintance, and probably never accused him of *bashfulness!*

But that's not what I was asked for, I know, and if you won't let me have any peace till I tell you how I got Dolly, and Dolly got me, I suppose I must make a clean breast of it.

Well, then, here it is : Joe and I were in Rockland then, keeping the post-office and working the wire between us, and chumming together as comfortably as could be, until what should we do but both fall in love with the same girl, like the pair of fools that we were. She was the student at Damariscotta, Dolly Vaughan by name, and although we had neither of us seen her, those long evening chats over the wire had done the business for me before I knew it, and at last, as I came in one evening and caught Joe in the midst of an earnest talk with her, and saw the smile on his face and the flash in his eyes, it came over me all at once that he was caught too, and for the first time in my life I almost hated him. I couldn't stand it, and out I went again into the open air to smoke away frantically, curse my unlucky stars— for Joe and I had been so long good friends that I wouldn't stand in his way—and finally went off and locked myself in my room, to lie awake half the night thinking of Joe and his happiness, and trying to tear out the fair image that I had pictured to myself, and had just discovered was grown dearer to me than I had begun to suspect. Well, the next day we both were rather quiet and solemn, though Joe did burst out occasionally in one of his merry whistles, and at "Goodnight" I was just reaching for my hat and coat to leave him alone for his chat, when what does he do but seize his before I could say a word, and disappear with only "Goodby, old boy ; engagement up-town," as the door slammed behind him. What could it mean? Well, I didn't stop to wonder long, for the temptation for just one more chat was too strong to be resisted, and down I sat and called Dolly, and soon we were in the midst of our talk, all the rest having cut out and left for home. But somehow Dolly's writing seemed changed to me—more easy and distinct. In fact, almost like that of Miss Warren, the regular operator. But that was out of the question, for she and I never could agree on anything; in fact, I didn't like Miss Warren at all, and the idea of *her* waiting so late to chat with me was utterly absurd. So that notion was soon dismissed, and, only casually complimenting Dolly on her improvement, I laid myself out to be agreeable, and spent one of the jolliest evenings of my life. She talked more freely about herself than ever, and gave me so many new insights into her character, her tastes and accomplishments, that before the evening was over I had decided that Joe shouldn't have her if I could prevent—no matter what the consequences might be.

Well, after that I got a few cups of main battery to use nights, and put in an extra relay on the desk, so that we could both "ground" and have a circuit of our own when we wished and still be able to connect it through whenever we heard a call on either side, and every night we would stay and talk without any of the others being the wiser. Joe fortunately took to billiards about that time, or something or other that kept him away in the evenings, and I had it all my own way, sometimes wondering at his sudden change, but thinking—if I thought of it at all —that what I had taken for a discovery of his love, must have been only a creation of my own jealous fancy. Well, it wasn't long before I determined to see for myself if my fair one were all that my fancy painted her; and, after arranging it with Joe to run the office for a day, I got myself up gorgeously, and drove down on one of the most charming spring days I ever enjoyed. By following the wires I easily found the office, and there, among window-gardens and hanging plants, a perfect bower of greeneries, and all the odds and ends of pretty things with which women know so well how to transform a room, if they only make up their minds to show their tastes—in fact, just the reverse of our

own dingy and ink-bespattered office at home—sat the object of my dreams.

I was received by two of the prettiest girls I ever gazed upon, and soon made myself at home within the railing which shut out the common crowd of customers and messengers. Of course, it was a little awkward at first, and Miss Warren struck me as somewhat cool and reserved, although friendly and polite enough; but that wore off in time, and after awhile she left us together, Dolly and I, making an excuse of "errands up town," and graciously accepting my offer to serve as operator during her absence, which I inwardly prayed might be a long one.

Well, I made good use of my time, I assure you; spent the day, took Dolly to drive in the evening, and finally returned through the gray morning to Belfast, with my head and heart in a whirl of the thoughts and aspirations which crowd the brain of an engaged man! Yes, I had done it; for one day of her company had been enough to complete what those months of wire conversations had begun, and the result had been what I had been longing for even more than I knew myself. Well, Joe took the news coolly enough, I thought, but was hearty in his congratulations nevertheless, and for the next few months everything went smoothly with us all, each of us taking occasional trips of a day or two—mine, of course, being to Damariscotta, and his—well, he never volunteered the information, and I never asked him, though I was pretty sure there was a "woman in the case" from his elaborate preparations. So I never knew till my wedding day.

That came at last in the following fall. You see, Joe and I had gone into partnership and bought out the store next the post-office, and had three strings to our bow; and when I was assured of a good prospect for the future, as far as business was concerned, I hurried up Dolly's preparations, and at last, one bright October day, leaving the office in charge of a sub and the store to the clerks, Joe and I drove down to Damariscotta, and in a quiet little church, with only himself as groomsman and Miss Warren as bridesmaid, we were married at last; and right there was where the cream of the joke came in. For after the ceremony, and just as we were about to pass on into the vestry and sign the book, what does Joe do but coolly remark that we "weren't quite through yet," and, stepping up before the altar, taking Miss Warren's hand, he goes right through the ceremony like a man, without half the blunders I had made after all my rehearsing, while I stood by with my bride on my arm, utterly speechless with astonishment. Well, I came to at last, and *such* a scene as there was, with the congratulations, kissings, and hand-shakings, I hope I may never forget to my dying day. Then we went to the vestry and entered our names, and just as I turned away toward the carriage, I glanced again at the register and stood spellbound; for there, in plain black and white, stood the record—my name in a rather shaky hand, below it "Mabel Warren!" and next, in bold, strong, flowing characters, "Joseph Sargent" and "Dora Vaughan." At first, of course, I thought it a mistake, but one glance at Joe was enough, as he stood cram-

ming his handkerchief into his mouth to keep from roaring, and like a flash it all came over me as plain as day. He had sold me completely, and for life! It was all simple enough. He had seen Dolly before I did, and when he found I was interested, had got the girls to change names as far as I was concerned, and, as they were alone in the office, and were both orphans and without relations in their town, there was no one to expose them. They did it at first by way of a joke, and then got frightened and didn't dare confess to me, and so I had actually fallen in love and married the manager after all, while Joe had secured his point and his "Dolly."

But of course I forgave him, and though my wife is still—as she always has been— "Dolly" to me, it was the girl that I loved, and not the name, and every year that has been added to our happy, quiet life, has only brought me more cause for thankfulness for the subtle exchange of my youthful passion from one "wire acquaintance" to another, and helped to teach me that I can never be sufficiently thankful for the entire success of Joe's little joke!

ONE morning in the spring of '65 a seedy-looking individual entered the operating room of a certain large office in Georgia. He was tall and thin, and wore a red shirt and linen duster coat. His shoes bore evidence of Georgia railroad mud. His pants were cut in "high water," and were at least six inches too short, which exposed the style of his "foot-covering," and showed them to be one boot and one fancy gaiter. His appearance forced one to believe that he had been "counting cross-ties," and his gaunt and cadaverous look showed that weeks must have elapsed since his stomach was astonished with what he would have called a square meal. He met the manager at the door and immediately negotiated for a job, but didn't specify whether as a lineman or what. When interrogated he replied that he could telegraph; in fact he said he was a "first-class" man. The operators crowded around him and induced the manager to give him a trial, in the hope of having some fun, as in those days the business was light, and there was only one busy wire, to the capital of the late lamented Confede-

racy. Press came from there at the rate of sixty words per minute, abbreviated. His muddy nibs sat down and answered press on this wire, but showed no activity about putting it down until he was fifty words behind, and the manager impatient. Then he asked for a pencil, and while they were looking for one he dove down into the pocket of that old red vest, brought out a stump of a pencil, and a "bit" on both ends. By this time Richmond was three items of press ahead, and starting on a Government cipher. The manager was furious, and yelled to the man with the visible lead-pencil to leave the desk. But he calmly asked the manager if he preferred the markets "deciphered" as he went along. He then asked all to wait until he got a drink of water in the hall. Richmond was still rattling along on Government messages, and the young plugs stood around in amazement to see a man carry so much in his head. Long and anxiously did they watch that door, but he never returned. His front name has passed from our memory, but the last was Schemy something.

Leander's Tour of Investigation.

POLITICAL investigation, of course. Leander fully realized the responsibility of his position. No doubt it had been his boyhood's dream to become a life member of a political investigation society, and be drawing a regular salary; to feel constantly under the influence of the active stimulant of promised success, as one feels who is pursuing the discovery of "perpetual motion," as well as to possess the sweet assurance that, as a political investigator, he will be kept just as far from a knowledge of the actual condition of political affairs as will insure his own self-complacency and a growing respect for the exploits of the political party under consideration.

It was a few weeks after election day. According to our bulletins, Hayes had been elected five times and Tilden three, "by a large majority." There was some uncertainty in Louisiana, and this was what Leander was going to look after. It was at a time in the national contest when men were sparing neither money nor time.

Leander was a little short of money, but had considerable "time" on hand, mostly "small hours," and Mrs. Leander, who sat up for him, can testify how many of these he gladly threw into the common National cause.

That "common National cause" has thrown a protecting mantle over many a "small hour" that would otherwise have had to bear the "lance of analysis." More than one family had a "common National cause" at that time. But this is a digression that cannot be followed up much longer without disaster. So, to return:

Leander was to start at once for Louisiana, and said he should take his life in his hand. Some people often take their lives along with them. Leander may, however, have meant a shot-gun.

His purpose was to disguise himself, upon his arrival in Louisiana, as a negro of the most unconstitutional stamp. This, in order to get unquestioned access to the negro, his hut, his political sentiment, if any, and his situation as a citizen and as a voter. While Leander was to be violently political among politicians, and let no occasion so to express an active interest in the issues of the hour, he should be kindly disposed and lenient toward all parties. He would inquire after the health of the White Leaguers and the Klux family. He should try to secure cheap board in the house of a poor but respectable individual. Like Mark Twain among the fixed stars, if there were any returns needed fixing, Leander was pledged to fix them. If it made trouble, he should be sorry, but firm.

The great need of the hour was a President —honestly, if he could be got honestly—but anyway a President. A President, even if he wouldn't "wash," and fell short a trifle of being "all wool and a yard wide;" so that it was understood, if, at any part of our investigator's route, an official and "truly" President should be announced as unquestionably elected, Leander should return home.

A slight accident to the train upon which he set out delayed him over night in the little town of Kennebunk, Maine. As he passed along the principal business thoroughfare of the town, he was struck with the general appearance of desertion everywhere along the way. Not even a dog or a rumbling wheel

"Rasped the mysterious silence."

Had it been a good day for foxes, they might have "dug their holes unscared," and no questions asked. Doors swung on their hinges, revealing cold and untenanted rooms. Even "meals at all hours," and the periodical depots, seemed to have "struck," and left the benighted traveler to shirk for himself. Perhaps even the telegraph office was on the retired list! The spirit of investigation came powerfully upon Leander. Shouting, "'Tis sweet, oh, 'tis sweet for our country to die," he took his life in his hand and followed the wires. Presently in the distance loomed up before ? m a dense, moving cloud. It had settled up's and around the telegraph office.

Sections of us/ black cloud trailed over the fences, art seemed to hang in festoons from the house-tops. The fact was as the gentle reader has no doubt anticipated. The whole town was out en masse to get the "latest" from the telegraph!

Ever then it was going up on the bulletin board. But what is a bulletin board where one an go behind the scenes, as Leander could, and have the wires and the operator to himself!

As the crowd surged away from the office, to press around the bulletin board, Leander pressed forward into the office. "What's the latest, William?"

"Here it is. Hayes elected by one majority."

"All right, William, thank you; I'll go back home on this train."

"Hold on, Leander, Portland says he'll have something definite soon. Everything depends on the next news."

Leander held on. The next news was that there was "fear of a turmoil in Louisiana."

Evidently that State was entirely out of political investigators. Leander concluded to resume his journey to Louisiana, but before he could get his life into his hands again the lightning was ahead of him with the news that "corrected returns from thirty-one counties, with eight to hear from, estimates based on the election of 1874, give Democratic majority in Florida of 1,700."

"'Rah for Tilden!" remarked a fellow from the roof of the blacksmith's shop.

Leander saw by the town clock that he had lost the "half-past" train, and concluded to take the train that left "twenty minutes of," and that would leave a margin to get the very latest news before starting.

And the news did come in time for him to reach the train had he gone trainward after learning that "dispatches received from most prominent men in New Orleans say that the dispatches claiming the State for Tilden are erroneous."

"'Rah for Hayes!" remarked a fellow in the door of the barber's shop. "Hold on, Leander. Here it is. Mr. Smith has been to South Carolina and says it is for Hayes by 10,000 majority. Official. Mr. Smith has seen Hayes, and seen the majority."

"'Rah for Smith!" remarked two fellows from an upper window of the dye house.

The train that left at "twenty minutes of" was whistling in the outward bound distance, but then there was another that left at "a quarter to," and surely, at a time of our country's peril, it is always best to know what that peril is, thought Leander, so he lingered yet awhile longer. Perhaps the next dispatch would settle it. Everybody said so; even the editor of the Morning Chirrup, and Leander was never known to question the veracity of an editor.

Toward noon the Boston Journal claimed North Carolina. Nobody objected to this. In fact, the people of the town seemed to be glad that North Carolina had fallen into such good hands.

The editor of the Chirrup did not remember of an instance where a State was owned by a private party. Still, he said, he should have claimed Florida years ago if he'd only had subscribers enough.

Leander was rewarded for waiting. Toward night something definite came, viz:

"There is nothing later than the Morning Chirrup."

Everybody knew this to be true, for there had been no bulletin all day. The Chirrup forthwith stepped upward one round on the ladder of fame.

Leander said he would wait one more day, if the general feeling was that a decisive result with regard to the election would be reached during the day.

The operator proceeded to find out what the general feeling was, with the following result:

9:30 A. M.: "The Globe is in doubt."

9:45: "Fears of trouble in Louisiana increasing. White Leaguers tuning their instruments."

9:48 : "Rumored that somebody in Wisconsin has spelled an elector's name wrong. This gives one vote to the Democrats."

10 A. M. : "The New Hampshire *Rainbow* says Hayes ran 600 to 800 ahead of his ticket in Florida. Official. Our special correspondent was there and saw him run."

11:06 A. M. : "President Grant and cabinet are going to compare views. All agree that it is the best time for ' views ' that we have had since the Beecher trial." •

1 P. M. (from Cranberry Isle) : "Democrats here have given up the struggle and gone to dinner."

9 P. M. : "No change. National pulse up to hundred and fifty. Symptoms of Hay(es) fever."

10:50 P. M. : Something definite expected before morning."

Leander was encouraged. He decided to give the national question one more day's consideration before leaving for the seat of war. Another day passed : another, and another, during which the "definite result," ever receeding from the pursuer's grasp, suddenly vanished.

Leander was getting somewhat muddled as to the best locality for his "investigation." Louisiana evidently needed him. Florida also; and North Carolina was spoiling for him, and certainly in South Carolina and Oregon an investigator need not perish for want of employment. The trouble with Leander was the same as with the man who had so much mind it took him a week to make it up.

He never swam that Hellespont of investigation. He came home.

Leander won't talk politics any more now. He is going to work in a sail-loft, and that kind of "canvas" is the only kind he wants in his.

Congressional Investigating Committee.

THE reader will only need to recall the action of the House of Representatives during the late Presidential contest to appreciate the following :

Ben Bilton sworn.

Chairman : What is your name?

Witness : Bilton.

Stenographer : Your initials?

Witness : I sign "F."

Chairman : What is your first name?

Witness : Oh ! Ben.

Chairman : How long have you operated in Florida, Mr. Bilton?

Witness : Well, first in the spring of 1855 me and Schemerhorn went from—

Chairman : We don't want to hear about Schemerhorn or '55 either. Did you work there in November, '76?

Witness : Yes, sir ; I subbed in Tallahassee that month.

Chairman : While subbing there, did you see or hear of a message from Chandler to Stearns, mentioning money and troops?

Witness : Yes, sir ; I received it myself, and asked about those two words.

Chairman : Asked who?

Witness : Oh, you don't " 18 ; " I mean I *broke* on " money." It's not unusual for operators to do that.

Chairman : Was this message delivered promptly ?

Witness : I don't know ; I think the money and soldiers were.

Republican Member : Please confine yourself to answering questions. Do you know Mr. Stearns ?

Witness : Stearns, the duplex worker ?

Members together : No ; Gov. Stearns of Florida ?

Witness : Not intimately.

Republican Member : How long can an operator remember a message ?

Witness : That varies according to circumstances. Some remember a " bulled " message eighteen months, when they could not repeat an ordinary message a day old.

Chairman : How long does the company preserve the originals ?

Witness : I don't know ; but judging from the date of changed checks and other errors, I should say they preserved them forever.

Chairman : That will do.

Republican Member : One moment, Mr. Bilton.

What influenced you to come so far to give this testimony? Witness: The eloquence of the deputy sergeant-at-arms and a morbid desire to scoop in that mileage business. But I didn't count on such a "roast" as this, and I am glad that it is at last over. Chairman: Bring in Mr. Orton again. When leaving the room, Mr. Bilton completely put his foot in it, by asking the door-keeper the way to the "bar" of the House.

The Song of the Wire.

Sing! wires, sing!
Ye iron threads of life, what tidings bear ye now?
Is't fortune's smile, or fortune's frown,
Or the blight of a broken vow?
Sing! wires, sing!
If not on evil bent;

And yet I know, your whisperings low
Are not unbidden sent.
Of joy or pain, of weal or woe—
Whate'er the message be—
Of death or life, of peace or strife—
Ye vary not your key.

Some Grave Thoughts.

When you are dead, what then? Will the deafening clatter of the little busy instruments at 195 or 185 Broadway die away? Will the quad and duplex be suspended and the automatic and combination printers be hushed as your former confrères gaze sadly upon each other and tenderly whisper that a great and good man, a model operator, and a faithful friend, has passed to his long home? Will the flag on the Western Union building be lowered to half mast, and the elevators cease to run because the funeral bell rings out the solemn fact that one we knew and loved will walk with and among us no more forever? Will merchants close their stores and pedestrians leave the streets to sorrow over the passing away of one whom the telegraphic profession held dear?

"When I am dead" some one will grieve. A father and mother, a sister or brother, a particular friend, perhaps a distant fellow operator whose face I have never seen, and one or two may feel a twinge of genuine sorrow at the heart as they see the crape on the door, or hear the low thud of the earth as it falls upon my coffin in the lowly grave. Great New York will not know it, or knowing will forget it in an hour, and I shall not be missed. Another will occupy my desk in the office, and few will remember that I ever even worked there. If one man turns off Broadway the passing throng does not seem the less in number; if one vehicle turns aside the monotonous roar continues just as loud. Messages will be sent and received as before, operators go on duty and return as now, and the man who carves my name upon the marble stone will remember me longest. There are dead whom we remember as we sit in the twilight and muse—there are no dead whom we remember as we sit at our desk in the office or walk the busy streets. Passing away they left no foot-prints by which they can be traced while daylight lasts. The feet of the living press on as before, and obliterate all trace that one ever walked up and down ahead of them.

"When I am dead" in a village, men will come and look soberly and sadly upon my closed eyes and pale face. Death will seem so near to them that they will feel awed and silenced. Women will come in and shed tears as they leave a flower on the lifeless breast. Children will walk in on tiptoe, whispering softly as if a word loudly spoken might bring me back to battle with the world for another lifetime. Neighboring operators and railroad employés, whose acquaintance I had formed, will look over the edge of the coffin upon eyes that never again will open and upon lips that will never again be parted, and they will be afraid of me even while they sorrow. Hundreds will gather to follow me to the grave under the young oaks, and as the man of God opens his arms and whispers, "Ashes to ashes and dust to dust," every face will wear a look of grief and every eye be moistened. My memory will live green in their thoughts for weeks and months, and a quarter of a century after grim death shall have folded me in his leaden arms perhaps some old man, sitting in the summer shade and waiting for the watchword, will recall my name and remember the far-off days when he and I worked a telegraph wire together.

But "when I am dead" in a great city people will miss me only as the ocean misses the shell dragged up by the fisherman's net. The tide of humanity will ebb and flow without pause, men and women and children will laugh and smile as before, and even telegraphers with whom I was familiar will fail to remember where I left their midst to accept a position somewhere in the Far West or to engage in other business; and acquaintances, whose hands I have pressed, will forget whether I sailed away

to some far-off country or was laid in the silent
grave. I hope, however, that, in the words of
William Cullen Bryant, I shall

So live, that, when my summons comes to join
The innumerable caravan, that moves
To that mysterious realm where each shall take

His chamber in the silent halls of death,
I shall not go, like the quarry-slave at night,
Scourged to his dungeon; but, sustain'd and
        sooth'd
By an unfaltering trust, approach the grave
Like one who draws the drapery of his couch
About him, and lies down to pleasant dreams.

The Volcanograph.

THE most casual observer of our professional peculiarities is aware, that in the long category of telegraphic offenses none is considered more aggravating than "breaking in" on a through press wire. The habit—it has grown to be a habit now—is cultivated especially by a breed of country lunatics whose knowledge of "adjustment" is very limited.

This much objurgated individual generally gets to his pranks about midnight, when the rain is falling in torrents and the wire working "hard." The sending operator, careworn and haggard-looking, is still plodding away, while at the other end of the line the receiver has "adjusted away out." He is not getting more than half of the signals sent, but with the spirit of a Bonaparte, and his head bowed down close to the instrument, he is bravely taking it in, in the vain hope of a speedy good-night. The two men know each other personally; they were out west together years ago, and years before that again they had earned reputations for themselves in the same office; and, owing to the entire confidence which each puts in the reliability of his friend, miles of Supreme Court decisions, political speeches, clerical investigations, and cables are literally melting away before their nimble fingers. But just about the time that bright hope is dawning, here comes our "way" student, and in his blind ignorance of anything like proper adjustment, commences to practice; or, as he says himself, to "6ractice."

To have one of these cadets of the telegraph practicing at any time is bad enough, but when the merciless ghoul's rule of life is never to begin before midnight, and his system of pursuing that variety of intellectual improvement extends no further than the alphabet, the numerals, the various stops and commas, and the headings of half rate blanks, it is infinitely more exasperating and atrocious. It is bad enough to have one of these hobgoblins break in in the midst of a two-column special, asking all kinds of unsolicited and unwelcome conundrums as to what you are "fi4ing" him, etc., but when you *know* he is not adjusted, and hear his melancholy "A, B, S, K, E," and so on, ground out with all the horrors and uncompromising continuity of a surgical operation, a faithful operator is to be excused for courting even death itself in his desire to be avenged.

Hitherto there has been no alternative but to get another wire by some round-about route, and to switch the electric clock on the abandoned circuit; send your special on the former, while on the latter the indomitable plug puts in the remainder of the night "fighting for circuit" with the steady and unyielding "tick, tick" of that reliable electric clock, which he fondly imagines is some irate first-class operator.

But science now comes to our relief in the shape of the volcanograph, a 2,000 cell dynamite battery, worked by a lever and crank in the main office.

Under ordinary circumstances I am unalterably opposed to the immolation of even plugs by means of disintegrated battery jars and giant sounders, especially since our ranks are being decimated by the axe of the official headsman, but for once I must attempt to justify a fell scheme which forever abolishes that delectable model of idiotic perversity, the embryo plug. Its operation is generally instantaneous, and, therefore, in the main, devoid of cruelty. The too confiding way station (I use the neuter gender in the same sense that lawyers speak of "the Court") breaks in to practice, and after legal argument has been exhausted, your chief turns on the volcanograph, and the devastation at the said way station is complete; that which was once a profusion of smiling confidence, jocularity, and tribute flowers, is in an instant turned to a blackened heap of keys, sounders, relays, and inanimate plug, and the good work of expediting good-night goes bravely on.

It was a bright, sunshiny day when we made our first official experiment with the volcanograph, but the rash victim at Thompsonville was just as perverse as on the dreariest wet night in mid-winter. His name was Junius B. Plugg, by the way—Junius Brutus Plugg, of Butler County, Pennsylvania.

He had his most intimate friends in the office, as usual, and was explaining to them, in his loftiest style, the fun of contending for circuit, and of compelling that champion operator in the main office to humiliate himself by meekly "backing down." His smoking friend, the gardener, was chuckling with delight at the thought of what wonderful mysteries his friend, young Plugg, had fought and conquered. A passing young man, who had often heard fairy-like tales of the telegraph—indeed, the operator had recently crossed him in love—strayed in at the door, and listened with mingled feelings of envy and astonishment to the running commentary on armatures and rheostats which his rival, young Mr. Plugg, was then indulging in. The doctor was there, too! "The doctor"— a mighty individual—the village druggist, and

a kind of wizard in the estimation of the country folks; one who passed his life like any other first-class rustic druggist, except when occasionally a vigorous outburst of intellect led him to inspect some such commonplace affair as a wayside telegraph office; one of those happy men who not only regarded himself with the greatest complacency as a representative American, but who was constantly detecting innumerable deficiencies in others. He was in the habit of standing off the same landlady for board as was his friend, young Mr. Plugg; so that, as they both owed astonishingly large bills, and fully intended to liquidate each other's account some day, their hearts beat in sympathy. As young Mr. Plugg was an operator, he was, consequently, "chock" full of technical telegraph talk, which the doctor used to cabbage and fire off as medical opinions and prescriptions at his patients; and, as the doctor was also one of those bright individuals of an investigating turn of mind, to whom the most trifling incident was a prolonged nightmare of disquieting mystery, they were again bound in sympathy. Furthermore, as "Sam" (that's the way he used to refer to Professor Morse) was an intimate personal friend of his, and as the telegraph itself was merely a hackney'd familiarity to him; and as he was entangled in several knotty questions at the Lyceum, and implicated in countless intricate and perplexing conundrums propounded anonymously from time to time in the weekly papers, he had no hesitation in accepting his young friend's humble invitation to be present. He would learn something, if that were possible; he could at least direct, so to speak, the scientific part of young Mr. Plugg's efforts to compel the main office to back down. He had brought his favorite goose along, a domesticated bird on the shady side of thirty which he was fattening on a purely scientific principle for Thanksgiving Day; a description of which and the fattening principle would occupy too much space in this sketch. Let it suffice to chronicle the important fact that his gooseship was here, alive and well, and that the countenances of all present reflected the inward

"GIVE THEM ANOTHER TURN," URGED THE DOCTOR.

feeling of confidence which was reposed in young Mr. Plugg and his wonderful machine, and, moreover, in that learned and profound thinker—the doctor.

The performance having got fairly under way, young Mr. Plugg explained to his admiring friends that the main office had got mad and said "go away," and that he (young Mr. Plugg) had promptly replied "73," a piece of witticism which elicited the most extravagant terms of approbation from the brilliant assemblage, and as the doctor went into the most alarming convulsions of laughter, they all did likewise.

Young Mr. Plugg next explained that the main office was threatening to bombard the way stations, a threat which the doctor laughed to scorn, remarking, by way of illustration, that when the key was open no communication could be had, and urging young Mr. Plugg to "give them another turn." The gardener, who couldn't tell a relay from the

yard arm of a ship, was wildly demonstrative in vouching for the accuracy of the doctor's theory. The young man at the door nodded his humble assent, well satisfied with the doctor's proposal, and the favorite goose on the shady side of thirty flapped his featherless wings with delight at the prospect. Young Mr. Plugg, feeling that he was being lured on to deeds of greater glory, proceeded to "give them another turn," as the doctor expressed it, but the volcanograph cut him short, and the next moment Philadelphia was again hurrying his special to Chicago, without the slightest resistance on the part of Junius Brutus Plugg, of Butler County, Pennsylvania.

There was a green Irishman on the roof fixing a leaky spot, and as the blazing liquid brass came whizzing through he mused on telegraphs in general, and wondered if it wasn't a hazardous business to work at. Not fully comprehending the situation, he, of course,

BUT THE VOLCANOGRAPH CUT HIM SHORT.

thought the racket was all in the regular course of telegraphic events, and watched

with much curiosity the old bootlegs and
broken office furniture and copies of "Oak-
um Pickings" that came whanging through
the shingles until they shot out of sight sky-
ward, and then he wondered how long it
would take those "messages" to reach New
York.

The young man at the door fared pretty
well—simply because he *was* at the door—
and any one who saw him two minutes after
he had been at the door, skipping through a
corn-field with a hole shot in his coat, would
be convinced that he was fully impressed
with the solemn fact; although he still
thought it was a put up job on the part of Mr.
Plugg and a certain fair but faithless one.

The learned doctor arose from a distant corner with a very kind but supernaturally sober
expression on his face, remarking that young
men should not be allowed to tamper with
those carbon batteries, especially in an atmosphere filled with oxygen, where they expanded to 9,000 their ordinary bulk, and explaining to nobody in particular that there
had been too much nitro-genic tension on the
electro-motor.   Indeed, so much taken up
was he with the logarimths and abstruse
technicalities of the subject that he never
noticed that one side of his whiskers had been
blasted off until the Irishman, who was then
looking down in horror through a hole in the
ceiling, called his attention to that trifling
circumstance.   This information seemed to
make him still more dignified, and noticing
the dead goose (the poor creature on the
shady side of thirty was stark and dead) he
stooped, seized it by the feet, slung its car-
cass over his shoulder, and with measured
tread and all due devotional sadness departed.

The gardener, who had been hit with seventeen million volts of dynamite battery in
seventeen hundred different places inside of a
second of time, and had lost his pipe and a
new Sunday hat beside, without knowing def-
initely what *had* struck him, was seen shortly
afterward on the grocery corner denouncing
his late friend, young Mr. Plugg, as a "gol

darned fraud," and exhibiting his nose
(which was a shocking wreck) to a sympa-
thizing crowd in proof of that sweeping accusation.   The people smiled at each other
and winked, for several of them had seen the
doctor staggering home with a dead goose
slung over his shoulder, and, therefore, they
were not quite sure that it wasn't another
"jamboree."

Years have rolled by since then.   Junius
Brutus Plugg, of Butler County, Pennsylvania, has left the business long ago, and
he now drives a team.   His face is forever
scarred and streaked with blue powder
marks like the tattoo embellishments on a
South Sea Island warrior.   His nervous system has been affected for many a year, and
he is always worrying about sudden accidents.   He resides with his wife and children
on the western shore of the Delaware Bay, in
the sixteen-inch steel turret of a monitor vessel
which was wrecked near there; and has
built himself a barricade all around and an
iron hurricane deck in front, to keep off the
mosquitoes, so he says.

Often on a bleak winter's night, after all
the young Pluggs have been dragged in
through the port-holes to supper, he tells them
queer anecdotes of the past; and in the mul-
tiplicity of subjects discussed on such occasions never fails to get in his well known
disquisition on the falsity and absurdity of
modern inventions.   Telegraphing, as he as-
serts, is a creditable occupation, but on the
whole, he prefers his present occupation—
driving a non-explosive machine.   He tells
the admiring young crowd that he was once
an operator, and, thank goodness, can lay
the flattering unction to his soul that in his
time he worked as fast as the best of them.
He had received from New York for three
days and two nights at a stretch without a
break, and made $173 extra in one month.
His writing used to go clear as a bell through
seven repeaters.   He never stuck but once,
and that was prior to '68.   Then there's a
long and painful silence, while the hot tears
roll down the veteran's powder-marked face,

and his daughter gets in her favorite solilo-quy on " never till life and memory perish."

It takes the old man a long time, together with many a strong dose from the domestic store of applejack, to compose himself; but as he reaches over the table for the last piece of custard pie, he gives his eldest son Junius a terrific back-handed whack in the jaw in answer to an innocent request to elucidate the mysteries of the volcanograph.

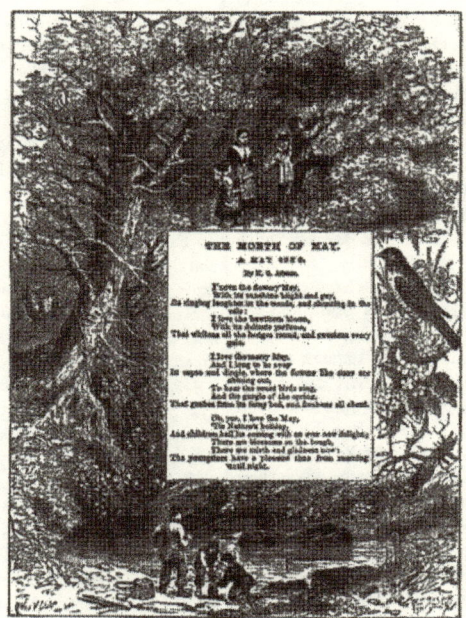

CIPHER messages are always more or less perplex-ing to the telegraphic fraternity, but the following one proved to be above the average. A gentleman recently stepped into a telegraph office in one of the large cities in Missouri, wrote out the following message to be sent to an eastern city, and handed it to the operator, who is a lady: " Darling, kick glutton to-day." The lady gazed at it in amaze-ment, nor was her surprise any the less when a re-ply was received which said, " Kiss glutton to-day." The gentleman called for his reply, whereupon the lady closely examined his appearance, wondering whether his mind was not impaired. He realized the situation, and in a few words explained that the first message as understood by the firm would read, " 325 brls. must be shipped to — to-day," and the reply, " Will ship to — to-day." The explana-tion proved satisfactory, and both enjoyed the joke.

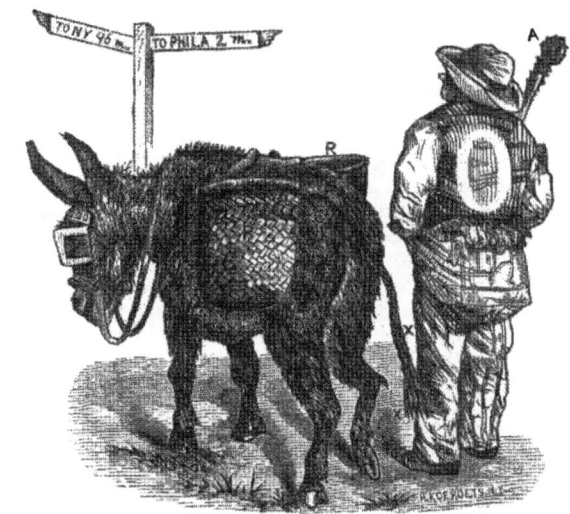

The Quadruplex!

EXPLANATION:

A, The armature lever, which the Operator grasps firmly.
C, The Condenser.
O, The Operator.
R, R, Receivers, constructed of wicker-work, on either side of the instrument, and into which messages are put, to be forwarded.
X, X, An extra local, for emergencies.

DIRECTIONS.

Put a whole day's business in the Receivers (R R). Then make a good, firm, and very rapid connection between the armature lever (A) and the condenser (C). If this does not result satisfactorily, give a few light twists (upward) to the extra local, (X X), and let the armature lever (A) vibrate pretty freely. In recent experiments the most astounding rates of speed have been attained in this manner.

As in the Duplex, an occasional return current, or "kick" is unavoidable, but with this invention it is more easily remedied. In Mr. Stearn's apparatus, a complication of devices and several problems in Euclid are necessary to counteract the "kick," whereas, in the Quadruplex, only a common piece of sheet iron (one foot square) is required, and which the Operator can easily adjust to suit himself—inside his wearing apparel.

A Perilous Christmas Courtship;

OR, DANGEROUS TELEGRAPHY.

I was walking leisurely along one of the bustling streets in classic Cheapside. It was noon, and the weather very pleasant. A patient crowd stood gazing wonderingly, and, melting away, being renewed and reconstructed almost ere it dissolved. There was I, a telegraphic idler whose train had rushed him too soon officeward, among that ever changing crowd. I was not "on duty" at the big Central office, the Titanic "TS," for half a listless hour; therefore, could I contemplate with fellings of awe-struck admiration, at my ease, and never a-weary, the comet-like galaxies, the brilliant "gilded youth," of all ages, who cleaved our rude clusters at one glittering stroke, leaving "obscurity blushing at being seen," behind them!

Perchance I was wishing that I were such an one as that lofty, elegant, and handsome man with the nut-brown "Albert Edward" beard, and faultless attire, who had positively honored me by approvingly glancing ever and anon at my lounging figure, while comparing his jewelled chronoscope with Gog and Magog's time piece; when *presto!* a flash of his white teeth and a merry brightening of his clear blue eyes transformed my erstwhile majestic ideal of grace and affluence into an old and dear friend of twelve years ago, "when we were boys together;" the quondam crack telegraph operator, and whilom chum of mine in the far north, Frank Willis!

"What! my Colossus of Wires!"—the sames old cheery tones and hearty greeting—"after all these years to come in contact within these antique precincts bounded by the sound of Bow Bells! It is meet and fitting, Jim, old boy," (that was me,) " that a festive occasion like this should be becomingly baptized. Man was made to imbibe, Jim. Let us absorb!" And, despite my vacillating and weak-kneed objections, in an adjacent caravansery of ostentatious exterior and finical decoration within, we *did* absorb.

Preliminary salutations and hasty but hilarious reminiscences of "good times" gone by were exchanged over fluids costly and exhilarating, until my impending "duty" compelled me to reluctantly say adieu.

"Well, if I let you go now, Jim, you must solemnly pledge yourself in this sparkling bumper of the rosy that you will dine with me *en famille* to-morrow, Christmas Eve—blessings be on its snowy head—when I will relate unto thee, dear boy, things that you wot not of, to account for my sudden and mysterious departure from you, telegraphy, and 'dear old Scotland' just twelve winters ago."

I "took the oath," fervently and reverentially—in a tumbler!

This is what I heard in reply to my anxious solicitations, next day, when the cloth was removed and the liquids sparkled:

"When last I saw your reverend features, my James, things were radically different with us; with me in particular. I enjoyed, aye, and felt proud of, the lavish stipend of eighteen weekly shillings which the 'Opposition and Informal Telegraph Company (Strictly Limited)' generously bestowed upon my dot and dashing labors. Many an evening 'prowl' have you and I enjoyed, Jim, among the saloons of gay Glasburg, during those heedless hours of our beardless youth, in a too, too successful endeavor to spend half our respective salaries (including extra) in as many hours as it had taken days to earn them! We were impecunious, but happy; hardworked, but content; dissipated, but unmindful of the world's care and troubles.

"You will remember that we were the closest chums, most particluar 'pals,' with no secret or reserve between us up to the time of my holidays in the year 1864. On my return, a change had crept over our relations somehow. You were the same, Jim; ever frank, open, and careless. It was I who was altered; not sad, not depressed, but grave, reserved, and reformed. A short fortnight had worked that change. You, not unnaturally, questioned and chaffed me, railing me, good naturedly, no doubt, but unconsciously touching me on tender points which 'riled' me considerably. A coolness arose between us, who had been inseparable friends till then, and you never knew what had happened to me to produce such a transformation. I had been in London, during those two eventful weeks, and I had met an angel. To encounter such a seraphic being sojourning upon our coarse earth for a brief span, and to fall inextricably in love with her, were to me then synonymous terms. She appeared to me first in a visit I paid to the main office, in London, the day after my arrival. Being shown in the instrument room, as I wished to speak to you on the Glasburg wire, I was led, nervous and bashful, through rows of tittering and whispering young lady telegraphers, who seemed to have no object on earth second to that of rendering a provincial youth awkward and shy. Arriving at 'Gb' wire, my *gaucherie* forsook me as if by magic. The lady seated at the key burst upon my dazed senses like a vision of transcendent glory and heavenly beauty. Probably she would not seem so to you, skeptical James, nor perhaps to other men, but to *me* she was everything lovely that imagination could depict—she was my *beau-ideal.*

> 'Her flashing dark eyes smiled upon me,
> Two ripe, pouting lips lisped my name,
> But her sweetness and innocence won me;
> Those charms that will never grow tame.'

"You will observe I grow poetical over the recollection. Well, I have felt so ever since when I reflect upon that meeting. But let us abbreviate, as we used to say on the wire. It turned out that she was the usual operator at our London wire, whom, you may remember, we could seldom tempt into talking. Unlike most other telegraphic ladies, she did not seem to care to 'do a flirt' on the wire. Violet Graeme was her name, you will recollect. Well, ere the first week had expired, I had so far improved our slight 'wire' acquaintance as to get an introduction to her family; and before that memorable fortnight

had all too soon come to an end, we were engaged, Jim, and I then had but one aim in life: to work, to save, to study—so that I might attain that position in which I could claim my sweet girl-lover of seventeen summers as my own—my wife. When I returned, sedate, but not unhappy, to the Glasburg end of Violet's wire, such a burning stream of affection, solicitude, and sentiment flowed over that senseless iron thread, when not ruthlessly interrupted by common-place dispatches, that I often thought, when our words grew warmer than usual, that the wire might positively *melt*, and so cut the only link that bound us in love together! That link was over four hundred miles long, as you know, old man, and yet we seemed as near to each other as if 'twere only a clothes line!

"Our correspondence went on thus, by letter and telegraph, growing sweeter and more tender each day until Christmas Day turned up; cold, wet, and dreary outside in the slush and rain; slow and miserable enough to me as I sat in the office alone, with one small messenger dozing in the anteroom. Our London main office had been closed all day except for an hour or so in the morning and again in the afternoon, so that there not being any ladies on duty, I had no chance of indulging in my daily delight, my diurnal joy, of a chat with my little Violet.

"Of course, in Scotland, we were unholy enough to keep open from morning till night, yet with a reduced staff; and I was the unlucky wight who had 'drawn' the lonely late duty. My soft-hearted little sweetheart had sympathized with and mourned over my sad lot the previous day, and tenderly wished she could have come and shared it with me. I sat there about eight in the evening, sorrowfully wondering if my darling was enjoying herself at the grand Christmas party her people were holding, when the London instrument, which had laid inert and silent nearly all that quiet day, to my intense wonderment and surprised delight suddenly chirruped forth 'F.' Why, that was our private signal! Could it be my darling at the other end of the wire, and, if so, how on earth came she there? The very huge building, on the very highest story of which the headquarters of the O. and I. Telegraph Company were situated, was shut up and sealed, as it were, from top to bottom. While I hesitated, bewildered, again the instrument clicked out sharply : ' F, F, are you there?' It was no illusion! It must be my Violet. I sprang to the key, and, giving our confidential countersign, 'V,' tapped back, hurriedly: 'Can that be you, darling mine, and what good fairy has borne you to my distracted loneliness?'

" Sweetly, but a little nervously, came back the response :

"'Oh, yes, dear Frank, it's your little girl herself! Are you not paralyzed with fright and astonishment? I could not bear to mix in the gay and festive throng while my poor boy was sitting lamenting and sad, perhaps jealous, all by himself! So, I annexed my younger brother, slipped out, and rattled off to Belham Buildings in a cab. Then I bribed the burly porter, who was fast asleep, and had to be roused up by hard knocks, to lend me the key and give me a light. John is downstairs propitiating the porter, and here I am alone and rather terrified, but pleased as Punch to give you a Christmas surprise!'

" You may guess, my dear Jim, that I was in the seventh heaven of delight at reading this, which I did off the Morse instrument without letting the paper run. My heart bounded fondly forth to that courageous girl of mine, petite, but plucky, and true-hearted as she was pretty. I hammered back, all aglow with love and rapturous excitement :

"'My own brave little heroine! may every blessing descend on your lovely little head! I am as happy now, my darling, as I was wretched before. But I do hope, Violet, that you have run no danger from this unprecedented visit. Whatever should I do if anything should happen to you, dearest, through your love and kindness?'

"'Oh, there is no fear, Frankie; I am not afraid of ghosts, and there is not a soul in this vast edifice but myself, my brother, and the big watchman; so how can there be danger, dear? Oh, I forgot to wish you the compliments of the season; I do so now, dearest Frank, and hope you will spend a very merry Christmas and a happy New Year. There, you naughty boy, you ought to have said it to me first!'

"'Ah, you little rogue, you didn't give me time, frightening a fellow out of his wits! But, here goes, darling mine, may you spend —and I hope you are now experiencing—the very merriest of merry Christ—.'

" Here, to my surprise, I was violently interrupted. A tremulous line, ending in a series of unconnected dashes and dots that seemed to shiver on the armature, just as if the hand that held the key wavered and shook with some strong emotion, and endeavored vainly to form characters almost mechanically, was all that appeared on the instrument; then the line went off and the instrument was silent.

" Struck with involuntary terror, I .called 'V' several times. No reply. What could be the matter? Perhaps the wire had got 'in trouble.' That would be annoying, certainly, but immeasurably better than any danger in that lonesome five-storied building to my beloved.

" Again I tried :

"' V, V, are you there, dear? Speak but one word if you hear me.'

" Almost with a shriek the trembling armature, after a second's pause, jerkingly said :

"'Help!—Frank—darling—help! Two—men—burglars—at—the—outer—door. I—have—fastened—it—but—they—are—breaking—it—open. Oh—Heavens—no—one—can—hear—my—screams!'

" Oh ! my God, I hope you will never feel as I felt then, old friend. My brain reeled; I shouted aloud in frenzy. I could not see the key for the blood that blinded my eyes. Staggering like a drunken man with the world whirling around me, I groped wildly for the key, and was about to say, I know not what, in my mad, helpless agony, when again the brass knell pealed aloud. Oh! Jim, *so* wailingly—

"'*They—say—they—will—kill—me. I— can—hold—out—short—time—yet—but—am too—hoarse—to—scream—now. Oh—help— me—my—own—Frank!*'

"Direct from Heaven must have come the sudden thought that inspired me then. Swiftly tapping to my sorely beleaguered darling comfort and hope:

"'Courage, my love. Barricade yourself in. I send help.'

"I rushed, hatless, across the muddy streets to the Voltaic Company's office, dashed into the instrument room, seized the key with which a busy operator was sending to London—the big company kept their office open all night—and crying to the astounded operators, 'Don't stop me for Heaven's sake! This is to save life!' I sent, fiercely and distinctly, the following message to London:

"'*I—am— Willis— of—the— Opposition. Murder—being—committed—in—our—main office. For — the — love—of— God — run— over—like—lightning. Take—policeman.*'

"A flurried 'all right' being returned, madly I darted, heedless of all inquiries, back to my office, fervently praying that aid might not arrive too late. Oh! if she could only hold out for three swift minutes longer—for the Voltaic office was not two blocks distant.

"I had left the paper of the Morse instrument running. I feverishly referred to the slip. 'Merciful Heavens! she is lost,' I groaned aloud. On the paper ribbon were the words, formed of maimed, halting characters, as from a dying hand:

"'*My—Frank!—good-by! They—have —forced— the— door! I — will —resi—!*'

Then a long blank slip.

"Forgetful of the four hundred miles which separated me from the cruel wretches who threatened all I held dear, I desperately shook the fatal instrument in a paroxysm of impotent rage, and fell swooning headlong on the floor.

"How long I remained in that comatose state I can not say.

"A cherry call of 'Gb' on the London instrument aroused me. I answered as one in a dream. Merrily the reply sung forth:

"'I am Coltmile, of Voltaic. Arrived in nick of time. Trapped burglars, who were after safe in board-room. Lady all right, had bravely barricaded herself in small testing-room. Gone home in cab, but sends love. Ta-ta, old man.'

"Down on my bended knees I sank.

"'Thank Heaven!' I exclaimed, forgetting to reply to the good fellow in London, so intently was I reading and re-reading the blessed slip. 'We shall have a happy New Year after all!'

"Then it was that I so mysteriously disappeared from Glasburg and from telegraphy forever, discarding all else but my love. I took the night train for London an hour afterward, saw my *fiancée* next morning safe and well, resigned my situation, and through her family's interest obtained a position on the Stock Exchange, where I have since prospered amazingly."

"And Miss Graeme?" I breathlessly inquired.

Willis rang the bell. A sweet-faced matron entered, a pretty babe in her arms.

"She is here to answer for herself," said he, introducing me to Mrs. Willis.

"Her flashing dark eyes smiled upon me,
Two ripe, pouting lips lisped my name,
But her sweetness and innocence won me;
Those charms that have never grown tame."

DURING a thunder storm a gentleman in Paris took a hack down the Champs Elysees toward the Faubourg St. Germain. He noticed that at every flash of lightning his driver piously made the sign of the cross, and remarked:

"I observe that you cross yourself. You do well."

"Oh, yes. It is always well where there are so many trees, but once we get into the streets I don't give a curse."

Playing with Fire.

"YES, I'll do it if I live ten minutes longer and can raise her, and I guess I can, for she is never slow in answering," and Rena Chelsey, operator at "M.," threw back her curls in an energetic manner with her left hand while she opened her key with the right. While her rapidly written "Bn" sounded along the wire without bringing an immediate response, she said to herself, in a low tone:

"I suppose it isn't just the thing to fool her, but I must do something to keep from stagnating in this dull office. Yes, I will sign a man's name and fool her in grand shape. She hardly ever receives from me, and has only been in that office a short time, so she won't know my sending."

Just then "Bn" sounded a brisk "i i," and in another half minute Rena had written "'G M:' Fine mng, isn't it? How is everything at 'Bn?'"

"'G M:' Yes, splendid. Everything O K, tuk u. Sign pls."

"My name is Isaac, but I sign 'Ia.'"

"U are joking, I fear. Is your name really Isaac?"

"I am not, truly. If you ever want me call 'Ia.' How are u getting along in ur new ofe? I saw u sitting near ur window the other day while I was passing there on the train, and u will pardon me, I trust, if I tell u that I compared u to a white rose I held in my hand. U are looking pale and shld take a vacation."

Then some one "broke," and Rena Chelsey threw her head back and gave vent to a hearty laugh.

"If I can make her think I am really and truly a man, I will have some fun of the first water," she said. "I hear she is fond of any attention from the masculines. Ha! that was a happy hit, telling her my name was Isaac. She will never imagine that my mother gave me that for a middle name because it was her last name before she was married. I fancy she liked being told she looked like a rose."

My descriptive powers are far from being good, but I must try to tell you how Rena Chelsey looked as she leaned back in her rocker with such a merry twinkle in her eyes.

She was not a small girl. A rather tall, but well-proportioned figure was hers. A shapely head and a good forehead, which was not covered with frizzed hair, as is the fashion. Lips which could form themselves into a very firm, loving mouth when occasion demanded it, closed over a set of strong, even teeth, or displayed them when they parted in a smile, as was often the case, for this Rena of mine was a merry body, and fond of fun. The skin was rather dark as the miscievous-looking eyes were blue, but take her as a whole she was a really fine looking girl, and had been called more than once the best looking operator on the line.

But those who were so fortunate as to know her well, valued her kind heart much more than her pretty face. Left an orphan at an early age, she had found life no play-day, though she had ever carried its burdens with a song instead of groans, making the most of its sunshine and groping bravely through its dark portions, and when I introduce her to you, my reader, she is grown into a brave, happy, self-educated, self-supporting girl, and a good operator.

Whenever the wire was not in use for business that day, Rena kept "Bn" busy talking with her, and in the evening, long after the other operators had gone from their offices, the busy click of the relays sounded in Rena's office and in that of "Bn's."

"Whew!" whistled Rena, as she leaned back in her chair after her late "G N" from "Bn," "I have certainly waded in pretty deep this day and evening. One would suppose from my talk that I was a regular lady-killer. Ha! I wonder how long I can keep this up? But she is much more sensible than I expected to find her. Stars and garters! Didn't she come down heavy on me when I quoted something from the Bible!

Well, I like spunky people. Mercy! it is nearly eleven o'clock! I must go directly home."

Scarcely had Rena seated herself before her instrument next morning when " Io," " Ic " sounded along the wire, and very soon she was writing in answer to a " G M " from " Bn."

" G M: It seems ages since u spoke to me. I dreamed of u last night, and it seemed to me that mng wld never come."

And as the day passed they found many minutes in which to chat, and that evening found them both in their offices till even a later hour than the previous one, and Rena went home saying to herself:

" I feel like a wicked wretch deceiving such a girl as she proves herself to be. If anybody ever tells me again that Miss Dwinell is silly I shall contradict it flatly. She seems to know all about every author of note, and is, I see, well versed in history, and in my opinion is a charming girl to know."

The days followed each other until three weeks passed, and every day our Rena kept up her seasons of chat with " Bn," while evening found each ready to talk and loth to say " G N."

At last letters were exchanged. " That's what I call a splendid letter," was Rena's remark as she folded her friend's first epistle. " Rather coarse writing, but I hate milk and water girls."

And so the weeks went on, filled up with letter writing, wire correspondence, and a few small presents such as Miss Dwinell would accept from Rena.

One evening as Rena was sitting in her office a letter was handed her, and on opening it she read:

" BN OFFICE, TUES., SEPT. 8th, 18—

" DEAR FRIEND:—I write you a hasty note this P. M. to say that I am going to Albany for a few days, and shall change cars at your station. Shall have an hour and twenty minutes to wait, and will you think me bold if I ask you to meet me on arrival of train? I shall go on 4:40 train to-morrow A. M.

" Yours, as ever,   BN."

Hastily calling her friend, Rena wrote: " Come by all means. Shall be more than happy to see u."

" Now for it," she muttered. " Angels and ministers of grace defend us! What *shall* I say to her when she comes! If I had ever imagined that she was half as interesting as I have found her, I would have tried to make her acquaintance at once in a decent way. I shall be heartily sorry to lose her good opinion, for I am so deeply interested in her that I more than half wish this Isaac business was a reality. Heigho! Of course, she will be very angry with me, and tell me never to speak to her again, and then—curtain falls to slow music."

*   *   *   *   *   *   *

" Please, madame, can you point the operator at this station out to me ? "

Rena, who had been looking vainly for the last five minutes for a lady who might be " Bn," looked up with a start, to see a tall, fine-looking fellow of perhaps twenty-five years of age standing before her.

" I hold the position of operator here at present," she replied.

" And is there no other óperator here ? " he asked, with a very puzzled look on his face.

" There is not business enough to keep *one* busy," she answered, smiling.

" There must be some mistake," he said, in a hesitating manner, and then he asked suddenly:

" Do you know a person on this line who signs " Io ? "

Rena's face was scarlet as she answered: " And what do you know of Io? Have you any business with that person?" '

" I have," was the unexpected reply.

" Then walk into my office, please, for *I* am ' Io.' I came out to meet a friend whom I expected on this train, but she has not come." And then she added:

" Perhaps my friend sent *you.*"

" What does your friend sign ? " asked the young man, as he took the chair she offered him.

"Her office call is 'Bn,' " was the answer, "but I believe she signs 'D.' "

There was a very merry twinkle in the eye of Rena's visitor as he said:

"Miss 'Ic,' this seems to be a real case of 'diamond cut diamond.' The fact is, a number of weeks ago Miss Dwinell, of 'Bn' office, wished to go away, and I consented to remain in her office during her absence. I had been there only a day or two when some one who signed 'Ic,' and said his name was Isaac, opened a conversation with me. I knew by the tone that he thought he was addressing Miss Dwinell. But the spirit of mischief was strong within me, so I did not tell him his mistake. You know how it turned out. Believe me I came here to-day feeling so mean and guilty that I knew I deserved to get flogged, but guess we can call it even."

There was stillness for a moment, and then Rena's voice rang out in a hearty laugh, in which her companion cordially joined.

"But there is something I have yet to tell you," he went on, when their merriment had subsided. "You have yet to learn how much I have come to care for my new friend. Often have I wished I *was* Miss Dwinell, if Isaac would care for me as he seemed to care for her. But things are now just as they should be, and if you do not consider the action too abrupt I would like to ask you to be my wife. I have a comfortable income, and, better still, love you devotedly. I think you cared for me in my old character. Can you learn to love me in my new?

The merry look on Rena's young face had been growing graver during this speech, and it was in a sadly earnest, almost solemn tone that she replied:

"Yes, it would be an easy task, but it must not be. Home love is not for me. I have duties you know nothing of—a purpose in life which I must work out alone. Let us each go our own way, bravely walking in the path marked out for us; content, though no earthly reward come to us, if we are sure we have a 'Well done' waiting for us in the world beyond. I thank you sincerely. This brief friendship will ever be a pleasant memory to me, and from my heart I say, may God bless and prosper you."

As the closing words were spoken, the soft rays of the setting sun came in through the window and rested upon the brown hair like a golden crown. Herbert Stanley bowed his head as if he had received a benediction, and slowly and silently walked away from the office.

* * * * * * *

Among those who have reached a high place in the telegraphic profession is Herbert Stanley. He is a grave, quiet man, and people often wonder that he does not marry; but he only smiles sadly in answer, and his mind goes sadly back to that autumn afternoon when the earnest words were spoken which made him think for the first time if he, too, had not a work to do in life—a purpose to fulfill.

A few years later Rena died. Her work was done. The brave heart ceased to beat, and the tired hands were folded, and no one said that hers had been a wasted life. Thank God she has found a home at last.

* * * * * * *

Turning the leaves of Whittier's beautiful poem, "Snowbound," Herbert Stanley always lingers over the words:

"But Love will dream, and Hope will trust,
Since He who knows our need is just;
That somewhere, somehow, sometime,
Meet we must."

"Now, you see, Sam, s'pose da was a dog, and dat dog's head was in Hoboken and his tail in Brooklyn." "Go 'way, da ain't no such dog." "Well, s'pose da was." "Well, s'pose da was."

"Well, den de telegram is jest like dat dog. If I pinch dat dog's tail in Brooklyn, what he do?" "Dunno." "Why, if I pinch that dog's tail in Brooklyn, he go bark in Hoboken. Dat's the science.

What Came of being Caught in a Snow-storm.

It was the day before Christmas, and all day long the snow had been falling, completely filling the air with its soft density, gaining upon the ground with marvelous rapidity. It was a real old-fashioned snow-storm. As the night came on the wind arose, piling high the light snow, making huge drifts through the roads and fields of the quiet country village of N. Notwithstanding the severity of the storm, Farmer Osborne had been to the railroad station and brought his daughter home, that young lady having arrived on the late afternoon train to spend Christmas with her parents. And as the Osborne family are now all at home, and seated around their cheerful tea-table on this stormy Christmas Eve, let us glance a moment at its members, in one of which you will certainly be interested, she being with us a member of that numerous and happy family who with gratitude recognize their indebtedness to Prof. Morse for the pleasant and interesting, if not always lucrative, employment in which we are engaged.

Mr. and Mrs. Osborne are two of the best people in the world; very intelligent and pleasing, both in manner and person. They have three children, two are under ten years of age, and of whom we shall not have further occasion to speak in this sketch. The other is Miss Fannie Osborne, who, as we have previously intimated, has just returned home, after an absence of three months. Miss Fannie was at this time eighteen years old, very pretty, and as intellectual and good as she was handsome. She had lovely brown eyes, always dressed tastefully and stylishly, and would be noticeable at all times, even in the busy thoroughfare of a city. She had been in the telegraph business nearly two years, although she had not been manager of her own office until quite recently, but, like hundreds of ambitious young operators scattered through our land, had served long and faithfully as a substitute, waiting patiently for the first permanent position that should offer itself, practicing meanwhile with the greatest assiduity, endeavoring to make herself competent to fill any position open to ladies. And she had not labored in vain, having at length been appointed to fill a vacancy at M., a large and growing town between N. Y. and B., where the business required a fair sound operator. I use the latter expression in the sense of eligibility, not of beauty.

Very proud indeed were Mr. Osborne and his good wife of their handsome daughter, as she sat in her accustomed seat at the table, praising mother's light biscuit and delicious butter, giving ludicrous descriptions of same of the many different boarding places she had been obliged to patronize while substituting, and comparing the edibles she had lived and thrived upon with those of her own dear home. So pleasant did everything seem inside that the furious storm outside was nearly forgotten, when all were suddenly startled by a firm knock upon the door. Fanny being nearest, and not very timid, quickly threw open the door and beheld standing in the doorway what at first appeared to be a snow man; but a pleasant, frank voice proceeded therefrom asking for shelter at once dispelled that illusion, and the stranger was invited to walk in.

A removal of outer garments soon brought to light a fine looking, stylishly dressed young man, whose quiet ease and self-possession, together with his polite manner, proclaimed him at once a gentleman. He introduced himself as Fred Thorne, and explained to them the cause of his sudden advent, and, he feared, intrusion, into their quiet home. Having accepted an invitation to spend Christmas with some relatives who reside several miles from N., he had started from the city without a thought of what a storm he was to encounter fifty miles away. Arriving at the N. station he found there was no one there to receive him, as he was not expected in such a storm, and, as he could not return that night, he decided to try his pedestrian powers, but finding the drifts numerous and deep, he soon became aware of the magnitude of his undertaking, and after a short trial decided to seek shelter at the next house that should present itself, which accounted for his appearance there. Mr. Osborne assured him in his hearty manner that he was welcome to spend the night there, and also to remain until the storm should abate. He then introduced him to the members of his family, and insisted upon him taking tea with them. After tea they all adjourned to the pleasant sitting room. In the course of a few moments' conversation, our friend Fred acquainted them with the fact that he was a telegraph operator, occupying the position of day press operator at B. This to Miss Fannie's great delight, for she had never been acquainted with a main office operator, and here was a real live one brought directly in her path. Mrs. Osborne had casually remarked that Fannie, too, was an operator, or, rather, was learning to be one, and, of course, nothing more was needed to make our young friends perfectly at ease.

What a host of questions Fannie had to ask! And how much Fred had to relate! What other occupation on this globe of ours affords such a fund of interesting facts for conversation as telegraphy? Fred was personally acquainted with many nice operators, and as he was well educated, and had a pleasing address, he was listened to with great interest by the whole family, and especially by the operator of the family. He spoke of that most accomplished of our American operators, who has worked his way high up in literary circles, and whose past record as champion receiver has never been equaled, and not forgetting to render the well deserved praise due to that " departed one," whose exceedingly rapid and accurate transmission is at once the admiration and wonder of the entire telegraphic fraternity; he having transmitted, with " Mc " receiving, 2,500 words in sixty minutes, or

an average of over forty-one words per minute for one whole hour, this being accomplished without a break or a mistake on the part of either sender or receiver.

He told them of an acquaintance of his whom nothing seemed to disconcert. How one night a gentleman with an accordeon caused all the other operators to cease from receiving, except this one, who was receiving first press. He only smiled, and continued his work even when the accordeon was brought near to him with the express purpose of compelling him to break. Those who have tried it can judge how good an operator one must be to do this. At another time this same operator was in a small office one afternoon with several ladies and a gentleman companion, all operators. Presently the office was called, and the lady manager not desiring to exhibit her powers before so many, suggested that one of the gents should receive the prospective message, at the same time answering the call and closing the key. After considerable delay the situation was accepted by this same gentleman. All this time the message, which proved to be a long railroad dispatch, had been coming at a good speed. After three vain attempts to make a commencement, in which he was prevented by the roguishness of the other gentleman, who siezed from him three blanks in succession, he finally made a start just as the sender was finishing. To the great surprise of all present a prompt " O K " was given, and our friend copied down the long message, which he had secured in his head, amid all the confusion incident to such an occasion.

Perhaps you can imagine the pleasant excitement that lighted Miss Fannie's fine eyes, as she heard these and many more stories of first-class operators, and when the hour of retiring arrived, all expressed themselves remarkably well pleased with the evening's entertainment. The next morning was bright and pleasant, and Mr. Thorne, after thanking his kind host and hostess for their hospitality, bade them all adieu. He had not proceeded far on his journey when the thought flashed upon his mind that he had neglected to inquire of Miss Fannie at what office she was pursuing her studies, which proved a most depressing thought, even preventing his enjoying the rest of his trip. Three days later found him at work again, and as he copied "The latest from Europe," "All about the Electoral Votes," etc., his mind continually reverted to that pleasant Christmas Eve, and innumerable were the schemes devised for discovering Miss Fannie's office. On this morning the press news was light, and he was called upon to assist in getting off some of the way business. Accordingly he sat down at one of the wires between N. Y. and B. He was feeling very light-fingered, and was just in the mood to "salt" everybody he had dealings with. On the table before him lay several messages for M. He at once raised the station, and proceeded to "salt" that countryman, or woman, whichever it might be. He rattled quickly through the messages, and, much to his surprise, was not broken once. When he had finished, and his sig. "F." had been given, the quick response came "O. K." "FO.," with the added remark, "That's the kind of writing I like to receive, Mr. T." "What! you don't mean to say you received those messages by sound, do you? And how did you know my name was Mr T.?" was Fred's reply. A

merry laugh came rippling over the wire with the answer. "Oh, certainly, I received them by sound. And can it be possible that you have forgotten Christmas Eve, and that dreadful, or rather delightful snow-storm so quickly?" Fred nearly jumped from his chair at the reply, much to the wonder and merriment of the operators who chanced to see him. A few more remarks on either side sufficed to establish satisfactorily the identity of both; Fred remarking that his surprise was greater from the fact that he understood she was only a pupil, when she really proved to be a fine operator. It was surprising how many times during that and succeeding days, our pressman found time to run over to that way wire, and chat a few minutes with FO. And again it was equally surprising how often the trains to and from M. found him therein. And since his last visit we have a very suggestive fact to record, viz.: That Miss Fannie now wears a new and beautiful pearl finger ring, of which she seems to be very proud. Our young friends are apparently as happy as the days are long. But we are here compelled to leave them to await the development of future facts. In the meantime, we would advise "subs" generally to watch "M" office vigilantly, for at no distant day, one of them may obtain a pleasant situation, should their application be presented in season.